Puffin Books
Mr Browser and the Brain Sharpeners

Out of the mysterious, swirling fog came the Brain
Sharpeners. Their strange, pepperpot-shaped spaceship
landed on the playing field of Chivvy Chase School early
one morning, when only Michael Fairlie was watching.
Mr Browser had summoned the Sharpeners by mistake one
day when trying to teach Class 8 a simple point of
long division for the umpteenth time.

Mesmerized by the Brain Sharpeners, Mr Browser and the
whole of Class 8 trooped into the pepperpot and emerged
completely changed. Michael alone escaped the treatment,
and he watched aghast as his classmates became obsessed
with learning and homework – because Michael was the
only person who realized that the alien Brain Sharpeners'
evil plot threatened not only Chivvy Chase School but the
whole world!

Michael's desperate race against time to rescue his
classmates from the influence of the Brain Sharpeners makes
a thrilling and often hilarious story, ideal for readers of 8
and over.

Also published in Puffin: *Mr Browser and the
Comet Crisis.*

Philip Curtis

Mr Browser
and the Brain
Sharpeners

Illustrated by Tony Ross

Puffin Books

Puffin Books, Penguin Books Ltd, Harmondsworth, Middlesex, England
Viking Penguin Inc., 40 West 23rd Street, New York, New York 10010, U.S.A.
Penguin Books Australia Ltd, Ringwood, Victoria, Australia
Penguin Books Canada Limited, 2801 John Street, Markham, Ontario, Canada L3R 1B4
Penguin Books (N.Z.) Ltd, 182–190 Wairau Road, Auckland 10, New Zealand

First published by Andersen Press Limited 1979
Published in Puffin Books 1982
Reprinted 1984, 1985

Copyright © Philip Curtis, 1979
Illustrations copyright © Andersen Press Limited, 1979
All rights reserved

Printed and bound in Great Britain by
Cox & Wyman Ltd, Reading
Filmset in Monophoto Baskerville by
Northumberland Press Ltd, Gateshead, Tyne and Wear

Chapter 1

First contact with the Brain Sharpeners was made on a foggy morning in February, but Michael Fairlie insists that Mr Browser, Class 8's teacher, was in distant communication with them before that.

It seems that a few days earlier Michael had been standing by Mr Browser's desk, half listening to an explanation of how to do long division sums, when Anna Cardwell came out with a broken pencil. Anna is a round-faced girl with large innocent-looking eyes, but she's one of the champion pencil point breakers in the class – especially when there are sums to be done.

'Please, Mr Browser,' she began.

'Don't tell me, Anna – your pencil's broken.'

'Yes, Mr Browser – could you sharpen it for me, please?'

Mr Browser shook his head wearily as he looked at the broken-off end, but he took his ancient penknife from his pocket and set to work on the pencil.

'How are you doing with the sums, Anna?' he asked.

'I don't think I really understand them, Mr Browser,' Anna answered honestly.

'Nor does Michael,' said Mr Browser. 'If only I had a brain sharpener as well as a pencil sharpener, maybe we'd learn a little more quickly!'

Anna giggled, but Michael was looking at Mr Browser's face as he was speaking; as soon as Mr Browser spoke the words 'brain sharpener', Michael

was sure that his eyes took on a glazed look, and he
stared into space as though he were listening to something far away.

'I thought he had indigestion,' said Anna, when
asked to confirm this. 'He suddenly held the knife still
and stared, as if Michael and I and the rest of the class
were not there for him any more. After a few seconds,
he clicked back into consciousness again, and gave me
back my pencil.'

'Brain sharpeners,' said Mr Browser, as though the
idea appealed to him greatly. 'We could certainly do
with some for this class. Nice children, but they will
not listen. I've said this before, Michael, haven't I?'

'Yes, Mr Browser.'

At least a hundred times – he's always saying it,
thought Michael, and tried harder to listen as Mr
Browser began to explain once more about the sums.

Several days passed before the events happened which changed Class 8 and Mr Browser completely. In that time Michael and Anna had forgotten all about the unimportant incident with the penknife; Mr Browser was always making little jokes like that – they helped the mathematical medicine to go down for some of the class. Since then Anna had broken off two more pencil points, but had sharpened the pencils herself because she was afraid that Mr Browser would think she was overdoing it.

Monday was the day on which it was unusually foggy. Michael arrived in the playground very early that morning, at about twenty minutes past eight. This happened because his mother started work very early on Mondays – and she always took Michael to school by car because Chivvy Chase School lay on her route to work. Also, Michael was so forgetful and untidy – so she said – that she was pleased to know for sure that he had arrived at school in one piece.

So, on this foggy day Michael ran down the path to the playground, happy in the knowledge that no one else would be there. He enjoyed having the playground to himself; he could run without fear of being knocked over, and he could play marbles against himself without any danger of losing. Best of all, he could occupy the climbing apparatus and swing around as he wished without upsetting anyone else.

He made straight for the climbing frame and clambered up to the topmost bars. It was pleasant usually to sit there and look down on the empty playground and the deserted school. Even the precise Headmaster, Mr Salt, would not have arrived yet; his shining new car would usually be the first one to arrive in the car park – at about half-past eight.

The fog had changed the usual scene completely,

and Michael was, to his own surprise, a little uneasy as he sat and looked around at his kingdom. The fog seemed to be closing in on him. The houses adjoining one side of the playground were completely hidden, and fog was swirling round the dustbins at the far end of the playground. He couldn't see the football posts in the middle of the school field, and even the school building itself was hazy.

For once Michael wished that someone else would arrive. It would be good to hear another voice; the fog was dampening sounds and making the world a mysterious place. If only Spiky Jackson or Jason Little would come running across the playground towards him!

It was cool at the top of the climbing frame, with the fog swirling around him, and he began to consider how he might occupy himself when he climbed down to the playground again. He was about to drop to a lower bar when he thought he heard the wind blowing from the direction of the field. He stopped climbing down and frowned: wind and fog don't go together, he was thinking – when all the fog on the field seemed to start blowing across towards him. Clinging to the cold bars as the fog swirled past him as if being puffed out by some giant smoker, he was aware of a whirring sound, followed by a sudden plop and hiss, rather like the noise when a hovercraft comes ashore and deflates.

For a second or two there was a gap as the fog was blown away, and through the gap Michael saw a huge white thing with windows in it, sitting in the middle of the school field. Then the fog closed in again, and the sudden wind died away.

Michael climbed down and walked across to the edge of the field. Hard as he stared, there was nothing to be seen but fog. He shivered, as much with excite-

ment as with cold. The thing had looked most like a
huge pepperpot – and the holes near the top of it were
probably windows. Had a plane landed on the field?
Michael didn't want to admit to the truth, but deep
down he knew that either his eyes had deceived him,
or he had seen some kind of space craft. No aeroplane
on earth had ever resembled the object he had seen.

As far as he could tell, the playground was still
deserted. If only someone would come, he could tell
him what he had seen. But would he be believed? Not
a hope, he decided unhappily. So the only way in
which he could prove to himself that he had not been
dreaming would be to walk across to the middle of the
field and take another look for himself. He put one foot
on the grass, then withdrew it. To walk on the school
field before nine o'clock was to break one of the strictest
rules, and it might even result in a caning. Mr Salt
hardly ever used the cane, but there were stories of

times when he had done so. As the field was very wet and muddy, he certainly wouldn't be pleased to hear his rule had been broken.

Excuses! If he didn't dare go out there, he would never know the truth. He might be missing the biggest sensation of the century! A look round to assure himself that he was still alone, and Michael stepped courageously off the asphalt and moved slowly over the grass, looking and listening intently as he went.

Was there a faint ticking coming from the place where the thing had landed, or was it his imagination at work again? He stopped, listened, and moved on again. Now the playground was no longer visible, and he was lost in a sea of fog, with no buildings in sight. He was on his own with whatever might be standing there on the football pitch.

No buildings in sight – but suddenly there it was, the pepperpot object, hovering a few inches from the ground, and ticking like an old grandfather clock. Swift rays of light started shooting out of it, so that Michael was caught in a kind of tunnel of light which reached from the pepperpot to himself, and no further.

He intended to turn and run, but his feet wouldn't obey him, and as he stood there against his will a door opened in the side of the pepperpot, revealing a collection of illuminated gadgets in the style of a huge computer. A platform rose up just inside the doorway, and on it there appeared a miniature pepperpot, exactly the same shape as the big one but having a large aperture in the front of it, the purpose of which was soon revealed to Michael.

'Boy,' began a dry voice coming from the hole in the little pepperpot, 'you are in the class of Mr Browser, are you not?'

'I am,' replied Michael, and the machine repeated

his words in its harsh voice. Then followed a whirring and clicking; evidently the machine was translating the English into its own language. A pause, more whirrings, and the machine was prepared to speak again.

'Boy, inform Mr Browser at once that the Brain Sharpeners have answered his call, and say that they want to see him. He must come at once, and you must tell no one else that you have seen anything out here. We are already constantly checking on your brain, and we shall know before you speak exactly what you intend to say. If you are tempted to tell of what you have seen, be warned: we have the power to make you unconscious before the words even leave your mouth. Now – fetch your Mr Browser.'

'But he probably isn't here yet,' protested Michael, trembling all over. The little pepperpot whirred and clicked.

'Go and wait for him,' it said. 'He is approaching the school gates now. Depart – at once!'

The light from the big pepperpot died away and the fog swirled round Michael once more, thicker than ever. In a couple of seconds the big pepperpot was hidden completely. Michael turned and ran diagonally across the field in what he thought was the direction of the car park. His sides were aching by the time the asphalt of the path around the school came in view, but he dared not stop. The only car standing in the car park was the Headmaster's sleek Rover; Michael ran past it and down the drive towards the school gate.

Mr Browser's old Wolseley 1500 swung into the entrance just as Michael arrived there. Mr Browser braked sharply and wound down his driving window.

'Michael – what are you doing here? On a foggy day like this, too! You're breaking the school rule, and worse than that, you're asking to be knocked down. Back you go to the playground at once!'

'But Mr Browser! I've a message for you. Somebody wants to see you.'

'Come down to the car park, then, Michael, and I'll talk to you. If we stop here there might be an accident.'

So Michael ran alongside the old car until Mr Browser had driven it into its usual place in the car park.

'Now, boy,' he said, picking his briefcase up off the seat and climbing out. 'Who wants to see me so early in the morning? Mr Salt?'

'No, Mr Browser. There's something out there on the field and it asked me to fetch you immediately!'

'It? What do you mean, it?'

'Well, it's a kind of space craft, I suppose you'd call it. Looks like a big pepperpot. And there's all sorts of computer instruments inside.'

Mr Browser stared at Michael.

'Look here, Michael Fairlie,' he said, 'it's only February, not April the first. Stop trying to fool me. Were you watching a space film last night?'

'I'm not fooling you, sir, I'm not! Please Mr Browser, I had to make sure that you would come. Please go out on the field and you'll see for yourself that I'm telling the truth. They call themselves the Brain Sharpeners, Mr Browser!'

'The Brain Sharpeners!' Something registered in Mr Browser's mind. He stared hard again at Michael, and saw that the boy appeared to be trembling. 'All right, Michael. I'll take a look. But if I find there's nothing there, you can expect a hard day's work!'

'Yes, Mr Browser. Over there, in the middle of the field.'

'Aren't you coming with me, Michael?'

'Oh no, Mr Browser. It's you they want to see. You alone.'

It seemed to Michael as though his words had been directed by some power beyond himself.

'Calm down, Michael. You'd better go back to the playground.'

Mr Browser strode off into the fog. Michael, as soon as Mr Browser had disappeared, returned along the edge of the field to the playground, which was now filling up with children.

'Where have you been, Mike? What are you doing on the field? Your shoes are covered with mud!'

His friend Jason Little confronted Michael with these questions, and Michael hunted frantically to find an answer. He would dearly have liked to have told Jason about the pepperpot, but he dared not; he fancied his brain became dizzy at the very thought of revealing the truth about the Brain Sharpeners.

'I've been chasing a seagull on the football pitch,' he said weakly. 'It couldn't see me in the fog, and I nearly caught it.'

'You're daft!' commented Jason. 'Come on, let's have a game of marbles.'

'It's too cold,' objected Michael.

'Not as cold as standing there and staring into the fog,' Jason retorted.

'Oh, leave me alone!'

'All right – I will!'

Jason found it hard to believe that his friend meant what he said, but at last decided that he did, and ran off to find some more reasonable companions. Michael was left staring out into the fog, listening hard to see if he could hear any of the sounds which had come from the pepperpot earlier.

All was quiet on the field – and his listening was not helped by the noise coming from the children playing in the playground. Now and again his classmates tried to persuade him to join in a game, or darted past him with such comments as: 'What are you looking for, Michael? Never seen fog before?'

He ignored them all, and gazed intently into the fog, because by now he was becoming worried about Mr Browser. Perhaps he should never have passed on the message to him. Suppose the Brain Sharpeners had lured him into the giant pepperpot and made off with him? Michael looked at the playing children near him, and was about to risk walking out on the field again, when a piercing whistle brought all the children to a standstill.

Miss Toms, the Deputy Head, was on duty. She had come to the middle of the playground in order to be able to see as many children as possible, and she was glaring round as though the children themselves were to blame for the fog.

'No one will move until I say so,' she threatened them. 'Now – Classes 1, 2, and 3, lead in.'

The smaller children set off for the entrance door, and Miss Toms moved towards the field just as Michael made a half-hearted attempt to disappear into the fog on the field.

'Michael Fairlie!' shouted Miss Toms. 'Don't you dare move! One more step, and you can go straight to my room.'

Everyone knew that to pay a visit to Miss Toms in her room under such circumstances was an event to be avoided. Miss Toms took a hearty dislike to anyone who disobeyed her, and set out to make the culprit's life unpleasant for at least a week. Therefore Michael stood still, and left Mr Browser to his fate. Gradually Miss Toms worked her way up the year groups until finally Michael's class number was called, and he reluctantly joined his friends in making for the door.

'Your shoes are very muddy, Michael!' stated Miss Toms as he passed her. 'You've been on that field, haven't you! Stand still while I'm talking to you!'

'Yes, Miss Toms.'

'Yes? Why, Michael, why?' This time Michael found a more acceptable story.

'I ran to fetch my ball, Miss Toms.'

'Where's your ball now? Seems as though you were digging while you were looking for it, from the amount of mud on those shoes!'

Miss Toms favoured him with one of her sharpest looks.

'One of my friends has it,' countered Michael.

'Oh well – get along, and see you wipe those shoes well at the door.'

'Yes, Miss Toms.'

How Michael wished that he could have told Miss Toms the truth! Perhaps, for once, she wouldn't have been so sure of herself. More probably she would have sent him straight to her room for being cheeky. He tried to console himself with the thought that one day she might find out the truth from Mr Browser – if he came back!

He was the last to enter the classroom, after being delayed by Miss Toms and by the thorough cleaning of his shoes. He found Class 8 making the most of the absence of Mr Browser. Spiky Jackson – known thus because of the spike of black hair which was once again standing up straight from the crown of his head – was about to throw a paper dart, and Jason was risking an

indoor game of marbles with Elmer Smith on the floor. Anna Cardwell was doing a dance in front of the blackboard, and several of the girls were still standing in what Mr Browser called 'Gossip Corner', where the coats and slipper bags were kept.

Steven Simons was busy preparing his Action Man for an attack on Sarah Mount's doll, and Jennifer Charman and her friend Alison Gilpin, both mad about horses, were fixing saddles on two lifelike models. Graham Skene was about the only one who looked as though he might be working, but if you looked more closely you would have seen that he was lost in a picture strip about a space adventure. Michael saw this as he passed by, and was tempted to shout to them all to be quiet, because outside on the field a real life space adventure was going on, and Mr Browser was caught up in it. But even as he entertained the thought, he felt a little dizzy – the Brain Sharpeners were keeping in contact with him. This frightened him, and he sat down at his desk with his head in his hands.

'Whatever is going on here? The oldest children in the school, setting such a bad example to the rest! I suppose I couldn't expect Class 8 to come into school and settle down to work on their own! Sit down, all of you!'

The thunderous voice belonged to the Headmaster, Mr Salt. He crossed the classroom to Mr Browser's desk and banged his fist down on it.

'Just because Mr Browser isn't here' – and he looked around sternly to see where Mr Browser might be – 'we don't expect you to behave as though it's a holiday! Take out a book, each of you, and see that you're quiet until he comes!'

Meekly the class obeyed, and after a minute or two Mr Salt decided that he could safely leave them. As he walked across the classroom it occurred to him that he himself had not seen Mr Browser that morning.

'Has anyone seen Mr Browser?' he asked.

To Michael's relief there was silence at first; but just as Mr Salt set off again, Anna piped up.

'He's at school, Mr Salt. I saw his car in the car park – and I saw him talking to Michael Fairlie. I was coming down the road by the car park at the time.'

'Indeed,' said Mr Salt, intrigued. 'Michael, was Mr Browser talking to you? Yet you haven't put your hand up. What was he talking about – and where did he go afterwards?'

Michael was confused, and perspiration appeared on his forehead.

'Please, Mr Salt, he was only talking to me for a moment; he told me to go back to the playground.'

'And where did he go himself?'

'Out on the field, Mr Salt.'

'Indeed! And why do you suppose he did that, Michael? It seems an odd thing to do –'

'Please, sir –'

'Well, Michael?'

Michael's head fell forward on the desk.

'Please, Mr Salt, Michael's fainted.'

Mr Salt hurried to Michael's side, and to his surprise found that it was true: Michael was slumped, unconscious, over his desk.

'Open the window. Give him air,' the Headmaster commanded, and quickly loosened Michael's tie and shirt. 'You're all right, lad,' he said, as Michael groaned a little and began to come round. 'Haven't you had any breakfast? Perhaps it's the fog that's upset you. I was only asking you about Mr Browser. I'm not going to punish you, though of course you shouldn't have been in the car park. I shall have to ask Mr Browser about that when I see him.'

'I am here, Mr Salt.'

All the class, including Michael, turned and looked towards the doorway, where Mr Browser was standing.

'How odd he looks,' whispered Anna. 'Just like when –'

'Ah, Mr Browser,' said the Headmaster, 'we were just trying to find out where you were, and Michael here suddenly became ill. I think he's better now, though. Perhaps you'll take over the class – I have a parent waiting to see me downstairs.'

'Of course, Mr Salt. I'll look after Michael.'

'I'm all right, sir,' said Michael, who had begun to feel much better as soon as he saw Mr Browser had come back safely from his visit to the Brain Sharpeners. As for Mr Salt, his main concern was that Mr Browser was back to take his class, and he didn't bother to ask him where he had been. Anna, however, was still curious, and as soon as the Headmaster had gone she risked putting a question to Mr Browser.

'Where have you been, Mr Browser? Please tell us!'

She was ready for a mild rebuke from Mr Browser, but she was far from prepared for what happened.

'From now on,' declared Mr Browser in a grating voice, 'you will cease to be impertinent, Anna Cardwell, and you will settle down and concentrate on your work. Your ignorance is appalling, as is that of the rest of the class. I am going to turn this class into the cleverest set of children in this school. Yes, the cleverest, and not only in this school, but in this country, in the whole of Europe and the world!'

'What a hope!' muttered Spiky Jackson, and half the class burst out laughing.

'Enough!' ordered Mr Browser. 'The time for jokes is past. This morning, just as a beginning, we will learn all our tables to perfection, so that in the days to come we shall be able to work on the complicated mathematics we shall be learning. Books and pencils ready! Not a second is to be wasted!'

Silently the children took out their books. Michael took the opportunity to look into Mr Browser's eyes, and the change that he saw in them told him everything. The Brain Sharpeners had taken full charge of Mr Browser.

Chapter 2

Mr Salt, the Headmaster of Chivvy Chase School, was
a tall and serious man who wanted – even demanded –
that everything and everybody in his school should be
perfect. It was said that when he walked in the grounds
of the school each blade of grass stood up straight and
the birds all sang in tune. So what he had seen in Mr
Browser's classroom – such things as Spiky Jackson
throwing his paper dart and Anna Cardwell dancing
in front of the blackboard, and many other activities –
upset him very much indeed. He blamed not only the
class, but also Mr Browser for not being with his class
at the right time. He returned to his room and
immediately buzzed through to his secretary, Miss
Copewell.

'Fetch me the files on the children in Mr Browser's
class, please. Oh, and bring with you any letters of
complaint about the class which we have filed away.'

Miss Copewell knew from the tone of Mr Salt's voice
when the Headmaster was especially upset, and when
she brought the files in she saw that he had taken his
glasses off to clean them, as if to have a clear look at
whatever misfortune was in front of him, which was
another bad sign. He rubbed away hard at the lenses.
Miss Copewell put the files down on the Headmaster's
desk and departed without saying a word.

'Hm!' Mr Salt scanned the class list. A likeable lot,
he thought, and admittedly Mr Browser had no one

with genius in the class to work upon. When it came to brains, Class 8 was certainly a normal sort of class. He flipped through the cards, picking out a selection of them – including the ones of those children whose parents had for some reason written in to complain about their children's progress.

'Sandra Axford – slow worker.' Yes, thought Mr Salt, all she has in her head is hairdressing and dancing.

'Peter Brymore. Football mad.' Yes, agreed Mr Salt, the boy has a crick in his neck through looking out of the window when other classes are having games.

'Anna Cardwell. Loves acting. Mischievous. Hates writing and maths.' Better put in likes dancing, too, decided Mr Salt, recalling Anna's dance that morning.

'Jennifer Charman. Horse mad.' There were several like that.

'Jason Little. Careless. Plays about with marbles.' True. Mr Salt had twenty of Jason's marbles in his drawer – and he blamed Mr Browser for not taking them off the boy more quickly.

'Simon Jackson. In trouble in and out of school. Does not concentrate.' Mr Salt could only shake his head.

Then there was the boy Fairlie, who was quite bright, and enjoyed writing science fiction stories. Funny how he had fainted. A bit of a dreamer, the Headmaster decided. He gave a little groan and pushed the rest of the files away from him. The unread ones, he knew, would resemble those he had read in many ways. Still, Mr Browser should be stricter with them – and why hadn't he been in class at the right time? Mr Salt decided to go back to the class-room after assembly and have a word with him about it. With luck he would catch him when the class was noisy, and then he would have an extra excuse for being critical.

As soon as assembly was over, he returned to his room and waited for a while so that Class 8 could have time to settle down. Then he carried out his intention and strode down the corridor to see Mr Browser. He was somewhat surprised, when he reached the classroom door, to hear no sound coming from within. He took a quick look inside, and saw all the children bent over their books and Mr Browser striding up and down the rows with a very severe expression on his face. Mr Salt turned and crept away. He would find a better time to give his message to Mr Browser and the class. About every half hour he returned to the room, but still, to his surprise, he was greeted with complete silence and a hundred per cent concentration on work – even from Spiky Jackson.

It was uncanny – too good to be true. Well, Mr Browser had evidently sensed the Headmaster's anger and was doing his best to make up for it. I must give him credit where it is due, thought Mr Salt. And after playtime that afternoon he didn't bother to visit Class 8 any more.

This was a pity, for just before the end of the afternoon Mr Browser began to relax and to look and act more like his old self. Once or twice he went to the window and stared out of it with a puzzled expression. Michael, too, was able to think of other things than the Brain Sharpeners, and began to feel better.

'Close your books and put them away,' Mr Browser ordered the class at the end of the afternoon. Desks were tidied, and each boy and girl sat up straight, waiting to be dismissed. Mr Browser stared at a point over the tops of their heads.

'Tomorrow morning, if it's foggy,' he announced,

'we shall be going out on the school field in order to measure exactly how far we can see in the fog.'

'Hurrah! Hope it's foggy!' was the reaction of Spiky Jackson; the announcement was greeted with enthusiasm by all except Michael, who shivered as though he were already out in the fog.

'You may lead out,' said Mr Browser, and soon all the class had gone except for Michael, who was sitting at his desk staring at Mr Browser.

'Well, Michael?' asked Mr Browser uneasily.

'You're going to take the class out to that pepper-pot thing,' said Michael. 'They've told you to bring us out into the fog, haven't they? They make the fog themselves, Mr Browser. Did they take you inside that thing? What did they do to you, Mr Browser, and what do they want to do with us?'

Mr Browser stood in front of Michael, a struggle going on inside his brain.

'Yes, Michael, they let me enter their craft. They want us all to go in there tomorrow, so that they can begin a course which will sharpen and extend the brainpower of all the children in the class, and will give me the ability to teach at a very advanced level. They showed me all their equipment. Each child will have a sort of helmet put on his head, and rays which will develop the brain will be shot into their heads for ten minutes. Gradually the length of treatment will increase, until each brain will be capable of receiving knowledge direct from the Brain Sharpeners, without my help. Michael, there's no knowing now how you will end your days. Maybe you'll become a great scientist, or even a leader of the people. The secrets of the universe are going to be made clear to us.'

'I wish you'd never thought about the Brain Sharpeners!' declared Michael. 'Why are they doing all this for us? What do they want from us in exchange?'

Mr Browser looked down at Michael as though his brain had just returned to earth, and frowned.

'You'd better go home now, Michael,' he said, 'or you'll be late for your favourite TV programme.'

Chapter 3

'It's a foggy day again, Mr Browser. Are we going out on the field? You promised we could.'

Spiky Jackson was always keen to do anything which did not involve sitting at a desk and writing.

'Yes, all right, Simon,' replied Mr Browser. 'We'll be going out soon after assembly.'

'I think it's silly to go out in the fog,' said Anna.

'Don't be a spoilsport,' muttered Spiky.

As Mr Browser called the register, Michael crept out and stood silently beside him.

'What's the matter, Michael?' asked Mr Browser when he had ticked the last name.

'Do you think it's wise to go out there again, Mr Browser? I've been thinking about the Brain Sharpeners, and I'm sure they're not up to any good – not for us, anyway!'

Mr Browser closed the register.

'I wouldn't worry, Michael, if I were you. I don't believe the Brain Sharpeners will be back. In fact, I think I must have dreamed about that pepperpot thing!'

'But you didn't, Mr Browser. I saw it too, and the Brain Sharpeners tried to take charge of my brain. You saw how I passed out yesterday –'

'Lack of air, Michael,' said Mr Browser. 'No, I can't believe they'll do us any harm.'

'There's only one way to stop them taking us over

completely,' whispered Michael. 'We must try not to think about them. Refuse to concentrate while they're around. Otherwise we'll become their slaves!'

'Nonsense, Michael. Go and sit down!'

'What were you whispering about, Michael?' demanded Spiky. 'What's the big secret?'

Michael was tempted to tell Spiky, but just as he was about to explain, the bell rang and the class had to go to the hall for assembly. Perhaps it was as well he hadn't said anything, he thought, as he watched Spiky sliding down the banisters. Spiky would probably only have laughed at him. Michael sat through the assembly service unaware of what Mr Salt was talking about. The Headmaster's voice was a meaningless drone as he told a story of somebody's brave deed; Michael's mind was on the Brain Sharpeners. More and more he was coming to believe that it was his task to discover what they intended – perhaps even to save the whole class from some disaster.

When the service finished with a prayer, Michael prayed that he could withstand the power of the creatures who controlled the pepperpot, and who even now might be coming in to land again on the school field!

Class 8 led back to the classroom, and Mr Browser joined them after fetching his overcoat.

'Put your coats on,' he told them as soon as they were inside the room. 'We are going outside for a while to do a little maths. We are going to estimate how far we can see in the fog. We shan't be outside for very long.'

Nearly all the class greeted this announcement with enthusiasm. Like Spiky Jackson, they thought anything was better than normal work at their desks. Reluctantly Michael joined the end of the line. Mr

Browser led the column as they went down the stairs and out through the main entrance. Mr Salt was standing in the entrance hall.

'Taking them outside on a day like this, Mr Browser?'

The Headmaster's look was critical. He hadn't been able to catch Mr Browser out the day before, but he was still suspicious and ready to believe the worst about Class 8.

'Only for a short while, Mr Salt. We're doing some practical mathematics. Estimating how far we can see in the fog.'

'Indeed.' Mr Salt couldn't say no to this, but he was uneasy. 'Jackson, move quietly about the school, or you'll be staying inside.'

'Yes, Mr Salt.'

So the Headmaster let them pass, and they marched along the front of the school building and turned down the path which led to the playground at the back.

'There's something hissing!' said Spiky.

'Can't hear anything,' said Michael. But he could; he knew that the Brain Sharpeners were back, and either they had timed their visit perfectly, or Mr Browser had timed his little expedition to the field at precisely the right moment.

'There's a wind coming up,' said Anna. 'The fog's blowing away.'

'No it isn't,' said Michael. 'It's the pepperpot landing.'

'Pepperpot?' repeated Anna. 'What do you mean, pepperpot?'

'He's pepperpotty!' Spiky mocked Michael, but Michael kept calm.

'You'll see,' was all he said.

By the time Michael had stepped on the grass, Mr

Browser and the boys at the front of the line were lost
in puffs of fog. As Michael drew nearer to the middle of
the field, no shaft of light came to meet him as it had
done before, and he doubted if the pepperpot was
really there, for he had heard no sound from those well
ahead of him.

A few more steps and he realized why he had heard
and seen nothing. The pepperpot revealed in front of
him was this time protected by a circle of light, and it
looked ten times bigger than the first one he had seen.
Mr Browser was standing at the door, watching the
class file up some steps leading into the middle of the
craft. Michael was filled with fear at the realization of
the power of the Brain Sharpeners. Today they had a
pepperpot big enough to accommodate the whole of a
class – next time it might be one large enough to hold
a whole school. Who could tell what the Brain Sharpeners might attempt? If they were unfriendly they
could soon take control of large numbers of the

population – perhaps by using innocent teachers like Mr Browser who wanted the brains of their classes sharpened – and use them to suit their own ends.

'Mr Browser! This pepperpot is ten times bigger!' he called out as he reached the steps; but Mr Browser ignored him, and he could tell by the expression on his face that he was already under the influence of the Brain Sharpeners. Michael stood still.

'Inside, Michael!' ordered Mr Browser sternly.

Michael thought about running away – but he realized he would find it hard to persuade people to listen to his story, and besides, he had learned from the stories of old heroes that it is often better to fight your enemies secretly from within their ranks rather than to retreat openly from them. The story of the Greeks and their Trojan horse sprang to mind, and in a flash he knew what he was to do. After his first encounter with the Brain Sharpeners, as soon as he had begun to think of other things their power over him had lessened. This time, while pretending to obey them, he must try to keep part of his mind independent of them.

As he walked into their automatic brain sharpening classroom he tried to think about his favourite television programmes. He saw that each child was being seated in a small individual alcove. These alcoves were at different levels in the walls of the pepperpot. Each one was taken to his place by a crane which scooped up each child in a seat and hoisted him or her to the nearest vacant place. Michael was lifted to a place high up, and as soon as Mr Browser had been placed in a large central desk down below, the door of the pepperpot closed.

Each child's head was resting in a kind of half helmet, and soon the first sharpening was under way.

It began with gentle vibrations and rhythmic knock-ings, while rays of varying colours darted from the walls and made contact with the children, who were all sitting like hypnotized rabbits waiting to be pounced upon by hungry snakes.

This, thought Michael, is the way that brains like Spiky Jackson's will be encouraged to concentrate in the future! Everybody will come to school with the intention of learning, and will be given the powers of concentration to be able to do it.

As for Mr Browser, he was enveloped in an absolute rainbow of rays. Michael found the sensation tempt-ingly pleasant; it would be so easy to give oneself up to it and allow one's brain to be completely taken over. Michael determined to keep a corner of his mind free, and tried to recall in detail the whole of a children's television play he had seen the night before. Maybe the

Brain Sharpeners wouldn't like it, but he would persist as long as he could in protecting just one tiny part of his brain.

Meanwhile, the brain sharpening machines were hard at work, and Class 8 sat patiently allowing the rays to work their will. Like sheep, thought Michael, and began to count, this time not to call up sleep but to keep that little section of him independent.

The process took nearly ten minutes before the vibrations ceased and the rays died away. Perhaps the Brain Sharpeners were afraid that brittle brains like Spiky Jackson's and Jason Little's would not be able to survive too much at one go. Mr Browser stood up, and the crane returned all the class to the floor, upon which the door opened and Mr Browser walked out. He didn't have to control his class now; they all followed him, exactly in step, with serious expressions on their faces. Mr Browser didn't bother to count them – but in this he made a mistake.

As the door of the pepperpot closed, Michael hid himself behind a square, box-like shape on the right-hand side of the floor. The hissing sound began again, and the pepperpot was preparing to rise, when a powerful sound could be heard above the hissing. There was a pause, and then a sound in reply from the pepperpot; seconds afterwards, the machine translated the message and spoke in English to Michael.

'Boy – why are you still here? You have disobeyed your master. The Brain Sharpeners are displeased.'

Michael swiftly decided that attack must be the best form of defence.

'I don't believe in Brain Sharpeners,' he said, 'and I won't until I see one!'

There came a jumble of noise as the pepperpot

translated the message and received an answer back. The answer, clearly, was an order. The pepperpot began to rise. Michael was heading for somewhere out in space. The Brain Sharpeners had accepted the challenge.

Chapter 4

While Michael was being whirled away in the giant pepperpot the other members of Class 8 were marching in perfect formation back into school. Mr Browser walked behind them. You could have put a long piece of straight rope alongside them, and not a limb would have crossed it or looked out of place. Nobody spoke, nobody stepped out of line, which was not usually the case with Class 8.

They marched into school, along the corridor and up the stairs, and entered their classroom without a word

being needed from Mr Browser. Once in the classroom, books were taken out and pencils were at the ready, so that as soon as Mr Browser began to talk, everyone was prepared to write down his words of wisdom.

A dream class, many teachers would have said. Mr Browser later on told them about the importance of doing at least three hours homework a night.

'To start with, three hours will be sufficient,' he informed them.

'May we do more if we wish?' asked Spiky Jackson.

This would normally have brought a gust of laughter from the class; the thought of Spiky doing any homework at all would have been hard enough to believe. Now, nobody made any comment, nobody smiled.

'I don't wish to stop anyone from doing more,' said Mr Browser. 'Do as much as you like, Simon. I am pleased to hear that you are keen to make a good start.'

'So am I,' called out Anna.

'Let us continue with some maths. Since our batteries are freshly charged, as one might put it, I will explain the theory of Pythagoras to you, and for homework you can work some examples.'

Mr Browser began to draw earnestly on the blackboard, and the class watched him in absolute silence. At that moment Mr Salt entered. He had been worried about the visit of Class 8 to the field in the fog; secretly he had watched the class leading back, and had noticed that the fog had thinned out and almost vanished as the last one entered the school. He had a sneaky suspicion that the children had been wasting their time, and he decided to check up on Mr Browser as soon as he had allowed time for the class to settle down.

Mr Salt stood still when he saw the concentration with which Class 8 was watching Mr Browser's drawing, and when he also saw the subject of Mr Browser's work, he held on to the doorknob and decided to retreat. But Mr Browser wouldn't let him.

'Good morning, Mr Salt. We are just learning about Pythagoras and his theory,' he said, turning like an automaton towards the Headmaster. 'The sum of the squares –'

'Yes, yes,' said the Headmaster hastily. 'I used to teach Pythagoras to my brightest pupils when I was a class teacher. But do you think that this class will cope with it? I thought some of them were still rather weak at their tables!'

In truth, he couldn't remember much about the theory himself.

'We shall all have mastered this by tomorrow,' announced Mr Browser proudly. 'Then I shall go on to more advanced work. Logarithms for example.'

'Logarithms,' repeated the Headmaster, vaguely recalling that this was something he had been taught

when he was in his Grammar School, at the age of about thirteen, not in a junior school at the age of ten. He changed the subject.

'I hope you found your expedition into the fog worthwhile,' he said, addressing the class. Before anyone could reply, Mr Browser answered for them.

'We achieved what we set out to do,' he assured the Headmaster. 'It was well worth while.'

'And just in time, too,' observed Mr Salt. 'The fog seems to have cleared up completely.'

As he looked out of the window, he caught sight of Michael's empty place near one of those windows.

'One missing, I see. Is there someone absent? No, I remember. Michael Fairlie sits there, and he was here first thing this morning. Where is he, Mr Browser?'

The Headmaster believed that he had hit upon something wrong in the class, and awaited an answer happily. Knowing Michael, he thought that perhaps he had stayed outside and Mr Browser hadn't spotted this. Mr Browser looked confused for a second, until Spiky Jackson started speaking.

'I think Michael stayed behind with the Br—' he began.

The words died on his lips and his mouth hung open as if he had lockjaw. Mr Browser's confusion changed to anger.

'I'll certainly look into it, Mr Salt,' he said. 'I think he must have slipped out into the cloakroom. And now, please, we must waste no more time. We have much to do today. Excuse me please, Mr Salt. The sum of the squares –'

All eyes were directed to the blackboard, and Mr Salt's presence was at once forgotten. He stood there for a few seconds, feeling rather a nuisance – and he didn't like that.

'Carry on, Mr Browser,' he said, and left the classroom. On his way back to his room he looked into the cloakroom for Michael, but he wasn't there.

'There's something odd about Class 8,' he told Miss Copewell. 'They're all working hard in there, doing maths which ought to be miles beyond them. Yet they seem to be enjoying it.'

'You should be pleased about it,' said Miss Copewell, who was always optimistic. 'Perhaps it's the modern methods Mr Browser uses.'

The Headmaster gave her a sharp look and started studying some forms.

'Well, he's lost that Michael Fairlie,' he muttered. 'I must go back and check that he's returned in a while.'

When he did return to Class 8 half an hour later he saw at once that Michael's place was still vacant. The class was steadily at work copying something from the blackboard. Mr Browser walked across to the door to meet him.

'Michael has just gone out to the library, Mr Salt,' he said before the Headmaster could speak.

'So he's come back,' said Mr Salt. 'What was he up to?'

'Oh, too enthusiastic about experimenting in the fog,' said Mr Browser. 'He was far away when we came in. Lost himself for a while.'

'Oh,' said Mr Salt. 'It seems likely.'

'Perhaps you'd like to inspect our work,' went on Mr Browser. 'We have a considerable amount of maths to cover, but I think that with effort we shall be up to O Level standard by the end of the school year.'

'I beg your pardon? Do you mean the old eleven plus level? O Levels are for children of fifteen or sixteen, Mr Browser, may I remind you.'

'I said O Levels, Mr Salt, and I meant it. And by the way, have we any copies of Shakespeare in the school? I would like to study *Hamlet* with the class next term, if possible.'

'I thought you were reading *The Wind in the Willows*,' said Mr Salt weakly.

'That's kids' stuff, Mr Salt!' called out Spiky Jackson. 'Buy us some Shakespeare, Mr Salt. Give us something to think about.'

Mr Salt looked at Spiky Jackson as though he had never seen him before.

'We'll see about it, Simon,' he muttered, and made his exit quickly.

'Miss Copewell,' he gasped, when his secretary came in with a cup of tea. 'Simon Jackson wants to study Shakespeare. He'll be going for his O Levels this summer. This summer, Linda! Think of it! At eleven years old – and Simon Jackson, of all people!'

'Spiky Jackson,' said Miss Copewell, who knew that Mr Salt was under stress because he'd called her Linda. 'Have your tea, Mr Salt. It's nice and hot. Perhaps you'd like me to fetch you an aspirin to take with it?'

'Yes, please!' begged the Headmaster, and gulped down a mouthful of too hot tea to try and bring himself round.

Chapter 5

As the pepperpot shot up into space Michael expected to have trouble with weightlessness, but found that he was able to walk about as though he were still on the ground. Perhaps we are just circling the world, he wondered, and decided that he might as well try and find out.

'Where are we?' he asked. 'Aren't we out in space yet?'

The translating machine set to work, and soon an answer came back.

'We are a hundred thousand miles beyond your moon. We are on course towards our Intermediate Space Station, where you will be able to meet one of our Outer Space Commanders – a most important Brain Sharpener.'

'Thank you,' said Michael. 'Where is the home of the Brain Sharpeners?'

There was a pause while the translating machine did its work and while the answering system considered whether the question was one which could safely be answered.

'Our world is not far away,' replied the machine at last. 'We live on a planet in a nearby galaxy. It has a climate similar to yours, which is why we are interested in visiting you. We have discovered several other planets near us which we could develop, and we need to recruit more citizens for them. Life on your world has not developed as fast as on ours, and of course our brains are much superior. So no doubt many of your people will be pleased to have their brains sharpened by us and start a new life in one of our colonies, especially when they find out what we have achieved with your Mr Browser and his class.'

Big heads! thought Michael, and then, just in case the Brain Sharpeners were reading his thoughts, 'Thank you very much for the information!' he added, aloud.

The flight continued for another hour.

'We are preparing to land,' the machine told Michael. There followed the usual hissing sound, and the pepperpot gently sank down. The door opened.

'You may step out,' said the machine. Michael obeyed, and saw that the pepperpot had flown into a huge enclosed platform. Above him a transparent roof was closing in, after having opened up to allow their entry.

'Stand still!' a voice ordered him. 'You will be taken to the Commander.'

Michael looked around for someone to take him, but the floor beneath him began to move, and he looked downward, fascinated, as his section of the floor was shunted and shuffled on its way to the door of one of the many rooms at the back of the platform. A door slid open, and Michael's piece of floor deposited him in the doorway.

'Walk in,' said a voice.

Sitting behind a desk was a tall, human-like person with long arms and a large but handsome head. It looked at Michael with a gaze so sharp that it felt like looking into the sun.

'Welcome,' said the figure. 'You wished to see a Brain Sharpener, and now you are looking at one. Is there anything more you wish to know?'

'Yes, please,' said Michael, avoiding that penetrating stare. 'Why are you interfering with my world, and why particularly my class?'

'I thought the machine had told you that,' remarked the Brain Sharpener.

'I'd like to confirm it,' said Michael. 'Machines can make mistakes.'

'Not ours,' said the Brain Sharpener. 'However, I will answer your question. When we first discovered your world, we were dismayed to find out how backward the people living in it are. Dangerous, too. If they go on advancing technically they may destroy themselves and lay waste to the whole planet. We considered two ways of preventing this. One was to destroy your planet ourselves, but we would only do that if we were threatened ourselves. The other way was to improve your brains so that you would be fit to survive and also useful to us for the development of our other planets. Do you understand this?'

Too well, thought Michael. It's slavery for most of us – and then he decided he'd better try and do without critical thoughts, in case the Brain Sharpeners took a dislike to them.

'Why did you choose my class?' he asked, to change the subject.

'Your teacher, Mr Browser, spoke words which put him in direct contact with us for a short while. No one else has ever spoken about Brain Sharpeners while we have been listening in to the planet earth. We realized afterwards that the words had only been spoken by chance, but as we were already contemplating making contact with earth, why not with your class? Your brains certainly could do with some sharpening, I'm sure you will agree.'

'And you are already sharpening their brains?'

'Of course. And from reports already received, the work is going very well.'

'What will happen to them when you have sharpened their brains enough?'

The Commander's expression was an earnest one all the time – he never relaxed his concentration.

'We shall consider them for transfer to our fifth newly discovered planet, which we are trying to develop.'

'But they are only children,' said Michael.

'Precisely. We need children, because by the time they arrive at their destination they will be just the right age for settling down.'

'An excellent idea,' said Michael, hoping that his secret thoughts, full of fear, would not stand revealed to the Brain Sharpener.

What an awful prospect! His friends in Class 8 were already busy preparing themselves to be kidnapped! At all costs he must return to the school to warn them – if they would listen. If not, he would have to speak to the Headmaster, or contact their parents. Meanwhile he must try to keep out of the clutches of the Brain Sharpeners himself.

'As for you,' went on the Commander, 'I have satisfied your wish to meet a Brain Sharpener. If you were to stay here and take a concentrated course, you could travel on to the Fifth Planet before the others, and by the time they arrived you would already hold an important position.'

'Thank you very much,' said Michael, trembling at the idea. 'It's a great compliment. But don't you think that if I stay here people on earth will become very suspicious about what has happened to me? There'd be an awful fuss in the newspapers – perhaps you don't know what newspapers on earth are like. When I came back, if ever I did, there'd be newspaper men around me like flies round a honey pot. And if I came back

44

cleverer than I went up it would arouse suspicion. At the moment Mr Browser will be having all the credit, and no one will suspect the presence of an outside power. I think the cleverest thing would be to send me back quickly, just the same as when I left. If I work hard, I'm sure Mr Browser will help me to catch up with the rest. You don't want anything to go wrong until you've made sure that Class 8's brains can be sharpened sufficiently for use.'

'Sound sense,' observed the Commander. 'Once we have sharpened your brain, you should have a great future on the Fifth Planet. I will arrange to have you transferred back to earth. You will be deposited on your school field immediately after dark.'

Michael stepped outside on the moving floor again. This time it guided him to a very small pepperpot, only just large enough to hold him. The door closed behind him as soon as he entered it, the transparent roof opened up and the tiny pepperpot ascended through the gap and rocketed on its way to earth.

Several sightings of a UFO were reported that evening, but nobody saw Michael step out on the school field just after dark. As soon as he had done so, the little pepperpot began to disintegrate, and within two minutes there was nothing left of it except a small mark of burning on the grass.

Michael ran across the field and into school. In Class 8's room Mr Browser was still there. He was putting books into his briefcase and preparing to leave.

'Michael! You have come back! You have missed a whole day's work! You will have to make up for it tomorrow!'

'Yes, Mr Browser.' Michael was disappointed. In the old days before the Brain Sharpeners had started interfering, Mr Browser would have wanted to know where he had been, would have been worried as to whether he was still all right, and would have told him to hurry off home to his parents. Now all he was concerned about was the missing of a day's work!

Michael hurried off home, very depressed. The prospect of rescuing Class 8 from their outer space fate seemed far from rosy, for he clearly couldn't expect any help from Mr Browser.

Mr Browser was already beginning to react just like a Brain Sharpener!

Chapter 6

As soon as Michael walked into the school playground the next morning he realized how much the Brain Sharpeners had changed his friends in Class 8 in one day.

Some of them, including Spiky Jackson, Anna Cardwell and Jason Little were already there – but not playing around in the playground as they used to do. Instead, they were hanging around the entrance door, anxious to be first inside.

'What's the rush, Spiky? Are they giving toffee apples away this morning?' asked Michael.

'No, they're not,' replied Spiky, as though Michael

had asked a serious question. Anna and some of the others frowned at Michael, and he saw that they were all carrying notebooks.

'What's been going on yesterday? What are the notebooks about?'

For a while no one condescended to answer him.

'Haven't you done any homework?' Anna asked him eventually.

'Homework? Not likely. Time enough for that at the Comprehensive School.'

'I did four hours last night,' said Spiky Jackson, looking highly satisfied about it.

'Four hours? You, Spiky? Impossible! You haven't gone round the bend, have you?'

Spiky flipped over the pages of his exercise book, pages filled with neat writing of which Michael would never have believed Spiky capable.

'You'll have to work hard to catch up with us, Mike,' said Spiky.

'I shan't have much time to catch up today, what with a television programme this morning and games this afternoon,' observed Michael. 'Are we playing a class football match with Class 7 this afternoon?'

'There won't be any games lesson this afternoon,' put in Anna. 'We've agreed to cancel our games lessons from now on. Mr Browser says we need all the time available in order to achieve what he's set out to do this term.'

'You're joking,' said Michael weakly; but there wasn't a sign of mischief in Anna's expression.

'TV has been cut out too,' Spiky informed him. 'Waste of time, so Mr Browser said. Wants us to concentrate on maths and science this term. If we do enough homework, he thinks we'll be up to O Level standard by Easter.'

Other Class 8 children were now crowding round

the door, all as earnest as Spiky and Anna. Michael's heart sank. The Mr Browser he knew would never have cancelled games on a fine day or cut out the weekly television programme.

'You're being tricked!' he shouted to them all. 'You and Mr Browser are being used by the Brain Sharpeners! If they think they can make you sharp enough, they'll take you off to Planet Five, and you'll never come back. You'll be kidnapped!'

The other members of Class 8 stared at Michael as though he himself were something from outer space, then turned away from him. A bell sounded inside the school, and a few seconds later the door was opened by Miss Toms.

'Class 8 – you all seem keen to go into school today,' she remarked. She was used to having to round up Spiky Jackson – and sometimes Michael – from the far end of the playground.

'We've some work to give in to Mr Browser,' explained Spiky.

'Indeed,' said Miss Toms, giving him an odd look. 'Well, if that's so, I'd better let the fourth years in first. Here – careful! Don't knock me over!'

Michael followed in the wake of the keen Class 8 students, who were up the corridor and stairs and into the classroom in a flash.

'Good morning, Class 8,' said Mr Browser. They were all sitting at their desks waiting for him as he went and sat down at his desk like an automaton. 'I trust you have completed all the suggested homework?'

The class, with the exception of Michael, answered together with enthusiasm.

'Then I trust we can look forward to another day of concentrated learning,' went on Mr Browser. 'I'll call the register first.'

When he came to Michael's name he stopped uneasily.

'Michael,' he asked, 'have you done any homework?'

'No, Mr Browser. I was away yesterday.'

'I remember,' said Mr Browser, frowning. 'You will have to work extra hard today in order to catch up with the rest of the class, and perhaps do an hour or two of extra homework tonight.'

'Yes, Mr Browser.'

An hour or two of extra homework! Mr Browser had been turned into a slave driver. Michael decided that he would try and play along with him and with the rest of the class, but it was sad to see Mr Browser so much changed by the Brain Sharpeners. It would be no use trying to persuade him that he and his class were in grave danger. Another way of fighting the Brain Sharpeners must be found.

Several days passed in concentrated study at school followed by hours of homework each night. When the weekend came all of Class 8, with the exception of Michael, looked sad at the prospect of a break in the learning routine. Mr Browser, too, was worried about this, and tried to make up for it by giving out enough homework to keep the class busy all Saturday and Sunday. The Headmaster was taking an increasing interest in the class, and his opinion of Mr Browser was rising steadily. At first he had been suspicious and disbelieving, but once he saw the giant strides in progress which Mr Browser had made, he was only too keen to bask in some of the glory.

Michael was the only fly in the educational ointment. He was completely out of his depth in all subjects, and obviously was not doing a tenth of the amount of homework done by the others.

'Michael,' the Headmaster warned him, 'if you can't keep up with the rest, you'll have to be transferred to another class. You're the only one who is not taking advantage of the excellent teaching Mr Browser is providing.'

'I'm the only one who's not being brainwashed,' retorted Michael.

'Sit down, and don't be so impolite,' the Headmaster ordered him.

On Monday morning he resolved to make one last attempt to foil the Brain Sharpeners. Only the Headmaster could save the class, he reasoned, by having Mr Browser removed from the school. If the class had no more direct contact with the Brain Sharpeners and their machines, then perhaps the effect would die away and Michael would win back his friends. He knocked on Mr Salt's door as soon as he entered school that morning. The Headmaster frowned when he saw Michael.

'Well, Michael,' he greeted him, 'I trust that you are making more effort to please Mr Browser.'

'I've come to see you about Mr Browser and Class 8,' said Michael. 'It's very important. If something isn't done soon, it'll be too late to save them.'

'Save them? From what?'

'From the Brain Sharpeners. Mr Browser is in touch with them, sir. They come from another galaxy, and they're trying to sharpen up the brains of Class 8 in order to send them to a planet they want to populate. Unless we can show that their brains can't be developed as much as the Brain Sharpeners require, one day they'll vanish, Mr Salt, and they'll never come back. They'll be kidnapped by the Brain Sharpeners, Mr Salt, I'm warning you!'

Michael paused for breath, and Mr Salt sat back in his chair and stared at him. He didn't take kindly to anyone in his school warning him about anything.

'That's quite a speech, Michael,' he said.

'It's all true, sir.'

'Do you really expect me to believe it? I happen to be highly pleased with your class, and with Mr Browser. You are the only one who gives me cause for concern, Michael. Even if your story were true, I would do all I could to assist Mr Browser to keep in contact with any power which could turn Class 8 into such an excellent group of children. The way they are going, they'll bring honour to the school. I can just imagine the surprise of the Headmaster of the Comprehensive School when he discovers how far in advance the Chivvy Chase children coming up to him are – they'll be far beyond the children of any other junior school. I am proud of them, Michael. No, my boy, it is not the rest of the class for which I fear. I fear for you. I would advise you to return to your classroom and buckle down to work, my lad. That's all!'

'You're worse than the Brain Sharpeners!' burst out

Michael, but the Headmaster was already shuffling papers, and Michael knew he was once again beaten. The Brain Sharpeners were winning. As he left Mr Salt's room he had to admit that he should not have expected any different reaction from a man as proud of his school as Mr Salt.

All hope seemed lost, until, as he passed the door of Miss Copewell's office he heard voices from within.

'I'd like to have a word with Mr Salt,' a man was saying earnestly. 'I don't know what's the matter with my Simon lately. He's behaving in a most curious manner.'

'I'm sorry to hear it,' said Miss Copewell in her sympathetic voice. 'What's the trouble, Mr Jackson?'

'He's spending all his time working,' said Mr Jackson. 'We can't stop him. No time for anything else at all. It's fishy. He's not in trouble any more, it's true, but this behaviour is not normal.'

'They do go through funny stages,' Miss Copewell informed him. 'However, if Mr Salt is free, no doubt he'll be pleased to see you.'

Michael stood just beyond the office door and listened, and a ray of hope warmed him. This was Spiky Jackson's father, come up to school because he couldn't understand why Spiky had suddenly become a bookworm. Maybe other parents would be equally suspicious!

As Michael walked back to class, Mr Salt kindly agreed to see Mr Jackson. But before he did he gave Miss Copewell something to do.

'Please check in the file if there's anything odd about Michael Fairlie and his family,' he requested her. 'Have you noticed anything yourself lately?'

'I can't say I have, Mr Salt.'

'The boy's been in here telling me the most ridiculous story. Behaved like a lunatic. Maybe he's been seeing too many space adventure films, but I would like you to check. And now please send in Mr Jackson. There's no pleasing some parents. Why, his son has just begun to work hard for the first time. I shan't let Mr Jackson waste much of my time, I can assure you.'

Chapter 7

As the days passed, the gap between Michael's knowledge and that of the rest of the class increased vastly. As he wasn't under the influence of the Brain Sharpeners, Michael didn't stand much chance of keeping up. Mr Browser soon began to despair of him, and allowed him to sit in a corner reading books and even comics while the brains of the rest of the class were being further and further extended.

'I shall have to do something about you, Michael,' he said occasionally as he walked past his one unresponsive pupil. 'I can't understand why you don't

make any progress. I shall have to find out when next we . . .'

He didn't finish the sentence, but clearly, as he couldn't do anything about Michael himself, Michael concluded that he was expecting to see the Brain Sharpeners again, and would try to find out from them why Michael's brain had not responded. Each day, in the morning, Mr Browser would spend some time looking out of the window, and one day Michael thought he had realized why.

'Hoping for some fog, Mr Browser?' he asked.

Mr Browser frowned and went away from the window.

Mr Salt was becoming increasingly proud of the cleverness of Class 8, and was heard to declare to Mr Browser that he would fetch the Chief Inspector in to show him how clever the children of Chivvy Chase School had become under him as Headmaster. Not everything, however, was rosy in Mr Salt's life. First Mr Jackson had complained about his son's changed outlook on life, then Mrs Cardwell came up to protest about the amount of homework Anna was doing.

'But I am assured by Mr Browser that all the children love doing their homework,' said Mr Salt. 'They keep on asking him for more.'

'So does Anna,' agreed her mother. 'But it doesn't seem natural. She never has time to help with the washing up, and she never listens to her "pop" records. She's hardly human any more, Mr Salt.'

'You should be proud of your daughter,' insisted the Headmaster. 'She'll be a credit to you later on.'

'She ain't my daughter any more,' declared Mrs Cardwell. 'Never laughs or even smiles, these days.'

Parents are never satisfied, thought Mr Salt, and

told Mrs Cardwell so, just as he had told Mr Jackson. Then more parents came up to complain. The Headmaster became more and more irritable with them for not praising the school; his ambition always had been to have the best school in the country, and now these ignorant parents seemed to be standing in his way.

'Go home and be thankful that you have such clever children,' he told them. And to them Mr Salt was such an important man that most of them did as he told them, just as their children had to do.

Michael, reading his comics in the corner, was pleased to note after about a fortnight that Mr Browser was not quite as intense as usual. Instead of allowing all who wanted to stay in at playtime to remain in the classroom and continue working, he ordered everyone out into the playground. Michael went with them, and whereas the rest of the class went out against their wills and hung around the door waiting to return to work again, Michael crept to the classroom window by means of the emergency stairs and looked inside.

Mr Browser was pacing up and down, wiping his forehead with a handkerchief. He sat down at his desk for a while with his head in his hands, then stood up again and marched up and down. Something was worrying Mr Browser, but clearly he himself couldn't grasp what it was. His behaviour confirmed the truth for Michael; the influence of the Brain Sharpeners was weakening. Mr Browser's brain needed further charging, or he would gradually return to normal.

At first Michael was pleased at this thought – but then he realized the danger that could go with it. The Brain Sharpeners would do all they could to keep Mr Browser under their influence, so no doubt they would be returning now as soon as there was a foggy day. They might, indeed, be so satisfied with the progress made in the sharpening of Class 8's brains that they would start them on their journey to Planet Five straight away!

And only I can stop them, thought Michael. He recalled the little Dutch boy who tried with his finger to stop the sea breaking through the dyke, and he felt just as small and helpless. Beads of perspiration appeared now on his own forehead as he realized that the lives on earth of all his friends could depend on him alone. He looked up anxiously for signs of fog in the heavens, but it was a clear day. Mr Browser was again coming to the window, gazing upwards. How he needed those Brain Sharpeners again!

The day was so still and clear that there could very easily be mist and fog the next morning. Probably Michael had less than twenty-four hours in which to save Class 8. He came down to the playground and watched them pityingly as they hung around the school door, hungry to be back inside again. It would be no use at all to try and warn them – they were so much under the influence of Mr Browser that they wouldn't even listen to any suggestion of danger. All Michael could do, he decided, was to try and warn their parents.

He spent the rest of the day obtaining the home addresses of as many of the class as possible.

'I may be moving away from the town soon, and I'd like to be able to write to you,' was his excuse – and to his relief it worked in each case. The poor little mental robots gave him their addresses without any question. After that all he had to do was to endure the rest of the school day, reading comics and listening to the drone of Mr Browser's voice as he gave out notes like a professor. In the afternoon Mr Salt came into the classroom to check on progress – though to tell the truth the lesson, one on finding the optimum stress on the arch of a bridge by maths, was well beyond the mathematical capabilities of Mr Salt. Perhaps because of this he was attracted by the sight of Michael reading in the corner.

'I shall have to remove you from this class, Fairlie,' he threatened Michael. 'You just aren't keeping up with the rest. I can't have Mr Browser's time wasted. I shall have to see about transferring you tomorrow.'

Michael feared that if he lost all touch with the class any chance of foiling the Brain Sharpeners would be gone.

'Please let me stay, Mr Salt!' he pleaded. Mr Salt muttered something and walked away.

At last the bell rang for the end of the day, and Class 8 students stuffed their homework books into their bags and made for home – and more work. Michael hurried off as well – but not directly homeward. He had decided to pay a few calls on some parents of children who lived between the school and his own home. First he knocked at the door of the bungalow in which Anna Cardwell's mother lived. He had seen Mrs Cardwell in the office at school, and she was friendly with his own parents, so he hoped she might listen sympathetically.

'Hullo, Michael, Anna's not home yet,' said Mrs Cardwell in some surprise.

'It's not Anna I want to talk to, Mrs Cardwell. It's you. Have you noticed that Anna has been behaving oddly lately?'

'She's been working very hard,' admitted Mrs Cardwell.

'Well, I know why she's like it.'

'Do you?' Mrs Cardwell was not being as sympathetic as Michael had hoped. Grumbling to a headmaster is something very different from hearing your own child criticized by another child.

'Yes – Anna is in the power of some beings from another world. They're called Brain Sharpeners, and if we don't stop them, they'll take Anna and all the rest away to another planet, and we shall never see them again!'

Mrs Cardwell took a step back and looked at Michael as though he were an unwanted salesman.

'Oh yes? And why did these Brain Sharpeners happen to tell you all this, Michael? Won't they take you as well?'

'No – because I've defied them,' Michael explained. 'I know what they're up to, and I won't let them control me.'

Mrs Cardwell started laughing.

'Pardon me, Michael, but I can't see that you have a brain so much superior to Anna's.'

'I haven't, Mrs Cardwell. I just won't let it be sharpened!'

'Sharpened! That's a good one! Really, Michael, I can't afford to waste any more time. And here's Anna. She'll want a cup of tea while she settles down to her homework. Might I suggest that you run along and do the same?'

'He doesn't do any homework,' said Anna with contempt.

'Perhaps he's jealous of those who do,' added her mother. 'Good-bye, Michael.' And as Anna walked in her mother quickly closed the door after her.

Michael walked down the garden path with tears in his eyes. This was a victory for the Brain Sharpeners! He determined to try Spiky Jackson's house next.

'Excuse me, Mrs Jackson!'

'Oh, hullo, Michael. Simon is working at his home-work. I hope you don't want him to come out to play. He hasn't any time to spare for that.'

'No, Mrs Jackson, I'm here to tell you the truth about Spi – Simon. It's not natural that he's working so hard, is it?'

Michael was echoing the words he had heard Mr Jackson saying to Mr Salt – but the expected response did not come from Mrs Jackson.

'Natural or not, it's doing him no harm. One of these days he'll be a doctor, or a lawyer, or even an M.P. We never used to expect anything of him, but now that's all changed. I want him to make the best of himself – and I'd advise you to go home and do some work yourself, Michael Fairlie. According to Simon, you're the dunce in the class now!'

'But I heard Mr Jackson say he was worried about Simon, and I came to warn you about the Brain Sharpeners.'

'Brain Sharpeners? You could do with a bit of brain-sharpening yourself, my lad. Mr Jackson isn't worried any more, Michael. Mr Salt and I have persuaded him to be sensible, and now he wants Simon to work hard, just like I do. Good-bye, Michael!'

The wretched Spiky Jackson must have heard their voices, but he couldn't even spare the time to get up from his books and come and say hullo. After that defeat, Michael went sadly home to tea. The thought of Spiky Jackson becoming a lawyer or a Member of Parliament could have been laughable, but the know-ledge that the Jacksons were deceiving themselves made Michael despair. Long before Spiky could ever become an M.P., the Brain Sharpeners would have whisked him away to another planet. How could he persuade these fond parents that it was better to have normal children than clever ones under the control of the Brain Sharpeners?

After tea he visited the parents of a few more of his classmates. All of them greeted his message with blank looks and disbelief. Some laughed, thinking he was joking. One or two called their children from their homework and asked them what Michael was talking about.

Those clever, robot students, formerly Michael's friends, stared at him and said they were sorry, but he had been acting strangely lately, and could they please go back to their work or Mr Browser would be angry with them. Then the fond parents, proud of their children's new keenness to work, grew impatient with Michael and told him to go, closing their doors in his face.

At last Michael accepted the hard truth: the parents would give him no help; they were all as deluded as their children. He even wondered whether the Brain Sharpeners had been getting at them as well. If he wanted to defeat the Brain Sharpeners, it was clear he would have to do so on his own.

As he set off home, admitting defeat, he saw that a low mist was forming at the end of the road, and the moon was already hidden. He shivered, not so much from cold, as from the feeling that the Brain Sharpeners might be calling to collect their victims in the morning.

Chapter 8

Michael awoke early the next morning. Jumping out of bed, he hurried to the window and drew back the curtains.

'Oh, no!' he said. The trees in his own back garden loomed out of the mist, but the houses beyond were hidden. It was a perfect morning for another visit from the Brain Sharpeners. If they were capable of creating the fog themselves, they had worked hard this time.

'I've not seen a fog as thick as this for a few years,' declared Michael's mother, 'and certainly not at this time of year.'

As Michael dressed he prepared himself for his coming battle of wits with the Brain Sharpeners. If only his own brain could be sharpened – without their help, of course! He was thinking hard as he ate his cornflakes, thinking as he drank his tea, thinking as he cleaned his teeth. His mother had never seen him so thoughtful.

'Have you an exam to take today, Michael?' she asked him as he thoughtfully put on his coat, putting the buttons into the wrong holes.

'No, Mother.'

'You're not unwell?'

'No, Mother.'

'Well, be careful on the road in this fog,' said his mother, giving up her questioning in despair. 'Don't go walking along in a dream and hit your head on a lamp-post, will you! I really don't know what's come over you lately!'

Michael set off up the road, still trying to think. Thinking is seldom unrewarded if we keep at it long enough, and by the time he had reached the school gate a plan had formed in his mind. Putting it into operation would be risky, but there seemed no other way to fight against the Brain Sharpeners.

He walked down the path towards the school, and to his relief heard no sounds coming from the playground. He was very early, so there was a good chance that his arrival would not be observed. He rounded the school building and made for the playground. No one was about. Crossing it quickly, he ran out into the fog on the school field. He ran across the football pitch, and with his heart throbbing and his throat dry, made for the railings on the far side of the field. As soon as they loomed up out of the fog, he stopped running and walked along beside them to a gate which was not used by the children, but was for the caretaker and groundsman.

He tried it, and it opened. Relieved, for it would have been difficult to climb over, he went through to the road outside. A few yards along it stood a telephone booth. He had known it was there, but he wanted to confirm this, for the booth was to play an important part in his plan. He returned to the school grounds. In the corner of the field stood an old shed used by the groundsman, and he hid behind it, listening to the distant sound of the children who were now coming into the playground in increasing numbers.

The bell rang, and there was silence. He was tempted to rush across the field and join his friends as they went into school, but he steeled himself to stay and wait for the arrival of the Brain Sharpeners.

Each minute the fog thickened, and hiding behind the shed was absolutely unnecessary. It was most unlikely that the groundsman would turn up for work on such a morning. Michael came out from behind the shed and edged along the railings in order to be nearer the telephone booth. If the Brain Sharpeners did come, he would have a great deal to do in a very short time. He was considering what excuse he would make for being late to school if they didn't come, when from somewhere up above him there came that familiar whirring sound.

The pepperpot was coming! He waited for a second to be sure, then ran to the gate and down the road to the telephone booth, moving faster than he had ever done in his life. To his relief, nobody was making a phone call, and he pulled open the heavy door, lifted the receiver and dialled 999.

'Police!' he panted into the telephone. 'There's a body in the middle of the field at Chivvy Chase

School. Yes, the school in Chase Road. I was just passing by, and I could see it from the pavement. Please come quickly!'

He didn't oblige the person on the other end of the line with any further information, but rang off and burst out of the booth, praying that the police would come even if they suspected it might be a hoax. Back into the grounds he ran, along the edge of the field and towards the school. The whirring sound was stronger now. Perhaps ordinary people might have mistaken the noise for that of a plane or even a gust of wind, though the stillness of the fog should have ruled out the possibility of wind.

Michael hastened across the playground and panted his way into school. His first call was not his classroom, but the office, where Miss Copewell was busy churning out some sheets of duplicating paper. Michael knocked, because he knew that if he didn't knock first there would be delay while he was asked why he hadn't knocked and while he was treated to a lecture on manners. Miss Copewell's machine stopped.

'Well, Michael?'

'Please, Miss, Mr Browser would like the key to Class 8. The catch isn't working properly, and he wants to keep the door closed.'

'Oh, Michael,' said Miss Copewell. 'The trouble with these doors is that they're not childproof!'

'Yes, Miss Copewell. Thank you, Miss Copewell,' said Michael as she handed him the key.

He hastened down the corridor, up the stairs and into the classroom. Class 8 had their heads down as they copied some notes, and Mr Browser was sitting at his desk.

'Sorry I'm late, Mr Browser,' said Michael. 'I've just come from the doctor's.'

Mr Browser looked at him with little interest. He had his class working, but his attention was focused on the windows. Michael recognized the symptoms. Mr Browser was becoming restless, and in a moment or two he would be asking the class to stand. Then he would lead them out again to the pepperpot! It mustn't happen, thought Michael.

'Please, Mr Browser,' he said loudly, 'I want to catch up with the rest of the class. May I have a new book from the store cupboard, please? My old one is full, and if I'm going to do four hours homework a night I shall need a new one badly!'

Mr Browser stared at him, and saw only keenness and a desire for work in Michael's face. The Brain Sharpeners must be working on him, he thought, and he mentally welcomed Michael back like a lost sheep

that has been found. There might be just time to give him a book before the Brain Sharpeners arrived.

'Good, Michael,' he said. 'Come with me at once. We shall be going out on the field any moment now.'

'Of course, Mr Browser,' said Michael.

Mr Browser hurried across to the store cupboard, and Michael followed him. In went Mr Browser – and Michael closed the door on him and turned the key in the lock. He slipped the key into his trouser pocket alongside the key to the classroom door, and made swiftly for the door.

'Let me out!' shouted Mr Browser. 'This is no time for joking, Michael: I must get out – we have to go out on the field. Open the door! Somebody let me out!'

He began to bang on the inside of the door, but by the time some heads had come up from their books, Michael was at the classroom door. He opened it, stepped into the corridor and locked the door on the class.

Triumphant, he lay back against the wall to regain his breath. And just at that moment the Headmaster came along the corridor. He was coming to tell Mr Browser that a Government Inspector was coming down to the school in order to check on the marvellous progress of Class 8.

'What's the matter, Michael?' he asked irritably, remembering that he had threatened to have Michael transferred to another class. 'Why aren't you in class? Has Mr Browser turned you out?'

'No, Mr Salt.'

A brilliant idea had just come into Michael's head; it was as though the Brain Sharpeners had put it there.

'I've just seen something strange on the field,' he gasped out. 'It's the Brain Sharpeners, Mr Salt! Don't go out there! They're after Class 8 and Mr Browser.'

'What's that banging?' demanded Mr Salt as Mr Browser redoubled his efforts to make someone free him.

'I don't know, sir,' replied Michael. Mr Salt took a look inside the classroom, and saw some of the class trying to force in the store cupboard door.

'Where's Mr Browser?' demanded the Headmaster, all his old suspicions of Mr Browser flooding back.

'I don't know,' said Michael. 'Perhaps the Brain Sharpeners have him – or perhaps he's locked in that cupboard. If he doesn't come out soon, the Brain Sharpeners may go away –'

Mr Salt pulled vainly at the handle of the classroom door, and Michael watched anxiously, for he knew that back in his room the Headmaster would have a master key, and if he fetched that in time, all would be over.

'That thing on the field looked like a pepperpot,' mumbled Michael – and Mr Salt grew tired of struggling with the door and heard him. He didn't like being ordered about in his own school – particularly by children. Michael had told him not to go on the field. Very cheeky!

'You're talking utter nonsense, boy,' declared the Headmaster. 'I shall go out on the field, and when I come back, having found nothing, I shall, for the first time this term, take out my cane and use it!'

He strode off down the corridor, and Michael was glad to let him go, for it meant that there would be more delay before Class 8 could escape, and maybe the police would arrive on the field before Mr Browser could bring the children there. Maybe, too, they would be there when Mr Salt arrived.

The banging inside the classroom became frantic, and it looked as though some of the boys were weakening the store cupboard door. Michael moved out of sight along the corridor, and then decided to venture out on the playground to see what had happened to Mr Salt.

There was a strange light coming from the centre of the field – and then the whirring sound began again, as it had done when the pepperpot had taken off. The siren of a police car sounded nearby. The whirring sound became fainter, and the fog began to thin out. Two policemen appeared, running hard across the field.

'Hi, there, boy!' one of them shouted.

'Yes?'

'Take me to your Headmaster,' ordered the first policeman. 'Steve, you carry on searching the field in case there's anything,' he added to his fellow policeman.

Michael made a move towards the field, then checked himself.

'He'll be in his room,' he said. 'This way.' He led the policeman into the school and along the corridor to the office. From Class 8's room upstairs came a variety of banging and shouting noises. The policeman raised his eyebrows.

'Their teacher's out,' explained Michael. He took the policeman to the office door and knocked.

'Please, Miss Copewell, there's a policeman to see Mr Salt,' he announced. Miss Copewell came to the door.

'Mr Salt is not here,' she said. 'He was going to look in at Class 8.'

'He's not there,' said Michael.

'Then I don't know where he is,' said Miss Copewell, who was used to spending considerable time each day searching for the Headmaster. 'Would you mind waiting? No doubt he'll be back in a minute. What's the matter?'

'Not in front of the boy,' said the policeman, looking down at Michael.

'I'll go back to class,' volunteered Michael.

'Good boy,' said Miss Copewell.

As Michael turned the corner and climbed the stairs he heard the voice of Miss Toms quelling the noise from Class 8.

'I'll fetch a cloth and break the glass,' she called out.

Michael ran along the corridor.

'Don't do that, Miss Toms. I have the key!' he shouted.

'You? What are you doing with the key, Michael?'

'I went to fetch it, Miss,' said Michael, smiling at her. 'You see, I was late, and –'

'Open it up, then,' demanded Miss Toms. Michael obeyed, and when Miss Toms entered the room Class 8 moved back to their seats automatically.

'Where's Mr Browser?' asked Miss Toms. Loud knockings on the cupboard door gave her the answer.

'Who has the key?' she demanded.

'I have,' said Michael.

'You! But –'

For once Michael did not allow Miss Toms to finish her sentence, but went and opened the store cupboard. Mr Browser, coat off and his tie awry, shot out like a rabbit from its burrow.

'Class 8,' he commanded, 'out in line at once!'

'Where are you going?' asked the confused Miss Toms – and when Mr Browser saw her, he also became confused.

'It's too late, Mr Browser. They've gone!' said Michael. Mr Browser stared at him.

'Are you sure?'

'Quite sure, Mr Browser. I heard them taking off. The fog's lifted, and there's nothing on the field.'

'It's true,' said Mr Browser, looking out of the window. The sun was trying to break through low clouds. Mr Browser wiped his forehead with a duster he had found in the cupboard.

'Who's gone where?' demanded Miss Toms, who hated not to be in control of the situation.

'Never mind, Miss Toms,' said Mr Browser with sudden firmness. 'Thank you for your help. I can look after everything from now on. Class 8, take out your books. Sit down, Michael. Read quietly, everybody – whatever you like.'

Miss Toms edged out sideways, wondering whether she ought to report all this mysterious behaviour to Mr Salt. Michael sat down – and to his surprise saw that Spiky Jackson was reading a comic and grinning all over his face – happy as a man who's been on a desert island for months and has just seen a ship coming towards him. Michael looked around him – and there was Anna Cardwell, playing quietly with a tiny doll which she had found at the bottom of her desk, where it had been lying untouched since the arrival of the Brain Sharpeners.

'Spiky!' whispered Michael. 'Shouldn't you be getting on with some work? You're wasting time with that comic.'

Spiky looked up briefly and winked.

'You're a fine one to talk!' he said, and returned to the comic.

Michael was congratulating himself that the class was coming out of the spell put on them by the Brain Sharpeners, when Miss Copewell came along the corridor with Miss Toms and the policeman.

'Excuse me, Mr Browser,' said Miss Toms. 'Has anyone seen Mr Salt? He is said to have come this way.'

Michael's hand shot up.

'Please Mr Browser, Mr Salt went out on the field.'

'Indeed,' said Mr Browser. 'Carry on with your work, Class 8.'

Looking very grave, he set off with Miss Toms, Miss Copewell and the policeman for the field.

'We had this report, made by a child, we think –' the policeman was saying.

Five minutes later they all came back – without the Headmaster. The policeman went to the office with Miss Toms to discuss the strange disappearance of Mr Salt. Mr Browser re-entered the classroom as Spiky Jackson launched the first dart he had thrown since the Brain Sharpeners had set him to work. It glided through the air, then swooped and landed on Mr Browser's desk. The whole class looked up in anxious expectation.

'Simon Jackson,' said Mr Browser, picking up the dart, 'that's quite a well made dart. Yes, it's the best I've seen for a while. It's nice to know you haven't forgotten how to make them. But no more of them, please.'

Spiky Jackson's mouth opened wide, and then a grin spread all over his face.

'Thanks, Mr Browser,' he said.

'I think,' went on Mr Browser, 'that we'll have a change of lessons this afternoon. We'll go out to games – we haven't been out for weeks, owing to the weather, so I think you deserve a long lesson.'

Class 8 came back to life, for everyone now knew that Mr Browser had also escaped from the clutches of the Brain Sharpeners.

'Hurrah for Mr Browser!' cried Jason Little – and everyone joined in the cheering.

'And no more homework for a while,' added Mr Browser. 'Maybe we've been overdoing it a little lately.'

Michael marvelled at the smooth way in which Mr Browser had dismissed the Brain Sharpeners from his mind – even blaming the lack of games lessons on the weather. He decided it would be wise not to bring the subject up for a while, though there were questions he wanted to ask.

Policemen in uniform were replaced later on in the day by important looking men in plain clothes – but there was no sign of the Headmaster. Late in the afternoon one of the plain clothes men asked Michael questions in the presence of Miss Toms.

'You said you saw Mr Salt go out on the field?'

'I saw him going along the corridor in that direction, and he said he was going out on the field.'

'Did he say why?'

'No,' said Michael. He had decided that unless Mr Browser was going to talk, he would say nothing at all about the Brain Sharpeners – it was surely best to let sleeping dogs lie.

That evening the parents of the children in Class 8 were surprised to find that their sons and daughters wanted to play or watch television all the time instead of working. At first they were shocked and disappointed, but gradually they began to admit that they were pleased that their children were back to normal, even if it did mean that they were often more trouble to them.

At school, Mr Browser became his old self, demanding reasonable work but not being fanatical about it. Once or twice Michael approached him with the idea of asking him about the Brain Sharpeners, but each time Mr Browser sent him away because he was busy. As for Mr Salt, the Headmaster had disappeared, and there wasn't a clue as to his whereabouts. There were plenty of rumours, and there was a report in the local paper stating that maybe it was overwork which had made Mr Salt vanish so completely. His wife declared that he had been ever so happy at home.

A fortnight went by as though the Brain Sharpeners had never existed. Yet the continued absence of the Headmaster was a constant reminder to Michael of all that had happened, and at last he could no longer remain silent. He chose a time at the end of the school day when Mr Browser was alone at his desk, and took him by surprise by doubling back from the door instead of following the others out.

'Please Mr Browser, do you think Mr Salt will ever come back?' he asked. 'If they were just sharpening up his brain for use on us he would have been back before now, wouldn't he?'

Mr Browser at first put on his aloof look, but Michael's determined appearance persuaded him to talk.

'I think you're right, Michael,' he agreed. 'I'm sure that Mr Salt was the very sort of man they needed to develop their new territories. It wouldn't be a surprise to me if he became a sort of Minister of Education on Planet Five, if they've managed to sharpen his brains up enough. They couldn't very well let him come back after their attempt to sharpen up our brains had failed, so they cut their losses and made off with him. They might send him back to some other town to recruit other suitable people for brain sharpening, but that depends on how long they're prepared to keep their space platform in its present position. If they take it back to their own galaxy, they won't be back here for hundreds of thousands of years – that's my guess.'

'Then we're safe, Mr Bowser.'

'I think so. But we must always be on our guard, in case they do turn up in some form or other.'

But to this day there has been no sign from the Headmaster or from the Brain Sharpeners. Miss Toms was appointed Headmistress in Mr Salt's place, and Mr Browser became Deputy Headmaster. The Inspector invited by Mr Salt arrived and found the children no cleverer or stupider than the children of most other schools, and went away saying that Mr Salt must have been a little deranged before he vanished into thin air.

So life returned to normal at Chivvy Chase School, and so far there's no sign that the Brain Sharpeners have yet struck in any other school.

Heard about the Puffin Club?

... it's a way of finding out more about Puffin
books and authors, of winning prizes (in
competitions), sharing jokes, a secret code, and
perhaps seeing your name in print! When you
join you get a copy of our magazine, *Puffin
Post*, sent to you four times a year, a badge
and a membership book.
For details of subscription and an application
form, send a stamped addressed envelope to:

The Puffin Club Dept A
Penguin Books Limited
Bath Road
Harmondsworth
Middlesex U B7 OD A

and if you live in Australia, please write to:

The Australian Puffin Club
Penguin Books Australia Limited
P.O. Box 257
Ringwood
Victoria 3134

A NOVELIZATION BY DAVE STERN
STORY BY KIRK M. PETRUCCELLI & LLOYD LEVIN
AND JAMES V. HART
SCREENPLAY BY DEAN GEORGARIS

POCKET STAR BOOKS

New York London Toronto Sydney Singapore

This book is a work of fiction. Names, characters, places and incidents are products of the author's imagination or are used fictitiously. Any resemblance to actual events or locales or persons, living or dead, is entirely coincidental.

An *Original* Publication of POCKET BOOKS

A Pocket Star Book published by
POCKET BOOKS, a division of Simon & Schuster, Inc.
1230 Avenue of the Americas, New York, NY 10020

ISBN: 0-7434-7709-X

First Pocket Books printing July 2003

10 9 8 7 6 5 4 3 2 1

POCKET STAR BOOKS and colophon are registered trademarks of Simon & Schuster, Inc.

Manufactured in the United States of America

For information regarding special discounts for bulk purchases, please contact Simon & Schuster Special Sales at 1-800-456-6798 or business@simonandschuster.com

PROLOGUE

For the first time in almost a month, Lara Croft was comfortable.

She was back home, in the study at Croft Manor, sprawled out in a red leather chair. On the table to her left was a mug of tea and a plate of scones—cinnamon walnut, fresh from the oven. *Plutarch's Lives* was open in her lap, there was a warm compress on her neck, and Coltrane playing gently in the background.

She did not intend on moving for several hours and only then to make her way into a hot bath. Then to bed. Up in the morning and repeat again till relaxed. A week or so should do it, she calculated—dispel the ghosts of Von Croy and Eckhardt from her mind, give the bruises she'd obtained in Prague and Paris time to heal.

When she heard the study door creak open, she frowned.

"No," she said without looking up. "Resting. Incommunicado."

She waited for the door to shut.

Instead, she heard the sound of a throat clearing. High-pitched, hesitant.

Bryce.

"Don't make me get out of this chair," she said. She wet a finger, and turned a page.

"Er," Bryce replied. "It's just . . ."

His voice trailed off. His footsteps edged closer. She looked up from the book.

Bryce was staring past her, at the scones.

"Oh my." He sniffed the air. "Are those cinnamon?"

"Cinnamon walnut."

He smiled, and actually licked his lips. "Really?"

She glared at him.

Bryce was her tech man—resident geek. Kept her equipment—weapons, communications systems, transport vehicles, etc.—in tip-top shape. She was glad to have him around . . . usually.

"One," she said, holding out the plate.

He snatched the biggest and started cramming it into his mouth.

"Now off with you," Lara said, putting down the scones. "I'm on downtime. Unavailable. System maintenance, to put in terms you'll find easily comprehensible."

"Mmm," Bryce said. "I understand." He licked his fingers. "Delicious. Hillary never makes these for me."

"It's because you're a pain in the arse."

Bryce looked shocked.

"I mean that in the nicest way possible," Lara said. "Now shoo—exit stage left. Close the door behind you."

"I—"

"Go," Lara repeated firmly. "Don't make me lay hands on you."

She turned to the *Plutarch* again. She was skipping around in it—no reason for her to study up any further on Pericles or Alexander, she'd done those two to death, and she never bothered with the Romans because she'd long ago decided that they were soldiers and nothing more—as far as culture was concerned they'd simply followed in the footsteps of the Greeks and appropriated whatever they . . .

Her musings puttered to a halt.

Footsteps, she thought. She hadn't heard Bryce's.

She looked up. He had, in fact, not moved at all.

He smiled. "Good stopping point?"

She sighed heavily and pinched the bridge of her nose.

"Bryce. Am I not making myself clear?"

"You're clear, you're clear," he said quickly. "I just thought you'd want to see this."

"This" was a sheet of paper, which he held up with both hands, turned toward her. A computer printout—a photograph.

"That looks like the ocean," Lara said.

"It is," Bryce agreed.

"Why would I be interested in the ocean?"

"You're not. What you might be interested in is this." He pointed at the middle of the picture, though from where she sat Lara couldn't see at what.

"Come closer," she said.

"It's a wooden something or other," Bryce supplied. "An artifact, to put it in terms you'd find easily comprehensible. With a very interesting carving on the face of it—" He pointed again. "Here."

Bryce was closer now—close enough that Lara could just barely make out the object he was talking about, floating in the middle of the sea. And on it, a geometric design of some sort—a representation of the sun, she realized. No, a star—an eight-pointed star, with—

Lara bolted upright. The *Plutarch* slid to the floor with a resounding thump.

An eight-pointed star.

"Let me see that," she said, standing.

Bryce shrank backward, mistaking her interest for anger.

Lara crossed the remaining distance between them in two quick steps and snatched the photo from him.

It was, indeed, an eight-pointed star.

The emblem of Alexander the Great.

"Where?" she demanded, shifting her focus from the picture to Bryce.

"The Aegean, as I said. Thirty-six point seven-four degrees north by—"

She grabbed his arm. He winced.

"Show me," she said and marched him out of the study, double-time.

Less than a minute later, they were standing in front of a huge flat-screen monitor. The screen displayed a landmass shaped like a backward C. There were two small islands in its empty center and another, slightly larger one to the northwest of it.

She recognized the area immediately.

"This is Santorini." She pointed at the largest island, the backward C. "That's Thera."

"Yes." Bryce smiled. There was a walnut stuck in between his two front teeth. "Very impressive."

Not really, Lara thought, but didn't bother to say it out loud because any archaeologist—and certainly any tomb raider—worth their salt would have recognized the island group just as quickly, Thera having been the site of a spectacular eruption almost four thousand years ago, an event that destroyed Minoan civilization and gave rise to the myth of Atlantis. And of course there was Akrotiri, a Minoan-era city on Thera itself, an excavation that had unearthed some of the most spectacular finds of the last twenty years. An excavation that her father had played a prominent role in, which had fixed the island—and its importance—permanently in her own mind.

"There was an eruption fifteen minutes ago," Bryce was saying. "Fairly minor—three point eight on the Richter, but what it did—here, I'll show you." He began feverishly typing on the keyboard.

Lara sat back again, letting Bryce do his thing, taking in the whole of the tech center—what he liked to call the mansion's "control room"—and shaking her head.

The place was a disaster area—a mess of cable, and monitors, and spare parts scattered haphazardly around the room. He'd put the helicopter simulator back online, as well, if she wasn't mistaken—and given the size of the joystick controller off to the right, she didn't think she was—which she'd told him more than once was a disastrously bad idea. The notion of someone as easily distractable as Bryce flying a helicopter . . .

Not for the first time, Lara wondered if actually sectioning off part of Croft Manor for Bryce's use had been a good idea. Perhaps she should have done as Hillary suggested—build him a shed next to the trailer he insisted on living in, right next to the manor. But Bryce had been so persuasive about the benefits of having the house "wired," she'd gone along with his desires.

Someone laid a hand on her shoulder. She turned and saw Hillary standing over her.

"This does not look like rest," Hillary said.

She smiled and laid her hand over his. "Don't worry—Bryce is doing the work. I'm just observing."

He frowned. Hillary was her man Friday—his family had served the Crofts for more than a generation. He'd lived in the manor longer than Lara had, knew things about it—about the Crofts, about Lara—that she'd long ago forgotten.

He also knew about Prague, and ever since Lara's return, had been watching over her like a mother hen.

"Where's your tea?" He frowned, and looked around the room. "I'll get you some more tea."

"Not necessary," she said. "I'm fine."

"Won't be a minute," Hillary said, heading off in the direction of the kitchen.

"Here we are," Bryce announced. "This is fifteen minutes ago."

Lara turned back to the monitor. It showed Thera as it looked from several hundred feet up, whitewashed stone buildings coating the hillside, the narrow cobblestoned streets, the churches, a tavern—

"Bryce," Lara said, suddenly realizing something. "Where are these images coming from?"

"No need to worry." He spoke without turning around to face her.

Lara frowned. "Tell me you're not tied in to Langley again." She did not want to have to deal with the Americans again. The last time they had caught Bryce hijacking their signals, she'd had to fly to Washington and kiss ass for a week to prevent them from starting extradition proceedings.

If he was doing it again . . .

"No, no," Bryce said quickly. "These are courtesy of a ZY-Three out of Jiquan command center. And it's all legit, believe me. Well, at least as legit as you can get doing this sort of thing."

Lara frowned. "Out of where?"

"Jiquan Command Center. Gansu Province."

Lara looked at the images again, and shook her head. "These are off a Chinese satellite?"

"Yes, that's right."

"The Chinese don't have anything nearly this powerful."

"Not officially." He smiled again. "But I've made a friend, recently—on one of the AI forums the other night, and we got to chatting, and of course I asked him what he did, and it turns out he's one of the surveillance monitors for—"

"Enough," Lara said, holding up a hand. "As long as it's not Langley, I can deal."

"It's not Langley," Bryce said. "Ah." He pointed at the monitor. "Watch this."

Whoever was controlling the satellite's focus—Bryce's friend, perhaps?—had found something of interest. The camera zoomed in closer on the town—Fira, or Oia, possibly even Merovigli, where she'd spent one idyllic summer as a teenager—and stopped.

They were looking at a wooden deck, perched precariously on a cliff overlooking the ocean. A large portion of the deck was covered by a white tent—no, not a tent, a thinner cloth, a canopy, almost transparent to the satellite. Beneath the canopy, Lara saw movement—people, dozens of them. On the portion of the deck not covered by the canopy, tables were set up, filled with people eating, drinking, in mostly formal wear . . .

Lara suddenly realized she was looking at a wedding.

The people moving underneath the canopy were dancing.

"Your friend," Lara said, smiling, "is somewhat of a voyeur."

"Well," Bryce said. "Er."

The camera moved away. Naturally—as high up as the satellite was, it couldn't focus on such a small area for long.

Except that a split second later, the satellite was focused on the wedding again. From farther off, and at a different angle this time—one that let it peer underneath the tent. Lara caught a glimpse of guests in formal dress, arms clasped around each other, making a circle—she marveled at the resolution the satellite was capable of—when suddenly the image on the monitor wavered.

The dancing stopped.

"That was shock number one," Bryce announced. He pointed to another monitor just to the right of the one they were watching, which showed an X-Y graph. "Two point seven on the Richter."

Guests milled about on the screen.

The image wavered again. This time, Lara saw objects on the monitor actually shake. For a second, she feared the entire deck might topple off the mountain and plunge into the sea.

"Shock number two," Bryce announced. "Three point eight."

The white canopy collapsed, covering dozens of people. The cloth rippled and surged. The bride sat down on the deck, and put her head in her hands.

The satellite moved off again. A second later, she was looking at the ocean. And as she watched, something popped to the surface and rested there, bobbing on the current.

The artifact Bryce had shown her, bearing the symbol of Alexander the Great. The eight-pointed star.

The earthquake had clearly disturbed something, but what . . .

"Can you go in closer on that?" she asked Bryce, pointing at the screen.

Bryce nodded. She watched the image grow larger, theories about what might have happened—what the earthquake might have disturbed—running through her mind. A shipwreck, perhaps—that seemed the most likely candidate, although—

"Terrible resolution at this size," Bryce said. "Hold on a minute."

He keyed in a few more commands. Lara watched as the image grew sharper and sharper, till Bryce leaned back with a satisfied smile.

Lara leaned forward, and studied the carving intently.

The first thing that struck her was how sharp the lines of the carving were.

"No decomposition," she said.

"It can't be very old then, can it?" Bryce asked.

"One would think so." It couldn't be from a shipwreck, either, she thought. So then what—

"It has that look, though—something out of another time," he said. "That's why I came to you."

"It does at that," Lara said, trying to remember if had Alexander ever traveled to Thera during his lifetime, which of his generals had inherited that portion of the empire. Her memory of *Plutarch,* clearly, was not as up to snuff as she'd thought.

She looked at the artifact on the screen again, watched as it rolled over slowly in the current, as the eight-pointed star disappeared beneath the ocean . . .

And Lara gasped.

On the other side of the piece, just coming into view, was another carving, even more detailed. This was of the moon— and etched within it, the instantly recognizable image of Alexander himself.

Now she knew what the earthquake had disturbed. Where the artifact had come from.

Lara smiled, and stood up again. The aches and pains she'd been all too aware of for the last few days were suddenly no longer with her.

"I've got to go pack," she announced. "Make a few phone calls."

On her way out the door, she brushed past a surprised-looking Hillary, carrying another pot of tea and more scones.

"Lara?" he called after.

"Lara?" Bryce chimed in, his voice just reaching her as she reached the foot of the main staircase. "What is it? It's obviously something."

"Oh, yes indeed," she called back. "It's something, all right."

ONE

Gus Petraki came down the ladder from the wheelhouse to find his eldest son Nicholas waiting for him on the deck.

"Papa, hey. Papa, listen." Nicholas had stripped to the waist. He had diving tanks on, and held a mask in his right hand. "Let me go down, scout things out for you, all right? Take a quick look, come back, give you the lay of the land, okay?"

Gus shook his head. "No. I said we'd wait, and we'll wait."

"But—"

"No." Gus glared at his son. "Take the tanks off, and go keep watch off the back, all right?"

Nicholas glared, then spun on his heels, heading for the stern, cursing under his breath. Gus smiled, watched as his son shrugged off the tanks. Nicholas was a good boy, even if he was a little impatient. Not without cause—time was of the essence here, but it wouldn't do any good for Nicholas to go down, he didn't have the expertise, the knowledge to know what he was looking for. Or looking at, for that matter.

Gus turned his back on Nicholas and headed toward the front of the boat.

His youngest, Jimmy, staring off the bow through a pair of binoculars, turned at his approach.

"Anything?" Gus asked.

"No." Jimmy passed the binoculars to his father. "They're all still down there."

Gus took the glasses and scanned the horizon, then focused downward, into the ocean itself. The water was a deep, dark blue, and clear down to three meters, which was about as good as it ever got. There was no sign of Kristos, or Leyden, or any of their divers.

He passed the glasses back to Jimmy and looked at his watch. Half an hour since the divers had gone in the water. Too long—he had a sinking feeling in his stomach that they'd found something else.

"You know, Papa, we could call Kristos."

Gus glared, and started to open his mouth. Before he could squeeze out a word, Jimmy went on hurriedly.

"No, no, hear me out. I know him—you know him, twenty years, right? You know he'd rather work with us than with Leyden, Papa. Yes?"

Gus could only frown and nod reluctantly.

"Yes, but—"

"Yes, you see?" Jimmy smiled. "And we've got those, right? He doesn't have anything like those."

Jimmy pointed off toward the back of the ship, and Gus didn't have to look to know he was talking about the DPVs. Personal diving vehicles, three of them, the pride and joy—and the bread and butter—of his salvage business. Gus had been doing salvage for three decades now, hiring out the *Konstantinos* and himself to treasure seekers, fortune hunters, family members looking to find loved ones (or their remains) lost at sea—and only during the last five years, with those sleds, had he been able to turn a consistent profit.

Gus nodded. "Yes, Kristos doesn't have anything like the sleds. But neither did we before that business with the Natla woman, and the Scion. And don't forget who's responsible for that, hey?"

"I didn't forget," Jimmy said. "But look at how many

ships there are. How many divers are going down. We have to—"

"Wait," Gus interrupted. "We have to wait."

Jimmy frowned.

Gus ruffled his son's hair.

If Nicholas was impatient, Jimmy was just the opposite. Considered and calm—a little too much of the thinker, for his taste. Join forces with Kristos? Hah. That would be the day.

Thing was, his sons were right. He didn't know how much longer he could afford to stand by and watch. There might not be anything left to find by the time—

"They're moving," Jimmy said.

He pointed off the starboard side of the *Konstantinos,* to the other boats. They had indeed started moving, heading northwest, toward the straits between Thera and Therasia.

"Let's stay close!" Gus shouted up to his pilot, Stefano, in the wheelhouse.

A few seconds later, he heard the motor come to life, and the *Konstantinos* inched forward. Gus went and stood by the railing. Something was happening, that was for sure—the other boats were all converging on a single spot in the ocean.

He pulled out his cell phone, punched the redial button, and waited.

"We're sorry. All circuits are busy at this time. Please try your call again later."

He restrained himself—barely—from throwing the phone in the ocean and looked at his watch. It only confirmed what he knew already.

Close to two hours past their scheduled rendezvous time. He didn't think they could wait much longer.

"They found another one!"

That was Nicholas, behind him, pointing off into the distance. Where a handful of divers had just surfaced, holding something roughly the size and shape of a man propped up between them.

The divers passed it along to waiting crew on one of the other boats, who started lifting it up out of the water.

Another statue. Damn it.

"Mark their location!" He shouted up to Stefano as he walked around the wheelhouse again, to the back of the boat. Jimmy followed him, his binoculars out and trained on the divers.

"Can't make out the statue, but—that's the Frenchman," Jimmy said. He swung the binoculars around to focus on the other ship. "And over there . . . Kristos."

Gus shook his head. He picked up the cell phone again and punched redial. Got the same recording.

He sighed, and stared out to sea.

"They're all here . . . all except one." He made a decision. "Follow Kristos. When he dives, we dive. Maybe we'll get lucky and find whatever it is . . ."

He frowned. The phone was making a buzzing noise now. No. Not the phone.

He turned, behind him, in the direction of the harbor.

Something was coming up behind them. Fast.

Gus squinted into the distance. It was a boat—three boats, very small, moving very quickly, and—

No. Not boats at all. Jet-skis. Three of them. The one in the middle, now pulling ahead of the other two, going way too fast, but whoever was riding it was an expert, he was—

No. Not he.

Gus broke into a big smile.

"Hey!" he heard Jimmy shout. "Isn't that—?"

Gus laughed. "You're damn right it is."

"Better late than never. . . ." Nicholas said.

Gus nodded, still watching as the jet-skis got closer. Still moving very quickly.

Too quickly, he realized.

"She's not slowing down." Jimmy frowned. "Why isn't she slowing down?"

Jimmy turned to his brother, whose eyes went wide as the lead jet-ski approached the *Konstantinos*. Barreling straight toward them. Collision course.

Except at the last second, the skier cut her engine, and started to brake—sharply to the right, away from the ship.

Gus saw what was about to happen, and leaned back from the railing.

Jimmy and Nicholas watched, transfixed—

And got showered with a few dozen gallons of seawater. Jimmy sputtered, wiped his face.

"You were asking? Why she wasn't slowing down?" Nicholas said, glaring at his brother.

"Pay attention, boys," Gus said. "The wake."

He pointed off the side of the boat with one hand, holding onto the railing with the other. Jimmy and Nicholas just managed to get handholds, as well, and then the wake from the jet-ski caught up to the *Konstantinos,* and the ship rolled. Big wake. Big waves.

The skier wasn't done with her fancy moves yet.

She came in hard again, used one of the wake waves as a ramp, and shot high up in the air.

Gus's mouth dropped open as his head leaned back and he followed her flight. Up in the air, into a flip—a flip, with a jet-ski!—and then back down again, at a dead stop, six inches from the *Konstantinos*'s ladder.

The skier brushed the hair out of her eyes and looked up at the boat.

"Hello, Gus." She looked over at Nicholas and Jimmy. "Boys."

She climbed up on deck. Gus folded his arms, and tried to

look angry. "Half the world's raiders are already here. You make us wait."

"You know I can't resist a bit of fun . . . forgive me?"

The skier stood before him, waiting.

"Lara Croft," he said, shaking his head. "All grown up."

Gus glanced from her, then over to his soaking wet sons, and back again.

Then he broke into a big smile.

He could never stay mad at Lara Croft.

"Of course, Lara. You're here. All is forgiven."

He patted her on the cheek.

Lara smiled, then turned to look at Nicholas and Jimmy, who were helping unload her things.

"How are you two?"

"Wet," Nicholas called back, without looking up. "And I don't forgive you—not just yet."

Jimmy grunted his assent.

"You two ought to know me better," Lara said, bending down to give the boys a hand. Seeing the three of them, together again—Gus thought back to the summer that Lara had spent with the Petrakis, in Merovigli—Lara and Jimmy and Nicholas had been practically inseparable. Always fooling around. Diving off the boat, pushing one another into the water. It seemed like yesterday.

It was, he realized, close to fifteen years ago.

Lara straightened up again and smiled.

"It's good to see you again, Gus."

"It's good to see you, too, Lara."

"Thanks for waiting. I'm so sorry I was late." She looked off the starboard, to where the other divers were going down again, and laid a hand on his shoulder.

"It's all right." Gus covered her hand with his own, then turned toward the back of the boat. "Come on. Let's get to it."

*   *   *

Lara had been up before dawn this morning, just in time to pass Bryce on his way to bed, and stop him, ask him obtain one more series of images she realized might be helpful in her task. Getting those pictures proved more time-consuming than she'd thought, so she'd missed her flight at Heathrow, had to grab a second, later one, which hadn't gotten her into Athens till eleven, local time. Still, she'd been at Thera by one, and alongside the *Konstantinos* on her jet-ski half an hour later. Yes, two hours behind the schedule she and Gus had agreed to the night before, which she was sorry for, but there'd been no way of avoiding the delay. And Gus's anger had been almost entirely feigned, she decided—and the boys were simply mad at her for one-upping them with the jet-ski stunt. She was sure they'd be seeking revenge for that soaking soon enough.

It was wrong to think of Nicholas and Jimmy as boys—they were grown men now, and Gus—

Well, Gus was older. Five years since she'd last seen him, and he'd aged twenty in that time. Not recognizable at all as the man she first met, during that long-ago summer when she was thirteen and in the middle of a cross-continent "excursion" arranged by her guardian at the time, Miss Stehlik. The excursion consisted of attending every stuffy society event on the continent, doing the things that were expected of a "proper" young English girl, heir to the renowned Croft name, a few scant years away from her majority.

Lara had been bored to tears by all of it—the dances, the teas, the dinners, the talk of who was spending the summer where, which plays were must-sees, which restaurants must-experiences, what clothes were in style and what weren't . . . she just wasn't interested.

What made it even worse, of course, was that their travels

had taken them so close to places she'd been dreaming about all her life, places her father, Lord Richard Croft, had drawn for her in bright, vivid detail in the stories he used to tell her before bedtime. Stories about Lascaux, and the cave paintings found there—the Great Hall of the Bulls, the Shaft of the Dead Man, the most miraculous example of paleolithic art on the planet—

—And they'd passed a sign for it, *Lascaux Cave*, right on the highway from Bordeaux heading east, and Lara shouted for the driver to stop, and Miss Stehlik ignored her request completely, insisting they were on a tight schedule.

Lara hadn't spoken a word to her guardian for a week.

It wasn't that long afterward that they'd found themselves on the road to Naples, and suddenly, there was Pompeii—Pompeii, for God's sake, she didn't need her father to tell her stories to know about Pompeii—though she did have to refresh Miss Stehlik's memory about the town in order to get her to pull off the road for even an hour so Lara could run through the site, which had resulted in a temporary truce between the two of them . . .

Until they were on the road to Athens, heading south from Thessaloniki, and drove right past Philip II's tomb—Philip of Macedon, Alexander the Great's father, inventor of the phalanx, the cavalry formation with which his son conquered the world. Without Philip, Lara's own father had been fond of saying, there would have been no Alexander.

"Daddy surely would have wanted me to see this, Miss Stehlik," Lara had pleaded—all to no avail, no chinking her guardian's armor on this one because they were on a tight schedule, on the clock. So she never got to see Philip's tomb—not that summer, at least.

Though she soon forgot about that disappointment, because a few hours later they were in Athens, and that was the worst of all. They were scheduled to lay over in the city for only two days—and she spent the better part of the first of those trapped in a hotel ballroom, mingling with her "peers" as they listened to speaker after speaker drone on about the benefits staging the Olympics would bring to Greece. Dinner turned out to be on the agenda, as well, so by the time Lara got back to her hotel it was nine P.M., and there was no time to do anything, Miss Stehlik told her, except get ready for bed and prepare for her busy day the next morning.

Lara said good night, locked her door, and raced to the hotel window.

She was three stories up, there was a tile roof just beneath her, pitch not steep at all, and a drainpipe that looked sturdy enough leading down to the ground.

Lara was going to the Acropolis, she was going to the Parthenon, she was going to the Piraeus, and any other sight that struck her fancy once she was out and about in Athens, come hell or high water.

She had just changed out of her nightgown into black jeans and a T-shirt when someone knocked on the door. Miss Stehlik, as it turned out, who announced that they had a visitor, an old friend of her father's who wanted to see Lara "all grown up."

"Just for a moment, of course," Miss Stehlik had said, an odd lilt in her voice, "because you need your rest," and then the door had swung open, and Gus Petraki walked in.

He'd stopped dead in his tracks when he saw her, and laughed out loud.

Lara looked to Miss Stehlik, trying to understand his re-action, and was surprised to see her smiling, as well. Odd be-havior from her guardian.

"A perfect combination of your parents," he said, smiling. "You don't remember me, do you?"

"No." Lara shook her head, and to her surprise found she was smiling, as well. She didn't remember him, but she liked him instantly, this smiling stranger with the full head of dark, dark hair, the olive skin, and the infectious laugh.

"I'm Gus Petraki," he said. He held out his hand, and the two shook. "Last time I saw you, you were two months old, and glued to your mother's breast."

Lara flushed crimson. Few adults in the circles she traveled in used the word *breast*. She expected Miss Stehlik to remark on this, as well. But instead her guardian merely giggled. More odd behavior.

Lara ignored it, and focused her attention on Gus again.

"You knew my mother?" she asked.

He nodded. "And your father, as well. You stayed in my house for a month, the two of you, while your father and I worked at Akrotiri with Professor Marinotos."

"Akrotiri?" Lara asked, unable to keep the excitement out of her voice. "You were at Akrotiri?"

Yes, Gus had replied, and then Lara couldn't stop the questions, about Akrotiri, about her parents, and once she learned that Gus had worked with her father on several other occasions, about every moment the two of them had spent together. They'd talked for hours that night, about all of it, and Lara went to sleep no longer angry over what she was missing, but excited about what she'd learned.

The next morning, things got even better. Somehow Gus had talked Miss Stehlik into canceling their plans for the week, and visiting his home on Santorini instead. It was another day of sharing memories, of good food and good times for both Lara and her guardian (it took Lara until the following winter to realize the obvious, that Miss Stehlik and the recently divorced Gus had been having a torrid affair that entire summer, one that lasted for several years afterward).

Those good times continued for several weeks thereafter, as the two of them stayed the remainder of the summer season on Santorini with Gus and his young sons, Jimmy and Nicholas, eight and nine at the time. At first the two boys had been a constant nuisance, harassing Lara endlessly. They were the younger brothers she'd never had, constantly in her face with requests to take them here, take them there, do this, do that, and every time she'd complain to Gus about his sons, he would smile and ruffle their hair and simply shrug at Lara, as if to say "boys will be boys."

She smiled, thinking about Gus then, and realized that he had been the spitting image of his sons.

Now the thick black hair she recalled was gone, and he was—well, to put it charitably, thicker—and nowhere near as imposing a figure. He looked tired, looked—as he'd put it in their conversation last night—ready to retire to a little island somewhere, and hand the business over to the boys.

Well. If she was right about what was down there, he'd definitely be able to do that. Maybe even buy an island all of his own.

She followed him now to the back of the boat, where there was a table set up. The four of them—her, Gus, the two boys—gathered around it.

"So fill me in," Lara said.

"They've brought up two statues," Gus said. He pointed at one of the charts. "Found here, and here. That's about all we know that you don't."

"Mmm," Lara said. "Did you get a look at them? The statues?"

The three Petrakis exchanged glances, shook their heads.

"No, not really," Gus said.

"What does it matter what they found?" Nicholas interrupted. "They don't have sleds. We have the sleds. We can cover more ground, we should get down there, we should—"

"You should know what it is that we're chasing," Lara said.

Gus nodded. "All right, Lara—tell us. What's all this fuss about? What do they think is down there?"

In answer, she reached down into her pack and pulled out a stack of paper. On top were copies of the images Bryce had shown her yesterday, pictures of the wooden vessel that had bobbed to the surface immediately after the quake. The eight-pointed star, the image of Alexander in the moon . . . she dropped the entire stack of paper on the table in front of them. Gus and the boys all leaned in close to get a good look.

The elder Petraki was the first to speak.

"The eight-pointed star. Alexander." Gus smiled, and clapped his hands together. "What is it, you think? A shipwreck? Something from one of the garrison towns?" He looked around the table, at Lara and his sons. "This could be big. We should—"

"Gus." Lara shook her head. "You're missing it."

"What?"

"Look." She jabbed a finger at the image again.

"The moon." He frowned. "I see it, so what does the moon—"

Abruptly, he stopped talking and leaned forward again.

"The moon," he repeated. Lara saw his hands tighten, grip the edge of the table until the veins on the back of them stood out. "Lara, is it . . ."

She nodded. "The Luna Temple."

"The Luna Temple?" he whispered.

"I think so, yes."

Nicholas and Jimmy looked at her, then their father, and then finally at each other. Both were frowning.

Lara realized they had no idea what she was talking about.

Gus looked at them and realized the same thing. He rolled his eyes.

"My sons, if it's not on TV, forget it!"

Lara smiled.

"The Luna Temple was built by Alexander the Great."

"Who was Greek, in case you don't know!"

Now it was Jimmy's turn to roll his eyes. "We know who Alexander the Great was, Papa."

"You know what he did, then," Lara continued. "Conquered the known world, at the age of thirty. Europe, Persia, India . . ."

She pulled another piece of paper from the bottom of the stack, and laid it on top so all could see. It was a map—showing Greece, and Macedonia, Cappadocea, and Armenia, Northern Africa and the Middle East, stretching out into what was now Afghanistan, and into the Hindu Kush. Athens, and Gaza. Babylon, and Persepolis. Damascus, and Nicea.

She pointed from one edge of the paper to the other.

"This is his empire, at its height. He collected treasures from all over the world. He stored them in two places. The majority went here, to his library at Alexandria—" she pointed to the Northern Coast of Africa—"which the Romans torched in an act of historical stupidity. But his most prized possessions went here . . ."

She set aside the map, pulled out another set of images. These were sketches of a massive temple, typical Greek construction, columns on either side, and at the center, a statue. This statue, however, was not of Zeus, or Herakles, or Apollo, or any of the other Greek gods, but of Alexander himself, seated on a throne. Presumptuous, one might say.

Or given the man's accomplishments, perhaps not.

"This is the Luna Temple. By law, no one was allowed to record its location. Then, in 350 B.C. it was——"

"Swallowed by the sea," Gus put in.

Lara nodded. "Destroyed by a volcanic eruption. Lost forever. Until yesterday." She looked around the table, making eye contact with first Nicholas, then Jimmy. "If the temple contains even half of what was rumored to be in it——if even half of that temple is intact——this will be the greatest find since Tutankhamen."

The brothers exchanged a look.

"So what are we waiting for now?" Nicholas asked. "Let's get down there."

"Yes——we're already way behind," Jimmy chimed in. He reached underneath the table, and pulled out a set of nautical charts, laid them over the temple drawings. "All morning, the others are heading here, along this shelf——going almost due west."

Lara looked at the charts. Jimmy had penciled in the exact locations where the other boats had stopped, and the length of time they'd spent there.

"Right here," he said, pointing to two Xs on the chart, "these are the places where they found the statues."

"They're following the currents," Lara said.

Jimmy nodded. "Of course."

Lara smiled. "No they're not."

All three of the Petrakis looked at her quizzically.

Lara pulled out a photograph from the stack on the table. It was a satellite image of the Santorini group, the one she'd waited for Bryce to get for her from his friend in Jiquan this morning.

"This is why I was late," she said, showing them the image. "It's a geological taken two hours after the quake.

The epicenter was here, five miles northeast of us. Look at the currents along the shelf now."

She drew a finger across a reddish swirl that went from the upper left-hand corner of the photo to the lower right.

Nicholas was the first to see it.

"They've shifted."

"That's right," Lara said. "I don't know how long it will last, but for right now, the currents are moving north—not west."

"So . . ." Jimmy looked from Lara's photo to his charts. "So while they're all diving there, the ruins will actually be—"

Lara put her forefinger down on the other side of Therasia—out in the open Aegean.

"Oh boy," Jimmy said. "They're nowhere near it."

"But we will be," Lara said.

Nicholas and Jimmy looked at each other, and grinned.

"I'll do the tanks," Jimmy said.

Nicholas nodded. "I'll do the sleds."

They took off like a shot.

Gus smiled, watching them go. "That is the fastest I've ever seen them move."

"I'm moving, too." She picked up her backpack, hefted it over her shoulder. "Where can I change?"

"Any cabin you want," Gus said. He picked up the charts, and the satellite image. "I'll go plot our course."

Twenty minutes later, the *Konstantinos* was anchored off the southern coast of Therasia, and Lara was standing on the deck in her wet suit, frowning. She'd used the time not only to change and get her gear unpacked, but to call Hillary at the manor. No one had been there to answer the phone—which was strange. The way Hillary had been fussing over her last night when she was getting ready to leave, the way he'd insisted on her taking full GPS equipment, so they could find her if there was any trouble . . .

She would have thought he'd be pacing next to the receiver, waiting for her call. Ah well. Hers not to reason why.

Lara climbed up to the wheelhouse, and took a look back toward the islands. No other boats, anywhere in sight—she had worried someone might follow them.

She looked starboard, saw Nicholas and Jimmy in their wet suits, prepping for the dive. The sleds were hanging by the side. In the water, they looked like motorbikes, submerged from the seat on down—though beneath the surface, of course, the sleds had no wheels, no engine block, no exhaust pipes, not even a footrest. They were electric-powered, propeller-driven—and Nicholas was rotating the propellers now, checking the blades, the batteries, the electrical systems. Jimmy, meanwhile, was up on deck, looking over a row of oxygen tanks. Seeing him bend over, squint at the gauges on the tanks, suddenly reminded her that she had a few instruments of her own to check over.

Lara looked down at her belt, swung it back to front, and glanced at her D1000C. Bryce had outfitted her camera with new housings from Subal just last week. The housings added several new controls, more than worth the expense of the retrofit, she decided after a few seconds of fiddling—she'd wait to fine-tune the camera until they actually got underneath the water.

Bryce had also spent quite a bit of time last night on the newest addition to her photographic arsenal, a miniature camera housed on the outer rim of her diving mask itself, set to record whatever she was seeing. And speaking of arsenals . . .

She swung the belt back around, and pulled the retrofitted Colt out of her holster. This was Subal work again, the weapon sealed and armored so that it worked underwater, firing true at almost any depth. She slid the clip out—saw she had five rounds left, she'd squeezed off a test back at the manor—then back in again with a satisfying thunk. Checked the spare clips on her belt, slid the weapon back in its holster . . .

And looked up to see Stefano, the pilot, frowning at her.

She smiled. "Just in case the boys misbehave down there."

Off his confused expression, she descended the ladder, from the wheelhouse down to the deck.

Up front, Gus was standing with arms propped up on the railing, staring out across the ocean, a pensive look on his face. She walked over to join him.

"Something wrong?" Lara asked.

He shrugged. "First Alexander doesn't record its location. Then God wipes it from the earth with a volcano. Now even the currents change . . ."

"And your point is?"

Gus avoided her gaze. "Did it ever occur to you that maybe this temple's not meant to be found?"

She leaned in closer. "Everything's meant to be found."

"Hey, Croft! Lara!"

She turned and saw Nicholas and Jimmy standing on the deck, waving to her. They'd put the DPVs in the water, moored them to the *Konstantinos* with motors running.

She waved back at the boys and smiled at Gus.

"Showtime," she said.

Less than a minute later (after a bit of clowning around that reminded her of other times she'd spent with Nicholas and Jimmy, back when they really were boys) she was on her sled.

Lara put her mask over her face, felt the oxygen flowing

immediately. She set the digital camera to record, and sat up straight on her sled.

The boys were on either side of her. She pointed forward with one hand, then gunned her vehicle straight ahead. They followed an instant later.

Just before they submerged, Lara turned back to the *Konstantinos*. Gus was still at the railing, watching. He waved now, his face expressionless.

Lara waved back, and as she did, Gus's words came to her again.

Maybe this temple's not meant to be found.

Suppressing a sudden chill, she descended into the inky blackness of the Aegean, in search of the past.

TWO

In 332 B.C., Alexander the Great conquered Egypt. He was crowned Pharoah at Memphis, and proclaimed the son of Ammon-Ra—making him a god on earth.

His ascension into divinity was not fiat, imposed by the will of his army. No, Alexander was loved—beloved—by the Egyptians, who hailed him as deliverer, saw in him the glories of their fabled past come to life again. They brought him their country's most priceless treasures, mountains of gold and precious gems, statues and relics bearing the emblems of long-vanished empires, papyruses and cuneiform tablets relaying secrets thousands of years old.

The celebrations lasted for weeks; Alexander held ceremonial games for his new subjects, and his old ones, too, issuing invitations to athletes from throughout the known world. Among the messengers that went forth was one directed to Pella, capital city of Macedonia, Alexander's home. This messenger carried not only an invitation to the games, but (according to a fragmentary reference Lara had found) a command from Alexander to his regent Antipater, a directive to start construction of a magnificent temple to be devoted to "the treasures of mankind." This temple was to be a twin to one Alexander planned to construct in his new capital, Alexandria. But whereas that temple was to be devoted to Ammon-Ra, the sun god, the one he commanded Antipater to build was intended to honor the goddess of the night.

This, as best as Lara could tell, was the first reference to the Luna Temple.

All other mentions she found (and every free moment she'd had, from the instant she finished packing last night to the moment she stepped on her jet-ski this afternoon, Lara had spent searching her library for those references, reading the extant sources, the fragments of descriptive history that had survived, reviewing her notes on the bits and pieces of rumor she had heard over the years) were as maddeningly elusive as that one. All told, what was truly known about the Luna Temple—its construction, its contents—didn't amount to much more than what she'd told Nicholas and Jimmy.

The temple was, in short, more the stuff of legend than historical fact. And unlike other legends—Atlantis, El Dorado, the Cave of Kyir-Banoff—this one was virtually unknown to the general public.

But if it existed . . .

If it could be found . . .

It would be easily the most historically significant discovery of her career. Never mind the treasures the temple was rumored to contain (which included a laundry list of items from the ancient world whose very existence was surely apocryphal—the armor Achilles had worn in the Trojan War, the pelt of the Nemean lion killed by Hercules, Pandora's box itself, and so on), extant sources hinted that the diaries of Alexander's royal biographer Callisthenes had been sent to the temple, and that alone was enough to make her blood race, a contemporary account of history's greatest hero which she would be the first to see in over two thousand years.

Which was why, a scant two meters down from the surface, she had the throttle full-out, headlights (the sleds each had four, two groups of two that could be independently operated) blaring, and was streaking toward the ocean floor like a guided missile.

She was in front, the boys behind her in single-file formation, Nicholas first, Jimmy lagging. She turned and gave them a smile, and then focused her attention downward again, leaning so far forward on the sled that she was laying straight out, just like she sometimes did on her Norton; in fact, now that she thought about it, riding one of the DPVs was a lot like riding her bike. No roads here, of course, no yellow lines or guardrails to help ward off danger, but that was part of the fun then, wasn't it?

The ocean floor appeared just beneath them, and Lara leveled out, slowing slightly as she began scanning the bottom.

Not for the Luna Temple itself—they weren't going to find Alexander's treasure out here, in the open, the lack of decomposition on the artifact Bryce had found was proof enough of that. The *Konstantinos* had anchored at what Lara calculated to be the extreme southern position of the temple's possible location—their plan was to follow the current north, looking for clues to the temple's presence.

The smooth floor gave way to jagged rock. Spectacular formations created by the Santorini volcano seemed to rise up and surround them, lava flows thrusting from the ocean floor at odd angles, encrusted with barnacles and coral, filled with numerous nooks and little caves, home to no end of sea creatures. Beautiful.

But hard to follow a straight path through. Lara glanced down at the compass on her wrist to orient herself. Nicholas and Jimmy shot past her as she calculated their location.

When she looked up, the brothers had slowed. She pulled closer and saw why. Just beyond where they waited, the sea floor came to an abrupt end.

Lara rolled her sled sideways, slipped in between them, and dove straight over the edge without hesitation.

She caught the surprised expressions on the boys' faces as she shot by, and smiled.

She really did have to stop thinking of them as boys.

The cliff face was sheer, and smooth. She counted one, two, three seconds before the ocean floor came into view, four, five, six before she had to slow the throttle. Sixty-one meters, at a rough guess. A long way down. They were going to have to decompress on the way up.

She leveled off. Nicholas and Jimmy appeared alongside her, none the worse for wear. Jimmy pointed to his oxygen tanks, and held up one finger. An hour's worth of oxygen—half of that time they'd have to spend decompressing, Lara knew. Which left them another half hour of dive time to find the temple.

She nodded her understanding to Jimmy, and turned to examine the cliff face.

Right in front of her was a narrow opening in the rock. She frowned, and scanned it with the DPV's headlights.

The opening itself was barely more than a gap in the rock. But farther in . . .

It looked like the gap widened, became a tunnel.

Lara frowned, and looked up at the cliff again, then at the tunnel.

Her mind began to churn.

Alexander had ordered construction of a temple to house the treasures of his empire. He'd decreed that no one record the location of the temple.

Ridiculous, on the face of it. How could you possibly keep such massive construction—such a splendid temple—a secret? Only one way, really. Do what the pharoahs had done with those who'd helped build their tombs, who knew where their treasures were buried and how to get at them.

Kill them.

Which was what most who granted the possible existence of the Luna Temple assumed that Alexander had done.

But Lara had never bought into that line of thinking. Indiscriminate slaughter was simply not Alexander the Great's style.

Next to her, she sensed Nicholas and Jimmy eager to move forward. She held up a finger.

Wait.

Alexander wanted a place to keep his treasures safe, she thought. A place that wouldn't be found, and ransacked. If he couldn't build it, he would have to find it.

And these islands were honeycombed with caves.

Smiling, she gunned her sled forward into the dark, foreboding tunnel.

The three of them went single file again—this time, because there was only room for one to squeeze through the tunnel at a time. Lara had to lay flat on the DPV, and even then, the runners of the sled scraped against the tunnel walls.

As she came around a particularly tight curve, she glanced down.

The headlights reflected off something unnaturally white. Lara bent even farther forward, stretched out a hand, and scraped dirt away with it as she passed by.

The white surface was smooth as glass. No, not glass. Marble.

The edges of her mouth twisted up into a grin.

A second later, the headlights caught another glimpse of white stone, this time embedded in the wall. No need to touch it to know what this was. A column fragment, embedded in the tunnel.

The grin turned into a full-fledged smile. Her instincts had been correct—about Alexander, about the temple. How he'd managed to keep its construction—and its location—a secret.

But her satisfaction was short-lived.

Around the next curve, the tunnel came to an abrupt end, blocked by a rockfall from the roof above. Lara's smile disappeared with it.

She turned. Jimmy and Nicholas were stopped in the tunnel behind her, their expressions grim, as well. She saw Jimmy glance down at his wrist, knew that he was checking to see how much oxygen they had left. By her guess, they'd been traveling ten minutes, so another twenty before they had to start surfacing.

Half an hour to the *Konstantinos*—half an hour, roughly, before their tanks were full and they could dive again, armed with explosives to clear away the rock. An hour all told before they were back here, in this exact position.

A more prudent person might have waited.

But Lara Croft had never been prudent. And she wasn't going to start now.

She turned back to the rockfall, and focused both sets of headlights on it, searching for something—a passageway narrow enough to squeeze through?—that might allow her to continue.

The headlights found the rockfall, and lit it up—really lit it—this time.

And suddenly, Lara's smile was back.

She gunned the throttle and drove her sled straight for the center of the collapse. Gritted her teeth and bent over the nose of the sled as it strained forward . . .

And smashed into not rock, but coral, the blockage had been coral, solid enough, sharp enough if you scrape against it while diving, but if you hit it hard and fast . . .

Not much of an impediment at all, really.

The DPV burst through the coral, and shot straight up into open air.

For a split second, despite everything that she'd worked out before, Lara thought that she'd miscalculated the depth of their dive, that the tunnel had led them right back to the surface, only it was somehow dark outside and the *Konstantinos* had disappeared and the air had gotten dank and stuffy, just like the inside of . . .

A cave. A massive, underground cave.

The sled bobbed in the water, came to a rest. The glow from her headlights lit up the cave interior, and as her eyes adjusted, gave her just enough light to see by.

She smiled, and took off her mask.

Jimmy, then Nicholas surfaced. One by one, they removed their masks, as well, stared around in wide-eyed wonder.

"My God . . ." Nicholas said.

"Is this . . . ?" Jimmy whispered.

"Yeah," his brother said. "I think so."

Lara nodded. "Welcome to the Luna Temple."

They had come up through a hole in the floor, in the middle of the temple. Great columns, fifty meters tall at least, lined the walls around them, and just beyond the columns, Lara glimpsed the original cave walls, the cave that Alexander had found, and converted, into a storehouse for his most valuable treasures. The cave that had been buried, entombed intact by the eruption on Santorini more than two thousand years ago.

The cave that was now tilted almost twenty degrees to her left.

A drop of water splashed down from above, striking the floor near her.

Lara looked up and saw the drop was coming from one of countless leaks in the ceiling. Were the leaks—the structure's tilt—the result of the quake that had sunk this whole portion of the island—or the one that happened yesterday? No way of telling.

Better safe than sorry, she thought, and turned her attention to the temple floor, intent on checking its structural integrity.

The floor was marble—composed of tiles perhaps two feet square. The ones closest to them were mostly broken, some shattered into small pieces, others split into one or two large fragments. The tiles looked in better shape toward the rear of the temple.

Where a seated statue of Alexander himself waited.

Lara squinted, and studied it closer.

Odd position to find Alexander in. Most statues of him—not only those still extant, but those which only survived in the pages of history—depicted the man in action. This was Alexander at rest, a position he'd rarely occupied in real life—caught in a rare moment of repose, as if he was contemplating something.

Possibly the treasure that lay strewn at his feet.

Lara saw gold and silver coins, jewels and other precious objects, piled high before the statue and on either side of it, all along the temple wall.

Jimmy and Nicholas saw the treasure at the same time as she did, and laughed. They began to climb off their sleds.

Lara held up a hand.

"Patience." She pointed to the tile floor.

"They're broken," Jimmy said. "So?"

"So we need to be careful." She didn't think this temple was booby-trapped—again, something about Alexander's character—but she was worried nonetheless. Any structure tilting the way this one was needed to be approached with a certain degree of caution. Besides, Alexander himself wouldn't have decided whether or not to booby-trap the temple. He'd never been here. Luna had been built by people who may have had their own ideas of how best to protect their king's treasures.

They needed to be very careful indeed.

She climbed carefully off her sled, and set foot on the cave bottom. Coral crunched beneath her feet. A step away, the temple floor proper began.

Lara stepped forward, and set a foot down lightly on one of the broken tiles.

It sank into the ground.

One of the columns on the wall to her right began sinking, as well.

Above them, the ceiling creaked ominously.

Lara withdrew her foot, and frowned. Jimmy cursed under his breath.

"Damn," Nicholas said. "What do we do?"

Lara looked at the floor again. About six feet straight ahead of her, there was a series of unbroken tiles.

She took a deep breath, and swung her arms. Back and forth, back and forth, back and forth—

She crouched, and jumped, landing square on one of the unbroken tiles.

The columns stayed as they were. The ceiling didn't creak.

She reached into her pack and pulled out a handful of nylon bags. Turned, and tossed them back to Jimmy and Nicholas.

"Fill these," she told them. "And stay off the broken tiles."

*   *   *

Lara was interested in the treasure, of course—she kept a close eye on what Nicholas and Jimmy were filling the bags with. Caught sight of what looked like a primitive abacus, and made note of which bag that went in. Saw something that looked like a sextant, and made a mental note of that, as well. Some spectacular necklaces that looked Egyptian, a crown in the shape of—of course—an eight-pointed star, and a scabbard encrusted with more diamonds than she'd seen in quite a long, long time—all of those piqued her interest.

But as they'd approached the treasure, her primary focus had shifted to the wall behind it, and the mural that ran the length of that wall. The colors had long ago faded, and parts of it showed signs of serious water damage, but nonetheless, as she drew close, she knew that she was looking at something quite spectacular indeed. A few seconds of up-close study confirmed her intuition.

She switched on the new digicam Bryce had prepared for her, the one affixed to her mask, and began recording.

What she saw was an illustration of Alexander's journey across Europe and Asia—his triumphal march across the known world, laid out in pictures. The images were reminiscent of something—a memory that tugged briefly at her consciousness, and then flitted away.

No matter—it would come to her again. She returned her attention to the glyphs on the wall.

There was a young Alexander fighting with his father, Philip, while Philip was still king—and here, the newly crowned Alexander, leading the destruction at Thebes. A few panels down, there was the cutting of the Gordian knot. Then, the triumphal procession into Egypt, the sacking of Persepolis, the death of Darius, and the long march across Persia. Here, his marriage to Roxanne, and here, the launching of his final campaign, the journey into India, and here was his army—

Lara frowned.

Here was his army, in a scene she didn't recognize at all.

Soldiers lay strewn by the score across a battlefield. Dead, obviously, but not from fighting—they looked untouched by any weapon.

"I could get used to this tomb raiding," Nicholas said, interrupting her train of thought. "Lara—what do you say to two handsome Greek partners?"

"I'll be gentle," she replied, giving him a brief smile before returning her attention to the battlefield scene. The more she studied it, the less sense it made. No weapons were drawn, the men had fallen in formation as if struck by lightning—

Here was something—a soldier off to the side of the battle, holding a small box in his arms. A treasure chest of some kind, perhaps? Something they had died defending?

It still made no sense. Was this a battle that history had failed, for one reason or another, to record? A defeat for the legendary Alexander the Great? The glyphs on the wall were arranged chronologically—which, looking on either side of the battlefield scene, put this between his first conquests in India, and his death in Babylon.

Right about the time, she realized, that Alexander had stopped his march eastward, and turned for home.

Lara had always been puzzled by that decision. According to the history books, the army, tired of fighting, tired of marching, had simply refused to go any farther. Alexander's initial response to those complaints had been to tell those who wished to turn back to do so—that he would proceed with his auxiliaries.

That's what she would have done—by herself, if she'd had to. One of the reasons why she'd always felt such a kinship for Alexander—his unshakable determination to push the envelope, to fulfill his destiny—to dream the spectacular, and then to live it. Not for him an ordinary life—nor for her.

(Which put her in mind, for just a split second, of the other men she'd allowed to share her life—Alex West, Tobias Grayson, Terry Sheridan, even—all of them had that same thirst for adventure.)

So why had Alexander changed his mind?

Because that was what he had done, just a few days after the declaration that he would continue, he'd turned his back on his most cherished dream, of finishing his eastward exposition in the Bay of Bengal—what he believed to be the Eastern Ocean, and the veritable edge of the world.

Why?

Did it have something to do with the scene before her? A disaster history hadn't recorded? One that necessitated his sudden about-face?

She zoomed in on the battlefield scene, let the camera linger on it a moment.

"Bad day . . ." she murmured, frowning.

There were other symbols underneath the glyphs, she saw now, barely visible even this close up. They looked like writing—but she didn't recognize the language. Odd. Lara was familiar with virtually all the Hellenic dialects.

Time enough to puzzle it out later, she thought, and recorded the new symbols, as well.

Then she turned away from the illustration to the statue in front of it, the seated Alexander. It was not a particularly noteworthy sculpture, she decided—and no wonder, since whoever the artist had been had to work from memory, as Alexander himself had been half a continent away. There was something off about the figure, and she couldn't quite put her finger on what. The mouth, perhaps, was just a little too angular—or was it the nose that was angular? In any case, the eyes . . .

The eyes. Lara stepped closer, and saw that one of them was covered by something. A medallion.

She stepped closer, reached up, and removed it from the eye socket.

The medallion was copper, turned dark with age. Lara had to hold it close to see that there was an image on one side.

A seated figure, playing a musical instrument.

Details were hard to make out in the semidarkness. More light might help, she thought, reaching for the flash on her belt.

It slipped from her grasp, and struck the temple floor.

The impact switched it on, and a beam of light shot straight up into the semidarkness. All at once, the temple was showered in a kaleidoscope of reflected light.

Lara looked up, and saw that the beam of light had struck something hanging from the ceiling. A cage of iron, suspended in the air by narrow horizontal bars, resting on a formation that seemed totally out of place in the temple—a black cone-shaped rock.

And within the cage, the source of the multicolored rays that flooded the interior of the temple—a shining, black Orb.

"Hey!" That was Nicholas. "How did you know that was up there?"

"I'm a professional," Lara said, without a trace of humor. She set down her guns, most of her gear, and the medallion.

"So what is it?" Jimmy asked, as the brothers picked their way carefully across the temple floor to where Lara stood.

"I haven't a clue," Lara admitted. "But I'm damn sure going to find out."

She looked up at the Orb, and the cage, and the bars. Frowned at the statue, at the sloping walls of the temple, and then up at the Orb again.

"Come on," she told Nicholas and Jimmy. "I need a boost."

THREE

They helped Lara up onto the statue. She perched on Alexander's hand for a second, then, using it as a platform, leapt straight up. Caught on to the protruding cornice of a column, and hung a moment, studying the route before her. The temple walls sloped inward, coming to a point high above the tiled floor. The Orb, and its cage, hung from a point perhaps halfway up. Not an easy climb. She'd have to—

Something within the column cracked. Lara felt the stone beneath her fingers begin to crumble.

"Lara!" Jimmy shouted.

She leapt again, just as the stone gave way. Her fingers closed on a handhold, and she hung in space a moment, suspended by one arm.

"No worries!" she called back, and started to climb. Within seconds, she was sweating like a greased pig—the humidity was much worse higher up, and Lara realized that it couldn't have been this humid in here for two thousand years, nothing would have survived, which meant that the recent quake had affected things inside the temple much more than she'd previously surmised.

They should not, she reflected, plan on staying long.

She had reached the cage now, was practically back-to-back with it, level with that strange, cone-shaped rock formation. Holding on tight to the wall with her right hand,

Lara brought her left behind her body, and grabbed hold of the iron bars. So far, so good—she'd planned this maneuver since she'd spotted the Orb from the floor below.

But now came the hard part.

Lara took a deep breath and then let go with her right hand, at the same time pushing off with her heels.

For a minute, she hung in midair.

Then her heels slammed into the wall again, chipping off stone, sending it crumbling to the temple floor below. At the same instant, both hands stretched out, and she grabbed hold of the cage.

There. Lara smiled and hung a moment, gathering herself as she lay suspended in space, parallel to the temple floor far below.

Then she looked down, and gasped.

The tiles of the floor formed a pattern, one visible only from high above.

A giant figure, drawn on the floor. A threatening, foreboding image—some sort of warrior—one whose like she'd never seen in Greek art before.

Another mystery, Lara reflected, thinking of the battlefield scene she'd spent so much time studying earlier. Neither of which she had time to puzzle through right now. She turned her attention to the black Orb, and the cage that held it.

Steadying herself with one hand, holding her legs straight as steel rods for support, she reached down and pulled the small acetylene torch off her belt. Thumbed on the flame, and brought the torch up to the cage bars.

As she did so, Lara happened to glance down again. The cool blue light of the torch's plume caught the eyes of the mysterious figure on the floor below, making them glitter like a thing alive, and casting shadows all about the cave, as well.

The earth shook.

Lara' s heels slipped on the temple wall. The cage started to swing away from her. She almost lost her grip—almost dropped the torch, as well.

"Aftershock!" she heard Jimmy shout from below.

The walls shook again, harder this time—and this time, Lara couldn't keep her legs in place. She slipped free of the temple wall—her body swung out into space, and she dangled in midair, suspended by one arm from the cage, her other hand gripping the still-lit torch.

Drop the torch, the voice of common sense told her. Grab onto the cage with both hands, and hold tight. No telling how long the aftershock will last, no telling what might happen before it stops, and you'd better be prepared for anything.

You'd better hold on to that torch, another little voice in her head whispered, a voice that told her if she dropped it she might never get it back, might never cut through the cage to get what instinct told her was the most valuable treasure in the entire cave, the black orb that hung just out of reach in front of her.

Lara gritted her teeth and held on with one hand.

The temple was vibrating like a tuning fork now. Chunks of stone, and marble, and dirt fell past her head like rain. She caught a clump of clay smack in the face, swallowing some, and turned away to spit it out.

The support column closest to her was separating from its base, sliding off it inch by inch, propelled by the force of the aftershock.

If it slipped all the way off, the whole temple was going to come down around them.

Lara opened her mouth to shout at Nicholas and Jimmy, to warn them, tell them to get out before—

The shocks stopped.

Lara looked all around her.

The small leaks from the temple roof were now streams. The temple was canted at closer to a forty-five-degree angle—the lower half was a wading pool.

Far below, the brothers were struggling to their feet.

"You all right down there?" Lara called out.

"Yeah. I think that's a sign to leave!" Jimmy shouted back.

"I think that's a sign to leave now!" Nicholas added.

They were right. No doubt about it, the Luna Temple was falling apart, about to disappear from the sight of man for a second and final time.

And yet, she still wanted the Orb.

Lara looked at it once more, trapped within the iron cage, so tantalizingly close and yet at least a couple minutes of cutting away. The light from the flash below was hitting the Orb at a new angle now, revealing details she hadn't been able to see before.

Including markings on the Orb's surface.

Intricate, gleaming carvings that shone like platinum against the black.

A pattern of some sort, clearly, but what . . .

No way to scan all the way around the object, get pictures of its entire surface while it—and she—were hung from the ceiling like this. Only one way to figure out what this pattern meant, really.

She had to have the Orb.

"Two minutes," she shouted down to Jimmy and Nicholas.

"What are you, crazy?" Jimmy shouted back up. "Get down here, we have to start packing up, we have to get out of this place—"

"Two . . . minutes . . ." Lara repeated firmly, bringing the torch to bear on the first of the iron bars.

Sparks began to fly.

Lara's mind raced as she cut.

She peered through the torch's plume at the markings on the Orb. She'd wracked her mind, trying to figure out what language the strange markings on the Orb were, but had drawn a blank. Not Greek, clearly, nor any of the Arabic languages that had dominated the Asiatic side of the Hellespont during this time frame. She was stumped.

She was through the first bar. She glanced down, and saw Jimmy and Nicholas busily loading the sleds with the bags of treasure, casting nervous glances up toward the ceiling as they did so.

Perhaps it was her imagination, but the water did seem to be falling faster, harder, from the holes in the temple roof. And the huge support column nearest her seemed inches away from coming entirely off its base.

She finished cutting through the second bar, moved on to the third. Six in all, on the side she was cutting, and now the cage hung at such an angle that the Orb was poised to roll out the second she'd finished slicing through.

Her mind returned to the markings on the Orb. Perhaps they had something to do with the circumstances of the temple's building, what treasures Antipater had decided to store there, and yet that was wrong, too, because all the fragments she'd found stated with no uncertainty that it was Alexander who'd decided which treasures were to be brought here, and which were to be stored in Alexandria.

It was a mystery all right.

She was through the fourth bar, and saw now that she only needed to cut one more for the Orb to fall free.

Sweat beaded on her forehead. Lara wiped it away.

She was halfway through the fifth bar—really, a hard punch would snap it now, and the waiting Orb tumbled right into her hand.

"Lara, watch out!"

That was Jimmy—with a panicked overtone to his voice.

The temple was collapsing—that was her first, instinctive reaction.

She looked up, expecting to see part of the roof falling toward her. Nothing. She looked down.

Her mouth fell open in shock.

They were no longer alone in the temple.

Six men, in full diving gear, armed with spearguns, had joined them. The boys were fighting them—they'd been surprised, as well, Lara saw, because both brothers were being held from behind. The Petrakis struggled, but the other men were well trained.

Nicholas elbowed the man who held him at the chest—hard enough to make a resounding thump. The man only grunted.

Light glinted off something in his hand—a knife.

The blade flashed—Nicholas fell to the ground, blood gushing from his throat. He flopped once on the ground, then lay still.

"No!" Lara screamed, but her shout was lost in the guttural noise Jimmy made as he saw his brother fall. Jimmy reached for Nicholas—

The man nearest him darted forward, quick as lightning, Lara had never seen anyone move so fast. He punched Jimmy square in the stomach.

The air went out of Jimmy in an audible whoosh.

Then the man dragged his hand up Jimmy's chest, and Lara saw that he hadn't just punched Jimmy, he'd stabbed him, sinking the blade of his knife deep inside his body, and now that blade was traveling upward, as well, gutting Jimmy, and Lara blinked. She couldn't see for a second, she felt ill, she—

Watched Jimmy fall backward, near where his brother lay. The two boys, side by side.

Boys. She had to stop thinking of them as boys—and yet in the instant she watched them die, that was all Lara could think of, images of the two of them as they had been.

Little boys, following her around like love-struck puppy dogs. Do this, do that, take me here, take me there—

Look where she'd brought them to now.

Spears flew through the air at her.

Lara dropped the torch, sprung off the cage, and landed on the wall. Another spear hit behind her. A second chunked into the wall above her head. A third passed right between her thighs, so close it tore the fabric of her wet suit.

She looked down and saw that the man who'd killed Jimmy had thrown that one.

The two of them locked eyes.

He was Asian, Lara saw. A face she didn't know.

But one that now she would never forget.

Lara watched as he walked over to the Alexander statue, which was now so tilted that its base was partially submerged, as well. He collected the equipment she'd left there, including her speargun—and the medallion from the statue's eye. Damn it.

She had to get down to the temple floor again to stop this man. Climbing was out of the question, though, she'd be a sitting duck, and it was too far to jump . . .

Unless she could land in water.

Lara scanned the temple—there. Halfway across the interior, she saw a pool that looked deep enough for her to risk a dive. One problem, though—there wasn't a handhold in sight.

A spear flew past, close enough to graze the hair on her head, reminding her that she couldn't stay where she was, either. She had to get moving.

The spear stuck in the wall next to Lara, deep enough that the wall vibrated with its impact.

Aah. That gave her an idea.

Lara faked a move forward, and another spear flew through the air, anticipating where she would be. It chunked in the wall, just ahead of the first.

Perfect.

She cursed out loud for effect, then faked the same move again. With the same result.

Another spear in the wall. And then a third, right on its heels.

That should do it, Lara thought, and launched herself for real now, diving forward through the air, and grabbing onto the spear closest to her.

It held for a second, then snapped off in her grasp, and as she tumbled the Orb dropped behind the statue.

Lara used the momentum from her jump to grab onto spear number two.

That broke, as well, but she used it to swing forward again, to number three, and even as number three snapped, she stretched out, hands above her head, and jackknifed into the water, even as another volley of spears flew past.

Lara went down as deep as she could and stayed there.

She waited ten seconds, fifteen, thinking about what had just happened up above, wondering who the men were, how they'd followed her, formulating a plan of action.

Kill them all.

Which she would need a weapon for. Jimmy's murderer

had her speargun. But—he'd missed the modified .45. Lara hadn't seen it, either. She thought—she hoped—that it was lying somewhere in the shallow water at the statue's base.

Only problem was getting there.

She swum twenty feet along the bottom, then quietly surfaced in front of the damaged support column.

Two of the attackers were poised over the water near where she'd entered it, spearguns at the ready. As she watched, first one, then the other fired into the pool, then stood over it a moment, waiting.

She noted they were Asian, as well.

The two men were firing blind, hoping to hit her. Not such a bad strategy, since the pool was not very big at all.

The two men exchanged a glance, then reloaded their spearpistols, and started circling the pool again.

Lara scanned the rest of the temple interior. Along the far wall, three other attackers were finishing what Jimmy and Nicholas had started—loading up the DPVs with the filled treasure bags. She didn't see the sixth man anywhere.

But there was the Alexander statue—now covered almost up to the knees by water. Lara took a deep, quiet breath and swam for it. Five feet away, she spotted the Colt. Without surfacing, she picked up the gun and released the safety.

Then she turned around. Closest to her were the two men circling the pool with spearguns, hoping to spot her.

Lara raised the gun, sighted, and fired.

The bullet exploded out of the water and caught her target square in the chest. He flew backward through the air, and even before he'd hit the ground, the other man was spinning, quick as lightning, raising his speargun and pointing it right at Lara.

But she was quicker. She fired a second time, and that man fell, as well.

Lara rose up out of the water and spun, aiming toward the first of the other three men, clumped near the DPVs.

Movement from above distracted her, and even as she squeezed the trigger, she knew her shot was off. That upset her.

What upset her even more was the source of that movement above her—the sixth attacker, Jimmy's killer, determinedly making for the Orb.

That was hers.

A spear whizzed past her.

Lara dove for the ground, and rolled, once, twice, then coming to rest flat on her back.

She raised the Colt, targeting the sixth man.

The sixth attacker raised his spearpistol. He smiled as he closed his hand around the Orb, and took aim at Lara.

The three remaining attackers—spread out along the far wall with him—did the same.

Lara's finger tightened on the trigger of her Colt. A split second before firing, she stopped herself.

This was her last shot.

She had four targets—four men to kill.

Only one way to take them all out.

Lara spun and fired at the base of the column behind her, shattering the last bits of supporting marble.

With a loud thunk, the column dropped five feet straight down, to the temple floor. A huge chunk of the temple roof came with it.

And then the entire cave began to collapse. Bits of earth and tile plunged all around her—from one of the leaks in the ceiling, a torrent of ocean water began pouring in.

Lara began to run toward the DPVs, and the treasure. Toward the hole in the temple floor that was the only way out of what was now a death trap.

A meter-square piece of tile plunged directly toward the attackers.

To Lara's immense disappointment, the sixth attacker—Jimmy's killer—shattered it with a well-aimed spear from his gun.

Even as he fired, he was pushing the others back toward the DPVs, shouting in Mandarin as he did so. On a course to intercept Lara.

She gritted her teeth, and willed herself forward, even faster.

As she passed the Alexander statue, a huge chunk of the petroglyph mural collapsed in front of her. She tried to leap over it, but her timing was off, and she clipped it with one foot, stumbled, and fell to the ground.

A cloud of earth and dust collapsed directly on top of her.

By the time it had cleared, the two men were dead, two had escaped, and the remaining DPV was useless.

She coughed up some of the dust she'd swallowed, and started crawling on her hands and knees toward where she knew the hole in the temple floor had to be. She found it, eventually. Only one problem.

Lara no longer had her breathing mask. Or oxygen. And by the most optimistic of reckonings, she was a hundred fifty feet from the surface. Surfacing without any sort of decompression was risky, but she'd have to take that risk.

Behind her, the temple rumbled again. Another portion of the wall collapsed.

First things first, Lara thought. Get out of here.

Taking a deep breath, she plunged headfirst into the tunnel.

Squeezing through the opening in the coral that she'd made with her DPV, Lara made her way through the winding passageway, out into the open ocean at the floor of the cliff base.

As she emerged, she nearly collided with a tiger shark, swimming by the entrance to the tunnel.

Lara reached reflexively for the knife at her belt. Brandished it in front of her, to warn the animal off. It paid her no mind whatsoever, and kept swimming—looking for an easier target, she supposed.

She slid the knife back into her belt and tensed her body, preparing to spring off the ocean floor for the long swim to the surface above.

But when she looked up, that surface—the dim light of day—seemed impossibly far away.

She'd been holding her breath for too long already—she would never make topside, even swimming as fast as she could now.

She needed to think this through.

She swam back into the tunnel, through the break in the coral, and emerged back into the collapsed ruins of the Luna Temple. To a rude surprise.

The air pocket above her was barely the size of a coffin.

Somewhere off in the distance, she heard a great rumbling. Soon even this little air pocket would be gone, she knew, taking one deep breath, then another. The last air she would get until she reached the surface.

And she would reach the surface, there was no doubt in her mind about that. She would find a way—she would have to—because she had to pay back the men that had killed Nicholas and Jimmy. Pay them back in kind, put a knife of her own into their hearts, make sure that those vicious killers would not get away with—

Vicious killers, Lara thought.

She pulled the diving glove off her left hand, and slid it, backward, over the glove already on her right. An extra layer of protection.

She would need it.

Lara pulled the knife out of her belt again, and slashed her right forearm. Blood welled up instantly in the cut.

She stuck the knife away again, and dove.

Through the coral, through the tunnel, toward the open ocean again. Felt a rumbling behind her as she swam that she knew was the final collapse of the Luna Temple.

Blood billowed from her arm as she emerged from the underwater cliff.

The tiger shark was nowhere in sight.

Come on, you cold-blooded bastard, Lara thought, waving her cut arm about in the water. Thrashing like a wounded animal. Come and get me.

The first attack came from directly behind her.

She spun just as the shark shot past. A bolt of blue-and-gray lightning. God, it was fast. But that run had just been a test—a feint to see how badly injured Lara was. It hadn't come within five feet of her.

Not close enough for what she planned.

Now the animal was circling. It came about and faced her again, its cold, dead eyes weighing her.

Lara let herself go limp.

And the shark struck—even faster this time, coming straight for her.

At the last possible second, Lara's left hand shot forward, clenched into a fist. She punched the shark right in the nose. An old diver's trick—the shark veered off, convinced again that this prey was not worth the risk.

As it swam past, Lara grabbed onto its fin with her double-gloved right hand, and held on for dear life.

The shark bolted for the surface, thrashing and weaving as it tried to rid itself of its unwelcome passenger.

For her part, Lara just concentrated on holding on. Her

breath was already gone, and she felt the beginnings of a faint queasiness that she knew could represent the bends, but she couldn't worry about either of those things now, as she narrowed her whole world down to her right hand and the fin, to squeezing with every ounce of her strength, ignoring the throbbing pain in her wound, the rush of the water sliding past her, the seemingly endless expanse of blue above . . .

The shark swam.

The animal thrashed hard to the left—Lara's body went with it.

Then the shark thrashed back to the right, and its tail caught Lara square in the stomach.

She went flying backward—her hand let go of the fin.

No, she thought.

"No."

She said the word aloud—and opened her eyes to find herself bobbing on the surface of the ocean. Calm, featureless, no sight of land or boat anywhere.

Her entire body was a bruise. Her right hand was numb.

She felt consciousness slipping away.

She reached out and grabbed a piece of wood as it drifted past.

Draped herself over it and activated the transmitter on her collar.

Everything went black.

Later. The sun burned down on her from high above. She felt something sticky, and wet on her face. Dried saltwater—dried blood, who knew which?

Not her.

She closed her eyes again.

*   *   *

She opened them with a start.

It was later now. The sun was at four o'clock, drifting toward the horizon.

Something was wrong.

Lara pulled herself up farther on the driftwood.

The water around her shifted.

Before she could move, something slammed into her from beneath.

The shark? No, too big for the shark, too hard for the shark.

Whale, she thought, adrenaline surging through her system as she rolled to the side and—

Touched metal.

The thing beneath her rose up, breaking the surface, sending her rolling backward.

It was a submarine.

Lara found a railing and held on.

The conning tower popped open. Hillary burst through the door, a panicked expression on his face.

Bryce followed a second later.

"Oh my God," Hillary said, stumbing down the ladder in his haste to get to her. "Oh my God."

He knelt down next to her, and from somewhere, produced a mug. It smelled like tea.

He held it up to her lips, and Lara drank.

It was tea.

"Oh. I needed that," Lara croaked.

Hillary continued to look stricken.

"Oh my God," he whispered.

"It's not that bad," she repeated, struggling to sit up.

"It's awful!"

Lara turned and saw Bryce poking at the remnants of her new digicam, which dangled off her shoulder.

"This is awful," he repeated, looking as distressed as Hillary had. "Lara, I spend countless hours making sure you have the best equipment. I don't think you appreciate that—"

"Bryce," Hillary interrupted, laying a hand on his shoulder. "Not now."

Bryce humphed, and glared at Lara. "That means you don't appreciate me."

She reached out and shoved him to the deck. He looked up at her, shocked.

"What did I say?"

"Not what you said—what you are. A pain in the arse."

It was only then she saw the piece of driftwood she'd been hanging on to.

With the word *Konstantinos* painted on it.

FOUR

Somewhere over the Atlantic, an hour out from the airport, the waiting finally got to Monza.

"Ridiculous!" He'd been holding his pen in one hand, flicking the point in and out, his impatience growing with each passing minute. Now he squeezed the barrel tight between thumb and forefinger, only for an instant, but his strength—like the rest of him—was prodigious.

The barrel snapped.

Monza laid the shards on the table in front of him, and cleared his throat. "Did you—did any of you know he'd moved the meeting to . . . this?"

As he spoke he spun in his chair, making eye contact with each of the five people sharing the main cabin with him in turn. First those seated behind him, San, Krev, and Al-Sabah—then, directly across the cabin, Duvalier—and finally, the sole woman in their group, seated directly across a small serving table from him, Madame Gillespie.

All shook their heads.

Monza snorted. He'd spoken more out of exasperation than anything else, wasn't really expecting that any of the others had any more advance knowledge than he had of the change of location. He was frustrated, that was all—moving the meeting had upset his schedule, ruined some carefully laid plans of his.

He glanced forward now, to the curtain that separated

the main cabin from the Gulfstream's forward compartment, said compartment being—presumably—where their host waited to make his appearance. As Monza looked, he thought he saw a shadow pass behind the curtain. He craned his neck, trying to peer around the edge of the fabric, but it was no use. The curtain was drawn too tight.

Monza snorted, and downed the rest of his wine. When Monza was frustrated, he tended to indulge. It was a fault of his, he knew it, but not one he had any desire to change.

As he settled back in his chair, one of the serving girls stepped forward to refill his glass. She avoided making eye contact with him—not surprising, really, people—particularly people of the opposite sex—had been treating Edgar Monza that way for his entire life. When he was younger, it was because his physical appearance—his size, the way he carried himself, the way he spoke, and acted—repelled them.

Now that he had earned himself a reputation—one that had clearly preceded him aboard this plane—it was because they feared him.

Which Monza far preferred.

"What's the matter? Don't you like me?"

The girl—she and the other server, the blonde, had introduced themselves as he'd boarded the plane, but Monza had forgotten their names immediately—forced herself to smile. Tried to laugh as she finished pouring his wine, but Monza could see through that.

She was terrified.

Monza reached for his drink, and deliberately knocked the glass over.

The girl bit her lip, trying not to show emotion. Monza smiled.

"Can I have some more. Please?"

She avoided his eyes, wiped up the spill. Then she picked up his glass and started pouring again.

Monza put his hand on her bottom, caressed her.

"I'm sorry, angel, if I seem irritated," he said. To her credit, she didn't spill a drop. Monza smiled even more broadly. She had more spunk than he'd given her credit for. He thought about taking her to the back of the plane, indulging some of his other desires with her. He wondered if their host would be annoyed.

He rather hoped so.

"I am not patient like my friends," he continued. "I don't like it when plans are changed for no reason—"

"Really, Mister Monza."

Monza looked up.

The curtain at the front of the cabin had been pulled back—

And Dr. Jonathan Reiss stood in the doorway.

"I should think you know me better than that."

The girl took advantage of Reiss's appearance to back quickly away. Monza let her go, took a sip from his glass as he studied their host.

Reiss was immaculately turned out, as always, in a tan suit—probably Italian, obviously custom-made, it hung off him perfectly, made him look like he'd stepped out of the pages of a catalog, his hair perfectly coiffed, matching shoes, tie, and handkerchief completing the ensemble. Monza, who had his suits made by the finest tailors in the world and yet could never quite avoid rumpling them, could never get them to fit properly, thought that another reason to dislike the doctor—as was the grateful smile the serving girl flashed at Reiss as she scurried to her post at the back of the plane.

"You'll all accept my apologies, of course," Reiss said, "but behind every choice I make, one will always find a reason. In this instance, the six of you in one room makes for a tempting target for NATO. Rather than move any of you, I decided to move the room." Reiss flashed a brief smile. "At six hundred miles per hour."

The others nodded understandingly. Mr. San, in the chair just behind Monza, even chuckled.

Monza was not as amused.

"That's not an apology!" he shouted, banging his hand on the table. "It's our money that pays for the shirt on your back, not to mention this jet! Yet you make us wait like dogs!"

There was silence after his outburst—a silence born out of tension, and expectation. Everyone—Monza included—waited to see what Reiss would do, how he would react.

The doctor locked eyes with Monza a moment, then nodded thoughtfully. He smiled.

"Then I apologize, Mr. Monza." He looked around the room, including the others in the conversation. "To you, and to everyone. Please—let's drink to it."

He waved the serving girls forward. They poured from new bottles—Monza swallowed what remained of his drink in a single gulp and held out his glass for one of the girls to refill.

To his surprise, the brunette—the one he'd been amusing himself with—stepped in front of the other server to see to his glass herself. Their eyes met as she poured, and Monza was surprised to see her so cool, so composed.

Odd, he thought, as she stepped away. Then her eyes went to Reiss, and he understood. Reiss was here, and she felt safe, protected. *False security*, Monza thought. His plans for today might have changed, but Jonathan Reiss would not be able to offer this delicate flower a safe haven for too much longer.

"Gentlemen—and lady," Reiss began, and he turned to the back of the plane a moment, seemed to study something there, though Monza couldn't tell what, there was only a painting of some kind, a clock, and the toilet of course.

"There is an expression," Reiss said, walking forward as he spoke. "It's not nice to fool Mother Nature. And yet, whether it be sarin gas for Mr. San—" he stopped next to San just then, and laid a hand on the other man's shoulder "—improved typhoid for Mr. Krev to use in the Balkans," he continued, lifting his hand and nodding toward Krev, "or enhanced cholera for Mr. Duvalier," and at those words, he and the Frenchman exchanged the briefest of smiles, "or the more exotic work I've done for you, Mr. Monza," Reiss said, and Monza looked up to find the doctor's eyes focused on him now, "that is precisely what I've been doing."

Something in the doctor's gaze unnerved Monza. He turned away, and took another sip of his wine. Different vintage, this, he decided. There was an aftertaste he didn't care for.

Reiss turned away, and glanced back at the rear of the plane again. Again, Monza wondered why. As he wondered, the doctor began speaking again.

"Yet while those weapons served their purpose, there are always limitations; stable diseases aren't lethal, deadly ones burn out too quickly . . . Mother Nature can only be fooled so much. So, after years of fighting her, I've surrendered. Rather than take a disease and attempt to transform it into a weapon of mass destruction, I've gone and found the one such weapon Nature ever gave us. Something meant for more than scaring the public into wearing gloves when they open their mail. This is why I've called you all here today— to show you the way that Mother Nature levels nations. And to offer you a chance to possess that power for yourselves."

Monza saw the others in the cabin exchange glances; he met Madame Gillespie's eyes and saw the hunger in there, felt that same hunger from all the others, felt it fill the sudden silence left by the doctor's words. Reiss had them.

And that didn't fit into Monza's plans at all.

The big man barked out a laugh.

"Crap," Monza said, the word slicing through the silence like a knife. "We've come all this way to hear crap. Forgive my crude outburst, doctor," and he made the title sound like a sneer, an insult, "but for years men like you have promised such a weapon and for years they have failed."

The doctor's eyes narrowed. "You've never heard the promise from me."

Monza laughed again, and felt a tickle in his throat. Some sediment in the wine—something stuck there. He coughed, and the slight tickle turned into a burning sensation farther down. Indigestion, acid reflux—he had them all. Nothing serious, never serious. He cleared his throat, and met Reiss's eyes again. Steel on steel—the two men eyed each other warily.

"Gentlemen—Madame Gillespie," Reiss said. "Your governments have attacked their enemies. Those enemies fought back. You've terrorized their citizens—those citizens rallied around waving flags."

Spare us the philosophizing, Monza thought, and opened his mouth to speak again, but instead let loose another cough. *Damn.*

He had a glass of water next to him, untouched. He picked it up now and drank.

"Deploy my weapon," Reiss continued, "and those same citizens will tremble at the sight of one another. As they begin to die, they'll blame their own government. Looting will erupt. Rapes, murders—your enemies, however great, will collapse from within like a house of cards. Or like . . ."

Reiss stopped, hung over Monza with a strange sickening smile.

"Like Mister Monza here," he finished.

Monza swallowed, and felt the burning in his throat again. Worse this time.

Looked up at the mocking smile on Reiss's face.

And looked down at the glass of water in his hand, the one he'd just drank from, saw red streaks in it, not wine, no, it was—

He gurgled, and set down the glass of water.

No. God, no.

Through the sudden fire in his chest, he was vaguely aware of Duvalier jumping to his feet, backing away from him.

"What the hell is going on?" Duvalier shouted.

"What's going on?" Reiss repeated, his voice sounding eerily calm, sounding to Monza as if it was coming from a million miles away. "He told M-I-Six about our meeting. That's why I changed the location."

The burning in his chest was unbearable now—Monza pulled the napkin from under his glass, and coughed into it. Felt something tear in his throat.

The napkin came away stained red, and white.

"Bastard," Monza whispered. "Bastard."

He looked up at Reiss, disbelievingly. The doctor continued to smile.

Monza knew he was dying—whatever Reiss had given him was sure to be lethal.

But perhaps—just perhaps—he could take the good doctor with him.

There was a gun inside his jacket—he had to reach for it without seeming to make a threatening move, disguise it somehow, yes, pretend he was reaching for a handkerchief, pretend—

A sudden spasm of coughing overtook him, and with it, an equally sudden attack of nausea. Monza felt his whole body wrenching upon itself, his insides twisting and turning themselves inside out and—

He moaned, and the moan turned into a gurgle, and a viscous stream of grayish matter poured out of his throat.

Monza stared, disbelieving, at the napkin, coated with what had just come out of him.

Everyone else in the cabin moved reflexively backward, seeking to put more distance between themselves and Monza. Everyone except Dr. Jonathan Reiss.

The doctor allowed himself a small shiver of pleasure, and then moved closer. He wanted to enjoy every second of Monza's death throes.

"He was going to turn me in, then seek asylum from the West," Reiss said. He noted sweat breaking out on Monza's forehead—the disease was progressing as rapidly as Holliday and the others on the team had said it would. Faster, even.

Monza was trying to get up. Reiss put his hand on the man's neck and forced him back into his chair.

"A smart man would have known I was on to him, would never have gotten on this plane. But I knew you would, because you actually thought—" Reiss found Monza's eyes, and a spark of whatever reasoning consciousness remained in the man, in the face of the unbearable agonies his body was suffering through right now "—you actually thought you could fool me."

The doctor shook his head pityingly.

Monza had another coughing fit, this one the worst yet. Halfway through Reiss heard a loud crack, and shook his head in wonder. That was a rib going, he thought. And there—another crack, another bone.

Marvelous.

Reiss had to hold Monza's neck even tighter to keep the man steady in his chair.

"These, my friends—" Reiss spoke without taking his eyes away from Monza's, he wanted to see every ounce of agony reflected there "—are the sounds of a traitor."

Then all at once, there were no more sounds.

The coughing had stopped. So had Monza's breathing.

Reiss stood over the fat man, whose head had come to rest against one of the Gulfstream's windows. Red matter trickled out of both sides of his mouth, and had stained his suit and one of the armrests on his seat.

There was some on the floor, as well, Reiss saw. And on the windows. The doctor didn't envy whoever was on clean-up duty after this flight.

He turned away from the corpse and focused his attention on his other guests.

"Please forgive that unpleasantness. It was necessary, of course, but—" Reiss shrugged. "I regret you had to see it. In case you were wondering, that was an accelerated form of ebola. It is the deadliest disease known to man. Highly contagious."

Duvalier, who still hadn't sat down (for someone with such an illustrious pedigree, Reiss thought, the man was a bit . . . well, jumpy), exchanged a nervous glance with first San, and then Krev. Even the normally unflappable Al-Sabah looked tense.

Reiss nodded sympathetically. "Yes, it is an airborne pathogen—I don't doubt the cabin is full of the virus. However . . ."

He nodded toward the two ladies at the rear of the cabin. They came forward and placed a single black pill in front of each of the other guests.

"Like all known diseases, there exist stockpiles of anti-serum in the West—ready to stifle any outbreak."

His guests all studied their pills for a moment. Then, one by one—Duvalier first of all, and Reiss made a mental note to speak with Sean about the man, he was too jittery today, he would fold under any sort of pressure, Reiss knew that now—they each picked up the capsules and swallowed them.

Only when they'd all done so did Reiss take his own dose of antiserum. He sipped from his water, and smiled at the others.

"My friends, there's no antiserum for what I'm offering to you. No treatment, no protocol, no vaccine, no cure. The modern world has never seen anything like what I've uncovered."

"Uncovered?" Mr. San asked.

"Yes," Reiss nodded. "I branched out. Archaeology."

San looked at him questioningly. Madame Gillespie frowned.

"I don't understand," she said.

"It's not important that you do," he told her. "All you need to know is zero-seven-seven-four-four-six-eight-one."

"I beg your pardon?"

"Zero-seven-seven-four-four-six-eight-one. That is the account at the Lardesbank in Bern. Nine-figure deposit—a fair price for what you're getting. Those of you who pay will see their enemies eliminated. Those of you who don't—" he looked from her to the others "—I hope for your sakes none of your enemies buy it. You have twenty-four hours."

Again, there was silence in the cabin.

"That's too soon," San said. "I'll need more time to gather that kind of money."

Reiss sighed. "Ah. Then I'm sorry for you, Mister San. Because this is, as they say in America, a limited-time offer. And the time limit is twenty-four hours."

Just as Reiss finished talking, a soft chime sounded in the

cabin. The two serving girls made their way toward the back of the plane.

"I'll leave you now," Reiss said. "But the girls will be serving dinner shortly—after we've had a chance to clear the cabin of—" He nodded in the direction of Monza's body. "That."

"Let me prevail on you to stay with us a moment, doctor," Al-Sabah said. "I would like to discuss exactly what it is you've found. Since you're asking us to take an awful lot on faith."

Reiss shook his head slowly. "I cannot believe, sir, that after my demonstration here—" he nodded again at Monza's body "—that you doubt my ability to deliver what I promise."

Al-Sabah, to his credit, Reiss thought, met his stare.

"I don't doubt your abilities—I just don't like paying that kind of money blindly."

"Not blindly, sir," Reiss said. "I believe you have more than enough information to make a rational decision here. And now, if you'll excuse me . . ."

Without waiting for an answer, Reiss spun on his heel and walked forward to his own cabin.

The doctor spent the next several hours resting. He preferred plenty of rest—ten hours a day, not necessarily in contiguous time chunks, blocks of an hour at least, though, at a minimum—though he did not use the time solely to sleep. Reiss spent much of it just thinking. The most valuable time he had, and the hardest to find, particularly in a world that seemed determined to supply a sound track—be it music or commercials or what passed for news—for one's every waking moment. It really was astounding to him, every time he went out in public, how anyone got anything done with the constant din of so-called civilization howling in their ears.

Among the things he considered now, as he sat in the half-darkness of his cabin, were the implications of Monza's contact with MI6. He of course knew the British Intelligence organization was on to him—Rankin, and Calloway, and Stevens, all three of them had been tracing his activities surreptitiously, and not-so-surreptitiously over the last several years. But if Monza had given them even a clue as to what he was up to now, that surveillance would turn into active pursuit. Relentless pursuit.

So what had Monza known? What could he have told them?

The invitation Reiss had sent to all his guests for today's meeting had been the same tersely worded message, delivered by fax to their respective offices.

Something of interest has just become available. Please join me at one P.M., our usual rendezvous point.

And of course, when Sean had spotted the MI6 operatives at the Harrod's salon, Reiss had moved the meeting, and Sean had moved to discover who was behind the betrayal. Monza topped his list of suspects from the start—Reiss had a profound distaste for the man, his crass, deliberately revolting manner, his poor hygiene—and a cursory survey of Monza's cellular calls was all it took to prove his instincts right. Thus, the enhanced ebola.

But what could he have told them before he died?

That Reiss had something new. So MI6 would right now be looking in the usual places for clues as to what Reiss had found. They would corral scientists who'd worked with him before, visit facilities he'd utilized, countries whose stockpiles he'd raided . . . no, there was simply no way that MI6 could suspect what he was up to. They—like everyone else—thought the newest, most dangerous weapons would come from the development of new technologies. They were looking forward, keeping their eyes on the future. Where Reiss's attention had been focused for the first two decades of his professional life.

But the problem was, everyone was looking toward the future, exploring the same techniques, technologies, treatments, seeking the cutting edge. What he had said earlier was true—as fast as the new diseases were being developed, there was always a cure also being tested.

Over the last few months, Reiss had been looking somewhere else entirely. The ancient, dimly remembered past.

He'd gotten the idea from a book, of all things—which was more than a little surprising. Reiss was not a man who read frequently, not even within his chosen field of expertise. Scientists today published because the universities or corporations who employed them demanded it, and their conclusions were always predetermined matters, driven by the bottom line. Reiss preferred to do his learning in the laboratory—or through experience.

Which is just what had happened, several months back, when the Gulfstream had been forced out of service for repairs. Reiss had been forced to fly a commercial plane out of London into the States. First class, of course, but still . . . a horrendous experience.

A baby in coach, sneezing and spreading all sorts of God-knew-what germs throughout the plane (luckily, Reiss had taken a half-dozen immune-system boosters before boarding), a woman next to him—a taut, tense, business executive a few years older than him, late forties—who'd flirted shamelessly throughout the flight, and the way the flight attendant prepared his steak . . .

Reiss shuddered, remembering how closely she'd leaned over his food, the minted scent of her breath, the stifling musk of her perfume—good Lord, there were no doubt traces of that horrible stinking liquid underneath her fingernails, all over her hands . . .

He'd passed on lunch.

He'd also passed on all the businesswoman's attempts at engaging him in conversation, preferring instead to stare intently out the window, pretending to focus on the view but instead working a bit of third-level calculus, working out the diffusion matrix for a cannister of Tyrolean flu, delivered via a low-flying airplane—a skydiving school having just presented itself as the perfect cover for such an attack.

And then at some point during the flight, he'd turned away from the window to find that his seatmate had picked up a book.

Plagues and Peoples in the Ancient World.

Reiss's interest, of course, was piqued.

He cleared his throat.

"May I take a look at that?" he asked.

The woman's eyes flickered from the page to Reiss, and she shook her head.

"In a moment," she said absently, obviously no longer interested in engaging Reiss in anything.

He reached into his pocket, and pulled out his billfold. Extracted a five hundred-pound note, and laid it on the woman's tray, next to her drink.

"Please give me the book," Reiss repeated.

She looked from the bill to Reiss, and shook her head.

"Really." She looked insulted. "I don't see how you can simply ignore people and then expect—"

Reiss pulled out another five hundred-pound note, and laid it next to the first.

"The book, please."

She frowned. "This is quite ridiculous."

Reiss couldn't help himself. He was getting angry.

"Please don't waste time," he said. "Give me the book."

She opened her mouth to speak again, then saw the look on Reiss's face.

He saw the look on hers, as well, and smiled.

Then he slid the book out of her hand, and settled it on his lap.

"Honestly," the woman said a moment later—after she'd picked up the bills and put them away. "What makes the book so—"

Reiss held up a finger to silence her and began reading.

The author's position he gathered at once, it being identical to not only his but that of several other popular works. The idea that disease played a pivotal role in history—in allowing Cortés to take Mexico, the English to overrun the North American continent—none of this was new to him.

What was new—and quite interesting—were the less-credibly documented examples the author drew on from ancient times. Rumors of what really caused the downfall of Minoan civilization, where the Anasazi had actually gone . . .

What had stopped Alexander the Great's march east.

It had put Reiss in mind of a story he'd heard as a child, a story that had made quite an impression on him at the time. Over the years, while he hadn't forgotten that story, he had tended, more and more, to dismiss it as apocrypha. Now, as he sat there on the plane, greatly intrigued by the book's discussion of ancient catastrophes, he wasn't so sure.

Over the last several months, Reiss had followed up on those discussions. Several promising lines of research had developed.

And now, through a serendipitous series of events, he was very close to reaping the rewards of that research. A thousand pounds well spent, he thought—and he was also convinced now that there was no way MI6 could have a clue as to his current plan of attack. Not from Monza, not from any-one, in fact. All in all, a very satisfactory state of affairs.

His train of thought was interrupted by the sound of a soft chime, followed a second later by Ms. Kelly's voice at his door.

"Landing in five minutes, Doctor."

"Thank you," Reiss called back.

He stood up, flicking the lights on to full, and checked his appearance in the mirror. Straightened his tie, dabbed water on his temples—there.

That was satisfactory, as well.

Reiss's chief of operations—Sean O'Sullivan—was waiting for him on the runway. Three bodyguards—Reiss had made more than his fair share of enemies over the years—waited with him.

Suddenly, Reiss was not happy.

There was supposed to be a fifth man.

"Where is Chen Lo?" he asked.

In response, Sean handed him a piece of paper. A faxed photograph, Reiss saw.

The Orb.

"And?" he asked Sean.

"Chen Lo got the Orb, but M-I-Six is on to him."

Reiss was stunned. "How . . . ?"

He had just gone over this, in all possible permutations. There was no way for MI6 to have known about the Orb. Or Chen Lo.

"He doesn't know," Sean said. "But rather than risk bringing the Orb here, he's waiting."

Reiss shook his head. This was unacceptable.

"I just told a cabin full of people about Pandora. That clock cannot be reset. Tell Chen Lo to bring the Orb at once."

"Are we sure that's wise?" Sean asked. "Let me find out more from him—what M-I-Six knows, check my sources, as well . . ."

"No," Reiss interrupted. If he had to gather those five again, ask for more time to make good on his promise to them . . . he would never get the money he'd asked for. Besides, the Gulfstream was gone, taking off behind them even now. Not that he couldn't have told them to turn around, but . . .

No. He had set his plan in motion. He would see it completed.

"Have Chen Lo bring the Orb," Reiss repeated. "Now."

Sean nodded, and took out his satellite phone, dialing even as he walked toward a waiting car. Reiss followed, so preoccupied with the impossibility of MI6's knowledge that he accidentally dragged the cuff of his trousers against the side of the car as he climbed in.

Grease. That would stain.

Reiss frowned.

At that moment, he was not a happy man.

FIVE

The funeral was to be in Merovigli—a week from today. Lara had already rescheduled her entire calendar so that she could attend. A single ceremony, for all three men.

She'd heard from Miss Stehlik this morning, the first time in years, asking for transport down to the island. Lara hadn't been able to face calling her back yet, risk a conversation that would certainly turn very emotional. She couldn't do emotional yet, not now. She had things to do. Revenge.

Hillary thwacked her on the arm.

"Pay attention," he said.

It was midmorning. They were in Lara's study, at Croft Manor, drilling with kenzai staves—wooden sticks five feet long. Hillary was wearing a padded vest and trousers for his safety. Lara was in a long flowing skirt.

"Are you sure this is a good idea?" Hillary asked. "Doctor Johnston said the only reason you're still alive is because you're in such good shape."

"No comments about my shape, please." Lara feinted to her left—Hillary went for it, and she thrust to the right, hard.

He took the blow square in the gut.

"Whoof," he said, and stumbled backward.

Lara pressed the attack.

Hillary righted himself, looking a little green, and blocked her next thrust. He thwacked her again, hitting her left forearm. Right where she'd cut herself yesterday. The wound sang with fresh agony.

Lara smiled.

This was exactly what she needed: action. To be moving, to get her blood flowing again so that when she tracked down the men who'd killed the Petrakis—

She thrust forward again, propelling Hillary back through the study door and into the library—

She would be ready.

Lara pushed through the library doors. Hillary stood in the middle of the room, holding his stave defensively, waiting for her.

Bryce was sitting in the red leather chair, fussing with her digicam, his laptop open on the table next to him.

"Bryce. What have you got?" Lara asked.

He snorted in frustration. "Well. I haven't even finished loading the images from your camera yet."

Lara pursed her lips in frustration. That wasn't what she wanted to hear.

She stepped forward and smacked Hillary good.

"Hey!" Hillary looked at Bryce, sensing the reason for Lara's attack. "Thanks."

He glared at Lara, and raised his stave once more.

They started drilling again.

Lara had to give him credit—Hillary had been practicing. A few months back, when he'd first volunteered to help with her training, she'd thought the idea preposterous. Hillary's performance during those first sessions hadn't convinced her any differently.

Now, though . . . he'd improved tremendously. Enough so that she had to give him her full attention. Well, ninety percent of her attention anyway.

"Bryce," she called out as Hillary danced around her.

"What about references to an Orb? If we find out what it was, it might help us find who attacked me."

"Shite," Bryce mumbled, hunched over in his chair. "Damn camera."

"I took the liberty of checking," Hillary interrupted. "What historical inventories there are of the Luna Temple do not list any Orb."

Lara frowned.

Hillary smacked her on the side—hard.

She looked at him and raised an eyebow.

He smiled back. "I believe I was fairly thorough in my examination."

"Fairly thorough won't cut it," Lara said, deciding to devote her full attention to him. She stepped forward, raising the stave in front of her.

"I want both of you to make a list of every Orb mentioned in Greek history."

"Every one!?" That from Bryce, behind her.

"Every one," Lara repeated.

"But," Hillary began, feinting forward, "that's—"

Lara, seeing his weight remaining on his back foot, ignored the feint and stepped forward herself, through his defenses, and struck his stave hard.

"Liable," Hillary continued, fending off her assault. "To—"

She whapped his right hip.

"Be—" He stepped back, and she brought her stave forward again, then jabbed out.

"Thousands!" he finished, stumbling backward to avoid the point of her stave.

She changed the forward motion to an upward one, sending his stave flying out of his hands. Hillary continued to move away, till his back was pressed up against a wall of books and he could move no farther.

"Then we'll read thousands." Lara drove her sharpened stave just past Hillary's ear, into the spine of a volume whose title had caught her eye. *Greek History* by Biester and Conant.

She pulled the book off the shelf with her spear, and flipped it to Hillary.

"You can start with that one," Lara said, lowering her stave. "I'll be in my office, making a call."

On the way out of the library, she whapped Bryce across the back of the head.

"Ow," he said. "What was that for?"

"Speed it up," she told him. "You've got a lot of reading ahead of you."

Lara wasn't able to make her call right away though. She had to wait almost an hour—time needed for the embassy not only to locate her party, but to set up a secure line. She had time to shower, change into her riding clothes, and sort through the day's correspondence before her phone rang softly.

"Hello?"

"Is this Lady Croft?" The voice was clipped and very upper-crust.

"Yes."

"We have your call." A moment's silence, then a click over the line, and then—

"Lara?"

"Kosa. My God, it's good to hear your voice." Lara smiled, thinking of the man on the other end of the line, at the British Embassy in Nairobi. Kosa Maasai—one of the chieftains of that near-legendary African tribe, the Maasai. Tall, elegant, skin as black as night, and a sense of humor just as dark.

"And yours," Kosa said. "I'm so sorry about the Petrakis."

"Not as sorry as whoever did it is going to be. You received my fax?"

"I did, yes."

Lara had woken early this morning, with the sudden knowledge of what it was that the petroglyphs in the Luna Temple had reminded her of. She'd had Bryce (who'd finally finished downloading the images from her digicam) print out the relevant shots, and faxed them off to the British Embassy, for Kosa's attention.

"I appreciate the look, Kosa. The drawings reminded me of work you showed me in Kenya."

"The Gloman exhibit? Yes, they are reminiscent. And I am happy to help." He chuckled. "Any excuse to give your diplomats a scare."

She laughed, too—the first genuine laugh she'd had since what had happened in the temple. She could just picture Kosa, prowling the halls of the embassy, wearing traditional robes and headdress, the bureaucrats scurrying by him, trying not to look fearful, while keeping a respectful distance.

"I'm looking at the fax now, Lara," Kosa said. "Page three."

Lara picked up her copy, flipped to the third page. It was an image of the mosaic of Alexander's journey across Asia—specifically, the scene that had puzzled her, the one of Alexander's army, lying dead on the battlefield.

"What do you think?" she asked.

There was silence for a moment. As Lara waited, she opened a drawer in her desk, and pulled out her hunting rifle. To call it hers was perhaps inaccurate, it was a family heirloom, an Enfield full-bore, dating back to the mid-nineteenth century. Originally the property of Lord Winston Croft, her great-great-grandfather. Made an even more satisfying recoil than her Colts—when you fired the Enfield you knew whatever you shot was going down, and was staying down. Winston had used it to hunt boar—specially freighted in for the occasion on the grounds.

Lara was planning on using it for a little target practice of her own.

"I'm looking at the glyphs beneath the drawing," Kosa finally said. "The symbols are a primitive version of Ol Maa. They read: 'with life comes death.' "

"Ol Maa?" Lara thought for a second she'd misheard. "I'm sorry, did you say Ol Maa?"

"Yes."

"That makes no sense." Ol Maa was the Maasai language—scant wonder the drawings from the temple had reminded her of the ones Kosa had shown her in Kenya.

But why were there Ol Maa inscriptions in a temple built by Alexander the Great? Yes, his triumphal march through Egypt had included a brief visit to the African continent, but history recorded no contact between Alexander and the Maasai, or any other African peoples. He had stopped there for all of three months, at most, and then headed eastward, never to return.

"I can't explain it, either," Kosa replied. "I can only give you the translation. Now. Turn to the next page of the fax."

She did. It was an image taken while she was suspended high above the temple floor, trying to get at the Orb.

"The figure on the floor is a shadow guardian. A mythical creature brought to earth to protect the treasures of the gods."

"This is from Maasai mythology?"

"Maasai, Chagga, Hadzabe—all tribes in this part of the world have legends pertaining to the shadow guardians."

"What are they guardians of?" Lara asked, turning the Enfield in her hand while she did so. The barrel shone, and the stock had been recently oiled, as well—Hillary had obviously been taking care of it.

"I don't know. I'm sorry, that's all I can tell you."

She sighed. "Well. It's somewhere to start. Thank you, Kosa. Try not to scare anyone on the way out."

"I'll do my best, Lara."

He hung up.

Lara stood there a moment, phone in hand, frowning.

Ol Maa? How could that be? What did the Maasai have to do with Alexander the Great? Who were the shadow guardians? And the Orb—where did that fit in?

Lara glanced down at the desk, at an image of the Orb Bryce had left lying there for her. Staring up at her like a great shining eye—

She dropped the rifle to the floor with a clatter.

An eye. That was it.

The *mati*.

"Hillary!" she called, heading for the library.

She found the volume in short order. Huge, massive pages coming out of the binding, she lifted it carefully from the shelf and set it down on the table.

"*Apocrypha of the Hellenic Age*," Hillary read off the spine. "I've been through this, you know. There's no mention of an Orb."

"It's as I said," Lara told him, as she began flipping pages. "The reference is not to the Orb at all. It's my fault for not seeing the resemblance sooner."

Hillary held up the image of the Orb, and turned it sideways.

"An eye? I don't see it at all," he announced.

"You have no imagination," Lara said. "Ah. Here we are."

She'd come to the section on Alexander the Great, and now began scanning the text, translating from the Greek as she read. Assembled in the early fourth century, the book was a collection of stories and myths associated with Alexander, offered by various writers as proof of his divinity. Like the tale of the two snakes who had magically appeared to lead him and his army safely through the Sahara to the oasis at Siwa. The Gordian knot. His victory over the Persians.

The *mati*.

Lara cleared her throat, and read out loud.

"It was at this time that word reached Antipater of Alexander's decision to turn for home. The messenger who brought word of this also brought a leather pouch he had taken directly from the king's hand, and borne in secret across the continent. Alexander had commanded him to give this pouch only into the hands of Antipater, and failing that, to see it destroyed."

"Within this pouch," she continued, "Alexander had placed the key to a terrible secret. He called this key the *mati*, and commanded Antipater to hide it far from the sight of men, forbidding anyone to look upon it. For according to the king—"

She stopped reading.

"What?" Hillary leaned over her shoulder. "What does it say?"

Lara paused a moment before answering.

"Some things are not meant to be found."

Alexander's words, now nearly two millenia old, were an exact echo of Gus's last words to her.

The resonance made her uncomfortable.

She closed the book.

"The literal translation of *mati* is eye. It, and the Orb, are one and the same."

Hillary nodded.

"So the Orb is the key to some terrible secret?"

"I think so."

"Such as . . ."

"That's the question, isn't it? When we find that out, we'll know why someone was willing to kill for it."

Lara stood up. At least she now had some idea of what the Orb was, though she was no closer to discovering who the men in the tomb were.

Enough of flipping through books. Right now, Lara needed action.

Shouldering the rifle, she headed for the stable—and the target practice she'd promised herself.

Lara entered the grove cautiously, sitting side-saddle (like the proper English girl Miss Stehlik had raised her to be), with the rifle poised on her shoulder.

The trees made a canopy above her, blotting out the sun. A thick, seemingly impenetrable wall of green surrounded her.

The first man popped out from behind a pine to her left.

In one fluid motion, she swung the rifle around, targeted, and squeezed the trigger.

She'd fired true. The bullet caught her target square in the forehead, and he simply exploded, disappeared from sight, shattered into a thousand pieces.

Cardboard pieces, of course, but Lara pictured the Asian man from the Luna Temple—Jimmy's killer—in the target's place, and smiled, tight-lipped, with satisfaction.

A second target slid down from a branch high above her and to the right.

She fired again—another hit.

And before she could even lower the rifle, another target came swinging toward her through the canopy of trees and she hit that, as well.

Lara reloaded.

In her mind, she put all the targets she'd just killed in diving suits, placed them in the Luna Temple, and stood over their bodies.

She rode on. There was a slight breeze in the grove, from out of the north. Leaves rustled above her.

A target shot up directly in her path, swinging back and forth like a pendulum.

Lara aimed . . .

And just as she fired, her horse reared up suddenly, and her shot went wide.

She frowned. Something had spooked the horse—what?

Then she heard the noise, as well—a thrumming from up above.

Lara looked up and saw a helicopter plummeting from the sky—a government copter, heading straight for the launching pad behind Croft Manor.

MI6, Lara knew instantly. What other branch of the British government wouldn't even bother phoning for an appointment?

She didn't know what they wanted, didn't care. She didn't have time for them right now.

She dug in her heels, urging her horse forward. As they rose past the target Lara had missed, she frowned.

She pictured Jimmy's killer, holding up the Orb in his grasp, smiling. Escaping on her DPV while the temple collapsed around her, burying Alexander's treasure, Jimmy and Nicholas's bodies.

Without easing up on the reins, Lara swung the rifle back over her shoulder. A quick glance behind her to sight the target, and she fired again.

As she swung back around, she heard the target explode.

And another popped up right in front of her, barely five feet away. No time to bring the rifle to bear.

So she punched it square in the face.

Lara rode on, her knuckles stinging. She didn't mind a bit. Hitting things was much more viscerally satisfying than squeezing a trigger. Part of her even hoped that whoever MI6 sent would give her a hard time.

She wouldn't mind dealing out another punch or two.

Lara burst through the door into the long hall, and saw two men—strangers to her—sitting at the table.

Bryce and Hillary stood over them, looking uncomfortable. Hillary was talking.

"Perhaps you gentlemen would like some tea while you wait—"

"No, they wouldn't," Lara interrupted. "Tea is for guests. The door is for intruders."

She nodded to the entryway behind her.

Give them credit—neither of the two men blinked.

"Lady Croft," one said.

"Or should we call you Lara?" the other asked.

"In any case," the first continued, "we need your help. I'm Agent Calloway. This is Stevens."

Bryce edged closer to her, lowered his voice. "Lara, these men are from M-I-Six—"

"I know that, Bryce," she said, folding her arms across her chest, not lifting her gaze from the two intruders for a second. "It's clear from their soft hands and pressed suits that these are men who make decisions then leave the dirty work to others. I have no interest in—"

Calloway reached into his pocket and dropped a photo on the table.

Lara glanced at it quickly, then froze in place.

Her mouth dropped open in shock.

The photo was of the Asian man—Jimmy Petraki's killer.

"This man's name is Chen Lo," Calloway said, nodding at the picture. "Along with his brother Xien, he runs a ring of Chinese bandits known as the Shay Ling."

"I know the Shay Ling," Lara said, which wasn't exactly the truth; she knew of the Shay Ling, knew their reputation, she'd come close to run-ins with them once a few years back, and had only on the advice of a certain person who at that point in her life she'd trusted stepped aside to avoid that run-in, which was neither here nor there.

What was important was what had happened in the Luna Temple.

"Then you know what they do," Calloway said. "They deal in guns, diamonds, antiquities . . . anything Chen Lo can sell on the black market. They followed you from the moment you arrived in Santorini—"

"Why?"

"For this." Stevens stood and handed her a piece of paper—a fax.

It was a drawing of the Orb.

"After you were picked up at sea, a listening post in Malta intercepted that fax," Stevens continued. "It was sent from Chen Lo to a man named Jonathan Reiss."

Lara nodded. Another name she knew.

"The scientist?" she asked. "Won the Nobel Prize?"

"One and the same," Calloway replied. "He's now the foremost designer of biological weapons in the world."

She frowned. "No. That can't be right. He's a respected man, I've seen him at—"

Calloway handed her a sheaf of photos.

The first she recognized instantly—it had run on the front page of every newspaper, worldwide, two years ago last August sixth. The anniversary of the bombing of Hiroshima. There had been an attack on a group of tourists visiting the museum that commemorated the bombing. Two hundred and ten people killed—most of them Americans—by a nerve gas that had disrupted brain function in the most painful way conceivable, before death followed.

Lara stared at the image of the two women lying on the floor, their faces frozen in a rictus of horror, and flipped to the next picture.

It was of a small village—one- and two-story houses, some of them with chunks of building missing. The image brought to mind someplace in Europe, the Balkans most likely. The focus was on the burning stack of bodies at the center of the image, and their blackened, bloated faces.

"Enhanced cholera," Stevens said.

Lara nodded, and flipped again.

The third and final picture was from a battlefield somewhere—Africa, most likely, the soldiers were all black men. They were all dead, as well, sprawled unnaturally on the ground.

Calloway took the pictures back.

"Reiss's creations have been at the heart of every act of bioterror in the past fifteen years," he said.

"His disdain for life is legendary. He has no political agenda, doesn't care who his weapons kill or why," Stevens put in.

"A modern-day Doctor Mengele," Calloway said.

Lara nodded, her mind racing as she absorbed what the two agents were telling her. Reiss, after the Orb. The *mati*— the key to a terrible secret. What did he think he was going to find?

She paced the length of the room, once, twice.

It had been a day of surprising revelations. The Shay Ling, and Jonathan Reiss. Shadow guardians, and smatterings of the Maasai language in a Greek temple.

Her eyes fell on the fax she'd sent Kosa. The drawing of Alexander's army lying dead on the battlefield.

The picture Calloway had just shown her—the army of bloated, disfigured corpses—flashed before her eyes.

The connection struck her like a physical blow.

A plague, she realized. Alexander's army had perished from a plague.

Stevens started talking again.

"We know Chen Lo followed you to obtain the Orb. We also know that he'll deliver it to Reiss soon. What we don't know is why. Candidly, that terrifies us."

Lara was listening—barely. Her eyes were still on the drawing of Alexander's army.

On the soldier holding the small box in his arms. What she'd thought to be a treasure chest of some kind.

Not a treasure chest at all.

She thought of the objects the temple had been rumored to contain, and a chill went down her spine.

"Pandora," she whispered.

The ultimate biological weapon—the sum of all evils contained in this world.

"Reiss is not to be trifled with," Stevens was saying. "The doctor—"

"Pandora's box," she repeated, louder this time.

Everyone in the room turned to her.

Hillary cleared his throat. "I beg your pardon?"

"Pandora's box—that's why Reiss wanted the Orb," Lara said. "He's going to use it to find Pandora's box!"

A long silence followed.

"Umm," Bryce said. "Pandora? Like in the fairy tale?"

"You mean the Greek myth," Stevens said. "Pandora is given a box by the gods, told not to open it. She does and unleashes pain in the world?"

Lara nodded. "I'm afraid that's the Sunday school version."

"There's another?" Calloway asked.

"Several. There are analogues to the Pandora story to be found in almost every culture."

She crossed to the far wall, to her father's prized Loring—a globe close to a hundred years old. Until a few months back, she'd kept it in the room that used to be his study, where Lara had sat at his feet, enchanted, as he spun her bedtime stories night after night, tales of the long-vanished kingdoms that dotted the ancient globe. Stories of gods who walked the earth, secret societies that controlled mankind's destiny . . .

Creation myths from every corner of the world.

"How do you think life began?" Lara asked, spinning the globe. "Shooting stars, meteor, primordial ooze . . ."

Stevens and Calloway shook their heads, waiting for her to continue.

"Actually," Bryce said. "It's fairly well known that—"

Hillary whacked him.

"My father told me a story once," Lara said. "In 2300 B.C., an Egyptian pharoah found a place he named the cradle of life; where we, life, began. There he found a box. The box which brought life to earth. The pharoah opened it, but all that was left inside was the Ramante: a plague which came as a companion to life."

"Companion?" Stevens asked.

"In nature there's always balance. The world comes in pairs. Right and wrong. Yin and yang. What's pain without pleasure—"

Calloway cut her off. "What did this plague do?"

"It leveled pharoah's army."

She met Calloway's gaze, held it with her own. "That's right. Just like the army in your photo."

The two agents glanced at each other, and sat a little straighter. Leaned a little closer.

"Go on," Calloway said.

"The pharoah's son dispatched his finest soldier to take the box and transport it to the end of the world, beyond the reach of man. The story ends there." Lara spun the globe again. The room was silent a moment.

"I don't understand," Calloway finally said. "What does this have to do with Reiss? With the Orb?"

Lara stopped the globe, with her finger stuck square in the middle of India.

"Two thousand years later, Alexander the Great reached India. His army was ravaged by a plague—"

She passed her copy of the fax she'd sent Kosa to Calloway—

"—after one soldier discovered a small box among some remains."

"India." Stevens frowned. "So you're saying—that's where the pharoah's man brought it?"

"That's right," Lara said. "India—specifically, the Bay of Bengal—was commonly regarded as the end of the world in Alexander's time. No one knew about the Americas, or China."

"And Alexander found it?"

"I think so." She was going on conjecture now, based on what she knew of the man, but it all made sense to her. "Found it, and realized the box was too powerful to be trusted to any man. So he returned it to its home—at the cradle of life. It's never been seen since."

"Is this still a story? Or is any of this fact?"

"That's the question, isn't it?"

"And this cradle of life is where?" Calloway asked.

"I don't know. But Alexander did. He found a map that

led him to it. The name he gave this map was *mati*." A literal translation of the word *mati* is—eye."

Lara picked up the fax Stevens had shown her of the Orb.

"The Orb is the map, hidden in the Luna Temple by Alexander. Reiss wants it to find Pandora's box. When he does, when he opens the box, he'll unleash a weapon more terrible than any you can imagine."

"Good Lord," Calloway said.

Hillary exhaled. "I'll go fetch that tea now."

Lara looked at the pale white faces of the two MI6 agents in front of her, and managed a smile.

"I should think something stronger than tea," she said.

Calloway looked up at her and nodded weakly. "Yes. Much stronger, if you've got it."

Hillary cleared his throat and Lara knew he was about to launch into a detailed description of the contents of their liquor cabinet.

She clapped Bryce on the shoulder. He looked up at her quizzically.

"You. Come."

SIX

A half hour later, she and Bryce had downloaded and cataloged all the still images from her digicam onto his laptop. They were in the library, him sitting at Lara's desk, her leaning over his shoulder, watching as he arranged the shots she'd managed to take of the Orb into a rough semblance of order.

Lara heard the door open, heard the rattle of silver on a tray, and spoke without looking up.

"How are our friends from intelligence?"

"Gone outside to make more phone calls." Hillary stepped over to the desk, set the tray down next to the laptop. Tea and scones. "Thought you two might like some sustenance."

"Ah." Bryce looked up and sniffed the air. "Cinnamon walnut, yes?"

He reached for one of the scones.

"No," Lara barked. "Focus."

He grumbled and bent over the laptop again. Hillary came around behind the desk, stood next to Lara.

"What do you have so far?" he asked.

Bryce pointed at the screen. "The markings are definitely a pattern, but even if I figure out what they represent, we won't be able to read the full map because we don't have a full view of it . . . see?"

Hillary nodded. Lara shook her head impatiently.

"Full view or not—get to work on how to read it." She straightened, turned to Hillary. "I have to start packing."

A noise at the door made her turn.

Calloway and Stevens were back.

Before Lara could open her mouth to speak, Calloway stepped forward.

"On behalf of Her Majesty, we formally request you find and recover this box before Doctor Reiss."

"Oh. Well." Lara smiled. That was just what she was planning to do. Find Reiss and the Orb. A worthwhile mission in and of itself, with an added bonus: where the good doctor and the Orb were, there she would find the men who'd killed the Petrakis, as well.

"Now that I have Her Majesty's permission," she said, "tell me where to find the Orb."

"Last we heard, it was still with Chen Lo and the Shay Ling. Somewhere in China," Stevens said.

Lara cursed under her breath. She'd thought the Orb would have made its way to Reiss by now. Taking the Shay Ling on in China, that would be tantamount to a suicide mission, the only reason she'd even contemplated it before was because of the relationship she'd been in at the time, and it was only because of that person she'd been in the relationship with that she'd even been able to locate them; they moved from hideout to hideout, they had local help in every province, there was no way she could do it again, not without . . .

She cursed again, out loud this time.

"Lara?" Hillary asked. "Is something wrong?"

"I'm thinking," she said, and she was, but she didn't like the direction her thoughts were going in.

Stevens cleared his throat and spoke.

"I suspect you're aware of the difficulties involved in locating the Shay Ling. You're right to be concerned—I'm afraid finding them will be next to impossible. But we'll assign you two of our best agents to help—"

"I don't want them," Lara said softly, her hands resting on the back of Bryce's chair.

Calloway and Stevens exchanged a glance.

"With all due respect," Calloway began, "expertise in archaeology doesn't qualify you—"

"I didn't say I don't need help," Lara said, cutting him off. "But your agents will never get me to Chen Lo in time. I need an insider. Someone who knows the Shay Ling. Their methods, hideouts . . ." She sighed. There really was only one person who could help with this, could help her avenge Gus and Nicholas and Jimmy, and just realizing that cost her, but she didn't see any way around using him, the conclusion was inescapable, it had to be him, and only him.

"I need Terry Sheridan," she said.

Bryce, in the middle of sneaking a mouthful of scone, spit up crumbs all over his laptop.

Hillary, standing next to her, used a four-letter word she didn't even know he could pronounce.

Calloway's expression hardened into stone.

"Not if he were the last man on Earth," the MI6 man said.

Stevens looked puzzled.

"Someone fill me in on who Terry Sheridan is, please," he said.

While Lara was debating how she wanted to answer that, Calloway spoke.

"Terry Sheridan. Formerly a commander in the Royal Marines. Quite possibly the finest, most lethal soldier ever to serve this country. Who one day, for reasons known only to him, disappeared. He resurfaced as a traitor—a mercenary selling his skills to the highest bidder." He glared at Lara. "You don't expect me to put him on the trail of a weapon he'll turn around and auction?"

"I'm not any happier about the idea than you," Lara shot back, "but Terry is the only man I know who can get me to Chen Lo in time."

Calloway shook his head. "Lady Croft, some men are capable of betraying their friends, but Terry Sheridan is the only one I know who enjoys it."

"Then it's lucky for us Terry's friends include Chen Lo and the Shay Ling, isn't it?"

Calloway had no response for that.

Hillary did.

"Ah," he said. "May I point out that at one time, Terry's friends also included—"

Lara spun and silenced him with a glare. Then she pointed upstairs, in the direction of her bedroom.

"You'll recall what I said earlier? About packing?"

Hillary sighed heavily, and left the room.

Lara turned back to the MI6 agents.

"You'll get me to him?" she asked Calloway. "Or do you need to make more phone calls?"

"No more phone calls," Calloway said, his expression grim. "We'll get you to him. But we want access to everything your man here finds," he said, pointing to Bryce, "so that we have a backup in case Sheridan betrays you again."

"When," Bryce mumbled. "When he betrays you again."

Lara thwacked him on top of the head.

"Focus," she told Bryce.

"Agreed," she told Calloway.

"I know what I'm doing," she told Hillary a few minutes afterward, upstairs in her bedroom, as she changed for her journey.

On the landing pad an hour later, walking toward the helicopter MI6 had sent for her, Lara said her good-byes, trying to make them short and sweet.

Bryce and Hillary were having none of it.

"I know you may well hit me again," Bryce said, handing her the digicam as he escorted her toward the waiting copter, "but a leopard doesn't change his spots, Lara."

"I know," she said, not breaking stride for an instant.

"You know," Hillary said, coming up alongside her on the left, opposite from Bryce, "you know, and yet the first chance you get, you run and save him."

Lara stopped suddenly, and both men stopped with her.

"I'll handle him," she said firmly. "Now good-bye."

She ducked low, under the whirling blades, and ran for the open chopper door.

Hillary's shouted response followed her.

"Even if it means killing him?"

Lara slammed the door shut without answering, without looking back. The copter rose immediately into an overcast sky, until the landing pad, Croft Manor itself, Bryce, and Hillary all disappeared from sight.

And yet the questions continued to echo in her mind.

What would she do when she saw Terry Sheridan?

Lara wasn't quite sure she knew the answer to that.

She drifted in and out of sleep, dreaming—daydreaming—about North Korea. And Terry Sheridan.

Five years ago. She had airlifted into Chasong, right along the Chinese border, to try and preserve what she could of an archaeological site dating back to the Silla dynasty, before alliance bombs started falling.

SAS had arranged for her rendezvous with the advance squad of marines on the ground already, working to pinpoint targets. Commander in charge, one Terence Patrick Sheridan.

"You must be Lady Croft," he'd said, stepping out of the bush right as she was climbing out of her chute.

"No lady necessary. And you're Sheridan." They shook hands. Sheridan was lean and muscled——the veins on his arms stood out like ridges against this skin. The backs of his hands were calloused, and bruised—Lara had seen similar marks on other SAS soldiers, those on "special force" assignments the nature of which they could never talk about.

Sheridan had no doubt been on many such missions himself. According to her briefing, he'd gone through SAS training and come out with the highest markings ever given in unarmed combat.

He had a knife strapped to each forearm, and guns—decidedly nonregulation guns—hanging off his equipment belt. He looked dangerous. Lara had been impressed. Even a little intrigued.

Sheridan also had a very big scowl on his face.

"This isn't going to be tea and crumpets, Croft. You sure you're up for it?"

Lara had sighed heavily.

Might as well get this part over with, she thought, and dropped her pack to the ground. She assumed a fighting stance.

"Shall I knock you on your ass now—or later?"

Sheridan had smiled. He looked her over.

"Nice stance. But you've left yourself open here—" and as he'd spoken, he swung a leg and knocked her feet out from under her.

She rolled as she fell, landed both hands on the ground, and kicked back with her feet, catching him square in the mouth.

"Nice move," she'd said, getting to her feet. "But you left your mouth open there."

Sheridan rubbed his lip, and his hand came away bloody.

His smile got broader.

"All right, Croft," he'd said, getting to his feet. "Let's see what else you've got."

A week later, they were living together in her tent.

Four months after that, Terry had deserted his unit—and sold the most valuable pieces she'd found from her dig to the Shay Ling.

"We're here."

Lara opened her eyes to see the copter was landing. It was twilight, and much, much colder. Men in uniform hustled her into a waiting half-track. The driver smiled at her as she climbed up into the cab alongside him.

Once they were underway, he turned to her and offered a gap-toothed smile.

"You're a beautiful woman," he said in halting English. "I have much whiskey."

Lara glared at him until he turned away, red-faced.

Nobody else spoke to her the entire trip.

Night fell as they drove deeper and deeper into rugged foothills, covered with snow, devoid of life. More snow was falling now, big flakes that danced in the headlights before fluttering down to the road and melting away. Then they began to fall harder, stopped melting at all. The road grew slick, the windshield white with accumulated flakes—the wipers couldn't keep up. Every few minutes, the driver had to open his window and clear the windshield by hand. A bitter, arcticlike wind entered the cab every time he did so.

Lara burrowed further into the fur coat she was wearing, and stayed warm.

Sometime after what was probably midnight, Greenwich Standard Time—if her internal clock was accurate—a light appeared in the distance, and grew closer. The truck slowed to a halt.

Lara climbed out.

She was standing on pavement, in the middle of a fenced compound. Soldiers patrolled in formations of three men, AK-47s at the ready. Half-tracks, marked with the red star of imperial Russia, were parked haphazardly around her truck.

Directly before her, in the center of the compound, was an old Soviet-era missile silo—a massive blockhouse of a building, albeit only a single-story tall. Above ground, that is. Below . . .

In the days of the cold war, not so long ago, upward of a half-dozen ICBMs had no doubt been hidden in this structure, buried beneath the ground, along with the requisite crew needed to send those missiles flying toward the United States of America should Moscow give the signal. The missiles were long gone, but the cavernous space they'd occupied still existed, in a slightly reconfigured format.

The silo was now a prison—Barla Kala, the locals called it. It housed the most feared, most wanted men and women on the planet. Abu Sayaaf, Hezbollah, Al Qaeda—this was the place where the civilized world sent those who would never learn to be civilized. Once they arrived, and were locked behind the massive steel doors in front of her, they were never heard from again. There were no parole boards or rewards for good behavior at Barla Kala, no such thing as easy time or exercise yards or movie night here. Prisoners at Barla Kala went in, and they never came out again.

Terry Sheridan had gone in five years ago, and Lara hadn't heard a word about him since.

A bearded, balding blockhouse of a man detached himself from a group of soldiers nearby and approached her.

"Lady Croft?"

Lara nodded.

"I am your host, Armin Kal." He laughed, and spread his arms in welcome. "Welcome to Fantasy Island."

Lara was in no mood. "Take me to Sheridan, please."

Kal frowned, his smile disappearing as quickly as it had come.

"Perhaps we can discuss this a moment, Lady Croft. To see this man is not a good idea."

"I'll grant you that," she said. "But it's necessary."

"May I ask why?"

"No." Lara put a little extra bite into the word—she'd only known this fat little man for thirty seconds, and already she disliked him intensely. "You may not. Now please—I'm on a schedule."

Kal shrugged. "As you wish. Come this way—I will take you to him."

Twin ramps, built to accommodate the wheels of a missile transport trailer, led up to the prison entrance. Kal turned and headed up one of those ramps, Lara staying a step behind.

As they reached the top, the main doors to the prison opened. Two men emerged, carrying a stretcher. The someone occupying the stretcher was covered by a sheet—one hand dangled from underneath it. The fingers looked wrong—it took Lara a second to figure out why.

They were twisted around, front to back. Broken, each one of them, not once, but several times.

Fantasy Island indeed.

Kal was waiting for her at the steel doors.

"Please—we don't get many visitors here," he said, allowing her to enter first. "Not like you. You're very brave."

Lara felt him leering at her without turning around. She didn't say a word. No way she was going to get drawn into a conversation with this man. She had business to do here, she was going to get it done, and leave—with or without Sheridan.

Kal preceded her down two sets of stairs, then into a long concrete shaft wet with ground water, and finally through a series of locked gates. At the last gate, he paused, reached underneath his coat, and pulled out a set of headphones.

"What are those for?" Lara asked.

"You," Kal said. He gave a thumbs-up sign to a guard standing on the other side of the gate. "Go ahead."

Lara frowned, but before she could ask him what he meant by that, the gate hissed open, and Kal entered the cavernous main cell block. Lara was a step behind.

The space before her was huge—five times the size of the Luna Temple, big enough to hold a football pitch, and that tall again. There were three levels of cells, surrounding a central atrium—she saw guards everywhere, again patrolling in groups of three, and an old missile gantry that was now doing duty as a guard tower.

She took a step forward, and the prisoners caught sight of her.

They erupted.

All at once she understood why Kal had donned headphones, why he'd said they were "for her" as he put them on.

The residents here, Lara realized, probably hadn't seen a woman since they'd been locked away. The things they were shouting at Lara, about her . . . well, nothing she hadn't heard before, though never in so many languages at once. Only one way to deal with that kind of verbal abuse, really.

She shut off for a few minutes, and simply moved her feet forward, one after the other. Staying behind Kal, her eyes focused on the back of his coat, until he stopped walking.

"We're here," he said, pulling off his headphones.

Lara looked up. Four guards stood ramrod straight in front of a single steel door, two on either side, rifles slung across their shoulders.

She stepped past Kal and walked to the door. A set of bars at eye level covered a small window in the door. Lara peered through the opening.

The only light in the cell came from a window directly across from her. She could make out a cot against the wall to her left and the outline of someone sitting on it. The light touched his hands.

The backs were calloused, and bruised—even more so than the last time she'd seen him.

Sheridan rose from the cot.

"I always knew one day you'd rescue me," he said, taking a step out of the darkness.

Lara's first thought was, he can't have been in here five years. He looks exactly the same as he did the day I last saw him.

Terry was unshaven, in a military-issue T-shirt and trousers. He looked strong and healthy. Like he'd spent the last five years at an island resort—not in a prison cell.

"Hello, Terry."

"Croft." He frowned. "You're favoring a leg. What happened?"

For a moment, Lara was taken aback.

She'd forgotten all about the injury—it had happened two weeks ago, in Prague, chasing Eckhardt through one of the catacombs. It had hurt like hell at the time—faded to a dull roar in the days following, and now to a barely noticeable twinge.

No one else—not even Hillary—had even noticed it. For Terry to pick up on it so quickly . . .

Time in prison clearly hadn't dulled his senses.

"Argument," Lara told him. She saw that there was a cut on Terry's hand. "What happened to you there?"

"Argument."

"Ah. I'd hate to see the other bloke."

"Maybe you did. They're offloading him now."

The corpse she'd seen while entering the prison, Lara realized. The fellow with the broken fingers.

Time in prison clearly hadn't dulled Sheridan's skills, either.

Terry smiled. "What do you think of the place?" he asked. "Not quite Croft Manor, is it? A little more like Chasong, wouldn't you say?"

She glared at him.

"Let's cut to the chase, shall we?" Lara asked. She pulled a set of keys out of her pocket.

"Ah." Sheridan smiled. "Key to your heart?"

Lara shook her head. "To a flat in Zurich. You can pick another city if you want. Your record will be expunged, citizenship restored—"

"By?"

"M-I-Six."

He was silent a moment.

"Would that make me Faust, or the devil?"

"No need to be melodramatic—it's business, Terry. You do a service for them, they'll do one for you." Lara shrugged. "You can be Faust, if you want. You can be anyone. Pick—they'll arrange a new identity for you."

"If I was out of here . . ." He shook his head. "You think I'd need their help—to disappear? Become someone else entirely?"

"Having two faces doesn't count," Lara snapped.

"Temper, Croft."

"Just making a point. Are you interested?"

"What do I have to do?"

"Is there anything you wouldn't?"

He laughed. "You like that about me."

"Answer the question."

"Sorry." Sheridan smiled. "Just making a point."

"Noted. So again—are you interested?"

"And again—what do I have to do?"

She met his eyes. "You have to take me to the Shay Ling."

Sheridan suddenly found something interesting to look at on the cell floor.

"The Shay who?"

"Ignorance doesn't become you." Lara pressed closer to the bars. "A man named Chen Lo took something from me— I want it back."

"You—or M-I-Six?"

"We're in this together."

"Now who's being two-faced?"

Lara bit back the first reply that came to mind, which was she'd get in bed with Satan himself if it meant her getting a shot at the people who'd killed the Petrakis. Damned if she was going to tell Terry Sheridan about them unless she had to. Damned if she was going to expose any of her feelings to him at all.

"As I said," she told him, "it's business."

Sheridan moved closer to the bars as well, till his face was scant inches from hers. "The Shay Ling are hard to find, but then you know that—or you wouldn't be here."

"The government will wire you five million pounds when we succeed. Call it second chance money."

"I don't need any second chances," Sheridan said.

"Happy where you are?"

"Don't press me, Croft." He smirked. "Maybe we should call it life insurance for you."

"Ha." She met his eyes. "I don't need any life insurance."

Terry shook his head.

"You and I, Croft—working together. I can't see it, some-how."

"Easier to see through you that way."

Terry paced back toward the window, disappearing from her view. "What happens afterward, Lara—when M-I-Six decides that having me back in the world is not such a good idea?"

"Then I'll feel sorry for whomever they send to get you."

"Who they send is not the point." He stepped forward again, stared straight at her. "It's you I'll hold responsible."

"Naturally."

"Doesn't that frighten you at all?"

"Do I look scared?"

"No." Sheridan smiled. "You have authorization to kill me."

"Anytime, any reason."

"That must have pleased you."

"You have no idea."

"What is it they say, 'Hell hath no fury . . .'?"

"Oh, please." Lara shook her head, and laughed. "You weren't that good." Her voice hardened again. "Are we going to do this or not, Terry? Make up your mind—the clock is ticking."

"Don't rush me."

"Fine. On to candidate number two." Of course, there was no candidate number two, there was only MI6 itself, and Lara didn't like the idea of working that closely with them, but if Sheridan was going to pass . . .

She'd do what she had to.

Lara spun on her heel, and walked back to Arman Kal, who was standing a discreet distance away from Sheridan's cell. "Let's get out of here," she told the man.

Terry called out from behind her.

"The Shay Ling are ghosts, Croft! They move constantly, their home base is the most remote region of mountains in

China. Maybe on Earth. I'm the only one who can get to them without being killed."

Lara stopped.

"Is that a 'I'm interested in your deal, Lara', and 'All right, I'll take you to the Shay Ling, Lara?' If so, you'll have to be a little more exact than 'region.' "

"Get me into China—I'll get you to them in a day."

"That's about what we have." Lara turned to Kal. "Unlock the cell."

He shook his head. "This is a very bad idea."

"It's my call, and I want him out."

Kal sighed, and shrugged his shoulders.

"As you wish."

He waved the guards forward. There were four locks on the door—each of the guards took out a key and unlocked one.

Terry Sheridan stepped out into the hall. Cracked his knuckles, smiled at Lara, at Kal, and then turned to the guards.

"Boo!" he said suddenly.

All four flinched as one, and took a step backward. One tripped over his own feet, and stumbled to the ground with a clatter.

"Priceless," Terry said.

"Stop showing off," Lara told him. "Come."

The two of them, walking side by side, followed Kal down the corridor.

"Five million pounds, Croft," Terry said. "I'll be able to hobknob with the same crowd as you."

"When the job is done," Lara said. "Until then—no money, no guns, no weapons of any kind."

"Talk about taking the fun out of life."

"You don't have time for fun, Terry. Your only concern is

Chen Lo. Run, you'll be hunted. Give me trouble, you'll be back here. Are we clear?"

He nodded. "We're clear."

Kal slipped on his headphones again, and Lara saw they were about to reenter the main cell block.

"Brace yourself," she told Terry. "They're quite loud."

The noise started up again—and just as quickly died down.

Lara was puzzled. Then she realized everyone was looking past her, at Terry. Assuming that she was with him, so she was under his protection, so she was no longer a target for their abuse.

She didn't like how that made her feel.

"Keep moving," she told Terry.

"Sure, Croft." He smiled thinly, then, as if he knew exactly what she was thinking, "You're in charge."

She'd forgotten what a cold bastard he could be.

They climbed in the half-track. Lara and Terry sat opposite each other on the bench seats in the back. A guard sat on either side of each of them. Add in the driver, that was six of them to handle Sheridan. All of them armed, while he was weaponless.

Good odds, she thought.

And then a memory came to her—

Working on one of the dolmen—the burial mounds—in Chasong. She had been surprised by a squadron of NVA soldiers. They'd marched her to a base camp twenty miles away, near Chosan. Bound her hand and foot, left her with two guards in a tent and four outside.

Terry had killed all six without making a sound. Without using a gun, or even a knife.

She looked up, and saw him casting surreptitious glances around the interior of the half-track. Lara followed his eyes, saw his gaze stop on the guard sitting to his right. She saw it the same time Terry did—

The guard had left the flap on his holster unbuttoned.

"Tempted?" she asked.

Terry turned and smiled at her.

"Not by him."

Another memory came to her, and she chased it away.

She didn't have time for this now.

"This isn't some second-chance honeymoon, Terry. This is business, understood?"

"All work, and no play—is that it, Croft?"

She nodded. "That's it."

"Well then." Terry settled back in his seat. "Let's talk about work. What do I need to know?"

"That we have the better part of a day to find Chen Lo. And get back what he stole."

"Well. We'd better get cracking then." He leaned forward. "The Shay Ling will be in Luoyang. But they have spies all over China, so we have to get into the country undetected. If we slip into Beijing, we can go by truck—"

"Truck?" Lara shook her head. "How about something a tad faster?"

"I'm game," Terry said. "What do you have in mind?"

She told him.

As Armin Kal watched the half-track pull away. Karenkov, his second-in-command, came up alongside him.

"Good riddance, yes sir? That Sheridan."

Kal shook his head. "I can't believe we're rid of him so easy. He'll be back, I suspect."

"I hope not, sir."

"As do I, Vasily. As do I." Kal shook his head. "That woman has balls to go off with him."

"She has balls to come in here at all, sir."

Kal nodded. "Mmm. Well. Sheridan's cell being empty, we now have a space to fill, don't we?"

"Yes sir. I was thinking Mr. Donovan."

"Yes. Mr. Donovan. Good." Kal patted Karenkov on the shoulder. "Take care of it, will you?"

Karenkov turned and headed back toward the prison.

When he was out of earshot, Kal took out a satellite phone he'd been given several months back as a way of maintaining exclusive contact with a certain party interested in "undesirables." It seems this certain party had a usage for experimental subjects no one would miss—should said experiments ever go wrong.

This certain party also had an interest in the Shay Ling, who were known to frequent this Godforsaken part of the world from time to time, and had phoned Kal just a few hours earlier asking him to be on the lookout for—in particular—the group's leader.

Surely this certain party would be curious to know of someone else's interest in the Shay Ling, as well.

Kal dialed the number he'd been given. The phone rang—once, twice, three times.

On the fourth ring, a woman answered.

"Yes?"

"I need to speak to Doctor Reiss, please," Kal said.

"Doctor Reiss is not available," the woman said.

"Then please give him a message for me." Kal looked off into the distance, where the half-track's taillights were just now vanishing into the storm. "This is Armin Kal. You can tell him that someone else is looking for Chen Lo. A woman named Croft—Lara Croft."

SEVEN

"A tad faster." Terry shook his head, as the scenery outside the cockpit whipped by. "You always were the master of understatement, Croft."

Lara was about to reply when the pod hit a wind shear, and they were smacked sideways. Her head slammed into the canopy glass next to her.

Even wearing a helmet, her ears rang with the impact.

"Christ, here we go again," Terry said, grabbing hold of the single lever in front of him. "Trying to control this thing is like trying to fly a rock."

The only controls in their pod were directional, passive—they had no infrared signature for the Chinese to lock missiles onto, no e-m signature to trace or identify. They might as well have been a meteor, hurtling through the atmosphere—which was the idea, after all.

They didn't want anyone—not the Chinese, or the Shay Ling—to see them coming.

They were in north China now—Barla Kala lay half a day and two thousand miles behind them, the NATO base in Turkey an hour in the past. They'd launched from there at o-four-hundred after catching a few hours of sleep in the belly of a cargo transport. They'd flown in through Russian, then Mongolian airspace, the glider strapped to the belly of a Blackbird SR-71 stealth fighter, Terry and Lara crammed into the small craft like sardines.

"There it is," Lara said, raising a hand and pointing directly ahead of her. "Our landing pad."

Directly in front of them was a tranquil lake, surrounded by mountains on three sides. They were coming in from the open end of the formation.

"Hope it's deep enough," Sheridan said, frowning. "We're going to hit pretty fast."

Pretty fast was an understatement—they were rocketing in like a missile, no surprise really, considering they'd cut loose from the SR-71 while that craft was moving at Mach five.

"Going to change the angle of impact just a little," Terry said, grabbing hold of the lever again. "So we don't slam into the surface and snap in two."

Lara nodded, and then suddenly they were out over the lake, hundreds of feet of open water going by in a heartbeat, impact seconds away, and then they slammed into the water—

And shot back up into the air again, like a skipping stone.

There was a little rowboat directly in their path. The image barely had to register—an old man standing up in the boat, staring right through the windscreen into her eyes—when they shot past him (Lara hoped he'd ducked in time), and headed straight for—

A rock wall on the opposite side of the lake.

All the maneuvering in the world couldn't stop them from slamming into it.

Lara reached down, and yanked the only controls she had access to—

The eject levers.

With a loud whump, the canopy flipped open, and flew backward. Lara and Terry's seats shot high up into the air, the force of the wind snapping her head back against the top of the seat as—

The canopy snapped off the glider, smacked into the lake—

The glider smashed into the cliff, shattering on impact—

And with a puff barely audible over the roar of the air rushing past them, their chutes shot open, and Lara and Terry fell to earth.

They landed in a field near the lake. Stashed the chutes, changed their flight uniforms for less conspicuous clothes.

"So you going to tell me a little more about this job now?" Terry asked. "Like what it is Chen Lo stole from you?"

"Not important." Lara paused a moment, got her bearings, then started off down a dirt path at the side of the field.

Terry caught up to her. "Bloody hell, Croft. Don't take me for thick. Look at what M-I-Six has gone to just to get us this far. A Blackbird, Croft, you know how much that little flight back there cost?"

She smiled. "Not as much as the glider."

"Ha. What I'm really wondering, though, is why send a tomb raider? What is it we're after—a scepter? An obelisk?"

"At the risk of sounding like the proverbial broken record—worry about the Shay Ling, Terry. Ah. There we are." Lara smiled, and pointed straight ahead.

"'There we are' what?" Terry frowned. "That?"

"That" was a farm, a hundred yards down the road. There was a small wooden house with a thatched roof, and a one-story wooden barn. Chickens and goats, horses, and a single, massive cow wandered aimlessly about the yard.

"That," Lara said.

"Welcome to the nineteenth century," he said as they drew close. "Ah, Croft. The ditching was good—well done. But expecting to locate a vehicle in a place like this? You planned badly."

Lara pointed to a pair of old horses nibbling next to a stack of hay.

"How about them? Will they do?"

"Hardly."

"Well, how far do we have to go?"

"Farther than that—hey, hang on a minute." Terry had caught sight of a truck on the far side of the barn. He strode toward it confidently . . .

And stopped.

No wheels.

But now he started forward again, heading for what looked to be a motorcycle, hidden beneath a plain canvas cloth. He whipped the cloth off—

To reveal a bicycle—a rusty two-wheeler, no gears, a flat front tire.

He shrugged.

"Ah—the proverbial bicycle built for two, Croft? What do you say?"

"Hardly."

"Thought you had a thing for wearing tight little shorts."

She pushed past him, headed for the side door of the barn, and pushed on through, Terry a step behind.

"I expected better, Croft. I expected much, much better. Now let me say I do have a contact in Beijing who might be able to get here with a car in a few hours—I stress the might, and we'd have to pay her handsomely for . . ."

He came up beside her and stopped short.

"You were saying?" Lara asked.

Terry shook his head. "Never mind."

The two of them were looking at a small arsenal of equipment. Motorcycles, guns, gadgets, clothing . . .

A woman—middle-aged, dressed in traditional Chinese peasant garb—stepped out from behind a large equipment locker. She looked incongruous among the gleaming steel gear.

Lara felt Terry tense beside her.

"It's all right," she said to him. "This is our contact—Shumei."

Contact was perhaps an understatement, considering how long Lara had known the woman before. Shumei had been the first person Lara had met, on her very first expedition into China, looking for the dagger of Xian. Over the last decade, their paths had crossed half a dozen times during Lara's trips into Asia.

"Lara. I saw you come in over the lake." She shook her head. "I expected better. You know how much that glider cost?"

"I know." Lara turned to Terry. "He was driving."

Sheridan frowned. The two women laughed and hugged.

"Everything ready?" Lara asked.

"Of course. Your clothes and guns are there—" Shumei pointed to one corner of the barn. "Knives back there." She pointed to a table nearby. "And I took the liberty of tuning your bike."

"You're a saint." Lara caught sight of a stack of communications gear on a table. "May I . . ."

"Go on." Shumei turned to Terry. "So. This is him."

"That's him," Lara agreed, picking up one of the satellite phones.

"Imagine that. I'm world famous," Terry said.

Shumei shook her head. "Infamous, I would say. Come on—let's get you some gear."

Lara dialed. Hillary answered.

"Croft Manor."

"It's me," Lara said.

"Ah. What is the happy couple up to?"

Lara ignored the jibe. "Accessorizing. Where are we on reading the Orb?"

"Bryce is doing a lot of frowning. Here—I'll put you on speakerphone."

There was a click, and then Bryce's voice was in her ear.

"No key."

"I beg your pardon?"

"Maps have a key, Lara. A legend, a scale—yes? The Orb's key is not on the Orb. It must have been lost—"

"Or was somewhere in the temple," she responded. "Go through every image I took. Start with things near the Orb. The key would have been linked to it in some way."

"Right."

"Right. Tell Hillary I'll call back later." Lara hung up the phone, just in time to catch the tail end of the conversation between Shumei and Terry.

"It's not like Lara to take a partner," she was saying.

"Oh, we've worked together before."

"So I understand. So where are you two going?" she asked, helping Terry on with a jacket.

"Maybe a nice walk, fresh mountain air." He shrugged. "Stop by and see my friends."

"You have friends here?"

"The Shay Ling."

"The Shay Ling?" Shumei looked past Terry to Lara, and shook her head. "You need more weapons." She walked over to a table piled high with ordnance, and began sorting out clips for Lara's .45s.

Five minutes later, the pack was full, and digging into the small of Lara's back. She and Terry were perched on motorcycles, the farm and Shumei to their rear, the dirt road and the mountains in the distance before them. A sliver of orange and red off in the distance caught her eye.

It ran up one side of the nearest mountain and down the other.

She squinted, and saw that, in fact, the sliver continued as far off into the distance as she could see.

"The Shay Ling watch all the roads," Terry said. "We'll have to go around the back—"

Lara was still looking at the sliver. "We'll go straight."

Terry looked at her like she'd grown two heads. "Ah— maybe you didn't hear me, Croft. They'll have men on every road from here to Luoyang."

Lara smiled and shook her head.

"What?"

"Not every road," she said.

If only Alexander had kept going, Lara thought. If he hadn't stopped at the Hesperus, who knows what might have happened. Perhaps the Bay of Bengal wouldn't have seemed like the end of the world to him. He might have reached Cambodia. And from there, China. And maybe, just, maybe . . .

He might have made it far enough to see this.

She brought her bike to a stop, and looked ahead and behind her, down the length and breadth of the Great Wall. Almost twenty-five-hundred kilometers long, supposedly the only manmade object on earth visible from the moon. Finished sometime in the third century B.C., if she was remembering right, although sections of it certainly would have been complete in Alexander's time. Probably this section, in fact—running as it did right along the old China–Mongolia border, it would have been one of the first to be built.

They'd been traveling on this part of the wall for about two hours, heading west. So far they'd only come across a single group of elderly tourists, standing outside a tour bus parked near the base of the wall. The look on their faces when Lara and Terry had driven by high above, on their motorcycles—

Priceless.

"Hey!"

She looked down. Terry, traveling for the last few miles on the road running alongside the wall, had stopped, as well.

"We need to think about heading south!" he called up.

She nodded and gave him a thumbs-up. Terry was right, they needed to turn for Luoyang soon. Which meant coming down from the wall.

Five minutes farther on, she found a long, sloping stairway that led to the ground. A minute later she was back on terra firma and searching the road ahead of her for Terry.

Ah. There he was—looking up at the wall, hoping to catch sight of her.

Suddenly, she felt like a bit of fun. Terry was always fun to play with, she remembered. Mainly because unlike ninety-nine point nine percent of the population, he could keep up with her.

Lara smiled, and gunned the motor. Came up behind him on a curve, shortcut through the brush, and—

Shot past him, close enough that he struggled to maintain control of the bike.

"Bit rusty, are we?" she called back.

Terry's only answer was a smile.

A second later, he'd blown by her, gotten twenty feet ahead.

At which point, he started slaloming across the road, weaving from left to right in front of her to block her way.

"I think it's coming back!" he shouted.

Lara shot straight down the center line.

"I expected better from a Scot!" she yelled as she flew past.

"I don't expect anything from an Englishwoman!" he replied—and just as she was almost past him, he accelerated, and their wheels locked.

Lara needed every bit of her strength to keep the bike from flying out from underneath her. She wrestled the bike upright, slammed on the brakes, and came to a dead halt.

Terry was right next to her when she stopped.

"Another thing that's coming back to me," he said. "What it feels like to get tangled up with you—Lady Croft."

"Don't, Terry. That's over and done with."

"Is it?" He smiled. "You sure you don't want to knock me on my ass? Now—or later?"

Lara glared.

Then she gunned her motor, and shot off down the road.

Three hours on, the sun just reaching its high point in the sky, Terry pulled off the road and stopped his bike.

"From here it's by foot."

Lara looked around. There was nothing in sight, just scrub and a few isolated trees. And off in the distance, mountains.

Terry saw where she was looking.

"Yeah," he said. "Those hills—that's our destination. A good few hours of walking."

"Let's get started then." Lara dragged her bike over behind a bush, hiding it from any passersby. She checked her Colts, then slipped on her pack.

When she turned around, Terry was standing right in front of her.

"Best to reconsider that no gun rule," he said. "Anything that happens is going to happen very fast."

Lara shook her head.

"No."

"Come on, Croft. Do you really think I'm going to turn on you?"

"It has happened before," she said.

"That was then."

"And this is now?" She shook her head. "One thing about archaeology, Terry—it forces you to learn from the past. Which I have done."

"Fine. Have it your way then." He threw up his arms in defeat and started walking.

Lara was soon on automatic—one foot in front of the other, hand up to push aside the occasional brush, eyes focused on the mountains ahead, Terry walking right at her side.

She turned around at one point and saw that the road they'd been on had vanished from sight. As had all signs of civilization. No sounds around them either, save the occasional birdsong. She and Terry could have been the last man and woman left on earth.

As isolated as they'd been in Chasong.

She looked up just in time to avoid walking into Terry.

"Keep moving," she said.

"Sure. But tell me something Croft—where do I fit in?"

"You're my guide. Keep moving."

"That's not what I meant." He sounded serious. "When you think back on the vast scheme of your life—where do I fit in? Was I a bump in the road? The love of your life? Was I time well spent? Four months, Lara—was it more good than bad?"

"I know what you meant, Terry. I'm just not going to answer that question."

She pointed ahead. The mountains loomed over them like silent, disapproving guardians.

They moved on.

EIGHT

What a fascinating woman, Reiss thought, setting down the dossier on his desk.

Lara Croft. Lady Croft, sole surviving member of one of England's most revered and influential families. A prize-winning photographer, an avid outdoorswoman, and—most important from Reiss's perspective—one of the most controversial figures in archaeology today. A "tomb raider," the papers called her.

Reiss wondered why he had never heard of her before. Especially given her connections with MI6, which his sources had been able to outline in some detail. Croft had done a considerable amount of work for Her Majesty's government—though only, he noted, when her interests and theirs meshed. Unfortunately, none of that work had involved cooperating with the MI6 agents Reiss had in his pocket, which made it harder to assess the potential threat she did represent.

Nonetheless, Reiss decided, her abilities were formidable. He would treat her with a considerable degree of respect—especially now that she'd added the Sheridan fellow to her team.

He wondered if he could persuade the two of them to change sides—to come work for him. They were exemplary specimens, both prime examples of what the human species was capable of achieving. Sheridan was a lethal weapon, and Croft—

Well. In addition to being very well trained herself, she was a superbly attractive woman.

Reiss flipped through a few more pictures.

Yes, he decided finally. If circumstances developed to the point where he could reach out to either of them, he would endeavor to do so. In the meantime . . . he had work to do.

The doctor sat down and logged on to his computer. Ah. Here was a message from Madame Gillespie—the last of the five he'd offered Pandora to respond. She, like the others, had agreed to his terms, had promised the doctor would see the money deposited in his account before the close of business.

He was in the middle of composing a reply to her when the soft shushing of the entrance doors caused him to look up.

Sean, Reiss's chief of operations, walked into the lab, followed by one of his operatives, and a stranger. This third man carried a crate.

"From Chen Lo," Sean announced.

Reiss took a closer look at the man, and the crate he carried, and frowned. Wrong size, wrong shape.

Chen Lo had gotten greedy—broken their deal. The ingratitude. The duplicity. The cheek. The doctor had paid him millions, in American dollars.

"That's not the Orb," Reiss said, rising.

Two frowns—one from the messenger, the other from Sean.

"What?" Sean asked.

Reiss waved dismissively at the crate.

"The Orb. It's not in there."

The doctor rose and walked to a plain white filing cabinet at the back of the lab. He punched in the proper combination and a drawer popped open. A moment later Reiss had found the file he was looking for.

He turned around, folder in hand, to see that the crate was now open and the messenger's hands cuffed behind his back.

Sean held out a satellite phone to him.

"You were right. This was all that was inside," he told Reiss.

The doctor took the phone, noting the number displayed on the screen. Chen Lo's, if his memory served. All he had to do was punch send to speak to the man.

Reiss composed himself and turned to the messenger. The unfortunate fellow looked confused—nervous. His eyes darted hurriedly from Reiss to Sean to the crate and then back to Reiss.

"Is there anything you can tell me about this?"

The messenger shook his head.

Reiss nodded to Sean, then hit the send button.

The tones sounded at exactly the same instant as Sean's gun. A second later, the messenger's body crumpled to the floor.

Chen Lo answered on the first ring.

"Doctor."

"I hope you didn't like your messenger," Reiss said.

"I didn't. But I did like the men I lost in the temple."

"You underestimated Lady Croft."

"I underestimated how much this Orb is worth."

Reiss opened the folder in his hand. It was a dossier he'd assembled on Chen Lo over the last several months. It contained not information on the Shay Ling or any of their operations, but rather more personal details. Information about Chen Lo's schooling, his parents, his years at university, his family . . .

Reiss turned to a picture of Chen Lo and his wife—sweet thing, didn't look a day older than twenty-one. She and Chen

Lo had two children already—a boy and a girl, featured in the next photo in the folder. Precious, precocious-looking children. And—as the file made clear—very important to Chen Lo.

Reiss had their medical records in front of him, as well. They'd been to the United States for all their vaccinations— TB, influenza, hepatitis, even smallpox. Drat. That would have been his first choice—he had so many choice strains, and the virus was so easy to transmit. Still . . .

"There are so many horrible diseases," he said to Chen Lo. "Things we are susceptible to as children. You never know when you could find yourself holding little Shiho and Tai's hands as a mysterious ailment begins to ravage their bodies."

Chen Lo cut him off.

"You kill them, and I'll just give your Orb to Lady Croft. My scouts tell me she's a few miles from here as we speak. I wonder how much she'd pay—"

"I'll transfer an additional twelve million dollars to the twelve currently awaiting release," Reiss said curtly, cutting him off. He didn't have time to quibble over money, not with Croft so close. A few miles away? This was not good news at all. He no longer had the luxury of trying to turn her anymore. She was moving *fast*—best to kill her quickly, and proceed with his plans.

"I will release it all once you've delivered to me the Orb. And Lady Croft's body."

"That will be a pleasure," Chen Lo said. "The Orb will come by truck to the flower pagoda in Shanghai. Nine P.M. You'll find Croft's body with it."

Reiss was about to hang up when he realized he'd forgotten something.

"Croft has company," the doctor said. "A former British commando—a Royal Marine, by the name of—"

Chen Lo laughed out loud.

"What?"

"It's Sheridan, isn't it?"

"In fact, yes. Terry Sheridan. You know him?"

Chen Lo's voice hardened. "Terry and I go way back. It'll be a pleasure to see him again."

From the way Chen Lo talked, the pleasure would be one-sided.

"Enjoy yourself," Reiss told him. "I'll expect the Orb in Shanghai tonight."

He hung up, and shook his head. It was a shame about Croft, really. He was sure she would appreciate what he was trying to do, or failing that, would at least have appreciated the opportunity to see Pandora. Too bad.

For her.

The scrub was long behind them. There was no sign of civilization, or life of any kind. No trace of the Shay Ling, either. Lara would have thought they were lost, except that over the last few moments Terry had actually picked up the pace, as if they were close to their destination. But all she could see, stretching out before them like an impassable obstacle, was a sheer, rock mountain face. Were they going to try and find a way up? Go around? Was there a trail somewhere that she hadn't spotted?

She watched Terry's eyes as he surveyed the route ahead. He hadn't spoken in quite some time, had stopped trying to quiz her about their shared past, or what they were hoping to take from Chen Lo and the Shay Ling. He was concentrating on the task at hand—and while part of her welcomed that focus, part of her was worried.

She wouldn't put it past Terry to be leading her into a trap. A place where he could surprise her, get the gun away, and make his escape. Leaving her with egg on her face, leaving Reiss with the map to Pandora, leaving the Petrakis unavenged. Not that he cared about any of that.

As Terry had proven to her several years back, he didn't care about anyone, or anything, except himself.

They came around a bend in the cliff and found themselves in a cul-de-sac, with an old mining tunnel directly ahead of them.

Terry stopped walking.

"Straight through?" she asked, coming up alongside him. "Or go up, and around?"

"Doesn't matter."

"Excuse me?" Lara frowned.

Terry smiled. "Doesn't matter, I said."

Lara stared at him. "You don't have any idea where they are—do you?"

"They're close."

"Which means what?" She was furious. "Tell me you haven't been pretending to know where they are all along, just so I'd get you out—"

"Croft, this isn't some tomb, and the Shay Ling aren't mummies. They're killers. If you don't trust me—"

"I don't. And I don't have any time to waste."

She had to get back to Shumei, she had to get in touch with Calloway, she had to find the Orb, yes, but even more importantly, she had to find Chen Lo.

She drew her gun and pointed it at Terry.

He glared at her. "Normally you hand it to someone butt first."

Lara motioned with the gun. "We're turning back."

Terry didn't move a muscle. Lara was about to speak again when something changed in his eyes.

"Go ahead, pull the trigger. I'd rather you than them."

She froze where she stood.

All around them, the rocks were coming to life.

The Shay Ling weren't ninjas—they were dressed like street punks, Lara thought, as they stepped forward, weapons at the ready—but they were nonetheless experts in the art of camouflage. Three had hidden themselves in the cliff formations near the tunnel, another handful had been right behind them, but somehow Lara had missed them altogether—

Another came up and ripped the gun from her grasp and Lara's eyes widened in surprise.

It was Nicholas's killer.

Lara knew there were guns trained on her all around and yet she couldn't stop herself from charging forward.

Not that it did any good.

She was shoved to the ground, kicked once in the side. She tasted dirt and spit it out. She rolled over onto her back—

And found herself staring straight down the barrel of not one, not two, but three machine pistols.

She looked to her left, and saw Terry facedown on the ground, getting the same treatment. Worse, actually. They were still kicking him.

"So, Terry." Nicholas's killer was standing over Sheridan, shaking his head. "What part of 'never come back here' didn't you understand?"

"Xien. Always a pleasure." One of the Shay Ling had a boot on Terry's neck—somehow he still managed to turn his head toward Lara. "Lara, this is Chen Lo's brother, Xien. Xien, this is Lara Croft. Lady Croft—treat her nice, or Her Majesty's Secret Service will want a word with you."

Xien shook his head. "Good to see prison hasn't cost you your sense of humor, Terry. Where was it, Barla Kala?"

"That's right."

Xien bent down next to Sheridan. "You should have stayed."

He punched Terry in the mouth. Blood dribbled from Sheridan's lower lip.

Xien stood up.

"Search them both—thoroughly."

The Shay Ling swarmed over her.

Lara gritted her teeth, and endured their none-too-gentle probing.

"All right, Croft?" Terry asked at one point.

"Fine."

"Don't get mad at me now. You wanted to find the Shay Ling."

"Find. Not be found."

"The only way we can get into their place is as their prisoners, okay?"

"You might have told me that little gem before."

The searching stopped. Someone wrenched her arms away from her sides, bound her hands in front of her. Her guns were gone. Her pack was gone.

She turned and saw Terry being bound, as well.

"Wonderful planning," she told him.

"Relax," Sheridan told her. "Now all you have to do is make Chen a better offer than his buyer. He'll cross them."

"Even if his buyer is Jonathan Reiss?"

Terry closed his mouth. Gave her a hard look.

"You might have told me that little gem before."

"Shut up, both of you." That was Xien. He nodded to his men, who dragged Lara and Terry to their feet.

"Now," Xien said. "March."

NINE

"Out of the country completely," Chen Lo said. "And don't tell me where."

"But—"

"Move them," Chen Lo ordered. "That is my command. You are to contact me at this number again in two days time. That is the only contact you are to attempt. Do I make myself clear?"

"Yes sir. But your wife—"

"She will understand. Do you?"

There was silence. "Yes sir."

"Good."

And with that, Chen Lo hung up. So. His family was—for the moment, at least—safe. Which gave the Shay Ling's leader time to consider his position.

Sheridan and Croft would be here in a moment. They would undoubtedly offer him considerably more money than Reiss had to turn over the Orb. Money was important, but it was not everything. Chen Lo had already taken one grave risk in the name of money—asking Reiss for more of it—and he was not prepared to take another. Grave risk was an understatement—Chen Lo knew that once Reiss had the Orb, the doctor planned to do exactly as he'd threatened. Kill Chen Lo, and his family, and anyone and everyone unfortunate enough to be associated with the Shay Ling. He estimated his grace period—once Reiss got the Orb, of course—to be a matter of days. Hence, the decision to move his wife and children.

That grace period would disappear entirely, Chen Lo knew, if he were to cross the doctor again.

So no more bargaining. He would kill Sheridan and Croft.

Well—kill the woman, at least. Terry, he would leave to other hands. But the Croft woman—before she died, perhaps she could enlighten him as to the significance of the Orb. Its historical significance, its practical application. Perhaps . . .

An audacious idea occurred to him. What if he cut a deal with MI6? Not for money, but for Reiss. Give up the Orb and the doctor's location, take cash and his safety in return.

Or perhaps . . .

If Croft could be made to tell him what the Orb was, what power it represented, then—perhaps—Chen Lo could utilize that power for himself.

He frowned, considering that path in his mind. Not a road one set out on lightly, for once you began traveling upon it . . . there was really no turning back.

That decision was one he would have to make very, very carefully.

Chen Lo heard footsteps scuffle on the cavern floor, and looked up.

Xien was bringing in Croft and Sheridan through the cliff entrance. The two had their hands bound in front of them, and were being escorted by a dozen Shay Ling warriors. Lu Yao was not among them.

Chen Lo motioned a subordinate to him, and sent the man to go fetch Yao.

Xien left the two prisoners and came forward.

"It is Sheridan," were the first words out of Xien's mouth. "Unbelievable, that he could show his face here again."

"Unbelievable indeed," Chen Lo agreed. "They put up a fight?"

"Didn't give them a chance. Why?"

"Because Terry always has an angle. And if he didn't fight . . ."

"He brought the woman here to negotiate for the Orb," Xien said. "Isn't that obvious?"

Chen Lo nodded thoughtfully. Of course, it was obvious. What was less obvious was the proper course for him to take in this instance. The Orb was clearly of immense value—Sheridan and Croft were willing to risk death for a chance at it, Reiss seemed willing to pay almost any amount of money for it . . .

Chen Lo frowned. He was operating at a distinct disadvantage here. The others knew what it was they were bargaining for, and he didn't.

He needed to find out what the Orb was. He needed to talk to Lady Croft.

But he had promised the doctor delivery of the Orb by nine P.M. Shanghai time, which meant he needed to send it on its way now.

However . . . that decision, Chen Lo realized, could always be rescinded with a simple phone call.

His mind made up, Chen Lo clapped his brother on the shoulder.

"Get the Orb on the road to Shanghai. Reiss has doubled his price. I'm going to find out why."

As Xien left to do as he was told, Chen Lo turned his attention to the prisoners. The two of them—Croft and Sheridan—stood in the main cavern, their backs to him, talking softly to each other. As he approached, he caught the tail end of their conversation.

"Were you really going to shoot me?" Terry was asking.

Before Croft could respond, Chen Lo spoke.

"Oh, I bet she would have." He crossed in front of them, came around to face Croft. "I've seen her work firsthand."

The two of them locked eyes. Chen Lo saw fury in her gaze. For a second, he thought she might actually attack him then and there, despite the presence of the armed guards at her back. The reason for her anger puzzled him for a moment—then he remembered the two boys he and his men had taken out at the cave. Could that be it? It seemed the most likely explanation.

He let his gaze linger on Croft a moment longer, and allowed himself a small smile—which only increased the rage smoldering in her eyes. Good. Anger was something he could use—an emotion he could play on, perhaps, to get the information he desired.

He turned away from Croft then, and clapped Sheridan on the shoulder. The file said he'd been in Barla Kala, but Chen Lo wondered about that. Sheridan looked fit, healthy, and as always, Chen Lo could see the gears in his mind moving at a million miles per hour.

Best to kill him quickly.

"Did Terry tell you," Chen Lo asked Croft, "the last time any of us saw him he was riding away in a truck. It was filled with Ming vases I found near the Longmen grottoes?"

Croft looked at Terry, but Chen Lo's attention was drawn to one of the side passageways, and the man making his way toward them.

Perfect timing.

"And that next to him in the front seat was . . . his sister?"

Lu Yao stepped past the guards and stood facing Sheridan—though facing was perhaps the wrong word, as Lu Yao was more than a head taller than Terry and considerably wider. Chen Lo was pleased to see Croft's eyes widen as she took in the whole of the man.

Lu Yao spoke in Mandarin to Terry.

"I will crush your bones," the giant said.

Sheridan shrugged.

"How is your sister?"

Chen Lo laughed. Sheridan—making jokes in the face of his own death. Some things never changed. But this was not a laughing matter.

"You shouldn't have come here," Chen Lo said.

"It got me out of prison." Terry nodded toward Croft. "Besides, the lady's got a good offer. Better than Reiss."

"Really? Should I take it?"

"Take it." Sheridan nodded again, and then a smile crept slowly across his face. "Or better yet—you and I ransom her and the thing back to the British for triple."

Chen Lo had to laugh again. From the look on Croft's face, she couldn't tell if Sheridan was serious about the offer or not. Neither could Chen Lo, truthfully. Not that it mattered.

"Let's discuss it," he said.

Sheridan started to step forward. Chen Lo shook his head.

"Not you, Terry. Lady Croft and I. You wait here and . . ." Chen Lo looked up at Yao and smiled. "Catch up."

The giant returned his smile.

Terry muttered something under his breath.

One of the guards jabbed a gun into Croft's back and pressed her forward.

It had taken several minutes, but Lara felt under control again at last. Seeing the men who'd killed Nicholas, Jimmy, and Gus, having both of them scant inches away from her . . .

She'd almost snapped, been on the verge of attacking them even though it went against what she'd promised MI6 she'd do, and would have certainly meant death for her and

Terry. Not that she cared about that, all that she'd cared
about for that first few seconds that she'd seen Chen Lo and
had him and Xien within her reach was killing them.

She was better now though.

Her focus was back on the Orb. On obtaining it, and
some idea of Reiss's whereabouts. MI6 had given her a blank
check to do so, authorized her to promise Chen Lo however
much money he wanted, as well as safe passage to any destination in the world for himself and his family. The idea of
Chen Lo sunning himself on a beach somewhere for the rest
of his life stuck in her craw, but Lara had promised she'd
make the offer, and so she would.

Part of her was sincerely hoping he'd turn it down though.

As the guards pushed her forward, she pretended to
stumble. Righting herself, she passed close enough to Terry
to whisper in his ear.

"I'll need three minutes," she said.

She heard a mumbled "terrific" from Terry and then she
was being pushed past him, and toward Chen Lo.

The Shay Ling's leader waved the guards away as she approached.

"Let's walk a bit," he said. "Please."

Not waiting for her answer, he turned his back and
started down one of the half-dozen passageways that
branched off the central cavern. Lara followed, catching up
after a few steps.

The passage was new—as this entire complex seemed to
be. The Shay Ling's headquarters was located at the top of
the sheer cliff Lara and Terry had stood in front of moments
before being captured, at the end of a narrow, winding trail.
And the complex appeared to contain not just their opera-
tional headquarters, but the Shay Ling's massive smuggling
outfit, as well.

As Lara and Terry had begun their march up the mountain, they had seen two Shay Ling carefully loading a life-size terracotta warrior—as impressive an example of Tang dynasty sculpture as Lara had ever seen—into a waiting wooden coffin. Climbing to the top, she'd seen a half-dozen other coffins being lowered down the cliff face by ropes, as well. And then, in the central chamber where they'd first met Chen Lo, she'd seen wooden crates of varying sizes stacked everywhere.

Lara took the whole smuggling thing personally—to her way of thinking, it gave tomb raiding a bad name.

She turned to Chen Lo, about to make a comment along those lines, when light flashed on something hanging from a chain around his neck. A medallion—copper, turned dark with age. It took a moment for Lara to recognize it.

The medallion from the Luna Temple. The one that had been hidden in the eye of the Alexander statue.

A sudden chill ran down her spine.

Her own words to Stevens—talking about the map that led Alexander to the cradle of life—came back to her.

The name he gave this map was mati. *A literal translation of the word* mati *is eye.*"

The Orb was the eye—the map to Pandora.

And intuition told her this medallion—hidden in Alexander's own eye—was the key to reading that map. Lara was certain of it.

Chen Lo saw her staring, and smiled.

"You remember it." He held up the medallion for her to examine more closely. "I took it as a trophy."

Lara forced herself to return Chen Lo's smile.

"I'll have to do the same."

He let go of the medallion and let it fall back around his neck.

"You mean that."

"I do."

"You're not frightened?"

"Of what?"

Chen Lo smiled again. "I'm surprised we haven't met before today, Lady Croft. We have much in common."

Lara bit her tongue to keep from replying.

"Come." Chen Lo slowed as they passed a narrow opening in the passageway, flanked by two Shay Ling. "There's something I think you'll appreciate in here."

He led Lara through the opening. The light dimmed—it took a second for her eyes to adjust. When she did, it was all she could do to keep her mouth from dropping open in wonder.

They were inside a large, low-ceilinged cave. A handful of lights were strung above her. And all around, as far as the eye could see, were terracotta statues—warriors—identical to the one she'd seen being loaded into the coffin below. All of them looked in perfect condition.

"There must be hundreds," Lara whispered.

"Thousands, actually," Chen Lo said. "This is the largest group of terracotta warriors I've found. The king of Qin made them for use in the afterlife. To fend off enemies he made in this one."

"You and I both need a set."

Chen Lo spread his arms wide. "I have many, as you see. I'll be happy to sell some to you."

"I hope," Lara said, choosing her words carefully, "you are as entrepeneurial with the Orb."

"Ah." Chen Lo smiled. "That is the question of the day, isn't it?"

"Most certainly." Lara paused. "Chen Lo—you lost men. I lost men. I see no reason why we should both lose again."

"Nor do I."

"So you're prepared to sell?"

"Perhaps."

"It's a yes-or-no question," Lara said.

"Suppose I want double what Reiss offered me?"

"We'd be prepared to pay that," Lara said quickly. "If the Orb is still here."

Chen Lo studied her a moment. "I believe you're serious." He sounded surprised; Lara wondered why. Surely he knew that MI6 would pay any amount to avoid the kind of casualties Pandora would . . .

Then, all at once, she was struck by a sudden realization.

Chen Lo didn't know what the Orb was. Didn't know why Reiss and MI6 wanted it so badly. Didn't know anything about Pandora.

Which explained a number of things that had been troubling her. Chief among them, why he was taking his time with her.

He wanted to pick her brain, to have her tell him everything she knew about the Orb.

Fat chance, that.

Three minutes, Lara had told Terry. She estimated half that time was gone already.

Lara took a deep breath and started again.

"We're your only chance, Chen Lo," Lara said. "You have no idea how important this Orb is—"

"It is very valuable," Chen Lo agreed.

"Really?" Lara asked, a cutting edge to her voice. "If you knew that, you would also know that Reiss will kill you the moment you give it to him."

"But your government will guarantee my safety?"

Lara nodded. "I will."

"That must hurt. Saying that to me."

She would have punched him out if her arms weren't still tied in front of her. Then Lara realized Chen Lo was trying to bait her, get her angry again, perhaps inspire a careless outburst.

She forced herself to stay calm.

"Take the offer."

He laughed—not a laugh of amusement, but incredulity. "You presume to give me orders?"

"Take the offer. Before it expires."

He shook his head. "No thank you, Lady Croft."

The amusement had disappeared from his voice. His eyes were suddenly cold, as well.

"Then I'll have to force you," Lara said.

"No." Chen Lo shook his head. "Then I'll have to kill you."

"You're welcome to try," Lara said, letting her voice grow cold, as well.

The two locked eyes then, and somewhere deep inside Lara was glad it had worked out this way. The thought of paying Chen Lo money, of keeping him safe . . .

It turned her stomach.

Jimmy, she thought. *Nicholas. Gus.*

"Killing me's not going to be easy," she said. "Not as easy as, say . . . killing innocent people from behind."

"Sure it is," Chen Lo said, and in a blur of motion, he brought his gun up to fire.

But Lara was moving even faster.

She kicked out, sending the gun spinning from his hand. It flew off toward the recesses of the cave and skittered away out of sight.

She kicked again, catching Chen Lo in the side with one foot and then in the head with the other, a roundhouse blow that sent him sprawling to the floor, unconscious.

At least, that's what it should have done.

But Chen Lo merely frowned, looking annoyed.

Then he looked past Lara, off to his left, and smiled.

Lara glanced that way and smiled, too.

Directly behind her, just barely visible in the dim overhead light, was a rack of spears. Intended for the king of Qin's terracotta warriors to use in the afterlife, they nonetheless looked solid enough to use in the here and now, as well.

Lara pivoted and ran, reached the rack first. Hands still bound, she grasped the haft of one spear and began to draw it out—

Chen Lo got there and kicked the entire rack to the floor. Spears flew everywhere—Lara had to let go of the one she had to dodge another flying at her—

She looked up just in time to see Chen Lo successfully do what she'd failed to—grab a spear out of midair.

In one smooth, fluid motion, he charged, jabbing and thrusting the spear at her. Lara backpedaled furiously, evading his attack as best she could. Twice the spear point came uncomfortably close to connecting, and Lara stumbled, almost falling the second time.

Which would be the end for her, she realized. With her hands still bound, she'd have no way to move with any sort of speed or precision once her legs were out from under her. She couldn't let that happen.

She had to get herself loose, and fast.

Of course she also had to stay alive and Chen Lo was making that difficult. He attacked relentlessly, always moving forward, chasing her now around one row of statues and then down another. Lara slammed backward into one of the warriors and grimaced as its outstretched hands dug into her back.

She slid between that warrior and the one next to it.

Chen Lo followed with a grin and a quick glance over her shoulder told Lara why.

She had backed herself into a corner. There was only five feet of floor left between her and the wall, and that space was disappearing fast as Chen Lo closed in, spear jabbing toward her like an angry, spitting cobra. The blade flashed once, twice, in the dim cavern light.

And suddenly, Lara had an idea.

She turned and faced Chen Lo straight on, a smile tugging at the corners of her mouth.

"Death wish, Lady Croft?" he asked, twirling the spear in the air once, twice—like a baton. The man wasn't even breathing hard, she noted with admiration. Which was fine with her.

Neither was she.

"On the contrary." Lara rocked back and forth on the balls of her feet. She could feel the wall behind her, scant inches away now. "Bring it."

Chen Lo obliged.

With one quick, lightning-fast stroke, he closed the distance between them and thrust the spear forward—a death blow aimed straight for her gut.

The man's speed was incredible.

Lara, though, was faster.

Even as he was moving, Lara whirled, turning her back to Chen Lo. She brought one leg over the oncoming spear, straddling it and the blade, which struck the wall behind her with a resounding crack.

Lara tensed her hands, stretching the rope between them, and chopped down on the blade.

The rope snapped with a loud thwack—one final emphatic burst of strength, and Lara's hands were free.

She raised her leg, spinning back the way she came, slam-kicking Chen Lo square in the chest as she did so—a solid shot that she felt in the bones all the way up her leg.

Then, back in her original position, back to the wall, she turned to face Chen Lo.

Only he wasn't there.

Lara had barely a split second to brace herself when Chen Lo's roundhouse kick caught her square in the face. She staggered and almost fell.

"Oh," Chen Lo said, bending to pick up his spear. "This is going to be fun."

Lara didn't necessarily think so.

Momentarily dazed, her ears still ringing, she slipped back behind a row of statues, seeking out the cover of darkness and a chance to recover.

This could be trouble, Terry thought.

He was surrounded by Shay Ling—four of them, arrayed in a circle. Terry didn't know any of them from the old days, but the way they stood . . . well. It would be a fight, that was for certain. It went without saying that Chen Lo trained all his people well. Each would know how to deliver the maximum possible pain with every blow.

And the four didn't even include Lu Yao, who was fifty feet away, talking to Xien. No doubt receiving the go-ahead to make Terry's pain as intense and lingering as possible.

And there, Terry thought, was the problem in a nutshell. Lingering.

Croft had said three minutes, but Terry knew she'd need at least five. Especially if it came to a fight between her and Chen Lo—which he suspected it would. No matter what MI6 had told Croft to do, he couldn't see her cutting deals with the Shay Ling. And there was something else there, too, something personal between her and Chen Lo.

Terry wondered what that something was, but that was all he could do, wonder, because Croft hadn't seen fit to tell him anything at all so far. Not about her dealings with Chen Lo, or this mysterious thing she and MI6 were after—hell, he was totally in the dark. Which—to tell the truth—pissed him off a little bit.

As did Croft's stonewalling him on the walk here, refusing to talk to him not just about the present but the past—their past—as well.

Terry was tired of it. He wanted to know what Croft and MI6 were up to, what Jonathan Reiss had to do with it, and what the cause of the bad blood between Croft and Chen Lo was. Thing was, he needed some kind of leverage, something that would force people to talk to him, divulge some answers.

Watching Xien head back toward the cave entrance, accompanied by a half dozen Shay Ling and a wooden crate roughly the size of a large milk carton, he suspected he might have that leverage.

Terry caught Lu Yao's eye as the big man approached.

"Where's Xien taking that crate?"

Lu Yao ignored him. With a nod and a few quick words in Mandarin, he dismissed two of the men from the circle and took their place.

Then the giant gave another almost imperceptible nod to the two remaining men in the circle, and all three began to move with slow, deceptively languid movements that had Terry instantly on his guard.

He braced himself for their attack.

"Listen to me," he said, turning as he spoke to keep Lu Yao directly in front of him. "While you're out here doing Chen Lo's fighting—he's making a deal worth twice as much as he's told you. Tell me where that crate is going and I'll give you each a full share—"

"Shanghai," Lu Yao said abruptly. "It's going to Shanghai. But don't worry, you'll be joining it. In a crate all your own."

He nodded to his left, where Terry saw two Shay Ling lifting another one of those gray statues into a coffin. Next to them, there was an empty coffin.

"Just your size, Sheridan," Lu Yao said.

"Don't go to the trouble of a formal burial on my account," Terry told him. "I'd prefer to be cremated."

Lu Yao launched a side kick. Terry made no attempt to dodge it.

The big man's boot caught him square in the side, slamming into his ribs with an ungodly force.

Terry dropped to the ground like a sack of potatoes.

Before he could get up, Lu kicked him again. Terry flew backward, rolling five feet on the ground from the force of the blow. He tasted blood in his mouth and climbed onto his hands and knees.

He glanced at the watch the old woman from the farmhouse had given him and felt a sinking feeling in the pit of his stomach. Lara had only been gone a minute or so.

He had to linger here for a little while yet.

Lu Yao drew closer, and Terry braced himself for another attack.

Come on Croft, he urged silently, as the giant loomed over him.

TEN

Head no longer spinning, Lara stalked silently through the vast cavern of terracotta warriors, her eyes darting in all directions, searching for Chen Lo.

She had thought his claim that there were thousands of statues an exaggeration, but now, after a few minutes of traversing through row after row of the unmoving warriors, she decided he'd spoken the truth. Which made this chamber a discovery on the order of the Longmen grottoes—the fabled treasure trove of the Qin emperors Chen Lo had spoken of earlier. She had no doubt there were experts around the world who would give their eye teeth to be where she was right now.

She'd have to appreciate the scenery later though. Right now she was more concerned with staying alive.

Lara paused a moment, sensing something.

Shadows flickered uneasily all about her—she looked up to see one of the strands of lightbulbs above swinging gently from side to side, as if stirred by a breeze.

She doubted very much, though, that the wind had moved them. Which meant only one thing: Chen Lo was close.

Lara pressed back tight against the statue behind her. She needed a weapon of her own—to face Chen Lo unarmed was like suicide. If she could—

The head of the warrior in front of her exploded.

Lara caught a glimpse of Chen Lo's face, grim, unsmiling, determined—and spun away to her left. Metal flashed—and the warrior on her right collapsed, suddenly carved into two.

Wonderful, Lara thought. Chen Lo has a sword.

She spun again and slammed backward into another statue, almost knocking it over. It wobbled, then unexpectedly steadied itself.

Move, a little voice inside her head told her.

Lara dove forward, just as a spear point burst through the stone, impaling the terracotta warrior and the air where she had just stood.

She did a forward roll and sprang up on her feet, ready to confront Chen Lo.

But the cavern was silent and still.

Lara drew a breath and slid forward. She moved behind one statue and then a second, her eyes scanning the cavern. Nothing. No one.

She listened a moment, then took a hesitant step out from the shadows. The warriors facing her held their swords (stone, unfortunately)—at the ready, prepared to attack.

Lara flashed suddenly on a memory from the none-too-distant past—of stone soldiers coming to life and trying to kill her. Their weapons had been rock, as well—but effective enough, if used correctly. She looked up at the statue before her, wondered about trying to remove its sword for her own use.

Angered, the statue lunged at her.

At least, that was her first surprised thought. Lara was so shocked to see the stone warrior move, all she could do was fall backward. She landed hard on the ground and looked up to see the statue falling straight toward her.

She rolled to the side, and its sword missed her by an inch.

A second warrior came crashing down toward her.

She rolled away from that one, too, and scrambled to her feet.

Chen Lo stood in the space left by the two terracotta warriors, sword in hand, smiling at her.

He'd pushed the statues, she realized. No stone-coming-to-life miracles happening here.

He took a step forward and Lara ran.

Blindly, at first, as fast as she could, hearing his footsteps behind her. Sliding between the statues, running at top speed through row after row of indistinguishable terracotta figures—

Then she burst into an open area, and all at once, recognized her surroundings. There was the entranceway to the cavern, ahead to her left. And directly before her—

Spears—from the rack Chen Lo had overturned—lay scattered on the ground.

He was a foot behind as she grabbed one up and—using it like a pole vault—leapt up onto the shoulder, and then the head, of the warrior nearest her. Then, using the terracotta figures as stepping-stones, she began to run again.

Chen Lo cursed as he came after her, chopping furiously, smashing statues out from under her even as she stepped on them. His relentless assault made it impossible for her to consider turning to fight—he would have gutted her had she tried it.

Lara stumbled, and almost fell. She literally felt the whoosh of Chen Lo's sword as he came within millimeters of cutting her off at the ankle.

She put on a renewed burst of speed. So did Chen Lo. He was going to catch her, unless she could think of something. And then . . .

Suspended from the ceiling directly ahead of her, Lara saw a string of lights.

Lara Croft (Angelina Jolie) is convinced that she knows the location of the tomb.

Bryce (Noah Taylor) and Hillary (Chris Barrie), with an assist from the Royal Navy, find Lara.

Terry Sheridan (Gerard Butler)—just released from an ultra-prison deep within the former Soviet Union—is singularly ungrateful.

Sheridan said he could take Lara to the Shay Ling—he just didn't mention how.

Chen Lo only *thinks* he has gotten the best of Lara.

Lara and Sheridan are determined at all cost to stop the truck carrying the Orb.

If recapturing the Orb kills a few of the Petrakis' killers, so be it.

Dr. Jonathan Reiss (Ciarán Hinds) watches with anticipation as his computers work to unlock the message of the Orb and the location of Pandora's box.

While she may enjoy his "company," Lara does not trust Sheridan.

The Orb reveals a map showing the location of the Cradle of Life and ultimately the box.

Kosa (Djimon Hounsou) and Lara secure help, hoping they can get to the box first.

When Lara sees no alternative, she agrees to lead Reiss to the Cradle of Life.

As an unseen force picks off Reiss's men, Lara knows it is the Shadow Guardians.

Lara has only to reach out and Reiss will possess the horrific powers of Pandora's box.

She raised her spear, and as she ran by the lights, swung her weapon like a bat. The bulbs shattered—a shower of tiny glass shards filled the air. She heard Chen Lo slow behind her, and curse.

Lara vaulted down from atop the statues and ran for the darkness.

He was standing in the middle of the Shay Ling fighters—three of them now, Lu Yao and two of the newcomers. Circling him, cocky smiles on their faces. A crowd had gathered to watch—Terry supposed that even if most of them hadn't been around when he was running with Chen Lo and Xien, they'd heard about his betrayal and wanted to see him get his comeuppance. Fine.

He was remembering faces. Making mental notes of who was saying what, and how often. They'd get theirs.

As soon as Croft got back here, that is.

Someone kicked him in the ribs and Terry snapped back to the here and now.

One of the Shay Ling fighters landed an uppercut to Terry's jaw. The other moved in, and dealt a combination kick and punch to his chest. Terry shot backward like he'd been kicked by a mule.

But he didn't fall.

He moved back to the center of the ring and glared at Lu Yao.

"You and I both know I could kill you right now," Terry said.

The giant responded by spinning into a massive roundhouse kick that connected square to Terry's temple.

"Why don't you fight back?" Lu Yao asked.

"I'm waiting," Terry said.

Lu Yao smiled, bobbing.

"Don't wait too long."

Amen to that, Terry thought, bracing himself for another blow.

Lara didn't know where the bamboo ladder led to, but the second she spotted it leaning against the wall at the far end of the cave she ran for it anyway. Anyplace, she decided, had to be better than here.

She ran full out now, no more trying to pad quietly through the cavern. That was Chen Lo's game—hers was to seek another battleground, and a weapon of her own.

She sprinted the last twenty feet between her and the ladder full out, and sprang for it. Grabbed the ladder, started climbing—

A sword appeared from nowhere, slicing the horizontal rungs in half.

The ladder split. Lara grabbed on to one of the poles with both hands. She slid down it like a fireman, reached the ground, and turned.

Chen Lo had two swords now. He flipped one head over heels in the air, caught it. Did the same with the second.

Then, wielding his weapons like machetes, he advanced.

Lara considered the bamboo pole still in her hand. Not unlike the kenzai staves she and Hillary had been training with.

Lara changed her grip on the bamboo, held it with her hands a few feet apart before her, and moved forward to parry Chen Lo's attack.

He sliced down with his sword and split her weapon in two.

Lara dodged by him and shifted her grip. She turned to face him again, holding both halves of bamboo together, in front of her.

Another flash of metal and she had four sticks of bamboo.

So much for training with Hillary, Lara thought.

She tossed the sticks at Chen Lo. As he knocked them to the ground, she spun and did a series of back flips across the cavern floor. She landed in a crouch and picked up the spear she'd seen lying there. Just in time.

Chen Lo was on her again.

Lara had to give ground as he slashed, backing her down a row of terracotta warriors. This spear was no better than the bamboo pole had been—bits of wood flew into the air as Chen Lo pressed his attack, slicing the weapon in her hands into smaller and smaller pieces.

She almost tripped over another spear and picked it up. Chen Lo's pace never faltered—he attacked like a man possessed. Lara tried to put a statue between the two of them and he pulverized it with a single blow from the sword in his right hand.

With the sword in his left, he split the spear in her hands. The force of the blow made her arms shiver.

Lara found herself holding a single stick barely as long as her forearm.

Chen Lo raised both blades again. Smiling, he moved in for the kill.

Lara cocked her arm back and threw what remained of her spear at him.

It flew like a javelin—not entirely straight, the stick had broken too jaggedly to fly true—but close enough. It caught one sleeve of Chen Lo's shirt and pierced it, pinning him to the terracotta warrior directly behind him.

Chen Lo screamed in rage and ripped the shirt free. She must have grazed his skin—blood stained the shirt where it had ripped.

No more measured moves for Chen Lo—he charged

wildly now, both blades swinging. Lara backed away as fast as she could, trying to keep from stumbling over her own feet, thinking that she usually preferred an angry opponent, rage made most people careless, but it only seemed to be making Chen Lo faster.

She bumped into something. A glance sideways showed her a wooden crate—she remembered seeing a stack of them off to the side when she'd first entered the cavern.

Chen Lo swung again and Lara spun to the side. He missed by not inches, but millimeters—the wind from the blade blew a lock of hair free from her cheek, where sweat had plastered it down.

The blade smashed past her and broke through the top of the crate, revealing its contents. Lara saw metal inside, and even before she consciously realized what she was looking at, her hands were darting into the crate and grabbing a rifle and she jumped to the side and aimed the weapon— an old 303, complete with bayonet at the end—right at Chen Lo.

Fear darted across his face.

Lara squeezed the trigger.

Click. She looked at the rifle more closely. No clip. No bullets.

Chen Lo roared and came at her with both swords again—she barely got the rifle up in time to parry his attack. Faster than ever he came, swinging one sword, then the next, and Lara's arms rang with the force of each blow.

But even though the 303 wasn't loaded, it was the best weapon she'd had yet in the fight. Unlike the spears or the ladder pole, the metal withstood Chen Lo's attack without shattering. And now, at long last, Lara had a second to breathe, to study Chen Lo's rhythm as he fought, the pattern of his attack, and she could see that there was no subtlety to his charge, anger had gotten the best of him, and Lara waited and watched, and then—

She saw an opening.

As Chen Lo brought the blade in his right hand down on the rifle, as the one in his left hung at his side for a nano-second before he raised it again, Lara stepped forward and thrust up with the rifle.

The blade in his right hand went flying.

Chen Lo looked surprised. No, not just surprised, shocked—as if such a thing had never happened to him before. Maybe it hadn't.

First time for everything, Lara thought, and thrust the bayonet at the end of the 303 down, toward the ground, and through Chen Lo's foot.

He screamed in agony.

She twisted the rifle hard, snapping off the blade, and then, still holding the barrel of the weapon, thrust up, smashing the headstock into Chen Lo's chin.

He screamed again, the blade in his left hand flew up in the air as he dropped to the ground, writhing in agony.

Lara caught the sword in midair. She tightened her grip on the hilt and held the point to the bare flesh of his neck.

Jimmy, she thought. *Gus. Nicholas.*

Lara pressed the blade forward. Chen Lo gasped involuntarily.

And then she remembered Terry. And MI6, and Reiss, and Pandora, and she lessened the pressure on Chen Lo's throat.

"Where's the Orb? Tell me and it spares your life."

Chen Lo gazed at her in fury. He spat and opened his mouth to curse her.

Lara decided she would be happy to kill him and find the information elsewhere.

Then suddenly, Chen Lo changed his expression. Almost smiled, and she could visibly see him swallow the curse on his lips.

"The flower pagoda. Shanghai. Nine P.M."

Lara looked him in the eye. No way of being certain, of course, but she would bet he was telling her the truth, that she would find the Orb then and there.

And to read it . . .

She ripped the medallion from the Alexander statue away from his neck and placed it around hers.

"Good luck, Croft," Chen Lo sneered. "Reiss will have you for breakfast."

"We'll see." Lara paused a moment, looking down at him. She let a fraction of the contempt and hatred she felt for him show on her face.

Chen Lo flinched.

Gripping the hilt in both hands now, Lara raised the sword over her head and quickly brought it down, point first.

She jammed the blade into the ground between his legs, missing his crotch by an inch.

"Now we're even."

Suddenly she heard a noise from behind her. Voices in the hall. Guards, no doubt coming to see what had happened. Damn.

She pulled the machete up out of the ground again and darted back toward the maze of terracotta warriors, hoping to escape the newcomers, or failing that, cut them off.

As she ran, she heard Chen Lo scrabbling on the ground behind her. Trying to get free. She wondered why he didn't just yell out, let the guards know where she was. Ashamed to have lost to her? That could be it, although—

Light glinted off the statue before her. Coming from behind, Lara realized instantly, and reacting on instinct, spun around.

She took in the scene in a split second—

Chen Lo, still lying on the ground, but now a few feet from where she'd left him, holding the gun she'd kicked out of his hands when they'd first entered the cave.

He raised the weapon to fire—

Lara threw the sword just as he squeezed the trigger.

The bullet went wide. The blade didn't.

Chen Lo gasped once, shuddered, and lay still.

Lara took a deep breath, and it was only then that she saw a trail of blood leading from the bayonet, still sticking up out of the ground, to where he lay.

Chen Lo had torn through his own foot to get to the gun, she realized. He must have hated her almost as much as she hated him.

The key word there being *almost*.

Voices behind her made Lara turn. Guards, bursting into the cavern. Raising their weapons now.

And she was out of swords.

Here we go again, Lara thought, and began to run once more.

It had been the longest three minutes of Terry Sheridan's life and, unfortunately, it showed no signs of ending.

All three of the Shay Ling that had been circling before were now taking turns kicking him. Now, that is, that he was lying on the ground defenseless. One would dash in and kick his stomach, then another his side (which side depended on which direction he rolled in, of course, they always attacked from behind), and finally he'd get a boot to the head.

For a split second there, Terry missed Barla Kala. The thought put a smile on his face.

"You won't be laughing too much longer, Sheridan," Lu Yao said.

One of the others spoke in Mandarin then—Terry didn't catch all of it, but it sounded to his ears like a slur on his manhood, his fighting ability.

Which was almost enough to get him on his feet and putting a fist down the speaker's throat. Then he remembered what he was supposed to be doing in this fight.

Lingering. For three minutes.

Lu Yao kicked him in the stomach. Terry doubled over and rolled to his left. One of the others kicked him in the back. He felt a boot in his face.

Terry rolled over and looked up at Lu Yao. Glared.

The giant spit on him.

"You're nothing, Sheridan," he said.

Terry smiled.

Lu Yao frowned. "What?"

Terry got to his feet and winked. Not at Lu Yao, but at Lara Croft, who had suddenly appeared behind the giant, hidden in the shadows of the cave, a smile of her own fixed firmly in place and a gun in each hand.

If it had escaped him before, Terry was beginning to remember why he liked her so much.

"Remember what I said before—how I could kill you any time I wanted?" Terry asked Lu Yao.

The giant laughed—Terry heard the two other Shay Ling behind him join in.

"Ha, ha," Terry said, the smile gone from his face. "You don't remember?"

"I remember," Lu Yao choked out between laughs.

"Well," Terry said. "Told you."

He took a deep breath then and moved—the way he'd been trained to, first by the marines, and then the Kon-shari, the way he'd practiced, in Afghanistan with Al-Hassari, and then by himself in his cell at Barla Kala for the last five years.

Terry Sheridan moved like the killing weapon he was.

He exhaled and snapped the rope holding his hands together, spun and broke the wrist of Shay Ling number one, and struck that same man's femoral artery with his clenched fist. As that guard toppled, Terry attacked the second man behind him, flooring him with a fist to the Adam's apple. He picked up the rope from the ground and wrapped it around the man's throat. Twisted tight, and heard his neck snap.

As that man fell, Terry looked up at LuYao.

"Next?" he asked.

The giant, to his credit, didn't run.

Not that he would have had time.

Even as he spoke, Terry kicked out Lu Yao's right kneecap. Kicked again, and snapped the man's left Achilles. As the giant crumpled, face twisted in agony, Terry punched up, thrusting underneath his ribs. Something cracked.

Terry stepped behind him and snapped his neck.

The other Shay Ling, who'd hung back while Terry was lying on the ground, allowing himself to be kicked, looked at him now in open-mouthed surprise, their minds still trying to process what had just happened.

The entire fight—such as it was—had taken three seconds.

Lara sprinted forward from the shadows. Terry started after her and a second later heard the Shay Ling following them.

Gunfire sounded. Terry dodged to his right. Lara went left.

"I was beginning to think you weren't coming!" he shouted after her.

"Sorry!" she called back, as they zigzagged again. "Chen Lo was harder to deal with than I thought!"

He caught up to her and they ran together, sprinting full

out for the main entrance. Terry saw half a dozen coffins scattered in front of them—loaded with terracotta statues like the others, no doubt—waiting to be lowered to the ground below.

He bounded over one. Lara, a step behind now, did the same.

The cavern entrance loomed ahead of them, twenty feet away. Through the opening, Terry saw the rocky face of the mountain due opposite them, lit up by the midday sun. He felt a cool breeze on his face, smelled the fresh air.

"Nice work back there," Lara said, and as she jumped another coffin, flipped him one of the guns she was carrying.

"I thought there was a rule—me and guns," Terry said. The cavern entrance was five feet away.

"I reconsidered!" Lara yelled.

And then she dove out the entrance into the open air beyond.

ELEVEN

The cliff face whipped by her.

Three meters down, Lara reached out and took hold of one of the ropes the Shay Ling had used to lower the coffins.

Next to her, she saw Terry do the same.

They continued to drop like stones, their fall guided by the hands they kept loosely on the ropes. It was delicate work—if she squeezed the rope too tightly, she would slow her smooth descent, turn it into a somersaulting tumble that would end up with her dead, either pancaked into the cliff wall or splattered on the ground below. Without the rope at all, though, she'd have no control over her descent, and end up just the same way. Done correctly, though, it was almost like being in free fall. Exhilarating.

Gunfire took out a chunk of the rock next to her.

Lara looked up and saw Shay Ling hanging over the cliff edge, firing down at them. She squeezed tighter with her left hand, removed her right, and unholstered one of her Colts. Which she'd recovered, along with the pack on her back and the other gun strapped to her leg, when she overpowered the last of the guards chasing her through the cave of the terracotta warriors.

She fired up at the Shay Ling. One man screamed and fell off the edge. A second crumpled.

The cliff emptied. But the gunfire continued—coming

from below now. Lara looked down and saw more Shay Ling. Before she could shift and bring her weapon to bear, she became aware of Terry at her side, drawing his weapon and firing straight down.

One, two, three shots. Three dead men.

Time in Barla Kala hadn't cost Sheridan any of his firearms skills, either. Even hanging upside down.

Lara made a mental note of that as she squeezed off a couple rounds of her own toward the ground—which, she realized with a sudden start, was hurtling toward them very quickly.

She dropped her gun and squeezed the rope tight with both hands. With a jolt, her fall stopped. Lara held herself straight up and down, hanging upside down, and looked around.

The ground was inches away.

She was staring straight into the vacant, glassy eyes of one of the men Terry had shot.

And speaking of Terry . . .

Lara looked up and saw him hanging upside down in midair, as well . . . a full meter above her.

"Losing your nerve?" she chided him, flipping over and somersaulting to her feet.

"The altitude must be affecting me," Sheridan said, as he did the same. "Where to now?"

"Shanghai." She wondered for a moment how they were going to get there—then saw that the Shay Ling, considerately enough, had left them a Jeep. Keys and all, Lara discovered as she jumped in. Terry climbed in, as well, and she started the engine.

She did a series of rough calculations in her head as she drove—time, her best guess at their distance from Shanghai, the condition of the roads they were likely to hit, how fast the Jeep was. After about ten seconds, she stopped calculating.

Shanghai was near the coast, and south. They were going to have to drive like a bat out of hell to get there by nine P.M. and meet the Orb.

And speaking of the Orb . . .

Lara had set her pack on the seat next to her—she reached into it now and pulled out her sat phone. Keeping one hand on the wheel, she keyed in a text message to Bryce and Hillary, letting them know she'd found the key to deciphering it.

As she hit the send button, she became aware of Terry staring at her.

"What?" she asked.

"Nothing." He adjusted the rearview mirror.

"Someone coming?"

Terry shook his head. "We lost them."

He was silent a moment. Lara recognized the look on his face. Terry was stewing about something.

"What?" she repeated.

He made a show of taking out his gun, checking to see how many bullets he had left.

"Look," Terry said, tucking the weapon into the waist of his pants. "You said get you to Chen Lo and I did. For me this is over."

Christ, Lara thought. *Same old Terry.*

She slammed the Jeep to a stop.

"Of course it is."

She set the emergency brake and waited for him to climb out.

Terry stewed a moment longer. Then he erupted.

"Tell me what this is about, Lara. Tell me what you're

looking for—or where it is. Do that, trust me, and I'll help you."

She snorted. "For another five million pounds?"

"Will I even live to see the first five?" He shook his head. 'Jonathan Reiss, for pity's sake? Come on, Croft, I'm involved now. Up to my neck. At least let me know what's going on."

Lara wavered. He had a point.

But he had a history, as well. And that history said that Terry Sheridan couldn't be trusted.

"I'll be fine," she said. "Thank you."

Terry stared at her, disbelief and anger warring on his face.

"You're welcome, Croft. See you around."

Without waiting for a reply, he opened his door and got out. Slamming it shut behind him, Terry walked off down the road, kicking and cursing every few feet. Looking for all the world as if he was actually, honestly, upset with Lara for not trusting him.

Lara watched as he stalked away and remembered Hillary's words to her.

A leopard doesn't change his spots.

But something seemed different about Sheridan—he seemed to honestly want to help.

Though there was that crack he'd made to Chen Lo, about selling her and the Orb back to the British. Was it a crack?

Only one way to find out, she decided.

She drove up alongside him and stopped the Jeep.

"We need to be in Shanghai by twenty-one hundred," she said.

Terry stopped walking. The beginnings of a smile crossed his face.

"I knew you'd miss me," he said.

Lara reached across and opened the door for him.

He climbed in and opened his mouth to speak.

"I have some questions for you," Lara began, her face grim. "But first, I want you to listen."

And she began to tell him of the map Xien was bringing Reiss, and what the doctor hoped to use it to find.

TWELVE

Reiss tapped his foot impatiently. The bodyguards on either side of him—Sean's men, he couldn't be bothered to learn their names, there were so many of them—shifted positions, scanning the surrounding buildings, their weapons at the ready. Off to the west, the sun was setting over the mainland.

Reiss looked at his watch: 7:03. They should have been in the air already. Sean knew better than to keep him waiting, he didn't understand what the holdup was here, he—

Suddenly the door leading onto the building roof slammed open and Sean raced out. From the expression on his face, Reiss knew it was not good news.

"Chen Lo is dead," Sean said simply.

Reiss shut his eyes and took a minute.

This was not a problem. It was not inherently a bad thing that Chen Lo was dead—he had been planning on doing just that himself. The only bad thing was how that death now might affect his timetable for obtaining the Orb.

He opened his eyes. "It was Croft, I suppose?"

"And Sheridan. They killed twenty Shay Ling, give or take."

"Impressive." And it was, but Reiss didn't give a damn about the Shay Ling. "Did she get the Orb?"

"No. Xien has it. He's on his way to Shanghai. Croft is, too, I'll bet."

"Of course she is." Reiss rubbed his forehead. Given her

background, Croft alone would be fully aware of the magnitude of the threat Pandora represented. She would never stop until she had the Orb.

He was beginning to get a migraine. He was beginning to wish he'd never heard the name Lara Croft.

All thoughts of turning her to his side had vanished. He wanted her dead now—almost as much as he wanted that Orb.

"We have to change the location of the rendezvous," Sean said. "We—"

"No." Reiss climbed aboard the copter. Sean followed, a confused look on his face. Both men strapped in.

"But if she comes to Shanghai—" Sean began.

"Oh, there's no if. Croft will be there waiting for us. So we will be there waiting for her." He leveled a thin smile at Sean. "In force."

Sean nodded, and pulled out his cell. "I'll get on it right away."

"Please have a contingency plan in place, as well, Sean," Reiss added as his security man began to dial. "Let's not underestimate Croft and Sheridan."

"No sir, I won't." Sean turned away then and began talking into his phone. Guns, personnel, diversionary operations to keep the local authorities occupied—Reiss listened with approval, then looked to the pilot and gave a curt nod.

Sean's men slammed the door behind them and the copter rose into the air.

Three fill-ups at gunpoint, one run-in with local authorities, and a frantic chase along the railroad tracks leading into Shanghai later, Lara and Terry were on the roof of a fish market overlooking the flower pagoda. Directly beneath them was a market square crisscrossed with a maze of handmade signs, banners, and rickety-looking telephone wires. The few scattered farmers and shopkeepers that remained in the square were hurriedly closing up their stalls for the night—almost as if they knew something bad was about to happen.

Lara checked her watch and realized they were right.

It was 8:58.

She checked her guns, reloaded courtesy of the local authorities she and Terry had encountered earlier, then crouched down next to Terry at the roof's edge. He lay flat out on the roof, scanning the area.

The flower pagoda was opposite them, in the center of the square. Behind it was a newer-looking brick building, with a helipad on top. On noticing it, Lara realized instantly that was how Reiss would come in, where he would want to make the exchange.

"There's one." Sheridan pointed toward a dimly lit alley to their right. Light glinted off the grille of a car, waiting there. "Another Mercedes. That's a half-dozen cars altogether—make it four men in each. Plus the ones we saw creeping in on foot." He shook his head. "The good doctor isn't taking any chances."

"We'll have to," Lara said. "To even things up."

Terry looked up at her now and smiled. "Seems like old times."

She smiled, as well, remembering what had happened after Terry got her loose from the NKA.

"Thirty, forty against two."

"Just once I'd like to go somewhere with you where there weren't people trying to kill us."

She had to smile at that.

"That's the first time you've smiled because of me, Croft. In a long while."

"It's the first time I've seen you in a long while, Terry."

"Yeah. Well . . ." He shrugged.

Lara turned to him, her face suddenly serious.

"Why'd you do it, Terry? How does someone wake up one day and leave everything they've worked for? They offered you a command—"

"They offered me a desk," Terry snapped. "A nice cozy office. A nice cozy life."

"All you had to do was say no—"

"That wasn't it, Croft." He stood up now, too. "I'd started asking the wrong questions. 'Why this mission? Why not that one?' I got tired of doing things somebody else's way. And it was always going to be somebody else's way."

"But deserting your men, your country—"

"I've paid my price for that." He looked her in the eye. "I don't know what it says about me, but leaving my men, my country, didn't hurt as much as I thought. Leaving you was what did. You're a hard act to follow, Croft."

She didn't know what to say. Terry had never—not in all the time they'd been together—opened himself up to her like this.

"The reason you and I got along? We both despise being normal. We both love what we do too much to leave room for much else. We're two of a kind, you and me."

"Terry." Lara shook her head. "We're nothing alike."

"I don't think we're alike. I think we're a pair. Opposite—and alone."

He leaned in closer. Almost as if he was going to kiss her.

"Wait," Lara said.

Terry looked up and then he heard it, too.

The sound of a helicopter, closing fast.

"On your command," the pilot announced.

Reiss looked down out of his window and saw the helipad lit up below.

"Hold here a moment," he said and nodded to Sean.

His security chief pulled out the thermal imager and aimed at the square. The imager looked for all the world like a videocamera with an oversize display screen—in its case, though, the screen provided a negative image of whatever the lens was pointed at. In this case, the area immediately surrounding the pagoda.

Sean pressed a button then and the screen filled with red dots. Each dot represented a heat signature—a man—more than likely, one of Sean's men. Reiss stopped counting at thirty.

"One of those is Croft," the doctor said.

Sean nodded. "She'll be somewhere with a vantage point of the helipad."

"I'll make the call," Reiss said. "Have your men start forming teams."

He picked up the phone and dialed.

"Speak."

"Xien?"

"Yes."

"This is Reiss. We are prepared to land."

"We're prepared to receive you. Give us your landing co-ordinates."

Reiss frowned. He wondered if Xien had any plans to duplicate his brother's foolish action—to try and hold him up for more money.

"We're using the helipad. My men have the situation well in hand," Reiss replied. "But I do appreciate your offer of assistance."

"Why don't you set down in the square instead? That way, my men will also have things covered."

Reiss was about to turn him down, and none too graciously, when he thought of Croft. No doubt she was in position already and, were he in her shoes, the helipad would most certainly be the place she was watching most closely. Surprising her at this stage of the rendezvous could only help them. And as for Xien's men being in control of the situation on the ground . . .

Reiss glanced over at the imager, and the handfuls of red dots scattered all over the square, and smiled.

His men were everywhere.

"Fine," he told Xien. "The square it is. And in case you weren't aware—Croft is here."

Xien waited a moment before replying.

"Oh, I'm aware." Even over the phone, Reiss could hear the menace dripping from the man's voice. "We'll deal with her."

"Please do."

Reiss hung up the phone then and thought:

And then we'll deal with you.

The helicopter was coming down.

But not where Lara had expected.

She cursed under her breath and then shouted to Terry.

"They're not landing on the helipad!"

"I can see that," he said. "They're going to use the square!"

Lara looked down. Two men were emerging from the shadows of the pagoda. One carried a large case in his arms. The other was Xien.

She started scurrying across the rooftop, looking at the maze of wires and signs directly beneath her, trying to figure out some way to get down there without getting killed.

"Croft."

She turned. Terry was looking left; she followed his gaze.

On the building next to the fish market, a huge neon

sign, shaped like a dragon, hung from a thick wire cable that stretched completely across the square. Lara smiled.

That would do.

She kicked her pack over to Terry.

"Extra clips. Another gun," she said. "You'll need them."

He nodded.

"See you down there."

As Reiss's helicopter roared by, Lara took a running leap and jumped onto the building next door.

They hovered just above the ground, the rotors kicking up dust clouds from the bare earth below. Xien stood almost directly beneath them, giving the all-clear signal. Reiss saw another man standing next to him, holding a case that—this time—looked the proper shape and size to contain the Orb.

Inside the copter, in the seat next to him, Sean was receiving signals from his men on the ground through his earpiece.

"All clear so far," he told Reiss.

At those words, the pilot glanced back, waiting for the go-ahead to land.

But the doctor hesitated. Something about the idea of touching down, of committing himself to the ground for however brief a period of time, made him suddenly uneasy. He didn't want those rotors to stop, or slow down, for a second.

Croft, he thought. *Sheridan.*

His fear was ridiculous, of course. Unreasonable. He had thirty-odd men in position, highly trained every one of them, plus however many Shay Ling Xien had waiting in the shadows. Call it an even dozen—which made the odds forty-something to two. But still . . .

His instincts told him not to land. And Jonathan Reiss always listened to his instincts.

"This is far enough," he said. "We'll make the exchange from here."

Sean nodded and reached below his seat for the suitcase.

Lara jumped from the roof directly onto the cable. Caught it with both hands and hung there a moment, suspended in the space between the dragon sign and the building. Then she pulled herself up and sat on the cable, her legs dangling.

The helicopter hovered in the center of the square. Xien and his man stood nearby. As she watched, the copter door opened and a man climbed out onto the landing skid.

Reiss wasn't even going to land, she realized. They were going to make the exchange right now.

Lara looked down. A secondary steel wire held the sign tight against the building, prevented it from sliding down the cable. She drew one of her Colts and shot that wire away—the sound of the isolated gunshot swallowed up by the roar of the copter's rotors.

She holstered her gun then and spun around. Braced her feet up against the wall of the building, reached behind with her hands, and held on tight to the dragon's neck.

Then Lara pushed off.

Slowly at first, then picking up speed, the dragon sign began to slide along the cable, heading toward the center of the square.

Reiss saw Sean holding onto the skid with one hand, holding out the suitcase of money toward Xien with his other. Xien, in turn, was holding up the case with the Orb in it toward the copter.

The doctor allowed himself a small sigh of relief. The exchange was going to come off clean. His fears had been for naught.

He glanced at the imager screen then, and froze.

A single red dot was moving toward them—very quickly.

Reiss spun in his seat and scanned the square.

Which made him the first to see the dragon.

He had a second of total disconnect, when his mind was simply unable to process the information his eyes were presenting to it. There was a dragon—a purely mythological creature, for goodness sake, nothing like it had ever existed on the planet—rushing out of the sky toward them.

It was, Reiss saw, even spitting fire.

For a second he thought he was dreaming.

Then one of the windows next to him shattered and Reiss realized that the sparks of fire were gunshots. He took a second look at the dragon and saw that it was simply a metal sign, sliding toward them along a cable that traversed the square, and that there was a person riding that sign, firing at them, and that person was—

Lara Croft.

Another window panel shattered. Reiss hit the floor. The imager landed next to him—Reiss saw red dots moving every which way on the screen.

All hell was breaking loose.

"Get us out of here!" he yelled to the pilot, and the copter rose into the sky.

Lara ducked just in time.

As the dragon shot past the rising copter, the main rotors chopped off its head, sending a shower of sparks everywhere. The copter wobbled and lurched right. It took out part of a balcony.

The man on the skid jumped to the ground. Lara fired at him and missed. She looked for Xien and the Orb, but they'd already vanished from sight.

All around her, guns were blazing. She returned fire as best she could, vaguely aware of Terry running parallel to her, along the rooftops to her right, providing some degree of covering fire without which she would have been long dead.

But at least she'd managed to prevent the exchange.

So far.

Reiss had to wait several long rings for an answer. In the interim, he imagined worst-case scenarios: Croft had the Orb. The Orb had been destroyed. Xien had been killed, the Orb was somewhere on the ground below.

He forced himself to remain calm.

There was a click on the line.

"Yes?"

"Xien. You have it?"

"Yes, I still have it."

"Good," Reiss said. The copter was making long, slow circles of the square—right now, the helipad was directly beneath them. He was about to have Xien rendezvous with them there when his eyes fell on the flower pagoda itself. Set off by itself in the middle of the square. Impossible to reach without being spotted, no wires running near it, the steep pitch of its long, sloping tile roof . . .

"All right," the doctor told Xien. "We tried it your way. Now listen carefully."

Lara had come to the end of the line.

She and her dragon sign had reached the far side of the square and the end of the cable they'd been riding, which was fastened to an uncomfortably solid-looking brick building directly in front of them. Time to get off.

Lara saw only one option: ten feet to the right of the cable tether, there was another large sign. A white rectangle with black lettering, fastened lengthwise to the building. It looked solid enough.

Not like she had much choice anyway.

Lara gathered herself and jumped. She landed on the top of the sign just as the dragon slammed into the building.

The impact was tremendous—dust and pieces of brick, glass from the sign's shattered neon bulbs rained down on her. The building shook.

Metal groaned beneath her. Lara glanced down to see a rickety-looking fire escape slowly detach itself from the building and topple to the ground.

The bolts holding her sign began to pull free, as well.

The top one went first: Lara slid down the sign as the next one gave, and then the next, her weight pulling out each successive bolt.

Lara was lucky: the last bolt held. The sign toppled toward the ground, falling over like a ladder. She walked down it to the ground below, shaking her head in wonder as she went.

Safe at last.

Windows shattered in the pagoda across from her. Gun barrels poked out and began firing at her.

A Mercedes screeched across the square in her direction. More gunfire.

Lara ran.

Reiss's phone rang. It was Sean, wanting to know what had happened to the money. Wanting instructions.

"Don't worry about the money," the doctor told him. "Don't worry about the Orb. I'll handle that end of things. Your job is to handle Croft."

Sean asked for clarification.

"Kill her," Reiss explained. "Slowly. Painfully."

The doctor hung up and directed the pilot forward, toward their new rendezvous point.

Terry reached the ground and paused a moment, listening.

No chopper. Isolated gunfire and the sound of men running.

He risked a quick peek out the building's front door.

Shay Ling were falling back toward the flower pagoda. Reiss's men were moving across the square, toward another building. Some of Xien's people, he saw, were headed down an alley, moving parallel to them.

They were chasing Croft, he decided. Probably thought they had her cornered.

The idea was laughable.

But he decided to go help anyway, on the off-chance it was true.

He reloaded his guns and stepped out the door. Hugged the front of the building, hiding in the shadows until the facade ended and the empty street loomed in front of him.

As he prepared to dart across, one of the Shay Ling—a straggler, apparently—hurried by. Terry walked quickly up behind the man and snapped his neck.

Then he continued on his way.

A Mercedes blocked the entrance to the next alley over—two men stood on either side of the car, talking to each other in hushed tones.

Terry shot each with a single bullet.

Three bodies later, he turned a corner and saw Croft hiding underneath a sign that advertised the best hot and sour soup in Shanghai. She was watching Reiss's men and the Shay Ling surround the building she was supposed to be in.

Terry approached from behind and laid a hand on her shoulder.

"I heard you two streets over," she said without turning. "You move like an elephant."

Terry was preparing an insult of his own when a low, rumbling noise from above made him look up.

Reiss's helicopter was descending toward the square again.

"They're going to try it again. Where this time, you think? The helipad?"

Lara shook her head and pointed.

Xien had just emerged from his truck and was now crossing the square, carrying the Orb case. Heading for the flower pagoda.

Terry frowned.

"The pagoda?"

Lara nodded. "The top. That's where they'll make the exchange."

She was right. Even now Reiss's men were pulling back toward the pagoda, as well. Surrounding it.

Terry scanned the square and realized that there wasn't a building within fifty feet of the pagoda that they could use for cover.

"How in the hell are we going to stop them this time?" he muttered.

Croft shook her head. "See any more dragon signs?"

"Ha." He kept scanning the square and the buildings around it. There was the fish market, there was the structure Croft and her sign had wrecked, and next to it, the building with the helipad, which would have been much easier for them to attack, sandwiched as it was between two equally tall structures. Good choice on Reiss's part to opt for the pagoda—even though Croft had disrupted their previous exchange, the incident in the square proved there was no need to actually land the copter, given the absence of any meaningful wind shears in the area. The windsock atop the helipad lay limp and still, fastened to the end of a long pole, which towered at least fifty feet above everything else in the square.

Fifty feet, Terry thought, and all of a sudden he had an idea. Crazy idea, but it just might work.

He turned to Croft, and by God if she wasn't looking up at the windsock herself. She turned to him and smiled.

"Are you thinking what I'm thinking?" she asked.

THIRTEEN

There was no direct route up to the helipad. So they had to improvise.

Under pressure, at times, because halfway up the side of the building a handful of Reiss's men caught sight of them and began shooting. Lara and Terry returned fire as best they could, all the while using whatever handholds they could find—signs, fire escapes, ridiculous midair jumps worthy of a trapeze act—to keep climbing up.

Finally, they reached the floor just below the helipad. The lip of the roof stuck out a good three feet from the face of the building. Lara was preparing to jump for it when she heard Terry curse under his breath.

She looked down and saw Shay Ling and Reiss's men pouring out of the pagoda en masse.

"Go," Terry said, and Lara leapt.

Gunfire raked the side of the building where she'd been.

Her hands caught the edge of the roof and she used her momentum to swing herself up and over and onto the helipad.

Lara ran for the windsock. The gunfire behind her continued, though she was no longer in range. Terry, still providing a target for their attackers. Awfully sporting of him—she'd have to thank him later. In the meantime . . .

She surveyed the helipad as she ran. The facility was in an obvious state of disrepair—and just as obviously, someone had made very recent attempts to bring it back up to snuff. A coat of fresh paint on the tarmac, a new array of lights fastened to the far edge of the roof. Very, *very* recent attempts, she realized, spotting some supplies stacked underneath a plastic tarp right by the light array. An old furniture dolly lay turned upside down atop the tarp, placed there to keep it from blowing away.

She'd bet good money that the work had been done on Reiss's behalf, in advance of a planned landing here tonight. Well—for whatever reason the doctor had changed his plans. Not once, but twice. Now the exchange was set for the pagoda and that was where she needed to be.

Which was when she heard the roar of the helicopter and looked up to see it descending toward the square.

Reiss was going to make the exchange now.

Time was up. She had to move.

Xien had done as he was told without a word of complaint or even suggestion, which at this point in the evening Reiss was thankful for. Not that the man had much choice in the matter—Reiss's operatives on the ground outnumbered the Shay Ling by more than three to one. On top of which, Sean had already given Xien the suitcase containing payment for the Orb.

But still . . .

Reiss appreciated a smooth transaction.

He intended to make his appreciation known to Xien shortly, but for the moment, the doctor was focused on completing the exchange—and making sure that Croft did not interrupt him this time.

He punched up Sean's number on his cell.

"O'Sullivan."

"Where is she?"

"The helipad. We have her and Sheridan pinned down on the top floor."

Reiss glanced across the square at the tall building, and frowned.

"I see movement on the roof, as well."

"Understood," Sean said. "We will redeploy."

"See that you do—and don't forget your previous instructions. Once I have the Orb—" Reiss glanced down, and saw Xien waiting on the roof of the pagoda "—I will be taking it directly back to Hong Kong. Follow me when—and only when—your task is completed."

Without waiting for a reply, Reiss hung up.

"Take us down," he told the pilot.

Lara ran for the pole with the windsock. She looked down: the anchors holding it to the roof were rusted almost clean through. One good push and that pole would fall.

She looked up, judged its height and the distance to the pagoda, and then frowned.

Not quite long enough. The little brainstorm Terry and she had shared—repeating her accidental stunt with the sign from before, when it had fallen and made a ladder for her to climb down the side of the building—wasn't going to work.

Time for Plan B. Only problem was, she didn't have a Plan B.

She watched the copter descend and realized she was not going to be able to stop Reiss. He was going to get the Orb—there was nothing she could do to prevent it.

On the plus side, she still had the medallion. If her instincts were right, and that was the key, Reiss would need it to read the Orb. Making the exchange would bring him no closer to Pandora.

If her instincts were right.

If the key wasn't on the parts of the Orb that she hadn't been able to photograph.

If Reiss wasn't able to find some other way to read it.

Hell, Lara thought.

Plan B it was.

Her mind raced. The pole. The dolly. One of the nifty little gadgets Shumei had given her.

She put the pieces together in her head as she ran.

The copter slowed its descent, leveling off a few feet above the roof of the pagoda. Xien stood there, holding out the Orb in its case.

Reiss slid open the copter door and leaned out to take it from him.

Down in the square, someone began setting off firecrackers.

As he took hold of the case, the doctor paused to look down. Odd. He didn't see anyone but his men. Most of them, as Sean had said, were gathered around the building with the helipad atop it.

They were all pointing up at something.

The copter, Reiss thought at first, but then he turned and saw what had drawn their attention.

The pole atop the helipad was falling right toward them.

And riding atop it, guns blazing, was Croft.

All of a sudden, Reiss's men stopped firing.

Terry wondered what had happened, but while he was wondering, he ran. No sense in looking a gift horse in the mouth, not in his situation. Which up until a split second ago had seemed quite bleak.

After Croft had leapt for the roof, he'd made a leap of his own—a jump back inside the building, into an office of some kind. He had no chance to look around, however, because hot on his tail came several hundred rounds of ammunition. He took refuge behind a metal desk, but the gunfire continued so hot and heavy that the walls themselves began to cave in around him. So he'd made a break for a window clear on the other side of the room, climbing out onto a balcony on the back of the building and what he thought was safety. For about two seconds—until the strafing started again, even heavier than before. He'd managed to slide down a fire escape ladder to the building next door, getting himself another momentary respite, and was just about to make another move when the gunfire had stopped.

Puzzled, Terry looked out the window. Reiss's men were still down there, all right, only they were all looking back toward the building he'd just come from. Toward the helipad.

Terry looked up and saw the pole with the windsock falling and smiled. Croft was heading for the pagoda. She'd need help when she got there.

Holstering his guns, he'd headed for the street.

The dolly she'd used for a skateboard.

The pole like a ski jump.

And the little gadget Shumei had given her . . .

Well, what were little gadgets for, after all?

Lara had grabbed the dolly from off the tarp and jumped on it with both feet, running full out. She built up speed with a circuit around the building's outer ledge, then jumped the board smack into the pole. The anchor bolts popped right away and the pole began falling. She rode it as best she could, sliding down the smooth steel surface toward the pagoda.

She fired as she went, but her aim was way off, distracted as she was by trying to maintain her balance. The gunfire caught Reiss's attention though—she was close enough to see him turn away from Xien and fasten his gaze on her. It was the best look she'd had at him yet, and the expression on his face was priceless. Equal parts disbelief and anger—or was that annoyance? Lara fixed the image in her mind—she looked forward to savoring it in the days to come.

For right now, it was the Orb she was interested in.

Good God, was there no stopping her? Was he surrounded by idiots and incompetents? Was he going to have to kill Lara Croft himself?

The answer to all three questions, unfortunately, appeared to be yes.

The case with the Orb was at his feet, just inside the copter door. Keeping one foot in front of it to prevent it from falling, Reiss reached back into the copter for his gun. Bullets pinged off the copter skids and he looked up just in time to see Croft flying toward him. Actually flying. The sight so unnerved him for a moment that he forgot to bring his weapon to bear.

Then he saw that her flight was actually a free fall, and that the pole she'd used to vault across to him was tumbling away behind her toward the ground below.

Croft was about to join it when she reached out and grabbed the bottom of the helicopter skid. I've got her now, Reiss thought, and raised his gun to fire.

She raised hers first and fired, and he had to duck away.

When he looked back, she was hanging from the copter door, with a hand on the case holding the Orb.

Reiss pulled the trigger. Behind Croft, he saw Xien's gun spit fire, as well.

She flinched—Reiss couldn't tell if she'd been hit or not—and fell.

He leaned out the copter door and watched her hit the pagoda roof and slide down the slick tile surface toward the edge.

Reiss pulled the Orb the rest of the way into the copter.

"This has been a messy business, doctor," Xien said. "I'm glad it's over."

"The mess has just begun, I'm afraid," Reiss said. "My regards to your brother."

Xien's eyes narrowed in confusion.

Reiss shot him in the heart.

Xien toppled backward onto the roof and plunged toward the street below.

Reiss, watching him fall, smiled for the first time in what seemed like days.

Then he saw Croft, hanging onto the edge of the roof, dangling over the alley, and his face fell.

"Up!" he yelled to the pilot. "Up!"

She couldn't hold on for more than another few seconds, Lara realized. Her grip was slipping on the slick tile surface already.

The trick was going to be deciding where to fall.

Unfortunately, the pagoda's isolation didn't work to her advantage in this instance, either. The paved surface of the market square looked like her only option, unless you counted Xien's truck, which had a nice soft canvas roof, but was parked a good twenty feet away from the pagoda. That roof might be reachable if she could get up some momentum and do a flip, but if she failed—

A body slid just past her right then and plummeted to the street below, smashing into the decapitated head of her dragon sign with a loud crack that made her wince.

It was Xien. Correction—it had been Xien.

Happy as she was to see him dead, the killing sent her

dislike for Reiss shooting up another notch. And sent an extra jolt of adrenaline through her body.

She took a second look at the truck and decided it was within reach after all.

Lara swung her legs back and then lunged forward, kicking out with all her might. At the height of her swing forward, she let go of the roof and soared out into space.

Her legs continued their backward motion, swinging out over her head.

She completed the flip, landing feet first atop the canvas, and immediately jumped down to the ground.

Reiss's men had seen her and were on the move again.

She took a step forward and then froze.

Someone was inside the truck.

She drew her gun and ripped the back flap open.

Terry hopped out and handed her another gun.

"Fresh clip," he said. "And how are you?"

Before she could answer, gunfire ripped through the canvas. They both dove to the ground.

"We've got to get out of here," Terry whispered. "They've got cars blocking all the alleys."

Lara pressed her back up against one of the huge rear wheels. Terry was right—if they didn't break through the cordon Reiss's men had set up, that cordon would tighten, and despite the faith she had in her abilities and his, they were outnumbered thirty to one. They would be killed and she wouldn't get to use Shumei's little gadget.

She leaned out from behind the tire and scanned the square, looking for a way out. Terry was snaking his way along the ground to join her.

"Bull," she said when he got there.

He misunderstood her. "What do you mean, bull? Look for yourself—every street is covered—"

"No," Lara interrupted. "Bull!"

She pointed across the square.

Squeezed in between two of the market stalls was an animal pen. Standing at the entrance gate, horns jutting out into the street, was a huge black bull. Other animals were visible behind it.

Terry snorted. "You've got to be kidding."

"Not in the least. Ferdinand there is our ticket out."

"If we can reach him, you mean."

Terry had a point. They had at least fifty feet of open ground to cover between them and the pen.

"Think we can get there?" she asked.

"You've been pretty good at dodging bullets so far, Croft, but . . ."

She waited for him to finish, and when he didn't, turned to face him.

He was staring at the shop closest to the truck. It looked to have been some kind of hardware store, though she couldn't be entirely certain since the sign above it had been shot to pieces. As had the windows facing the street.

But somehow, miraculously, the pyramid of spray-paint cans in the store display hadn't been touched at all.

"Do I think we can get to your bulls?" Terry repeated. "I do now."

Reiss's men seemed to be content to wait, to let Croft and him make the first move. Which they missed entirely—that move being Terry crawling to the store commando-style and retrieving the spray-paint cans—ten in all.

When he was ready, he gave Croft the high sign.

She stood up and ran for the pen.

Terry followed, facing back toward the truck. As he ran, he threw the first can high in the air and—taking careful aim—he shot it as it fell.

The can exploded, bursting into flames, sending drops of blazing paint shooting through the air. Some of those drops splattered Reiss's men—those unfortunate few dropped their weapons and brushed frantically at their clothes.

Terry smiled and threw another can.

Four explosions later, he and Lara had reached the gate. The bull had retreated a few feet back from the entrance and was now eyeing them suspiciously.

"Now what?"

"Now we wave the red flag," Lara said, pulling off her jacket. The inside, Terry saw, was a deep, deep crimson.

Just as he was about to tell Croft that he'd done the whole running-of-the-bulls thing before, and once was plenty for him, gunfire nicked the fence post right next to him.

"Hold them off," Croft said, turning her jacket inside out.

"I'll try—but hurry." Terry showed her five paint cans—all he had left from the display. "That's how long you have."

She nodded and leapt into the pen.

Terry turned. Reiss's men were coming, fast and furious.

"Here goes number five, Croft," he shouted, tossing the can in the air. As soon as it exploded, he threw another. "Four!"

Behind him, he heard a loud snort and the charging of something massive.

"Three," he shouted. "Croft—where are you?"

He turned, and almost got his head taken off by a piece of the gate, which shattered as Lara rode through it astride the huge black bull. Two others, even bigger than the first, followed.

Terry slipped between them, heading straight for a clump of Reiss's men, who looked bewildered and then terrified.

They broke and ran.

Terry used the last two paint cans to break up a knot of men massed together by one of the Mercedes.

The bulls brushed past the massive auto like it was a toy and continued full speed down the alley for several minutes.

Finally, when Lara judged they were clear of any possible pursuit, she jumped down from the black bull. The animal immediately slowed. With a slap on its rear, Lara sent it walking back up the street the way they'd come.

"Runaway," she explained to a crowd of curious onlookers.

Terry caught up to her at the next corner.

"You have a way with animals, Croft."

"And you have a way with paint."

"Thank you. Sorry we didn't get your Orb. Any idea where Reiss would take it?"

"Let's find out," Lara said.

She stepped into the shadows. At Terry's confused look, she reached into her pack and pulled out the second half of the gadget Shumei had given her—MI6's latest GPS display.

The other half, of course, was the transmitter—which she'd fastened on the crate with the Orb, while the copter hovered over the pagoda.

She flipped the display on and saw the signal was coming through loud and clear.

"You put a tracer on it," Terry said. "I'm impressed."

"I don't go skating down flagpoles, full guns, unless I know I'm going to succeed."

She watched the transmitter move off and smiled. She had the Orb again—after a fashion.

The question now, of course, was where Reiss was taking it.

FOURTEEN

A hot shower. A clean suit. A good Shiraz, a strong cheddar, a fresh loaf of olive bread, ten cc's of a rejuvenating cocktail specially engineered for his system . . .

Reiss felt almost human again.

He returned to the main lab, anxious to begin work. Dr. Holliday, who had been with him since the Nobel, the only one of his staff who could make that claim, was there waiting. They had already talked once this evening after Holliday had tested the Orb for biological contamination. He noted that she'd already changed, from biohazard gear into a standard lab coat.

The Orb remained where he had left it, in the clean room, still in its case. Reiss had taken a preliminary look at the delicate etchings on the object's surface and decided to prohibit his staff from handling it.

At a nod from him, Holliday began.

As Reiss watched, robotic hands gently lifted the Orb from the crate and held it motionless in the air. Reiss moved closer to the Plexiglas window separating him from the Orb. Seen up close like this, the object was truly amazing. Luminescent markings, silvery etchings reminiscent of nothing so much as computer circuitry, covered its glowing black core.

"There was always a part of me that allowed for the possibility Pandora's box was just a legend," Reiss whispered, as much to himself as the doctor. "But seeing this, I know it's there."

And the Orb, he knew, would tell him exactly how to find it.

He nodded again and Holliday activated the scanning laser.

The instrument would map every millimeter of the Orb's surface in the minutest possible detail and record it into his computers. Then the analysis would take place.

Reiss had recently purchased a handful of NEC Earth Simulators—the machines that had just taken the title of the planet's fastest supercomputer away from the Crays—for just that purpose. He looked forward to putting them through their paces.

Based on a sample he and Holliday had just completed, the doctor expected that deciphering the Orb should take the NECs approximately twenty-nine seconds. Give or take.

And then the real fun could begin.

Someone coughed behind him. A newcomer—Reiss had been so absorbed in his work he hadn't heard anyone enter.

He turned and saw O'Sullivan. Saw the look on the man's face and felt the tranquility begin to leak out of him like air from a burst balloon.

"She escaped." Reiss felt a faint pounding just behind his temples. He reached into his pocket for an ibuprofen—specially modified, of course, to suit his body chemistry.

Sean nodded. "She has no idea where we are."

Reiss swallowed the pill and shook his head.

"We'll take no chances." He turned to Holliday. "Start transferring everything we need to manufacture an antidote to the jet."

She nodded and waved a white-coated assistant forward to monitor the scanning. Sean left the room to begin preparations of his own.

Reiss stayed a moment longer, watching the laser's progress on the computer display.

Percent Surface Scanned Completed: .028
Time to Scan Completion: 7:12:29

Slightly under seven and a half hours until they had the Orb deciphered and were on their way. Reiss didn't expect to see Croft pop up before then, but if she did, he would order an immediate evacuation.

He planned to treat her like an infectious disease from this point forward. Or to put it more colloquially . . .

He was going to avoid her like the plague.

MI6 got a Chinese military transport to follow the copter. Someone high up was pulling strings—the plane (Lara and Terry met it at a base just outside Shanghai) had been reserved for their exclusive use. And not only were they the sole passengers, rations and sleeping hammocks had already been prepared for them.

Lara skipped the food and took a hammock, exhausted. Before closing her eyes, she took a final look at the GPS readout, but it only confirmed her previous guess and the intelligence MI6 had given her when she'd called for help.

The Orb was headed to Hong Kong. Intelligence had Reiss's operation based there, though no one could confirm its exact whereabouts.

We'll be taking care of that little item tomorrow, Lara thought, and immediately fell into a deep and dreamless sleep.

Daybreak found them at a Kowloon pier, waiting with a queue of early risers for the first hydrofoil across to Hong Kong.

When they were allowed to board, Lara made for the bow of the boat, holding the GPS display in front of her as they walked. Absorbed in the task of trying to narrow down the Orb's location, she didn't notice Terry bringing her breakfast until she looked up and the tray was on the rail at her shoulder.

"Eat," he told her.

"Thanks." She gulped down her espresso and nibbled at a croissant, all the while concentrating on the readout. Hong Kong was roughly split into two distinct regions—the urban north side of the island, whose gleaming towers they were fast approaching, and the suburban south. Reiss's headquarters were definitely in the north, probably the central district that was the heart of the island's shopping and financial community, but that was all she could tell from the readout at this distance. Still, it was good news. Central started at the pier and went only a few blocks deep. With any luck, they'd have his exact location within the hour, and the Orb not long after that.

"We did well back there, Croft," Terry said.

She glanced up to find him studying her intently, in a way that made her immediately uncomfortable. In a way that reminded her of other breakfast mornings they'd shared, in another life.

"We did nothing," she snapped. "Reiss has hours on us now. He may have already deciphered the Orb. He may be on his way to Pandora at this moment."

Terry frowned. "You said you had the key to reading the Orb. The medallion."

"I believe I have the key," Lara corrected. "I haven't established that yet."

An airhorn sounded. The hydrofoil was docking. Lara folded up the GPS, and hurried to join the crowd already gathering by the exit ramp.

Minutes later, she and Terry were forcing their way

through a crowded market plaza. They seemed to be swimming upstream, fighting through businessmen and women in freshly pressed suits, street vendors jockeying for sidewalk space, and knots of elegantly dressed shoppers seemingly intent on walking as slowly as possible. The air was thick and smelt heavily of diesel fuel—Lara found it hard to believe Reiss could find a quiet space to work in this madhouse, much less to build a laboratory.

Terry's thoughts seemed to be running parallel with hers.

"Are you sure about this?" he asked.

She checked the GPS again and nodded.

"That way," she said, pointing.

The signal led them out of the marketplace at last, and into a more upscale commercial district. The sidewalks here were slightly less crowded, but the streets were lined with taxis and limousines, double and triple parked. Office towers loomed overhead, circling them on all sides.

Terry stopped walking and shook his head. "A weapons lab in the middle of the city? No way. He dumped the crate."

Lara checked the GPS again. The signal had stopped flashing entirely, which meant . . .

"It's right here," she announced. "The Orb."

"One of the buildings?"

"No. It's exactly where we're standing."

"There's nothing here." Terry did a three-sixty, his eyes coming to rest on Lara. "It's like I said. He dumped it—"

"No he didn't." Lara was looking at the tall skyscraper right in front of them. Its facade was glass—beyond the entrance, she glimpsed an escalator leading up to the floors above. And another, leading down.

"New Central Shopping Mall," Terry said, reading off a banner that hung just above the building entrance. "Eight floors, eighty stores, International Food Court."

"Nothing about a biological warfare laboratory?"

Terry smiled and shook his head. "Hardly."

"False advertising," Lara said, snapping the GPS display shut.

She jogged for the entrance, Terry right beside her.

On sublevel four, she stopped and checked the display again.

"Down," she said, putting one foot forward, then stopped.

There was a bank of payphones right beside the escalator.

She'd been unable to reach the manor since Luoyang— since finding the medallion. And in case anything happened to her . . .

Both Hillary and Bryce answered on the first ring.

"Lara! Are you all right?"

"Fine." She heard the scrape of chairs pushing back from a table and realized she was on speakerphone. "Have you made any progress on reading the Orb?"

"Not really." That was Bryce, sounding guilty. Lara could hear a faint whirring noise in the background, which she recognized as the helicopter simulation. She hoped that wasn't all he'd been doing in the day or so she'd been gone.

"Well, I may have some help for you. I need you both to look at something."

She reached into her pack and pulled out the wireless digicam. She attached one end to her belt, tucked its lens over her ear, and turned it on.

"Do you have this?"

She waved a hand in front of the lens.

"Hello to you, too," Bryce said. "We're live."

She lifted the medallion out from around her neck, held it up to the lens.

"This was in the Luna Temple, close to the Orb. I'm betting it's the key to reading the markings . . ."

"Do that again, slower this time if you would," Bryce said. "I'm recording."

She did as she was asked, showing him both sides of the medallion.

"What's that figure?" he asked as she ran the lens over the figure on the medallion's obverse side.

"The musician?" Lara frowned. "It could be Pan, I suppose, though the face isn't exactly—"

Bryce whispered something.

"Say again?" Lara asked.

"Music," he said, his voice suddenly full of life. "Sound! Brilliant!"

Lara thought she knew what he was driving at. "A tonal language?"

"Maybe. Or maybe not a language at all. Maybe musical tones."

"A song?"

"Maybe."

"Maybe, maybe, maybe," Lara said. "Find out."

"Will do," he said.

She said good-bye. Next to her, Terry was finishing a call of his own.

He put a hand over the phone. "Escape route," he mouthed to her, then returned to the call.

"If that's the only way, then set it up," he finished, and set down the receiver—harder than necessary, Lara thought.

"Problem?"

He shook his head. "No, no—piece of cake. Escape Plan A in place."

"All right then." She started for the escalator, taking out the GPS locator again. "Let's go find the good doctor."

FIFTEEN

Percent Surface Scanned Completed: .934
Time to Scan Completion: 0:18:42

Reiss studied the display and frowned, wishing he hadn't taken the stimulant cocktail in a sleep-deprived state. It was affecting his judgment, making him paranoid. The closer the computer came to finishing its task, the more anxious he became.

He expected to look up at any minute and see Lara Croft staring out at him from the clean room.

Ridiculous. She was half a continent away.

"The jet is ready."

He turned to see Sean standing in the doorway to the lab.

"I'll be there in a moment." Reiss didn't like leaving before the scan was finished, but the delay Chen Lo had caused by not delivering the Orb immediately had put them behind schedule. Duvalier had already called twice and the others would no doubt follow suit very shortly. He had calls to make, ruffled feathers to smooth, tasks best accomplished from his office aboard the Gulfstream.

He motioned Sean forward.

"Call me with the location of Pandora, as soon as you get it. Until then, make sure the Orb is never left unattended. Understood?"

"Understood."

Reiss left the room. Two of Sean's men fell into step beside him.

He stopped to check in with Holliday, regarding the delivery system they'd set up for Pandora. She had questions regarding containment of the virus once it had been disseminated.

Reiss smiled and reassured the woman that containment would not be an issue.

Still trailed by Sean's men, he passed from the lab into the security room. A bank of video monitors lined one wall, tied in to cameras strategically placed throughout the lab and the mall beyond.

Reiss's laboratory occupied all of sublevel eight beneath the skyscraper. He'd personally supervised its construction, paying off the architect and his employees—in a manner of speaking—in a way that insured its existence remained secret. Research facilities, manufacturing equipment, living quarters for almost two dozen associates—the space had provided all the doctor could have asked for over the last decade.

As this was more than likely the last time he would pass through its doors, Reiss took a final look around, courtesy of the monitors.

A nod then, to the guard on duty, and the main entrance to the lab—a massive steel door—slid open.

Reiss, followed by the two men Sean had assigned to accompany him, stepped through.

"Sure?" Terry asked.

"You keep asking that. And I keep telling you the same thing." Lara snapped the GPS display shut. "The Orb is here. Right here, in fact."

They were on sublevel eight—the bottom level of the

mall. According to the display, the transmitter was less than fifty feet away. Where, though . . .

That was the question.

There were no shoppers down here, no shops, either, just empty storefronts boarded over with plywood, painted with ads promising exciting new shops, coming soon. They'd passed an emergency exit to the parking garage, offices for a Korean real estate firm, a rest room with an *Out of Order* sign hung over it . . .

They'd tried every door—all were locked.

Lara was studying the ceiling, looking for an access panel when Terry grabbed her arm and pulled her behind a support column.

"What—"

"Shhh." He put a finger behind his lips and pointed.

Jonathan Reiss, followed by two of his guards, was walking directly toward them.

"He came from there," Terry whispered, nodding toward the real estate firm.

"Think he's buying real estate in Pyongyang?"

"Hardly."

Reiss and his men walked past, on their way to the elevator banks. A car came and Reiss and one of his men stepped inside. Just as the doors were closing, a young boy burst out of nowhere, ran to the elevator, and stuck his hand in between the closing doors.

The doors popped back open and the boy—followed by a harried-looking couple Lara took to be his parents—dodged inside the elevator.

Lara caught a glimpse of a very annoyed-looking Reiss and then the doors shut again, this time for good.

Lara's attention was on the other security man.

"Take him?" she asked Terry.

"Take him," he agreed, and as the guard walked back past, stepped out from behind the column.

Terry's knowledge of pressure points was truly amazing.

Approximately twenty seconds later, Reiss's man had supplied them with details of the lab's security system.

About a minute after that, Lara and Terry were inside, and their guide—as well as two guards who'd been manning the control center—lay unconscious at their feet.

The guards all wore wireless headsets. Lara took one for herself and another for Terry, adjusting the frequencies so they could communicate directly.

"Croft." She looked up to see him standing next to a wall of video monitors. "We've got problems."

She joined him and quickly grasped what he meant.

The monitors were apparently wired in to cameras scattered through Reiss's lab. It was huge—and very well manned.

"So much for easy . . ." Terry muttered.

But Lara's attention was elsewhere.

She had found the Orb.

Seeing it on one of the monitors, she heaved a sigh of relief. Watching Reiss leave before, she had feared he'd already finished with the Orb, and was on his way to Pandora. But there it was, in an isolation chamber of some sort—a clean room, perhaps—surrounded on all sides by floor-to-ceiling Plexiglas walls. Cradled in a pair of robotic hands some five feet off the ground, while a laser beam traveled slowly across its surface.

There was a display of some sort next to it: Lara used the controls on the monitor to zoom in on the image.

Percent Surface Scanned Completed: .939
Time to Scan Completion: 0:17:06

"I've got your back." That was Terry, leaning in over her shoulder. "Go."

Lara nodded and ran.

It took her a full minute to sneak past a secondary security post, four doors down the corridor.

Another minute wasted hiding in the shadows outside the canteen, while white-coated technicians paraded by her.

She doubled back, guided by instructions from Terry over her headset. Finally she found a side route that brought her to the main lab entrance.

She paused there a moment, hidden in an alcove. Beyond a double glass door, three technicians in full hazmat suits were gathered around a centrifuge.

Just past them, she caught a glimpse of the Orb.

"No good." Terry's voice came over her headset. "There are two guards on the other side of the corridor and a good dozen technicians between you and the Orb, as well."

"Take me 'round another way."

"There is no other way. You've got to get everyone out."

"What do you suggest, the fire alarm?"

The doors to the lab hissed open then and a technician walked out. Lara squeezed farther back into the alcove. It was a tight fit—behind her, a supply cart, lab instruments scattered on top of it, filled most of the available space.

Lara grabbed a knife from the cart and crouched down, prepared to attack if she was spotted.

She needn't have worried—the technician walked past her hiding place without once lifting his eyes from the clipboard in his hands. Not his hands, actually—he was wearing thick rubber gloves. Full hazmat gear, as well.

The entire lab, Lara realized with a start, was a hot zone.

Hence the glass walls, with biohazard symbols pasted all over them.

Lara looked up at those walls, down at the knife in her hand, and smiled.

"Hang on a minute," she whispered into the headset. "I've got an idea."

Seconds later, alarms were whooping throughout the complex.

As he stepped out of the elevator, Reiss's phone rang.

Duvalier, no doubt, the doctor guessed, glancing at his watch. Or one of the others—he was all of ten minutes late with the update he'd promised them. Well, they'd be happy enough once they heard his report, heard that they were hours away from having Pandora in their possession.

Suppressing a momentary flare of irritation, Reiss raised the receiver to his ear.

"Yes?"

But it wasn't Duvalier.

It wasn't any of the five.

It was the distinctive sound of the alarm in his lab below—and hearing it, Reiss froze where he stood.

Normally, that alarm meant the elaborate containment system he'd designed had failed, that somehow, one or more of the toxins he worked with had escaped into the atmosphere. Cause enough for concern.

But he feared that in this instance, it meant something far worse had happened.

"Croft," Reiss said through clenched teeth.

He whirled, in time to see the elevator doors closing just behind him.

Cursing, he ran for the escalators.

*   *   *

"Rats fleeing a sinking ship," Terry said into her ear. "Only two men left—both of them in the Orb room."

Lara nodded and slid the knife into her pocket. The puncture she'd made with it was a small one and had only breached the outer glass wall of the lab, but—as she'd suspected—had done the trick. Set off sirens, sent the technicians and the guards—none of whom, she guessed, were paid enough to stick around to see how dangerous the breach actually was—scurrying out the buildings' emergency exits.

She walked silently through the now open lab door, past the centrifuge, and into a room whose walls were lined with row after row of sleek, silver boxes. The new NECs, she realized. The Earth Simulators.

If Bryce was here, he'd think he'd died and gone to heaven.

"Sorry?" Terry asked.

"Nothing," Lara said, realizing she'd spoken aloud.

She wondered how Bryce was faring with his own translation of the Orb—whether or not he'd managed to figure out what the markings on the medallion meant. She wondered if the computing power she saw would allow Reiss to decipher the Orb without that key.

A flash of movement up ahead caught her eye.

"Terry?"

"Careful," he whispered. "One of them's on the move."

Lara walked on. There was a glass door at the far end of the computer room. Through it, she glimpsed the next—and final—chamber between her and the Orb. It looked like some sort of office, or meeting room. Desks and chairs, a long low counter at the back and—oddly enough—a mirrored ceiling. Through the glass door at its far end, Lara saw a man, standing on guard next to the Orb. She recognized him from the flower pagoda—he'd been with Reiss aboard the copter, before all hell had broken loose.

"I see him," she said. "Right next to the Orb."

"No," Terry shot back. "He's the one I've got."

"Where's the other?"

"Lost him," Terry said, frustration evident in his voice. "Sorry."

"Guesses?"

"He has to be in that next room over—the one you're making for."

"You can't tell?"

"There's no camera in there."

"Wonderful." Lara took a deep breath. "All right. I'm moving."

"Careful."

"You said that already."

She stepped toward the door and it slid open automatically.

Lara ducked down, and rolled forward, coming up behind the counter.

There was no sign of the second man. Perhaps he'd gone in another direction—or decided to run off with the others after all.

She paused a moment, considering how to best mount her assault on the Orb, and its sole remaining defender.

Which was when, of course, the man attacked.

Only the flash of the gun barrel in the window opposite her alerted Lara to her danger. She spun and saw him slipping out from behind the half-shut door of a storage closet, the noise of the still-blaring alarm covering the sound of the door creaking open, the rustle of the gun being drawn, the scuffing of his shoes on the floor as he stepped forward.

She continued her spin, turning it into a kick, catching him on the wrist even as he squeezed the trigger.

The gun went off and skittered across the floor.

He slammed her back against the counter with his left hand, grabbing her throat like a vise. Lara dropped her chin, easing the pressure. He punched at her face with his right fist, or tried to—she caught that arm with both hands and yanked forward, twisting him up and onto the counter.

She jumped to her feet—just as bullets began flying everywhere.

The other man was firing at her from the Orb room.

Lara reacted instinctively, lifting the man lying on the counter by the scruff of the neck, raising him in front of her like a human shield.

His body shook like a leaf in the wind as gunfire tore into him. He gurgled once and was silent.

Lara dropped him and dove to the floor.

"Bloody hell."

That was Terry.

"What?"

"Our trigger-happy friend hit something in the walls—some wire or something. I've just lost visual."

"Where?"

"Everywhere. All I've got is static."

"Wonderful."

"Stay put. I'm coming."

"No—stay where you are. Likely he's called for help. You can catch them as they come in."

A sound came to her then, over the alarm, and she paused. Metal on metal. It took a split second to recognize it—a clip, being slid out of a gun.

The man in the Orb room was reloading.

Lara drew her own gun and sprang.

The wall behind her exploded and she hit the ground again, pieces of the counter flying around her. She heard a thump and turned to see a lab technician—where had he come from?—sprawled in the doorway to the computer room.

The man in the Orb room had tricked her. He'd had a second gun—kept that trained on her while ejecting the clip from the first. Hoping to goad her into attacking. It had worked—she guessed the technician's appearance behind her had distracted the gunman just enough to save her life.

In any case . . .

This boy was clever.

"I'm glad," the gunman called out. "That would have been too easy."

Good God, Lara thought in disgust. *One of those.* Men who liked a challenge, particularly when the opponent was someone like her. She seemed to draw them like flies.

"Mmm."

Terry again.

"What?"

"My turn for a clever idea, I think," he said—and then the lights went out.

"Ah. Thanks."

"Sure. That ought to even things up a bit."

"Let's hope." Lara slid sideways along the back of the counter, making her way across the room. She heard the other man's footsteps heading toward her.

She stopped. He stopped.

Silence, except for the low humming from another row of computers along the wall next to her.

"I'm waiting, Lara!" the man called out. "Give me your best!"

She risked a peek. He was standing in the very center of the room, a machine pistol in each hand, spinning slowly.

Lara frowned. From where she crouched now, she didn't have a good shot. She'd have to risk moving, but there was little cover to her left, none to her right, and up ahead—

Up, she thought, and raised her gaze to the ceiling. The strangely mirrored ceiling, directly above her, and the gunman.

She took aim and fired over his head.

The ceiling shattered, splintering into massive, razor-sharp shards. The gunman was moving even as the first of those shards began to fall. He dove to the ground, rolled, and a split second later was back on his feet.

Nice reflexes, Lara thought, measuring the distance he'd traveled.

She fired over his head a second time.

He dove to the ground again, rolled in exactly the same fashion, and got to his feet once more.

Lara stood right in front of him.

"Careful what you wish for," she said, and clocked the man. His eyes rolled back in his head and he fell to the ground, unconscious.

Lara raced into the Orb room. Her eyes fell on the display.

Percent Surface Scanned Completed: .962
Time to Scan Completion: 0:08:25

She pictured Reiss, wherever he had gone, checking his watch, anxiously awaiting word of the Orb's translation.

"Sorry to disappoint, doctor," she whispered, pulling off her pack, "but the only person deciphering this particular key is going to be me."

"Missed that, Lara," Terry said into her ear. "Say again."

"I said I'm going offline," she told him. "Can you give me the lights again, please?"

"Ah. Roger. Hold on a minute."

The lights came back up. Lara slipped off her headset, then pulled the digicam out of her pack.

Fastening it around her neck, she flicked the cam on and pressed the transmit button.

"Crop circles," Bryce said. "There's your proof—what about crop circles?"

Hillary raised an eyebrow.

"Crop circles?"

"Like in Devonshire. Farmer goes to sleep, next day wakes up and his whole cornfield's been whittled into the shape of a cigar. Who do you think did that, hey?"

"You've been watching too many Hollywood movies," Hillary said.

"It was in the paper."

"The Tattler, I suppose."

Bryce glared. The two of them were in his trailer working. Or rather, he was working, and Hillary was giving him a hard time. Being very close-minded, Bryce thought. The evidence was right in front of the man—what didn't he understand?

Bryce was about to go at him again when the computer beeped. He spun in his chair, turning away from Hillary to face a bank of video monitors.

Right now, only a single screen was active. It showed a portion of the Orb's surface—one of the images that Lara had taken in the Luna Temple. The beeping indicated that the computer's analysis of the image was done.

"That's the last one, isn't it?"

Bryce looked up to find Hillary leaning over his shoulder.

"Yes, that's the last one," he said. He keyed in a series of commands and the image disappeared, to be replaced by a series of wave functions scrolling down the screen.

"Can we hear what it sounds like now?"

Bryce nodded and punched in another command.

A series of tones issued from the speakers at the far end of his workspace. Cacaphonous, distorted—it sounded to him like someone playing the vibraphone—with a cat instead of mallets.

"Ow." Hillary wriggled a finger in one ear. "And this is supposed to be the translation?"

"It's not made for our ears," Bryce said. "My guess is, these tones will activate the Orb."

"And what happens then?"

"I don't exactly know," Bryce admitted. "But here's my point."

He held up a printout of the Orb. "This thing is over two thousand years old? Where on Earth did the technology exist to make something like this?"

"India, apparently," Hillary said.

"Be serious."

"Perhaps Egypt."

"No." Bryce shook his head emphatically. "Nowhere on Earth. This Orb is not a product of human civilization. This—" he waved the picture in front of Hillary's face—"is alien technology."

Hillary still didn't look convinced.

Bryce was about to recount the evidence yet again when the monitors at his workstation came alive.

A woman's face stared up at them.

"Lara!" Bryce and Hillary shouted in unison.

"Gentlemen. Keeping busy?" Her voice—marred by a burst of static—came over the speakers.

"We are," Bryce said hurriedly. "Breaking the code, as it were." He started to tell Lara his theory about the source of the technology they were dealing with, but she listened for only a brief moment before stopping him.

"Bryce. All that is very interesting, but besides the point. You understood the medallion?"

"Yes. The markings are sound waves. We've translated all we could see on your images, roughly half the Orb—"

"Good work. Let's finish the set."

"You're in Reiss's lab?" Hillary asked.

"I am. Though the good doctor himself is absent at the moment. Still, he's been good enough to leave the Orb for me."

"Sporting of him," Hillary shot back. "Where's Sheridan?"

"Watching my back," Lara replied. "No comments, please."

"My lips are zipped," Hillary said. "However . . ."

Their conversation continued; Bryce focused his attention on the images coming over the monitor. Lara had turned the digicam forward, so he could see the lab as she walked through it. The facility was state-of-the-art, from what he could tell of the electronics. There was a Cooper-Janson relay box, a half-dozen Nystrom servers, and—

"Hey!"

The camera passed over a brushed metal machine, about the size of a small refrigerator.

"Is that an Earth Simulator?"

"Down, boy," Lara said. "I'll see if I can bring one home for you."

Bryce was about to ask if she was kidding when the image on the monitor jumped—Lara focusing the digicam—and suddenly, filling the screen in his trailer, was the Orb itself.

"Beautiful," he said, staring at the delicate silver etchings on its surface.

"I'll record the rest of the images, then send them to

208 · DAVE STERN

you," Lara said. "Once you have them—finish the translation and transmit the sounds back to me."

"Hi-res images, yes?" Bryce asked. He didn't want to be dependent on the quality of capture they got at this transmission speed.

"Of course."

Lara got started then.

This should do it, Terry thought, and flipped the switch.

For a second nothing happened. The wall of monitors before him remained unchanged—row after row of screens filled with only static.

Then, one by one, those screens came to life.

Terry smiled. Look at that—he'd managed to do something useful while he waited for Croft to scan the Orb. Found a control panel and rerouted the system video feed, bypassing the circuitry that had been shot up. He could monitor the lab again. A quick survey of the facility told him that Lara was still the only one—or rather the only one conscious—in the entire lab complex.

Standing around like this made him itchy—Terry wasn't used to being support staff while someone else waded into the fray. Even if that someone was Lara Croft. It was part of what had raised his hackles about the military, the idea of living his life as a little cog in some big wheel's plans. Not for him taking orders blindly—nor sitting behind a desk and giving them.

He wasn't down on Croft for waiting here—not that at all. It made sense for her to be the one going after the Orb. Though he still wasn't certain about this whole Pandora business—sounded more like something out of a fairy tale than a legitimate bioweapon. Still, Jonathan Reiss was involved, and Jonathan Reiss had a pretty legitimate reputation in some of the circles he'd traveled in.

He flicked a second switch now and brought the cameras out in the mall back on-line. The crowds were out in full force now—

Then he froze in place.

Reiss and another guard were running flat out for the lab entrance.

"Croft!" he shouted into his headset. "Lara!"

A split second later, he remembered. She'd taken off the headset to use her digicam. He had no way to warn her Reiss was coming.

This was bad.

SIXTEEN

This was worse than he'd expected.

Not only was the command post deserted, but the doctor couldn't reach Sean at all. Given the very, *very* specific instructions he'd left regarding the Orb, how important it was to keep it guarded at all times . . .

Reiss shuddered involuntarily and tried hard not to dwell on the implications. Of what he would do if, in fact, the Orb was not where he had left it. One thing was for certain—this was no ordinary containment breach, not a case of something toxic getting out of the lab but of something—someone—breaking in.

And that someone had to be Lara Croft.

The guard with him keyed open the main door and reached to shut down the alarm. Reiss put a hand on his arm.

"No," he said. "We don't want to let them know we're coming."

The man nodded and stepped forward into the security room. At the all-clear sign, Reiss drew his gun and made to follow.

Suddenly he stopped and looked around.

The doctor had the strangest feeling someone was watching him.

Crouched in the shadows opposite the main door, Terry hesitated.

He had a shot at Reiss. Not a good one—the angle was bad, a filing cabinet near the door blocked most of the doctor's body—but Terry had made a career of taking hard shots.

Killing Reiss would end this whole thing. Pandora would never be found.

Terry hesitated.

Reiss walked through the door, and out of sight.

Lara came around the front of the Orb, stepping over Reiss's man, still out cold on the floor. She was somewhat surprised he was still unconscious—she hadn't hit him that hard, had she?

"There," Bryce said in her ear, and Lara stopped where she stood and focused the digicam on the Orb's surface.

"Excellent. This is the last one we need," Bryce said.

"All right, then." Lara clicked the capture button and heard the whir of the Panasonic writing to the flash card. "We're done."

"Not until you send me the images," Bryce said, and Lara was just about to pull the flash card out of the digicam when she heard a faint, just barely audible noise coming from behind her.

Her eyes darted around the room and came to rest on the Orb. And the reflection she saw in it.

Reiss.

She pocketed the camera assembly and, in one smooth move, drew her gun.

The doctor—and there was another man who'd entered with him, she saw now—dove behind the long counter at the rear of the lab.

Needlessly, as Lara hadn't intended on shooting them.

Instead, she turned to the NEC mapping the Orb and fired.

"NO!" Reiss screamed and charged, but she was already taking out the second NEC, which left only one, and she turned to blast that—

And a shadow passed over her.

The gun flew from her hand.

Someone took hold of the back of her head and slammed her face first into the desk in front of her. Lara's head rang and she tasted blood.

She felt a gun at her throat and at the same instant, her right arm being yanked up behind her back.

"I've had your best, Lara," a voice whispered in her ear. "Now I'm looking forward to giving you mine."

Reiss's man—the one she'd coldcocked before. So he'd been playing possum after all.

"That was hardly my best," she said. "Lackeys don't get my best."

He yanked hard on her arm and Lara grunted in pain.

This one could be rattled. She filed that information away in her mind and as she did so, a question that had been tumbling around in the back of her head marched front and center.

Where was Terry? And how had Reiss managed to get past him?

The doctor leaned over her and brought his face close to hers.

"Lady Croft. Lara. We meet in person, at last. Needless to say, you've already made quite an impression on me."

"Charmed, I'm sure," Lara said.

"I doubt it, but it's nice of you to say so. And I see you and Sean here have had a chance to get acquainted, as well. Wonderful."

"The pleasure's been all mine," the man holding her down—Sean—said. "Too bad it's going to be ending so soon."

The gun barrel pressing on her at her neck disappeared then, and Lara felt the point of a knife on her throat.

"Ah," Reiss said. "Not just yet, Sean. Not until we're sure the NEC here has done its job, and that we will have no further need of Lady Croft's expertise."

Lara turned her head and looked at the monitor.

Percent Surface Scanned Completed: .976
Time to Scan Completion: 0:04:13

Less than five minutes and Reiss would have Pandora's location.

She couldn't allow that to happen.

She had to do something—stall for time, hope that Terry would arrive, hope that Bryce and Hillary could get MI6 to their location . . . talk Reiss's ear off, perhaps?

"I'm curious, doctor," she said. "How does a man go from Nobel Prize winner to terrorist?"

"Terrorist? Please, Lara—I'd ask you not to use that word. It conjures up some very unfortunate images. Lice-ridden, religious fanatics in dirty robes—ugh." Reiss shuddered. "I remain what I have always been—a scientist, working for the greater good of humanity."

"I'd be very interested in hearing how Pandora ties into that vision, doctor."

"I should think that obvious," Reiss said. "Pandora is—"

Reiss's phone rang.

"Excuse me a moment." He flipped open the sat phone. "Jonathan Reiss. Ah. Madame Gillespie. Yes. I appreciate your concern, but we are now back on schedule. I'll have the item for you by the close of business tomorrow."

Lara stretched her neck, trying to see past Reiss to the monitor, to gauge how much longer she had.

Sean slammed her head back down on the table.

"It's not going to be pleasant, Lara." He leaned closer. "I can promise you that."

"And it's been such fun so far," Lara said.

Reiss finished his call and put the phone back in his pocket.

"That's all of them, isn't it?" Sean asked.

"Yes it is. Madame Gillespie was the last." He crooked a finger at the man he'd entered the lab with and pointed him toward a row of display screens on the other side of the room. "Check the network computers, if you would. I'd like to confirm the financials."

"You were saying," Lara prompted. "About Pandora."

"Yes. Pandora." Reiss folded his hands behind his back and began pacing. "In a way, it's been my lifelong inspiration. You see, when I was seven we moved to Calcutta. Filthy place. It was there I heard the local legend of a box that purged Alexander of half his army. I filed it away in the back of my mind."

"Planning ahead?"

"Hardly." The doctor laughed. "I just thought it fascinating—ironic—that a tiny germ, invisible to the naked eye, could succeed where the armies of the world had failed. That a disease could defeat Alexander the Great."

"Pandora isn't a disease," Lara said sharply.

"No," Reiss agreed. "Pandora is something altogether different. But I didn't know that then, did I? In any case—" he shrugged "—the story of that box started me thinking. About the function of disease—how in nature, it acts as a curb, a balance if you will, on the too-rampant spread of life. The ultimate predator. Certainly the only one that man still fears." He looked her in the eye. "I'm not boring you with all this, am I?"

"Not at all. It's rare I get a close-up glimpse of such depravity."

"And here I thought I was making your last few moments on earth pleasant ones."

"I'm sorry to disappoint you." Lara shook her head. "You really believe you'll be able to control what's in the box. Make it another of your weapons?"

Reiss stared at her a moment and shook his head.

"Really, Lara. Now you do disappoint me."

She frowned, suddenly lost. What on earth was Reiss driving at?

"Excuse me, sir." The doctor's man—the one he'd sent to check on the network—had returned.

"Go on," Reiss said. "Have we received payment from all the buyers?"

"Just confirmed, sir. As you can see on the monitor."

Reiss's gaze went to one of the display screens on the far wall. Lara's followed. The screen showed a map of the world, with five blinking green lights—one on each of the major continents. Lara supposed those lights represented Reiss's buyers. So despite his crack about terrorists—Reiss's clientele spanned the globe. And so would Pandora, once it was released. If the legends were true, it would indeed act like the ultimate predator Reiss had referred to. There would be no stopping it.

A sudden chill went down her spine.

"You don't want to control it," she said.

Reiss turned to her and smiled. "Ah. Well done."

"You're using the buyers . . . they release what you give them, thinking it's just another weapon . . . and the world blames them for what happens."

"What's *left* of the world blames them." Reiss moved closer to her. "Politics bore me. One side killing another over some god or some resource like oil. Trivial compared to the real challenge we, as a species, face. Look around and you'll see it, Lara. The human race is growing weak. As a species, we are failing."

His eyes glinted and Lara found herself wondering when the change had happened, when the Nobel Prize winner had become a madman.

"I grew up on a farm," Reiss continued. "On a farm, when the herd is at risk from disease or has simply grown too fat and frail for its own good, you thin the herd. That's what the box is for. To weed out our weak, our feeble. Those races which would have expired but for our ludicrous notion that all men are created equal—that we should help our weaker members to survive. Every organism has a state of balance. Mankind is out of ours. Properly thinned, we'll evolve and grow."

Sean's grip eased for a moment. Lara was able to twist her head just enough to see the other monitor again—the one displaying the laser's progress.

Percent Surface Scanned Completed: .994
Time to Scan Completion: 0:00:41

"You're insane. To think you can control something like Pandora."

"Not at all. Once I have it in my grasp—before I open the box—I'll make enough antiserum to spare the best and brightest. Heads of corporations, heads of state. Life will go on."

Reiss leaned closer.

"Are you telling me you haven't looked around and thought, the world would be better off without some of these people? Come now, Lara—the truth."

Lara looked up at him. "Well, I can think of a few I could do without."

A soft chime sounded.

Lara looked up at the monitor again.

Scan complete
Translation in progress

Reiss stood up. She heard footsteps—lots of them—entering the room. Reinforcements.

Which perhaps explained what had happened to Terry.

"I'm sorry to kill you, Lara. You would have been welcome in my world." He turned to the man who'd delivered the news about the financials.

"Take no chances. Shoot her right between the eyes."

"Damn," Sean whispered in her ear. "Looks like we aren't going to get to play after all."

He lifted Lara roughly to her feet and pinned her in front of him, his grip so tight that she couldn't begin to think of moving.

The man before them raised his weapon and pressed his gun right up to her forehead.

The barrel was cool against her skin.

Lara tensed and waited for the click of the trigger.

SEVENTEEN

A gun fired.

The guard toppled over backward and fell to the floor, crimson spreading across his chest.

A gun went off again and a bullet whizzed just past her shoulder, and Sean let go of her and dove, for the floor. Reiss dove, too, and it was only then that Lara realized what was happening.

The cavalry had just arrived.

Terry—somewhere up ahead, hidden in the shadows, in perfect sniper position. He'd gunned down Lara's would-be killer before that man could shoot her and was now spraying covering fire all over the room, pinning down Sean and Reiss and what looked to be a half-dozen newcomers, as well, providing Lara with a chance to escape. Which she fully intended to take advantage of—once she'd attended to two minor details.

Number one, Reiss's translation of the Orb.

She snatched her gun off the floor and shot out the last NEC.

Reiss roared out a series of curses totally out of character with the polished, urbane image he'd been so careful to project.

Lara somersaulted clear across the room and snatched detail number two—the Orb itself—out of its robotic cradle. She placed it carefully into her backpack.

"Good luck with the farm animals," she shouted to Reiss and turned to run.

One of the newcomers popped up from behind the desk in front of her and took aim.

She dodged and a bullet took him square in the shoulder—courtesy of the unseen Mr. Sheridan.

Lara jumped over the man's body and ran back the way she had come.

Two rooms down, she saw half a dozen more reinforcements heading straight toward her.

No good, she thought, and turned to her left. There was another glass wall directly in front of her.

She charged at it full speed, and at the last possible second, fired at it.

The wall exploded and she ran straight through.

A second wall loomed before her, and then a third, and she did the same thing—shot them out and ran through. Turning around, she saw Terry backpedaling right along with her, laying down covering fire as he ran.

"I was beginning to think you weren't coming!" Lara called out.

"Would I forget about you, Croft?" he shouted back.

Lara was about to respond when she looked up and saw a final glass wall straight ahead—final because just beyond it she could glimpse the mall concourse itself, sublevel eight, and directly ahead of them, the elevator bank.

She raised her gun as she ran, intending to blast away that last wall.

Click. Out of bullets.

Terry was catching up to her, still firing. Reiss's men were getting closer. Bullets ricocheted off the floor and zinged past.

Lara didn't slow down for a second.

She shouted out a war cry and jumped straight for the

wall, covering her face with her arms, aware that if she'd mis-
judged her companion, something very, very embarrassing
was about to happen.

But she hadn't.

Terry blew out the glass a split second before she smashed
into it.

Lara went sailing through the air and landed on the tiled
floor of the mall beyond.

A second later, Terry was running right along with her.

"The elevators!" he shouted, pointing straight ahead.

Lara shot him a glance. Elevators did not sound like the
best plan to her.

"Trust me," Terry said, seeing her look. "Escape Plan A."

They dashed into a waiting car. At that exact moment,
Reiss's man Sean—followed by at least half a dozen guards—
raced out of the lab's main entrance.

Terry hit the button for the top floor.

"A hundred and ten?" Lara couldn't keep the uncertainty
from her voice.

"Trust me," Terry repeated.

She shrugged. Not as if she had much choice.

Terry opened the elevator panel and pulled the emergency button. Smart, Lara thought. Now the car wouldn't
stop anywhere else. They were on an express route to . . .

Well, wherever.

The doors began to close. Sean and his men were running
full out toward them.

But they'd never make it.

Lara waved good-bye.

Inches away from shutting, a little hand poked in between the elevator doors and they popped open again.

Lara looked down at a little Chinese boy—the same boy,
she realized, who'd scooted aboard Reiss's elevator earlier.

"Kay-bee," the boy asked. "Toys 'R' Us?"

Lara looked up and saw Sean, twenty feet away.

She pushed the little boy firmly out the door.

"Not this car, sonny," she said.

Terry slammed the door close button and the car rose upward. It—like the walls of Reiss's lab, like the walls of the skyscraper housing the mall—was made of glass, giving them an incredible view of first the New Century mall, and then Hong Kong itself, as they rose up along the side of the skyscraper.

Lara looked down and touched Terry's elbow.

"Look," she said.

Two other elevators were rising right along with them. Each filled with Reiss's men.

"You know we're not going to be able to get back down," she said. "They'll have men covering the stairwells."

"We'll get down," Terry said. "Don't worry."

The car pinged to a stop then and the doors slid open. Terry raced out, Lara a step behind.

"There." He pointed to a staircase labeled in Mandarin, Portugese, and English: *Rooftop Access.*

He shot out the knob, and they jogged up a small flight of stairs onto the roof itself.

The naked sunshine, after so much dim, artificial light, was dazzling.

The rooftop was empty.

Terry spun about wildly.

"This is Escape Plan A then, is it?" Lara asked, folding her arms across her chest.

"Yes."

"What about B? Is there a B?"

"No," he snapped. "No Plan B."

Lara opened her pack. She was going to have to destroy

222 · DAVE STERN

the Orb. A fall of one-hundred-ten stories, she judged, ought to do it.

Perhaps she would accompany the object on the way down. That would be a relatively quick, relatively painless way to go. As opposed to what Reiss—and in particular, Sean—might have in mind for her.

"Ah."

She looked up and saw Terry running for the edge of the roof. Seconds later, he'd dragged two backpacks out from underneath the ledge and begun pulling out swaths of colored nylon from within one of them.

Lara smiled. "Parachutes."

"Not exactly." Terry tossed her one of the packs. "Something a tad faster."

She began to pull out the contents of the pack and soon saw what he meant.

Reiss paced back and forth in the lab, willing himself to remain calm.

"Excuse me, sir."

He looked up and saw Holliday, knelt over the last of the NECs Croft had shot out. She was shaking her head.

"I'm afraid the data is compromised. It will take approximately eighteen hours to reconstruct."

Reiss shut his eyes a moment. This was not happening. He'd been within seconds of Pandora's location. Now Croft was going to beat him to it.

"Croft," he said, opening his eyes.

"Sir?" Holliday asked.

He drew his pistol and shot her.

"If you'd stayed in position," he said, standing over her corpse, "instead of running, perhaps this wouldn't have happened."

He dropped the gun to the floor then, as angry with himself as anyone. This was his fault, for not shooting Croft himself when he had her helpless. Never again.

His phone rang.

"Team A in position." It was Sean. "Teams B and C are flanking."

"English please," Reiss said. "I'm in no mood for paramilitary acronyms."

"We're ready to storm the roof. We have the stairwells leading down blocked and surrounding rooftops manned, as well."

"Excellent. Proceed—but Sean."

"Yes, doctor?"

"The Orb is paramount. Croft and Sheridan are secondary."

"Yes sir. Understood. The pack is our target."

"Good work. Notify me when you have it."

Reiss snapped the phone shut.

The guards in the room shifted position and eyed him nervously.

"What do we have to reach?" Lara asked.

She and Terry stood on the roof ledge, looking out over Hong Kong, back toward the mainland.

"That ship." Terry pointed due west of the Kowloon harbor. Lara was barely able to pick out a spec on the horizon.

"Great," Lara said—and at that second, the door to the rooftop behind them burst open.

Sean and his men stepped out, rifles raised.

"Hands up!" he shouted. "Throw down the pack, Croft. And I'll make it quick."

"That's sweet of you!" She looked down and saw more of Reiss's men coming into firing range, on the roofs of the buildings nearby.

This was going to be harder than it looked.

"Backup plan?" she asked Terry.

"Stand here and get killed." He smiled. "Why? Losing your nerve?"

"Please." She adjusted the straps on her pack then, cinching them as tight as possible. Nylon—the jumpsuits she and Terry had donned over their clothes—bunched beneath the cloth as she fastened it securely.

"Last chance, Croft! Drop the pack."

Lara turned.

"Say hello to Reiss for me," she said, and jumped out into space.

Terry was right alongside her. They dropped twenty stories in a heartbeat.

Then she spread her arms and the webwings woven into her suit caught the air.

Gliding high above the city streets, she and Terry sailed toward the harbor, the Orb secure in her pack, whatever curses Sean was shouting after her lost in the swirling winds above Hong Kong.

Reiss did not kill anyone else.

Neither did he curse, or stamp his feet, or smash things.

He simply waited in silence for Sean's return, for an explanation of Croft's escape. When he heard it, he laughed.

"Jumpsuits—with wings?" Reiss had to chuckle again. Had to, because the alternative was simply to give up, and he refused to do that.

He had won the Nobel Prize twenty years ago, fresh out of university. He had evaded the intelligence agencies of every country in the world for the last decade—evaded with ease, and impunity. He was not going to have his plans thwarted by some dilettante of an archaeologist and her steroid-enhanced paramour.

He strode past Sean, surveying the wreckage of the lab. Guards gave way as he walked, his brow furrowed in concentration. Was there anything salvageable here? No. Croft had seen to that. She had been very thorough in her destruction of all the data relating to the Orb. And yet . . .

Destruction was not all she'd been intent on. Or she would have shot out the last Earth Simulator long before he'd arrived.

So what else had she been doing?

He cast his mind back in time and pictured Croft, standing next to the Orb, as she'd been when he first entered the lab.

She'd been wearing an earpiece of some sort.

Reiss walked to where the Orb had been and bent low, rummaging among the wreckage on the floor.

A second later, he rose to his feet.

"Sean. Have the field team assemble at the airfield."

"Where are we going?"

Reiss held up the object he'd found in the rubble. It appeared to be a digital camera of some sort—with a transceiver built right into it. A transceiver whose signal, he realized, could be traced back to its point of origin.

"Our destination?" He smiled. "Why, Lady Croft is going to tell us that."

EIGHTEEN

Terry and the ship's captain were arguing details of their passage in the hallway. Lara couldn't hear all of it—and her Tagalog was not up to snuff—but the conversation had something to do with money, of that she was certain. From Terry's tone of voice, the captain apparently wanted more.

She was inclined to tell Terry to pay it. The cabin they'd been given was surprisingly spacious and comfortable-looking, considering the condition of the freighter that housed it. Twin beds, clean sheets, and in an adjoining bathroom . . .

A shower. Hallelujah.

Lara turned the knobs and was even more pleased to discover actual hot water.

She returned to the main cabin area and found Terry juggling the Orb in his hands like a soccer ball.

"So . . . this rock is the map."

He didn't seem at all concerned about her finding him with it.

"That's right," Lara said.

"I've never seen anything like it, have you?" He held the Orb out at arm's length and studied it. "It's quite beautiful, actually."

"Yes, it is." Lara moved to take it—and Terry stepped back, keeping it just out of her reach.

"And it's the only way to find that box?"

"Pandora? Yes, that's correct."

They exchanged smiles.

"Just think," Lara said. "You could tuck it under your arm and go right out the door."

"Window's better, actually. Off the ship faster. Harder to track."

He kept grinning. Lara felt the smile on her face begin to waver.

She wondered if he was serious.

Terry set the Orb back down on the bed and laughed.

"Would I do a thing like that to you, Croft?"

That was the question, wasn't it?

Terry set about unpacking what little he had—his gun, a few spare clips. Lara put the Orb back in her pack.

"I'm going to take a shower," she announced, and took out a spare set of clothes. Then she changed her mind.

She took the entire backpack with her into the bathroom and shut the door.

She scrubbed every inch of her body clean and let the hot water pound against the sore muscles in her back until her skin was numb.

When she finally emerged from the bathroom, dressed in a silk wrap, Terry had fallen asleep completely undressed on one of the beds.

She went to the window and stared out at the ocean.

They were well out to sea now—far from Reiss, and any of his men. The Orb was safe—which meant Pandora was safe. She still needed to transmit Bryce the rest of the images, but that could wait. The clock had stopped ticking.

So why was Lara still worried?

A memory tugged at the back of her mind.

But before she could dredge it to the surface, a creaking noise from behind made her turn around.

Terry had risen from the bed and was coming straight toward her.

She looked over his shoulder and saw the pack safe on her bed, where she had dropped it after coming out of the shower.

Then she saw the expression on his face and knew what he wanted. Not the Orb.

Her.

He came forward and reached out to take her in his arms.

Lara grabbed hold of one of his wrists with both hands.

"Don't," she said.

"Break it, if you want," Terry told her. "I'm still going to kiss you."

And he did.

She let it happen—a long, slow, lingering kiss that for a moment made her forget about everything—the Orb, Reiss, Pandora. She dropped his wrist and relaxed in his arms.

They fell over onto one of the bunks, Terry on top.

"Shall I kick you on your arse now, or later?" Lara asked. "Never mind, I'll do it twice," she said, and rolled him over so she was on top.

Terry laughed and tried to push her over again. She resisted—they both laughed then, and looked into each other's eyes.

And at that second, the memory that had been nagging at her surfaced.

"What's wrong?" he asked.

Lara didn't answer—she leaned over and kissed him again, passionately, hungrily—one hand reaching into the front pocket of her pack as she did so.

Click.

Terry looked up at her in surprise. "What?"

She stood up and Terry pulled feebly on the cuffs she'd shackled him to the bed with.

After a second, he gave up, and smiled at her.

"This isn't exactly what I had in mind, but—"

"Why didn't you shoot Reiss?" Lara snapped. "He must have walked right past you in the lab."

"I didn't have a clear shot," Terry said. "And I had no idea where you were."

Lara looked into his eyes and knew he was lying.

"I'll inform MI6 you've completed your service. You'll get your money and your life. Don't waste it."

Terry laughed in disbelief.

"Now is no time to be splitting up, Croft—"

"You're wrong," she said savagely. "Now is exactly the time—before you're in a position where you make the wrong decision."

His face twisted in anger.

"You want to leave, go ahead, but don't pretend it's to save me. You're afraid. Afraid you might not be able to pull the trigger. Afraid of letting your guard down, letting anyone in—"

"I'm not leaving because I couldn't kill you, Terry. I'm leaving because I could."

He stared at her.

"And if you're wrong about me, Croft? What about that?"

Lara shook her head.

"I'm not wrong, Terry. You know it, and I know it."

She slipped on her clothes and collected her things, pausing at the door.

"Good-bye, Terry."

He gave her one last smile. "This isn't good-bye, Croft."

But she hoped, for both their sakes, that it was.

*   *   *

The freighter they'd landed on had two Zodiac speedboats strapped to the hull. Lara had seen them when they'd glided down to the deck.

She paid (overpaid) the captain for one, outlining Terry's history of abusive behavior and begging him for the chance to escape. She didn't know if he believed her or not—the important thing was that he let her go. She headed due east with the Zodiac. Taipei, she decided. Not only did she have friends there, but the political climate was favorable—MI6 would have no problem picking her up, should that become necessary.

She arrived within sight of the harbor by early morning, still bone-tired, having been limited to the occasional thirty-minute catnap at the wheel of the Zodiac. Coffee, she thought, and then communications. She would have good reception here for the sat—she could get the rest of the images to Bryce, have him send her the translation and be on her way to Pandora by midmorning. Well in advance of Reiss, even assuming he could somehow piece together the data she'd destroyed and translate it.

Even this early in the morning, the harbor was busy. Lara had to join a queue of ships trying to make their way down the single narrow channel to the docks ahead.

Glancing off to her right, she spied an antiquated Chinese junk—with a very modern-looking set of communications aerials.

Worth a try, she decided, and pulled out of the queue. She came up alongside the boat and tied off onto a gang wire next to it.

An elderly couple and two children were just sitting down to their breakfast when she rapped on their door.

"Good morning," she said, bowing. "Might I borrow your television? It's important."

The old man looked at her in confusion. The youngest child—a girl—smiled.

"This way," she said, grabbing Lara by the arm and tugging her forward.

Not only did Lara get the television, she got breakfast. Duck's eggs instead of the scones she'd been anticipating, tea instead of coffee, but a much-needed pick-me-up all the same.

She repaid the elderly couple's kindness by ripping apart their television set.

"I'll put it all back together once I'm done, I promise," she assured them in her best Mandarin, but they only looked on with mild curiosity as she went about her business. Combining components from her cell, their television, and the digital camera to put together a makeshift wireless video conferencing facility.

It took the better part of an hour to put the pieces together.

Then she set the Orb down on top of the television, and dialed up the manor.

To her surprise it was Bryce, rather than Hillary, who answered.

"Lara."

His image filled the screen—behind her, Lara was aware of the elderly couple hugging their children closer. He looked terrible—haggard, as if he hadn't slept all night.

"He's a fright, all right," she said without turning around. "But he is a friend of mine."

Bryce leaned closer. "Where are you?"

"Never mind that," she said. "I want to send through the captures from Reiss's lab. Are you ready?"

"In a second." Bryce leaned out of the picture a moment. Then he was back. "Ready."

"All right," Lara said. "Sending the last images of the Orb . . . now."

She'd already slid the photo chip into her phone—now she pressed the send button and the air filled with the squeal of the electronics handshaking and then the data being transmitted.

"Got them," Bryce said.

"Translate them."

"Already on it," he said, swiveling around in his chair to study a display screen behind him. The resolution on her end was well below snuff—she could vaguely make out lines of data scrolling by on the monitor.

"Done."

Lara repositioned the Orb on top of the television slightly, so that the speaker from her cell was as close to it as possible.

Then she stood back and nodded to Bryce.

"All right. Send the sounds."

"Hang on. I'll verify the data."

"Bryce." She shook her head. He knew her better than that. "No. Send the sounds, please."

"All right. Sending . . . now."

For a moment, nothing. Then a series of tones began issuing from the speaker. A simple melody at first, then a flood of noise, sometimes harmonic, sometimes utterly discordant. There was a curious, muted quality to some of the notes, as if they were coming from underwater.

Lara had no idea what was supposed to happen next—but after a minute of listening, and watching the Orb intently without anything on its surface changing, she knew something was off.

"Nothing," she said.

"Back to the drawing board," Bryce said quickly.

Lara shook her head. "Play them again."

Bryce sighed and did as she asked.

"Hang on," she said, half a minute into the playback.

"What?"

It was that muted quality to some of the tones; it had bothered her the first time through and now she knew why.

"The tones are being distorted."

Bryce frowned. "I don't think—"

"There's a phase shift," she realized. "Because of the phone line. The pitch is wrong!"

She looked up at Bryce, expecting to see the light of discovery in her eyes reflected in his.

Instead, she saw only disappointment.

"Bryce?" She frowned. "Are you all right?"

"Fine. I just don't see it, is all."

Lara tried again. "Have you ever listened to your voice on a tape recorder? It's the same thing."

"Maybe," Bryce said.

"Maybe nothing." Lara frowned.

"So what do you want to do?"

She thought a moment. "Send me the raw data."

"I could try to compensate on this end," Bryce said. "Send the tones again."

"No. The sounds came through this speaker distorted. So either send me the file or I'll bring back the bloody Orb to the manor."

"Sending it," Bryce said.

"To be honest, I'm surprised you missed that."

"Sorry," he said, looking anything but. He really did look terrible—not that she would ever say such a thing out loud, but perhaps she had been riding him too hard.

When this was over, she would send him on a long, long vacation. With one of those NECs she'd promised him for company.

A soft beeping announced that the file had arrived in her in-box. She picked the phone off the television and used its keypad to first open the file, and then set the tones to play.

Halfway through the playback, Lara realized that in using the phone to open the data, she'd accidentally bumped the Orb to one side, moving it farther from the speaker.

She reached out to push the two closer together—

—and as her fingers touched the Orb, the world around her suddenly changed.

It was as if the Orb was a movie projector, and the ship around her the projection screen. White light blanketed every surface, turning the junk, the elderly couple, the television into a blank screen.

And then that screen exploded with images. A jumble of them, rushing past Lara so quickly they barely registered. An endless black sky, a flash of light, an explosion—

The horror-stricken face of a young girl and then the crinkled face of a dark-skinned, elderly man.

The lid of a box, snapping shut.

A village of primitive-looking people, falling dead at her feet, their faces swollen and black with disease.

Warriors, wearing armor plates, carrying short swords falling, as well.

Darkness again, and then—

She was standing in the middle of a vast grassy plain. African savannah, she realized, but how—

She looked down at the Orb in her hands and tried to reason out what was happening. The tones had activated some kind of image projector, that was clear, but it was ungodly realistic, holographic in detail—technology so far beyond the capability of twenty-first-century civilization as to seem the stuff of science fiction.

And yet . . . the Orb was two thousand years old. So how on earth had Alexander and the astrologers who passed for his "scientists" managed to do this?

My father told me a story once.

She recalled her words to Calloway and Stevens, in the library back at Croft Manor.

In 2300 B.C., an Egyptian pharoah found a place he named the cradle of life; where we, life, began. There he found a box. The box which brought life to earth.

It was the only possible explanation. Bryce was right, after all.

The Orb in her hands, Pandora itself . . .

They were not of this world.

She tried to step forward then, to see how far the illusion extended, but her feet refused to move. Part of the illusion, as well?

She moved the Orb, then, trying to disrupt the projection.

Instead, the world around her slipped, as if she was actually tilting it with her hands.

She continued to turn the Orb, bringing it around a full rotation. Images slid past—hundreds of flamingos basking on a lakeshore, a herd of elephants trampling the savannah, impossibly green, impossibly leafy patches of jungle, filled with the chattering of a million creatures—one overlapping the other, moving faster and faster.

Lara suddenly realized she was moving through the projected space—it was almost as if she was strapped to the front of an impossibly fast train, hurtling through the African countryside.

And the second she realized that, she realized something else, as well.

The Orb was in control here, not her.

And the Orb had a definite destination in mind.

The savannah flew past. Drifting by her on her right, she saw the snow-capped peaks of Kilimanjaro. She was in Tanzania then—near that country's border with Kenya. A few hundred miles south of Nairobi.

A few hundred miles south of Kosa.

She remembered talking to him as he walked through the halls of the British Embassy—a conversation about the shadow warrior on the floor of the Luna Temple, and the seemingly incongruous inscriptions within written in Ol Maa.

Seemingly incongruous no longer.

She set that knowledge aside, as another mountain appeared, this time directly in front of her. Shrouded in gray clouds, its summit came not to a peak, like Kilimanjaro, but rather ended in a cone. A volcano? She didn't recognize it specifically, but from what she recalled of the geology of this part of Africa, there were a number of active volcanoes in this area.

The savannah came to an abrupt end, became desert. She saw no vegetation, no signs of life anywhere. She drove toward the mountain's summit, up a winding path through a barren, rocky canyon, past strange conical-shaped rock formations.

They reminded her, she realized, of the cone the Orb had rested on within the Luna Temple.

The images slowed. Lara sensed her journey had come to an end.

She stood before one of the cone-shaped formations—bigger than the others she had passed before. And black—a deep, midnight ebony exactly like the cone in the temple.

It exuded a palpable sense of menace.

Pandora, she thought. *It's right here.*

But where was she?

Lara began to turn the Orb in her hands, trying to get a better sense of her location.

A shadow fell upon her then and touched the Orb.

She heard something behind her—a low, rumbling sound, like the sound of lava bubbling in a volcano, only almost musical. Like something alive.

Suddenly the fact that she couldn't move, couldn't turn her body even an inch while holding the Orb, was no longer a curiousity.

It was downright scary.

The shadow covered her entirely.

The sound grew louder.

Out of the corner of her eye, Lara saw movement.

Move the Orb, she thought. Then you'll see it. But she didn't want to see it. She wanted to run.

Too late, though. It was upon her.

Bryce actually thought Lara was going to scream.

He had never seen her so scared before—scared at all, for that matter, and he'd seen her in a lot of fairly terrifying situations. Like that time with Gunderson and the Mai Tufari in Chango, or the ants in that Purepecha tomb in Tzintzantzun—she'd been cool as ice then. Cracking jokes, while he'd been sweating bullets. And he'd certainly never seen her actually turn white before.

Something quite extraordinary had obviously happened.

All at once, she let go of the Orb and staggered backward.

"Lara? Are you all right?"

She looked straight at the camera lens. Bryce had her, head-and-shoulders view, on the main console monitor.

"Africa. It's in Africa! Somewhere past Kilimanjaro!"

"Pandora?"

"Yes, Pandora. Of course Pandora."

Bryce sighed.

He wished she hadn't told him that.

"That's great, Lara," he said, in what he hoped was a convincingly enthusiastic tone.

"I'm half a day away. How long will it take Reiss to put his computers back together? He's mapped the Orb completely—he might be able to get Pandora's location, as well."

For a number of reasons, Bryce wasn't sure how to respond to that.

"Hmm. Err. Twenty-four hours at the fastest, I'd say."

She looked down at her watch and nodded.

"Then that's what we'll assume. Get in touch with Kosa. Tell him to pick up my car and meet me north of his village."

She cut the line then and the screen went dark.

Sean, who'd been leaning over the console, gun pointed directly at Bryce's head during the entire conversation, shook his head and smiled.

"Bit faster than twenty-four hours, I'd say."

"Indeed. I should expect we'll be in Africa before Lady Croft. Though we'll to wait for her to lead us to Pandora." Reiss, who'd been hanging back in the trailer entrance, turned to one of the guards standing over Hillary (who had remained silent throughout Lara's call, pressing an icepack to the large black-and-blue mark on his forehead), and spoke. "Tell Mr. Garner to have the Gulfstream fueled and ready to leave within the hour."

The man nodded and left the trailer.

The doctor turned back to Bryce.

"Now all we need is for you to call this Kosa fellow— whoever he is—and arrange for him to pick up Lady Croft. We don't want her aware that anything is out of the ordinary. Do we?"

Bryce sighed. What could he do? From the moment Reiss and his entourage had arrived at the manor in the middle of the night, they'd shown a willingness to use force to get what they wanted.

Hence, the ruins of his copter simulator in the manor's control room.

And the bruise on Hillary's face.

It was all his fault, anyway, Bryce decided, for having constructed the digicam in such a way that the transceiver signal could be traced back to its source. Bad design. The next revision would incorporate a completely different architecture.

Assuming, that is, he got the chance to build it.

He looked over at Hillary, then at Reiss.

"All right," he said. "I'll make the call."

Terry had a nasty cut on his wrist.

He was going to have to get it attended to soon, although he was certainly better off than Davos, who really should have known better than to ignore Terry's shouts for help, and who certainly shouldn't have stood there, laughing at him naked and chained to the bunk, while Croft made her getaway.

In retrospect, of course, it would have made more sense for Terry not to explode the way he had (and he really didn't care to dwell on the late Captain Davos, or his unfortunate crew), because it had taken several long, frustrating hours for him to get the second Zodiac in the water. He had an easier time tracking her to Taipei, thanks to the transceiver he'd stuck on her pack when looking at the Orb.

But she'd gone out of range by the time he reached the harbor.

Fortunately, she'd left her Zodiac anchored in front of an old junk, and it didn't take more than a few moments of polite conversation with the old couple who owned the boat to ascertain where she had gone after leaving them.

Africa.

Terry smiled. He'd pick up the signal there, then.

And—he guessed—have a good shot at Pandora, in the bargain.

NINETEEN

Kosa had done something to the Jeep. Lara saw that right away, though she couldn't figure out what that something was as yet.

She punched in his number on her sat phone.

"Kosa. I'm here."

"Lara? What do you mean? Where is here?" He sounded confused—she could understand why. She watched the Jeep swerve and barely miss going off the road entirely. That would have been a mess.

Ah. She knew what was different about the vehicle now.

"You cleaned my Jeep."

"I know how you like your equipment. But where are you? I can't see you."

"Don't worry. I can see you . . . just keep going straight."

Kosa was driving south from Nairobi, on a dirt road that ran parallel to the Namanga highway, some thirty-two kilometers north of the Kenya–Tanzania border.

Lara was about a three hundred meters off the ground, paralleling his course, several hours and several thousand kilometers away from Taipei, courtesy of MI6 aerial transport. She was thoroughly sick of air travel and looked forward to being safely on the ground.

She pulled down on the straps of her parachute, adjusting her angle of descent.

"Keep your speed steady," she told Kosa.

"Right. I'm switching to cruise control."

About thirty seconds and a half-dozen tugs of her landing straps later, Lara set down gently in the backseat of her Jeep. She cut away the chute and it flew off in the distance behind them.

Kosa slid over to the passenger seat and she climbed in front and grabbed the wheel.

The two of them embraced.

"I don't suppose you considered a more normal means of getting here?"

She adjusted the seat, then shook her head. "No time."

And she told him about Reiss, and Pandora, and what the Orb had shown her.

After she finished talking, Kosa was silent a long while.

"How long do we have before Reiss finds this place?"

"Hours, if we're lucky."

He shook his head. "Worse than I thought."

"I don't understand."

"I feared this," he said. "When you sent me the fax. When I saw the box."

She slammed on the brakes. "You knew about Pandora? And you didn't tell me?"

"You are my friend, Lara, but—" he hesitated. "You are an outsider here. And there are things that are not spoken of to outsiders."

"I see," she said tightly.

"You have no call to be angry with me. Had I known about Reiss, I would have told you everything. But as a matter of archaeological curiosity—no. Do you not understand what this box is—what it contains?" He shook his head again. "There are some things that are not meant to be found."

His words—an echo of Gus Petraki's, of Alexander's—struck her like a dash of cold water in the face.

"I'm beginning to think you might be right about that," she said.

They drove on in silence.

They stopped to eat and refuel the Jeep just before crossing the border into Tanzania. Lara tried the manor, but was unable to reach either Hillary or Bryce. Strange. Perhaps Bryce was sleeping off whatever strange mood had come over him earlier in the day. As for Hillary . . .

It was very, very out of character for him not to answer the phone.

Perhaps he needed a vacation, as well.

Once in Tanzania, the scenery started to look very familiar to Lara indeed. They were driving along the same route the Orb had shown her—there was Kilimanjaro, off in the distance, and to their left a huge soda lake with hundreds of flamingos baking in the sun. Jungle, and savannah, and then looming before them . . .

A mountain, shrouded in clouds.

"Kosa. We've never been here, have we?"

"No." He turned in his seat to face her. "That's the mountain you saw, isn't it?"

"Yes."

"It is Ol Doinyo Lengai—the mountain of God."

"The box is there somewhere. We have to stop Reiss from getting it, Kosa. You understand that, don't you?"

"I do." He nodded. "There is a tribe that makes a home on it. They might help us."

"Might?"

Kosa nodded. "When you see them, you will understand."

*　　*　　*

Ol Doinyo Lengai, it turned out, was an active volcano. One that had erupted as recently as 1983, so the entrance was clearly marked with danger signs, warning of possible seismic activity.

"In many ways, this is the last bit of pristine wilderness on the continent," Kosa said. "Tanzania is not as popular a tourist attraction as my country, so there is not as much pressure for development."

Lara nodded as they walked through a cloud bank. She hadn't realized they were that high up already.

And then she realized they weren't.

"This is all smoke . . ."

Kosa nodded. "To keep the tribe hidden from outsiders."

It got thicker and thicker as they climbed. She stumbled over an outcropping of rock and made it a point to keep her gaze focused on the path ahead of her to avoid a repeat performance.

"We're here," Kosa said suddenly.

Lara looked up and saw only thick smoke. She must have misheard him. *Turn* here, he must have said, and she stepped up behind him.

But Kosa had indeed stopped walking.

"I will be a moment. Stay in this exact spot."

He moved away from her and it was only then that she looked up and realized she hadn't misheard him at all.

They were in the middle of the village.

Not ten feet to her right, a group of figures, barely visible through the mist, were gathered around a bonfire, feeding wood to the flames. There was another group three meters beyond them. She turned and saw another fire directly behind her and another one to her left.

A man stepped forward out of the blinding white mist.

He was tall and thin, dressed in a plain brown, one-piece toga. Maasai, Lara thought at first, just like Kosa.

Then he moved closer and she saw his face.

There were markings carved in his skin—elegant, decorative patterns that were at once strange and yet completely familiar to her, and a second later she knew why.

They were undeniably reminiscent of the etchings on the surface of the Orb.

Lara became aware of voices behind her. She turned and saw Kosa talking to a man dressed in robes far more elaborate than any of the others were wearing. The village leader, no doubt.

He was angry, almost shouting—Kosa was trying to calm him down, reason with him. Both men pointed in Lara's direction several times—she was no doubt the focal point of their argument.

Time for her to get directly involved, then.

She pulled the Orb from her pack, and suddenly, the entire village got very, very quiet.

Kosa walked quickly to her side.

"I'm not sure that was the wisest move," he whispered.

The village leader walked up to her, as well, and began speaking. Kosa translated the words as fast as they were spoken.

"He says to leave this object and go. Never speak of it. To trespass on the cradle of life is to risk flooding the—"

Lara cut him off. "Men are coming for the box."

The leader's mouth dropped open and his eyes clouded with anger.

Clearly he wasn't used to being interrupted.

"Tell him," Lara said to Kosa.

He repeated her words in their dialect to the leader. The entire village listened. A wave of murmuring—fearful murmuring—swept through the crowd.

When Kosa finished, the leader's reply was abrupt and angry.

"He says the gods forbid you to speak of the box."

Lara took a step forward of her own then and met the leader's gaze.

"These men are not like me. They won't look at the box with fear or respect," she began, and then nodded to Kosa, who started translating as she spoke. "They will open it. They want to use it. Now, I am sorry if I have to disturb your gods to keep this from happening, but I will do whatever I must."

This time, when Kosa finished talking, the crowd was silent.

The village leader studied Lara intently. Judging her.

Then he folded his legs beneath him and sat. He looked up at Lara and Kosa and motioned for them to do the same.

Kosa translated as he began talking.

"Do you truly, truly understand what you are doing? Are you truly prepared for what you will learn? Some secrets must remain secrets. These are very heavy burdens, very lonely burdens. If you find the box, you will have to bear those burdens in solitude. Are you prepared to do that?"

Lara looked into his eyes and nodded.

"You must speak the affirmation," Kosa said, and gave the words to her. She pronounced them the best she could— African languages had never been a specialty of hers.

The leader nodded, satisfied, then began to talk again.

"He's going to give us ten men," Kosa translated. "They will take us to the cradle of life. To the box."

"Thank him," Lara said.

Kosa did. The leader stared at her then, and began speaking again.

"He warns that no one who has gone looking for the box

has come back. He says the land beyond the canyon belongs to the shadow guardians. They do not sleep, they never rest. To them sky and earth are meaningless. They move like a wind. Anything that walks their land will die."

Lara's gaze darted to Kosa and she thought of the figure on the floor of the Luna Temple. And then she remembered something else—the presence she'd felt hovering over her, the last few seconds of her journey with the Orb. Something dark, and deadly, something that had scared her so much she couldn't even bear to look at it. Now, at least, she could put a name to that fear.

Shadow guardian.

"What are they?" Lara asked. "Where did they come from?"

Kosa repeated the question. The leader looked puzzled a moment, then spoke.

"He says they came with life," Kosa translated. The leader pointed to the sky. "From up there."

Lara fell silent then, realizing any further questions were academic.

Ten minutes later, they were on the move again—Lara, Kosa, and ten warriors from the village, all of them armed with spears and shields. Lara wanted to phone up MI6 and have them airlift in a case of AK-47s. This was the twenty-first century, after all.

Then she reconsidered.

Who knew what weapons—if any—would work against shadow guardians?

Just outside the village proper, the jungle thickened, becoming a curtain of thick, green vegetation. Their progress slowed. Some of the warriors passed their spears to others and pulled out machetes. They began hacking their way through

248 · DAVE STERN

the forest. Lara joined in, glad to have something to do to take her mind off what lay ahead. Pandora—what she might have to face off against to protect the box from Reiss.

She fought her way through a particularly dense patch of brush and emerged into a bare patch of forest. Ol Doinyo Lengai—the mountain of God—was suddenly visible through the trees.

Lara stopped in her tracks and stared. The angle, the distance to the summit . . . she'd been this way before. With the Orb.

Kosa and one of the tribesmen stepped up next to her.

"Take a break," he suggested, misunderstanding why she'd stopped. "Let me go first."

"No, I'm not tired." She pointed to the summit. "It's just that we're getting closer."

The tribesman frowned, then spoke to Kosa.

"He said you're right," Kosa told her. "The cradle of life lies near the summit. He wants to know how you knew?"

"Tell him I had help." Lara reached behind her then and brought out the Orb. A flight of birds in the trees ahead of them suddenly squawked and flew past, startled by the sudden movement.

The tribesman looked from Lara to the Orb and nodded. Then he spoke to Kosa.

"He says he will not turn back with the others. He will go as far as we go. He will fight the shadow guardians."

Lara met the man's gaze and smiled.

"Tell him thank you. With brave men like him, we shall win. No, hang on—" she put a hand on Kosa's arm to stop him from speaking. "Tell me how to say that."

Kosa did. Again, she did her best with the pronunciation. Apparently it was good enough—the warrior smiled and raised his spear in acknowledgment.

LARA CROFT · TOMB RAIDER · THE CRADLE OF LIFE · 249

Then he said something else to Kosa and both men laughed.

"What?" Lara asked.

"He says you have a funny accent."

She frowned, then joined in the laughter.

The laugh turned into an exclamation of surprise as an animal came charging out of the brush ahead and ran right by her. She only got a quick look at it and then it was past her.

"Ducker," the tribesman said, or something to that effect.

Lara was about to ask him to repeat the word when another one shot past, followed quickly by a third. Something swung by in the trees above, moving fast. Moving in the same direction as the animal that had charged her, as the birds that had fled earlier.

Running from something, Lara realized. But what?

Then she heard it. A low, mechanical sound, a relentless thrumming that came on them so fast that she couldn't localize the source until it was directly above them.

Helicopters.

"Reiss," she whispered and exchanged a quick glance with Kosa. But how? It hadn't been anywhere near twenty-four hours—they should have had more than enough time to reach the summit and find Pandora before he showed.

The tribesmen were all looking at her now for direction, casting frightened glances around as the wind from the copters above whipped up dirt and debris from the forest floor.

She saw ropes dropping from the copters and camouflaged figures sliding down them.

"Run!" Lara shouted.

But it was too late.

Gunfire filled the air. The tribesman next to her—the one

who had sworn to fight the shadow guardians at her side—
was the first to fall.

It was over in seconds.

Reiss's men—there were at least two dozen, all in spank-
ing new camouflage fatigues, all equipped with AK-47s—
surrounded her and Kosa. The two of them were marched
through the jungle, past the bodies of the villagers sent to
guide them (she counted eight, which gave Lara hope that
perhaps the others had made it safely into the surrounding
jungle), and into a clearing.

The copters landed as they approached.

Reiss hopped out of the nearest one.

"Lady Croft. A pleasure to see you again."

"I wish I could say the same," Lara shot back.

The doctor looked confident and relaxed. He'd actually
managed to find the time to change clothes, even to shower,
and it was at that instant that Lara realized Reiss was actually
going to do it, he was going to find Pandora and release it
into the world. Unless she stopped him.

Unless she killed him.

She had a throwing knife hidden in her boot and a small
blade tucked into the small of her back, as well. One of those
should do the trick.

She shifted position, keeping her hands raised high in the air,
but taking the weight off one ankle—the one with the blade
strapped to it. Kick off her boot, grab the blade and throw.
Should take her somewhere between one and two seconds.

Lara tensed.

Reiss smiled and waved to one of the men behind her.

"Search her," he said. "Thoroughly."

Hands seized her and drew her back, away from the
doctor. Someone grabbed her pack and pulled it off her
shoulders.

"Hello, Lara," a man whispered in her ear. It was Sean. "Hold still—this won't take a minute."

He found the knife strapped to one ankle right away and took the gun tucked into her waistband, as well. His hands began roaming elsewhere then, all over her body. In between trying to keep the disgust off her face and herself from kicking him in the groin, Lara realized that in about two seconds Sean was going to find the butterfly knife hidden in the small of her back and then she would have no way to get Reiss.

"You missed something," she said. The tips of his fingers were inches away from touching the knife.

Sean's hands stopped moving.

"What?"

"My watch." She held it up for him to see. "It's really a small high-powered laser."

"Ha," Sean said, and returned to his search.

But she'd used the intervening seconds to turn her body, ever so slightly.

His hands, when they started moving again, were past the knife.

Sean finished his search. He stepped in front of Lara and handed the Orb to Reiss.

The doctor was kneeling down next to one of the dead tribesmen. He gripped the man's face in his hand, turned it to one side, and frowned, staring at the markings there. Then he studied the etchings on the Orb.

"Remarkable. The similarity of the patterns." He shook his head. "Primitives will do anything to please their gods."

Lara began, ever so slightly, to lower one of her arms. Despite the enthusiasm and thoroughness with which he'd conducted his search, Sean had left her shirttail tucked in. She was going to have to pull it out before grabbing the knife and that would add a second to her task. Any head start she could get on the maneuver, she would need.

Reiss stood and walked closer.

"Thank you, Lara, for leading me here. And for finding the Orb in the first place. I'm sure you are aware that if you hadn't found the Luna Temple, none of this would be possible."

"It had crossed my mind." The doctor was ten feet away—easily within killing range. The problem was Sean, whose gun was pressed right up against the back of her skull. The second she moved for the knife, he would fire. And if she tried to take him out, the other guards would get her.

"My getting the box is a foregone conclusion," Reiss said. "However, you've seen its exact location. You can save me hours—perhaps even days. I'll make you a proposal. Help me—and I'll make it worth your time."

She shook her head. "Thanks, but—"

Reiss took another step forward.

"Think about what I'm offering before you answer. The chance of a lifetime. The chance to find out how all of this began." Reiss's gaze bore into her. "Life, Lara—the origin of all we are. Don't tell me that's not tempting."

She smiled. "That's what got Pandora in trouble."

Reiss shook his head. "Ah, Lara. I admire your resolve."

He was within arm's reach now. She might be able to do it—have the knife in her hand before Sean could fire. A lunge forward, executed properly, and even a bullet would not be able to stop her.

It was a chance worth taking, Lara thought. Especially given the alternatives.

She tensed, ready to move—

"They told me you wouldn't do it," Reiss said.

Lara paused. "They."

The doctor snapped his fingers and a single guard emerged from one of the choppers, holding a machine pistol ready. A second later, two other men—dressed in civilian clothes—jumped to the ground.

Bryce and Hillary.

She felt all the air come out of her at once. The guard marched the two men toward them.

Both men had been beaten—Hillary had a particularly nasty welt above one eye.

"And I told them you would do it," Reiss said. "Rather than lose two more friends. These, your closest . . ."

"Sorry, Lara," Hillary said. "We couldn't stop them. They—"

"It's all right." She turned her attention to Bryce, who had remained silent. "I should have realized you'd never mess up those tones by accident."

He nodded. "I should have known you'd hear the distortion and found another way to throw you off."

"You should have," Lara agreed, which earned her a brief smile from Bryce.

Reiss stepped in between them.

"Take us to the cradle of life, Lara. It's your destiny to see what's inside. It would be foolish to stop when you're so close."

Her eyes darted over his shoulder and found first Hillary's gaze, then Bryce's. She could see the determination she felt in their eyes, as well.

Reiss could never be allowed to get to Pandora. No matter what the cost.

She steeled herself, more aware than ever of the knife, pressing against her back.

"He's right, Lara."

Kosa, who had remained silent several long minutes, stepped up next to her.

"It's foolish to stop. Especially when we are so close. Just through that canyon—remember? Such a short walk might save your friends."

For a second she didn't know what Kosa was talking about. Had he lost his senses? Take Reiss to Pandora? Yes, that short walk might save her friends, but—

And then it came to her.

The shadow guardians.

They were out there, in the canyon. And she suspected AK-47s would be as useless against them as spears.

"I'm up for a walk," Lara said. "If it spares my friends."

"Excellent," Reiss replied. "I knew you'd see reason."

He barked out a series of orders then, and split the group.

TWENTY

Bryce couldn't believe what had just happened.

"What is she thinking?" he asked Hillary, as the two were being marched back toward the helicopter.

"She's not thinking, she's feeling. A damned ridiculous time to start acting all emotional, if you ask me."

Bryce stopped walking. He'd never heard Hillary swear before—the words didn't sound right coming out of his mouth.

"Keep moving, you." The guard jabbed Bryce in the back with the end of his rifle.

He led them toward one of the copters. As they strode to the door, Bryce saw the pilot, night visor on his helmet down, studying the instrument panel with the oddest little smile on his face. The man had a nasty cut on one of his wrists—a ring-shaped bruise, gouged deep into the skin.

Odd. Bryce hadn't noticed that before.

Their guard slid the copter door open.

"The doctor wants them kept in here for the time being. Any particular place you want 'em?"

"Anywhere is fine." The pilot turned around in his seat then, and flipped up the visor on his helmet.

"Hillary," he said. "And you must be Bryce."

Hillary visibly blanched. "Sheridan."

"Bloody hell," the guard said and raised his rifle.

Bryce saw the flash of a knife in Terry's hand and threw himself to the floor of the copter.

*   *   *

Darkness fell as they marched on.

Lara and Kosa were in the lead, guards flanking them on either side. Sean followed, directly behind, his eyes never leaving her for an instant. Reiss and the rest of the eleven men he'd brought held the rear.

Lara was moving by instinct now—taking them out of the jungle, into a narrow, winding canyon. There was no trail to follow, no familiar landmarks for her to set a course by, save the occasional glimpses of the mountain's summit. The landscape was desolate and deserted, and as the sun set, shadows began to play tricks with her vision.

On a rocky path that snaked along one side of the canyon wall, she stumbled and Kosa caught her arm.

"Thanks." The two of them exchanged a glance.

"How close are we?" Kosa said, and she knew he was asking not about Pandora, but the shadow guardians. She had been wondering the same thing herself for the past several minutes—looking for the cone-shaped rock formations she had been looking at when she sensed the guardian's presence.

No such formations were in sight.

"I don't know," she told Kosa and started up the path again, hoping they hadn't bet millions of lives on creatures that didn't even exist.

Some time later, Reiss called for a break. He allowed them all a five-minute rest and directed one of the guards to pass out water and rations to everyone. Everyone, that is, except for Kosa.

"We should maintain a bit of urgency about this, after all," he told Lara.

She was about to protest when Kosa laid a hand on her arm.

"It's all right. You forget who I am—where I come from."

He straightened and stared at Reiss. "I have gone for days without food or drink in this country."

Reiss smiled. "Hopefully this won't take anywhere near as long as that."

They marched on, heading up the canyon walls. It was night now—the guards flanking her and Kosa took out flashlights and shone them on the path ahead. The landscape began to look familiar to Lara—the rock formations, the dirt beneath her feet . . . this was the way the Orb had shown her.

And then, all at once, the path came to an end.

They stood at the edge of a forest. Not jungle—the trees ahead of her were tall, slender, isolated shapes against the moonlit sky beyond. There was no brush in the space between the trees—no signs of life anywhere.

"The Petrified Forest," Kosa said.

"What?"

"I've heard of this place, but—"

A terrible scream came from the trees directly in front of them, followed almost instantaneously by a second and then a third, each louder than the next.

"Jesus Christ," one of the guards said. "What the hell was that?"

Kosa pointed to the treetops. Lara saw shapes darting about there, and a second later, her eyes had adjusted enough that she could pick out details.

"Baboons."

"Yes," Kosa said. "They're letting us know this is their territory. They will defend it aggressively."

"Filthy apes," Sean said, stepping forward and raising his gun to his shoulder.

"No, no," Reiss said. "Save the ammunition. They will fall back."

The doctor was right—even now, the apes were scurrying

away from them, into the depths of the forest. Lara followed their progress and then saw something else, in the distance beyond.

The final rise to the summit. The moonlight made it hard to judge distances accurately, but she guessed they had three more miles to go, at the most.

Reiss was within striking distance of Pandora.

If the shadow guardians didn't show soon, she was going to have to make alternate plans to deal with him.

The doctor stepped up alongside her.

"Through here or not?" he demanded.

Lara hesitated a moment, then decided that if it came down to a fight, the forest would provide her better cover—a better chance at turning the tables on Reiss.

"Yes," she said.

Sean stepped up on her other side.

"Then move," he said, pushing her—and then Kosa—into the forest.

It was like entering another world.

Petrified Forest was perhaps not an entirely accurate name—whatever the trees were that made up this patch of jungle, they were most definitely not petrified—but she could see where the term had come from. The trees looked as if they were made of stone—gray, sleek, branchless shafts that stood stock straight, spaced apart with what seemed like almost mathematical precision.

They didn't, Lara decided, seem like living things at all.

Shafts of moonlight shone down through the canopy, casting one patch of forest in brilliant white and leaving a second, right next to it, in pitch darkness. All the guards had flashlights out now and the beams, darting through the woods, catching the glare from the moon in places, turned the forest around them into an eerie, flickering light show.

Next to her, Kosa's head suddenly darted left and then right.

"What is it?" she asked quietly.

"Listen."

Gradually, she began to hear it.

A low, rumbling sound—like the distorted tremors of some angry volcano. There were subsonic components to the noise, as well—something felt as much as heard, a sound that reached right inside her and made her feel faintly queasy and more than a little bit scared.

Because she knew exactly what the sound was.

"Shadow guardians," she whispered to Kosa.

"Just in time," he nodded, casting a fearful gaze around, looking not at all happy about the news.

Reiss stepped forward.

"Keep moving."

Lara turned around and smiled at him.

"Your wish is my command," she said and set off again.

Bryce knew Sheridan was less likely to kill them than Reiss, but the man still made him very, very nervous. The way he had methodically dispatched every guard Reiss had left behind, betraying not an ounce of remorse or emotion as he went about his business . . . that MI6 man had been right. Sheridan was a killing machine. Best to stay out of his way entirely.

Hillary had the same idea, apparently. The two of them hadn't moved a muscle since Sheridan had gone after their guard. They stood outside the helicopter he'd been hiding in, watching as he scavenged among the equipment that had belonged to Reiss's men, picking and choosing his weapons.

He slung a single rifle across his shoulder and stalked over to them.

"Do you know where she's going?"

Bryce and Hillary looked at each other.

"No," Bryce said. "We don't."

Sheridan studied them carefully.

"What are you going to do?" Hillary asked.

Sheridan suddenly jabbed a pistol right up against Hillary's throat.

"Worried about your precious skins? Or your precious Lara?"

Bryce tried to clear his throat. It came out as a squeak.

"Both, actually."

"I don't blame you," Sheridan replied. "But you don't have anything to fear from me."

"I'd find that easier to believe without the gun at my throat," Hillary croaked.

Sheridan lowered the weapon.

"I don't suppose either of you can fly a helicopter?"

Bryce nodded. "I can."

"What . . . ?" Hillary shook his head. "Don't fool around, Bryce. He's serious."

"He" meaning Sheridan. But Bryce was serious, too.

"I have one hundred and fifty hours of flight time."

"Really?" Sheridan looked impressed.

"Yes. Between simulators and models."

"How about the real thing? How many hours have you actually spent flying a copter?"

"Eleven."

Hillary moaned softly. But Sheridan, to Bryce's surprise, didn't seem deterred by that revelation at all.

"You're only going to fly it once I'm gone, so . . ."

He threw Bryce a set of keys.

"Those are for the shackles. Undo yourselves and let's get this thing in the air."

He climbed into the copter.

A moment later, Bryce and a very reluctant Hillary followed.

They went another fifty feet through the forest when suddenly, someone screamed.

The noise came from the back of the group. Everyone stopped walking at once.

"What the hell was that?" Sean asked.

"Those baboons?" one of the guards asked hopefully.

"Not a baboon," Reiss said. His eyes went to Lara and he frowned. "That was a man."

Another guard—Lara didn't recognize him, he must have been with the group bringing up the rear—came jogging forward. "Cassovitch. He was walking with us a minute ago and now he's gone."

Sean frowned. He pointed to the guard who'd just joined them and then two others.

"You three. Check on him!"

The men nodded—somewhat reluctantly, Lara thought—and turned around, heading back into the forest the way they'd come.

Lara looked up to find Reiss's eyes still on her. The good doctor suspected something was up. Smart man.

For all the good it would do him.

They walked on. Kosa and she were alone at the front of the group now. He cast a nervous glance over his shoulder.

"Whatever they are. They're getting closer."

Lara nodded and thought: Just in time. The summit was getting closer, as well.

All at once, gunfire exploded behind them. One weapon, then a second, and a third. She heard screaming—sudden, intense, agonized. And beneath the screaming . . . other sounds, as well. Low-pitched, rumbling . . . not human.

A burst of staccato gunfire sounded again—then the forest fell silent.

"What's happening back there?" Sean asked. He looked at Reiss, and the doctor, in turn, looked at Lara once more.

They were all facing back the way they'd come now. The man at the rear group raised his weapon.

"There!" He pointed at one of the trees. Lara didn't see anything at first.

Then a shadow swooped down out of the forest and passed between the guard and the tree he pointed at—a bat? No. Too big to be a bat.

With a howl, the guard ran forward, firing as he went.

He got perhaps ten feet before something reached down from the trees and grabbed him up.

There was a single agonized scream and then nothing.

"The hell with this." Sean broke from her side and stepped forward.

"Two teams, epsilon formation. Shoot to kill," he barked to the remaining men and separated them. "Go."

They swarmed through the trees, spreading out, rifles at the ready.

Shadows danced around them.

One guard fired into the air, barely missing the man next to him.

"Careful!" someone shouted.

The guard on point, crouched over in combat position, turned around to Sean.

"Something in the branches over there," he said. "Give me cover, and I'll—"

A blur of black shot through the air and literally sliced him in two. He died with a gurgle.

The guard next to him broke and ran. Another began firing at the spot where the first had stood.

Shadows were suddenly everywhere. Gunfire and scream-ing filled the air.

It was a slaughter.

"Poor bastards," Kosa said.

Lara didn't share the sentiment. Those poor bastards had helped kill her friends. She didn't mind watching them die. Not in the slightest.

Sean fired into the air, screaming futilely at his men.

"Cease fire! Fall back! Cease fire!"

Reiss drew his gun and jammed it into Lara's face.

"What is this? What are you doing?" Anger distorted his features.

She smiled. "Thinning the herd."

He gritted his teeth and spun around again.

The four of them—Sean, Reiss, Kosa, and her—were sep-arated from the guards. Inching slowly away from the killings before them.

"The tribal leaders were right," Kosa said. "We don't be-long here."

"If you have a way out, I'm all ears," Lara said, backing up against one of the trees. Not that she was sorry she'd come—Reiss was going to be finished in a few more seconds and that alone was worth the price of admission—but she didn't think it right for Kosa—or Hillary and Bryce, wher-ever they were—to pay for her mistakes. Her arrogance.

The tribal leader's words—Gus's words—came back to her then.

Some things were never meant to be found.

And she remembered the tribal leader had had a few other things to say, as well.

"What did he say about them?" she asked Kosa. "The shadow guardians?"

Kosa nodded. "They move like the wind . . ."

A terrified guard came to a stop right before them and froze.

Shadows flickered nearby, hovering in the air.

" . . . earth and sky are meaningless."

"Whatever walks their land dies," Lara finished.

She stared at the guard, still frozen in fear, just as another of Reiss's men ran past.

The shadow darted away from the first man and blanketed the other. He screamed.

And Lara knew.

Whatever walks their land dies.

A black shape crossed before her eyes and stopped directly in front of her and Kosa.

She got her first look at a shadow guardian.

It ebbed and flowed before her, like a pool of dark oil spilled on the surface of a lake. Roughly the shape of a man one instant and formless the next. She glimpsed a single, dark red Orb in the center of it—an eye, a mouth—and the glinting surface of what could have been metal.

It looked like nothing on earth she'd ever seen before. Which only made sense.

The guardian flickered in the air and moved from her side to Kosa's. She felt him tense, ready to run.

"No. Don't move!"

He looked at Lara, the question on his lips, in his eyes.

"Whatever walks their land dies," she repeated, and nodded to the fallen shape that had been one of Reiss's men on the ground before them. "They only react to movement."

"Then we better not move."

The voice was Reiss's. He came around the side of the tree and put his gun on her throat. Jammed it right up against her windpipe so hard that for a second, Lara thought he was going to drive it right through her neck.

From the look on his face, he wanted nothing more than to do just that.

Sean came around the other side of the tree and put a gun on Kosa.

"Who wants to see if the coast is clear?" he asked, pushing Kosa forward.

Lara looked around and saw two things.

Reiss's men were all dead.

And they had come to the end of the Petrified Forest.

Just beyond, framed by the suddenly bright light of the moon, lay the summit of Ol Doinyo Lengai. The mountain of God.

"I know it's close," Reiss said. "I see it in your eyes. Take me to Pandora's box."

"I don't know how," she said.

Reiss shook his head. "Now."

"I can't—"

"DO IT NOW!" he screamed and lifted his gun to her face, on the verge of losing control and firing.

Then he pivoted the weapon around and pointed it at Kosa.

"You're the one who wanted to go on this walk," Reiss said. "Start walking."

He fired the gun into the ground.

Kosa flinched, but didn't move.

"The next one will be higher up," Reiss said, taking aim at Kosa's head.

"Don't," Lara said. "Those things will tear him apart."

"Of course they will." Reiss turned to Kosa. "Start walking. Do not stop walking until Lady Croft takes me to Pandora."

"He has nothing to do with this," she protested. "It was my idea, the shadow guardians—"

Reiss fired a second shot, right next to Kosa's foot.

"Shadow guardians, is that what they're called? Useful in-formation." He raised the gun again. "Of course I won't kill him, that would ruin my bargaining position but I shall put your friend through a great deal of pain if he does not— START—WALKING!"

Kosa turned to her and attempted a smile.

"I am not worried, Lara. Don't—"

"Enough already." Sean whacked him across the face with his pistol. "Shut up and walk."

Kosa turned to the forest. Hesitated a moment.

"Now!" Reiss screamed, and fired.

Lara's heart leapt into her chest—Reiss really was out of control, he had said he wouldn't kill Kosa and then he fired anyway—but then she saw the bullet had missed and relaxed.

Only for a second, though.

The bullet had missed because Kosa had started walking forward.

And the second he'd taken his first step, shadows began gathering in the forest. A low-pitched rumbling noise reached her ears.

What to do?

Her gaze fell on an oddly shaped rock formation just ahead of her. A small cone of volcanic rock, no more than three feet high.

And suddenly she saw there were at least half a dozen other, similarly shaped rock formations all around her.

Lara flashed back to this morning, when she'd stood aboard the Chinese junk, holding the Orb in her hands. This was the landscape she had seen then—with one difference.

She cast her eyes about the rocky summit, searching for the final image the Orb had shown her.

"I don't like his chances."

That was Sean.

Lara looked up, her concentration broken, and saw Kosa still walking toward the forest, his face impassive.

The shadow guardians were waiting for him—blurring and swirling behind the slender tree trunks, moving faster than the eye could follow.

Her friend was going to die any second, unless she made something happen.

And then she saw it.

A cone of pitch-black ash, dark ooze gurgling out of the top of it.

A cone identical to the one the Orb had shown her this morning.

Identical to the one she'd seen in the Luna Temple, a lifetime ago.

She turned to Reiss.

"Give me the Orb."

He took it out of the pack and held it. "Why? Why do you want it?"

She looked toward Kosa. The shadow guardians were coming out of the trees now. He continued to walk forward, seemingly oblivious.

Damn it.

Lara took a step toward Reiss and the Orb.

"You want to get out of this alive?" she asked. "You want to find the cradle of life—then *give me the Orb*."

He stared at her a moment then, and she could see his mind working, weighing his options.

"I don't think so." Reiss smiled. "Tell *me* what to do with it."

Lara met his gaze head on.

"No," she said.

Reiss frowned and hesitated.

Lara didn't.

She snatched the Orb from Reiss's hand and leapt forward, running toward the black cone. Behind her, the guardians' low-pitched rumbling literally doubled in intensity.

Lara had no doubt she was now their primary target.

But Sean had moved, as well.

He caught her from behind and grabbed hold of one arm. Lara tried to twist away and fumbled the Orb in her hands—

And then she caught it again and swung it behind her, toward Sean, using its weight to regain her balance. She continued her spin, moving like a discus thrower, moving through a full three hundred-sixty-degree turn, ending up with her right fist connecting squarely with Sean's jaw.

He rolled with the blow and came up on his feet, gun in hand.

And then the shadow guardians were on him.

He had no time to react, no time to do anything other than utter a wordless exclamation of surprise—and then he was jerked into the air and literally snapped in two.

The guardians slammed him down on the ground with such force that he disappeared into the earth.

Reiss stood motionless, shocked into silence.

Lara gathered herself and the Orb—and ran again for the black cone.

"Stop!" Reiss shouted. She glanced over her shoulder and saw him take aim.

Kosa blindsided the doctor, knocking him to the ground.

The shadow guardians flowed over them, leaving the two men untouched, coming straight for her.

Lara gritted her teeth and ran harder.

Two meters away from the black cone, she saw a series of smaller rock formations, arranged like stepping-stones. She jumped for the first and used it to reach the second, each formation taking her higher than the one before, until she stood opposite the top of the black cone.

She heard shadow guardians behind her and yelling that sounded like Reiss, and she set the Orb down on top of the cone, duplicating the arrangement she'd found back in the Luna Temple.

The second the two touched, both disintegrated into a fine black ash.

The rumbling of the shadow guardians behind her disappeared.

As Lara turned, the entire cone crumbled, giving way underneath her. She fell to the ground, only it was black ash, too, and she continued to fall.

She looked up and saw Reiss jumping down after her.

Then the earth swallowed them both.

TWENTY-ONE

All at once, the tracking device he'd put on Croft's pack stopped working.

Terry jiggled the GPS display. Nothing.

"Something the matter?"

That was Bryce, in the copilot's chair next to him.

"Don't know," Terry said.

They'd been tracking Lara and Reiss rather easily up until now, staying well behind them so as to keep their presence a secret. Then this. Terry frowned. He couldn't take a chance on losing them now—not when they were so close to the box.

He decided to move closer.

"Hang on," he told Bryce and Hillary and gunned the copter forward.

They flew up the side of Ol Doinyo Lengai, passing from jungle into a narrow, rocky canyon. The wind currents were tricky—Terry had to stay focused on the instrumentation, on holding the copter steady as they climbed.

So he missed the exact moment the canyon ended and the forest began. All he knew was that one minute he was flying over rock and the next . . .

"That's the weirdest-looking jungle I've ever seen," Bryce said, his nose pressed to the window.

Terry looked down. It didn't look like jungle to him—even in the dark, he could tell there was nothing green growing down there. The trees below looked as if they'd been covered with a thick coat of gray ash.

Terry glanced at the GPS display and realized they'd come to the exact spot where the signal from the tracking device had stopped working. He flicked on the copter's spotlight and shone it down on the ground below.

Bodies—no, make that parts of bodies—were scattered everywhere. Hanging in the trees at the edge of the forest, strewn across the sandy ground directly beneath them.

There was blood, too, wherever he looked.

"Ugh," Bryce said.

There was no sign of Lara, or Reiss, or any living thing, for that matter.

Terry frowned and set the copter to hover.

"Take over," he told Bryce. "I'm going to see what the hell happened down there."

Lara slammed into the ground and lay there a second, stunned.

She was in some sort of cavern. The walls, the floor, the ceiling above her—all were a dull, mottled shade of black. Anthracite.

That was all she had time to notice before Reiss plummeted to the ground next to her. His gun went skittering across the floor.

She dove for it, but Reiss was closer. He grabbed the gun and then dragged her to her feet, holding the weapon to her head.

"You took us through them on purpose!"

"Wouldn't you?"

He cocked the gun and pressed it harder into her head. His eyes blazed and she could tell he was using every bit of self-control he had not to shoot her right then and there.

Reiss took a deep breath. He eased the gun away from her head, still keeping it cocked and pointed directly at her.

"Do you have any other surprises for me, Lara?"

"No. What happens from here on out is a mystery to me."

"Then let's explore, shall we?" He looked around. Lara saw what he did—the cavern was closed on one end, but at the other, someone—something?—had carved rough steps, leading down, directly into the rock face.

Reiss waved his weapon in that direction. "You first. And don't think you'll be able to outsmart me."

Lara bit back her reply and started walking.

There was a small opening in the cavern above them— the one they'd made falling through to the chamber. Beams of moonlight shone down through that opening, just as they had through the trees in the Petrified Forest. Only here, the effect was different—not light and darkness, but light and shadow. As they descended, Lara noticed that shadow seemed to change texture, becoming almost solid one minute, transparent the next.

She brushed up against what she thought was a cavern wall and her arm went right through it.

Reiss noticed and frowned.

"Keep moving," he said.

But the farther down they went, the more pronounced the effect got. The more confusing the chamber around them became—what was solid, what was illusion.

Lara walked smack into a wall and Reiss ran into her.

She swung for him and he danced back out of the way, just out of her reach.

"Don't do that again," he cautioned. "Or I'll shoot you where you stand."

She turned without a word and started down the stairs again.

Except she was heading upward.

Lara stopped where she stood. Clearly this was no ordinary cave. Just as clearly, whatever sort of technology (or magic, if you wanted to call it that) had produced Pandora and created the shadow warriors as its first line of defense, had set up another obstacle between the box and whoever desired its power.

Reiss, on the step beneath her now, was shaking his head.

"What sort of place is this?" he asked out loud.

A place that was never meant to be found, Lara thought.

They continued onward. Lara began to lose her sense of direction—where the steps had turned, which way they'd come from. She had to concentrate on putting one foot in front of the other, on pushing her body through what at times felt like an amusement park attraction—the Incredible Chamber of Optical Illusions, where down is up, left is right, and nothing is what it seems.

All at once the steps ended and they were on level ground.

"There it is," Reiss whispered.

Lara looked around. The chamber they'd entered was empty, save for a small, star-shaped pool at the far end. The pool was filled with a thick, viscous, tarlike-looking substance—the same black goo, she realized, that had been oozing forth from the cone above.

In the middle of the pool floated a small box.

"Pandora."

She couldn't tell what the box was made of—stone? meal? It looked ancient, primordial.

Next to her, Reiss laughed out loud.

"Perfect, isn't it? All that power in such a small container. The gods don't need fire and brimstone to kill."

Neither did she, Lara suddenly realized.

She'd forgotten all about the blade hidden in the small of her back. All she needed to do was get close enough to use it.

Reiss pushed her forward.

"Let's have a closer look, shall we?"

Terry sat in the open door of the copter and lowered a rope to the ground.

He was about to follow it down when he noticed a sinkhole at the edge of the forest. He shone a light on the rim and saw flashlights scattered on the ground nearby.

He turned to Bryce, who had the helicopter in a hover, and motioned him to bring the copter closer to the hole. He saw scuffmarks on the ground near the hole.

"I think we've found them," he said.

He pulled the rope back up and let it down again. It passed through the hole and into the darkness beyond.

Then he grabbed his rifle and a pack full of supplies.

"I'll be back," he said to Bryce and Hillary, and jumped.

"With Lara?" a voice called after him.

He saw no sense in answering—whatever reply he made would have been lost in the roar of the chopper's blades.

Reiss stopped at the pool's edge and stared at the black liquid bubbling within.

"I don't like the looks of that," he said and took hold of Lara's wrist with his free hand. He turned her so she was facing directly toward the pool.

"I see no reason to break with tradition. I think a woman should collect the box."

Before Lara could tell him what to do with his tradition, he kicked her legs out from under her, sending her falling face forward toward the pool.

Only the fact that he hadn't let go of her wrist saved Lara from plunging in.

"Go on . . ." Reiss said, the gun in one hand pressed to her head, his other hand holding her up, dangling her over the bubbling, black liquid.

He lowered her closer to the pool.

Lara made a show of stretching out with her free arm, letting her hand dangle inches away from the box. In truth, she could have grabbed it from where she was right now. But she couldn't just give it to Reiss—he would kill her the second he had it.

He lowered her closer to the pool and a few loose strands of her hair brushed the surface of the black liquid.

They dissolved instantly.

Lara flinched and drew back.

"Go on!" Reiss repeated. "Take the box."

Her fingers touched the box and Lara knew she was out of time.

If ever she was going to make a move, this was the moment.

Terry landed softly on the cavern floor and unhitched the rope from his belt.

For some reason, his heart was going a mile a minute. He'd actually been apprehensive—all right, scared—sliding down toward the sinkhole, as if something was trying to get to him before he disappeared beneath the surface.

Ridiculous. There hadn't been a single living creature above within miles.

Terry let his eyes adjust to the dim light and got his bearings.

There was Croft's pack, on the ground in front of him.

So she was here. No surprise—there was no place in the

world Croft wouldn't go if it meant an adventure. Glory. And the money that went with it, of course.

All right, for her it might not have been so much about the money—only because Lady Croft didn't need it. She was fabulously, independently wealthy—to the manor born. Unlike some of us, Terry thought.

We need every dollar we can get.

The cavern was closed on one end, so Terry set off toward the other. Found steps going down and took them.

A minute on, he walked straight into a brick wall. He'd taken a wrong turn somehow. So he went back to the cavern he'd landed in and tried again.

The same thing happened.

He turned to start back up—

And stepped down instead.

He froze a moment and looked around.

The walls seemed to literally be changing shape.

"What sort of place is this?" Terry whispered, shaking his head.

Lara had decided. Reiss was not going to get his hands on Pandora, no matter what. Even if it cost her life.

Of course, she hoped it wouldn't come to that.

He pressed the gun closer to the back of her head. He lowered her closer to the pool.

"Pandora," he whispered. "Give it to me."

"I'll give it to you, all right," she snapped.

She swung her free arm behind her then and grabbed the knife from the small of her back. Then she did the last thing in the world that Reiss could have expected.

She stabbed him in the arm—the arm that held her wrist, the arm that was keeping her from falling into the acid.

Reiss cried out in pain and let her go. She released the

knife and dropped toward the pool. Reiss fired as she fell. The bullet passed close enough to literally part her hair.

Lara twisted in midair and kicked out.

Her foot found Reiss's chin and connected squarely, sending him flying backward through the air.

Her hands found the edge of the pool. She landed in a push-up stance, her face the width of a finger away from the acid.

She scrambled to her feet. Reiss did the same, picked up his gun again, and fired.

The bullet passed by her shoulder and smashed into the chamber wall.

Lara somersaulted through the air, landed on her feet, and ran back the way they came.

Reiss fired again and agony exploded across the back of her right thigh.

She stumbled, bit her lip to keep from screaming, and kept running.

Finally.

Reiss could just kill her and be done with it.

No more threats to Croft or her friends, no more false promises of wealth and power. He didn't need her to share some secret about the Orb, or to lead him to where Pandora had been hidden. He knew exactly where the chamber was now, where the box floated, and so he was free to hunt her down, shoot her like the dog she was, and feed her body to the acid. He would call for assistance then—have the box removed from the pool, brought to the lab in Yemen, whatever lay within it analyzed, the antiserum created, and Pandora itself passed on to his buyers.

Reiss could picture every step of the process in his mind right now and the part he was going to enjoy most was seeing Croft's body dissolve into nothingness.

The hunt was off to a good start. He had got her with that last shot—she'd been visibly limping as she ran. Reiss smiled and jogged after her, heading back up the steps.

The path widened suddenly and he looked up to find that he was teetering on the edge of a twenty-foot drop down to solid rock.

Reiss gasped and leaned backward, stopping himself from falling at the last possible instant.

Where had that drop come from?

He peered over the edge and noticed a beam of light shooting up at him from below. Its source was a hole in the floor that looked familiar to him. In fact, Reiss thought, it looked exactly like the hole in the chamber roof—the one he and Croft had fallen through.

He looked up and saw the path he'd been walking on, now directly above him.

"What on earth—" he began, and then he was falling, up toward that path . . .

Down to the ground.

Reiss pushed himself up on his hands and knees and shook his head.

More of what he and Croft had encountered on the way down. Annoying, but effective as a last obstacle to Pandora. He couldn't help but wonder what sort of technology was involved here—was gravity itself being manipulated? Or was some sort of optical illusion taking place? He favored the latter, given the way shadow and light had been manipulated here in the chamber, and above (Croft's shadow guardians), but he had no way of being certain.

Not that it mattered. Whoever—whatever—had created this place was capable of performing near-miraculous feats—which only made him want to eliminate Croft quickly and get back to the box that much sooner. Get it open and see what sort of biochemical miracles lay within.

Ah. And speak of the devil . . .

There was Croft on the path twenty feet below him, oblivious to his presence.

Reiss smiled and raised his gun. He had a straight on head shot, no obstacles, and Croft had obligingly stopped moving for a moment.

This was going to be even easier than he'd expected.

Then Croft looked up and saw him.

Reiss swore and fired. She gathered herself and sprang twenty feet through the air to her left—

And landed on the cavern wall, feet first, tilted ninety degrees from the position she'd started in.

"Impossible," Reiss said.

This whole place was impossible. It was like being trapped in an Escher painting, for God's sake. Down was up, left was down—how was he supposed to know which direction was which?

Silly question, he realized. He'd spent his lifetime acquiring knowledge, and there was really one correct way to learn anything. Experiment and deduction.

Croft had done the experiment for him. She'd jumped left and fallen down. Therefore, at this instant—

Left was down.

Deduction complete.

Reiss jumped left and dropped down through space directly toward her.

Except as he fell, the chamber twisted, and suddenly Croft was on a ledge, above him.

He reached out to try and stop his fall and lost hold of the gun.

Croft's eyes widened and she gathered herself and jumped down toward him.

Wrong, Lara. Reiss smiled in satisfaction as she flew past without stopping. You've miscalculated. Down is—

He didn't get to finish the thought.

Croft fell back *up* through the air at him and caught him square across the chin with her boot.

Reiss dropped to the ground . . . right next to his gun.

Croft saw. She turned to run.

Reiss grabbed the gun and stood. He brought the weapon to bear and fired.

Gravity was with him this time. Luck wasn't. The bullet missed her by inches.

Croft limped out of sight and Reiss lowered his weapon.

He only had two bullets left.

Better make them count, he thought, and started off after her.

"We can't wait any longer."

Hillary, leaning out the copter door, turned around at Bryce.

"You're not seriously suggesting we abandon Lara?"

"I don't know what the bloody hell else to do!" Bryce shouted, louder than he'd intended.

Hillary glared at him.

"Look," Bryce said, pointing at the instrument panel, where the low fuel light was flashing insistently. "I don't know how long that thing goes before we actually run out, but I have to think we don't have that much longer."

Hillary cursed (again, Bryce thought—bad habit he was picking up), and climbed back in the copter.

They rose into the air.

"We'll go back to the clearing," Bryce said. "We'll siphon off fuel from the other copters and we'll come back."

"In time, hopefully."

"In time," Bryce said. "Besides, don't forget Sheridan's down there, too. He'll—"

"No," Hillary snapped. "No one knows what the hell Sheridan will do."

The second he entered the chamber, Terry saw the box.

It floated in a pool of dark, bubbling liquid at the far end of the cave.

Pandora. His for the taking.

Somehow he'd managed to beat Croft and Reiss to the prize. Perhaps they were still lost on the steps leading here— God knows he'd had to turn back more than once. No matter. He'd be sure and tell Croft all about Pandora. Afterward.

He'd brought a lead-lined bag to transport the box in. He pulled it out of his pack and started toward the pool.

Halfway across the chamber, he stopped and sniffed the air.

Gunpowder.

Shots had been fired in here—and quite recently.

So Croft and Reiss had gotten here first after all.

He set down the bag and shone the flash in a wide circle. The beam fell on flakes of dark stone, scattered along the floor by the far wall. He found the spot where the bullet had struck.

A little farther on, he found the blood.

It was Croft's, he knew instantly—it had to be. She was a crack shot. If she'd fired at Reiss, Terry would have found his body.

So she was injured. Reiss was chasing her.

That changed things.

Terry might not wear the white hat these days, but he had been a marine once. Coming to the rescue was still part of the job description, as far as he was concerned.

The key word there being *part,* he thought, as his eyes went again to the box.

She was losing blood fast.

The wound was deeper than Lara had originally thought and running around on the leg wasn't helping. Not that she had much choice about that—Reiss was still coming. Apparently he'd decided that finishing her off was more important than getting Pandora in a timely fashion.

Fine. He might have the Nobel Prize, but Lara would wager she had considerably more combat experience than he did.

Unfortunately, being wounded tended to even things out.

Her vision blurred. Lara leaned back against the cavern wall a moment to steady herself.

Reiss had chased her into a part of the chamber they hadn't passed through before. A bridge of some sort, looming high over the pool of acid Pandora floated in. Who knows, perhaps it hadn't even existed before, the way the walls seemed to keep shifting on her.

She looked down a moment and blinked. Now she really was seeing things.

The box was gone. How was that possible? Had Reiss doubled back to take it?

She heard the sound of a gun being cocked and turned.

Reiss stood in front of her, smiling.

Then her vision blurred and two Reisses stood in front of her.

"Lady Croft," they both said. "You seem to be in a bit of distress. Something I've done, I hope."

Lara blinked. The two Reisses resolved into one again and he moved closer.

And as he moved, Lara realized that she had one final chance to end this—here, now, on her terms.

Because Reiss was one step away from joining her on the bridge. One step away from being directly over the pool of acid.

Wounded she might be, but Lara knew she had one good leap left in her. One good leap that would send her and Reiss over the edge and into the pool below.

Unfortunately, Reiss wasn't going to take that step.

"So it ends, Croft," he said, raising his weapon. "Survival of the fittest. And the wisest."

"I don't think you're either of those."

The voice came from behind Reiss and now Lara knew she was really injured much worse than she'd thought, because not only was she seeing things, she was hearing them, as well. Impossible things.

Terry Sheridan, who she'd left shackled to a slow boat in China, jumping down on the path behind Reiss.

Terry Sheridan, proving everything she'd ever thought about him wrong, and coming to her rescue.

Except the doctor seemed to be seeing the exact same thing he was, for he'd spun around at the sound of Sheridan's sudden appearance, as well.

"Give me the gun and I'll make it painless," Sheridan said.

Reiss took a step backward—the step she needed. She launched herself across the path, tackling Reiss and sending both of them off the ledge together, falling straight for the pool below.

TWENTY-TWO

Reiss's gun went off and fell out of the doctor's hand.

The doctor's eyes were wide with surprise. He had yet to react to the peril beneath them, had barely registered the fact that they were falling through the air.

Lara knew why—Reiss was a scientist, given to careful contemplation of events unfolding before him. Situations like this, however, didn't lend themselves to contemplation. They required split-second reactions.

Lara was used to dealing in split seconds.

Even as she'd leapt for Reiss, she was gauging the distance to the pool, weighing a half-dozen possible courses of action. As they'd gone over the ledge, she'd registered their relative positions in the air and decided instantly on the best way to insure not only Reiss's death, but her survival.

And that one, she acted on.

She pulled the doctor closer and flipped him over in midair, so that he was facing up toward her. Then she snapped her arms and her one good leg out, pushing off, putting distance between the two of them.

The shell-shocked expression on his face hadn't changed at all. Reiss still looked like a deer, caught in the headlights. An apt comparison.

He was about to meet the same fate.

The gun smashed off the rim of the pool and skittered across the cavern floor.

Reiss plunged into the acid.

For a split second, Lara saw the expression on his face finally change, from shock to sheer agony as the black, bubbling liquid touched him.

She jumped down on him, landing feet first, simultaneously pushing him farther down into the acid and pushing herself back up into the air.

She flipped and rolled to the ground just outside the pool.

The soles of her boots were smoking where they'd touched acid.

"Fitter? Wiser?" Lara shook her head. "You weren't either of those, doctor."

A skeletal hand shot out of the pool, clawed for the rim . . . and failed.

The last of Dr. Jonathan Reiss dissolved before her eyes.

She turned and saw his gun lying in the dirt. Operating on instinct, Lara picked it up and tucked it into her waistband.

And here coming toward her, through the far end of the chamber, was Terry.

"Nice work there." He smiled, nodding toward the pool.

"Thanks." She hesitated. "And thank you for coming back, Terry."

"You're welcome—Lara."

She smiled. "You know that's the first time you've called me that. In a long time."

"I know." He set down his pack on the ground. "Here. Let's take care of that wound."

"I'm fine," Lara said.

"Yeah. Just the same." He eased her down to the ground and pulled some supplies out of his pack.

"Hillary? Bryce?" Lara asked as he tended to her wound.

"They're fine. They're up there—" he nodded toward the surface. "In a copter."

Lara nodded, then frowned. "Wait a minute. Bryce is in a copter? He's not flying it, is he?"

"He is. Not doing a half-bad job, either. Though I'm glad it's not my copter." Terry started to wrap the wound—looser than she would have liked.

"Here—let me." Lara took the gauze from his hand and finished dressing the wound. Terry helped her to her feet when she was done.

"I'm not fooled, you know."

"About what?"

"I know the only reason you helped was to prove I was wrong about you."

Terry smiled back. "Come on. Let's get out of here."

He slung the pack over his shoulder and turned to go.

It was only then that Lara saw the other bag hanging from around his neck and the outline of what was contained within it.

Pandora.

The gauze in her fingers slipped through her hand.

"Terry."

He turned to look at her.

"No. We can't."

He saw where she was looking and his eyes widened in surprise.

"You're joking."

She shook her head.

"We just leave it here? When it's worth a fortune?"

"Millions of people could die."

"You're being melodramatic. No one will actually use it . . ."

"You'd take that chance?" She shook her head. "Terry—"

"WHAT?" He advanced on her, eyes blazing. "You want to tell me again about those millions who could die? It won't happen. And I'm not going to leave this here on the chance it might. I served my country, then I served my time for going out on my own. I've helped keep this away from Reiss. I deserve my reward. I'm taking it."

He turned to go.

Lara stepped in front of him.

"That's the longest speech you ever made, Terry. Congratulations. Too bad it's all just a load of self-serving bull." She stared into his eyes. "What happened to you, Terry? What happened to the man I knew in Chasong?"

"I became wise in the ways of the world, that's all."

He took a step forward and she blocked him again.

"You have authorization to kill me? Better do it then. Because if you think standing in front of me is enough . . ."

He moved then, too fast for her to do anything, and cracked her across the face.

Lara fell to the ground, stunned. She blinked away tears.

"You don't have it in you to stop me, Croft. Because when it comes down to it, all your beliefs, all your ideals—they're just words. They're not real. I am. And you've loved me. I don't care how strong you think you are. You're not going to choose them over me." He stared her in the eye. "Now move."

She hesitated.

Terry was right about one thing. It was time for her to make a choice. Her beliefs, her ideals . . . or him.

"Fine," he said, shrugging. "We can just stand here all day long and argue, and—"

But she wasn't listening. Because at the same time Terry had shrugged, his arm had started to move toward the gun in his waistband.

Split-second reactions, Lara thought, and her fingers closed around the grip of Reiss's gun.

TWENTY-THREE

Two thousand years, or twenty-five thousand—the force within the box knew no conception of time. It had no conception of space or distance, either.

One world was much the same as the next.

Life and death, shadow and light—all aspects of existence were contained within its being. It knew the essential, existential truths that lay at the heart of mankind's eternal, never-ending quest for knowledge.

Lara sensed all those things, somehow, as she held the box in her hands, on the verge of placing it back in the black pool. For a minute, she was tempted.

The lid seemed to lift a little, beckoning her to gaze within.

Just a peek, she thought. Just a glimpse of the knowledge, the power that lay within.

But she knew how that story went.

She set the box down in the pool and stood.

All at once, a shaft of white light filled the room. Daybreak so soon?

"Lara!" That was Kosa's voice coming from above.

She looked up toward the roof of the chamber and began to climb.

It wasn't just Kosa. Standing outside the crater that surrounded the entrance to the chamber, waiting for her, was the entire tribe. They had made the light she saw—all of them carried flashlights, or lanterns, or lamps of some sort.

Kosa smiled and walked toward her. She smiled back, happy to see that he was all right, that neither his fight with Reiss or his encounter with the shadow guardians—

Sudden terror filled her heart and she spun around, looking to the forest.

"They're gone. The shadow guardians," Kosa said.

"So is Reiss," Lara said.

The tribal leader stepped forward and spoke.

"The box is safe now, he says," Kosa told her.

Lara nodded. "Will you tell him something for me?" She looked the leader in the eye. "Tell him I understand now, what he was saying before."

She looked back across the summit, at the primordial, windswept landscape, the towering cones of black rock, the pools of bubbling mud, and the entrance to Pandora's chamber.

The mountain of God.

"Tell him he was right," Lara said. "Some things aren't meant to be found."

The descent to the village was a long one.

The whole way down, Lara found herself thinking about Terry.

She thought of him lying on his back in the chamber below, staring up to the heavens with a stunned expression on his face. To the last, he hadn't believed she would shoot him. And to be honest, up until that very instant that Terry had gone for his weapon, Lara hadn't known herself what she would do.

She thought, too, about why he'd done what he had. Why the five million pounds MI6 had promised him wasn't enough for him.

Why she hadn't been enough for him—either back in Chasong, or in Pandora's chamber.

Something had died inside him long ago, she decided. Maybe there was even a little part of him that had wanted to die, had wanted Lara to shoot. Maybe that was why he hadn't killed her right off in the chamber, why he'd only slapped her, telegraphing his intentions so that she was ready the next time.

Maybe. Lara didn't suppose she'd ever know for sure.

The sun was shining high in the sky now. Just ahead, she saw a clearing in the jungle. The village.

She heard Bryce and Hillary laughing in the distance. Well. At least somebody was having a good time.

Kosa came up alongside her.

"Sometimes it's a lonely path."

Lara nodded.

"But it is the right one." He smiled and laid a hand on her shoulder. "You did well back there."

His words—an exact echo of what Terry had told her, not once but twice over the last couple of days—stopped her right in her tracks.

"Are you all right?" he asked, frowning.

"Fine." She managed a smile now. "And Kosa—thank you."

"I did very little—but I do appreciate the sentiment." All at once he burst into laughter and pointed straight ahead, toward the village.

"I see your friends have made themselves at home."

Lara's eyes widened in surprise.

"What on earth . . ."

Bryce and Hillary were seated in the middle of a large group of tribespeople—most of them women. Both men had abandoned their clothes for traditional tribal costume.

Lara and Kosa joined the group. Both men were so involved in what was being done to them—Bryce was having

his hair braided and Hillary was having his face painted—
that they didn't even notice.

"That rather tickles," Hillary said.

"Be thankful you don't wear makeup everyday," Lara
said.

Hillary's eyes opened and he shot to his feet.

"Are you all right? Where's Reiss?"

"Pandora?" Bryce asked. "Sheridan?"

She avoided their eyes. "I'm fine. It's over."

"Lara?" Hillary frowned. "Are you sure?"

"Sure. Really. Even better now seeing the two of you.
It's . . . touching."

"You know us," Bryce said. "Always making friends, sharing a laugh—"

Kosa, who had been talking to one of the women in the
group, leaned forward and interrupted.

"Getting married."

Bryce's jaw dropped.

"What?" Hillary said, the smile suddenly frozen on his
face.

"This is a wedding ceremony. And these—" Kosa pointed
toward the two largest women in the group, who smiled
back at him "—are your brides."

"Er." Bryce stammered. "That was never explained to us."

"No. Definitely not." Hillary shook his head. "No propos-
als were exchanged."

"That we know about," Bryce said.

Hillary glared at him. "Definitely not."

"Don't worry," Kosa said, winking at Lara. "I'll explain
this is a miscommunication."

The tribal leader had joined them. Kosa and he began to
talk.

Lara discreetly backed off. She'd spotted her Jeep at the

edge of the village—Kosa must have had it brought up earlier.

He suddenly looked up and spoke in English to Bryce and Hillary.

"Run," he said.

The two men turned and headed straight for Lara.

She fired up the Jeep. They clambered into the back—Kosa ran up alongside and jumped in the front.

"This'll teach you to spend time with other women," Lara said, eyeing Hillary and Bryce in the rearview mirror.

Both men smiled back.

Lara and her friends sped away then, across the African savannah, heading for home.

ACKNOWLEDGMENTS

Special thanks to Margaret Clark, Scott Shannon, the Pocket Rocket, and all the other good folks at Pocket Books . . .

Thanks also to Paula Block at Paramount, Dean Georgaris, Larry Gordon, Lloyd Levin, Kirk M. Petruccelli, and the Fabulous Five high atop Mother Mary's Hill.